THE SORCERER

THE RETURN OF
THE SORCERER

Clark Ashton Smith

PRIME BOOKS

THE RETURN OF THE SORCERER

———

Prime Books
www.prime-books.com

For more information, contact Prime Books.

ISBN: 978-1-60701-209-2

CONTENTS

INTRODUCTION
Gene Wolfe

During his lifetime (1893 to 1961) Clark Ashton Smith was best known as a poet and a ladies' man. My own experience teaches that the writing of poetry is an easy occupation and pleasant one—far easier and far more pleasant than building birdhouses, for example. The relentless pursuit of a variety of women is (I am told) laborious, costly, and frequently frustrating.

At one point the two find common ground: neither is remunerative. Today we have forgotten both the poet and the womanizer and know Smith only as a writer of fantastic and often frightful tales, one whose best work is literally inimitable. In its heyday, he was one of the three musketeers of *Weird Tales*, the other two being H.P. Lovecraft and Robert E. Howard. Let us pause briefly to notice that although Lovecraft has had many imitators (he is in fact quite easy to imitate) and Howard more than a few, no one imitates Smith. There could be only one writer of Clark Ashton Smith stories, and we have had him. Klarkash-Ton, as Lovecraft called him, arrived in 1930 and departed in 1935, producing a staggering amount of fiction during those six brief years. May I give the barren years after 1935 a little personal perspective? I was four when Smith stopped writing his necromantic narratives, and thirty when he died.

No thoughtful reader should overlook the dates of his brief productive period. Smith began to write, and write frantically, at the time of the stock market crash. (Late October and early November

7

of 1929.) He continued to write through the depths of the depression and stopped as soon as the economy had somewhat revived.

The pattern strongly suggests that Smith was dependent on dividends for income, probably dividends from inherited stock. Today, when we have forgotten how much a single dollar would buy in the nineteen thirties, we sneer at the one-cent, two-cent, and even half-cent word rates paid by the old pulps. We would do well to remember that Howard, a doctor's son who wrote for those rates instead of going to medical school, had the highest income in Cross Plains, Texas. A recent issue of *Weird Tales* carried a cover price of five ninety-five. I have the May, 1940 issue, on which the cover price is fifteen cents. At two cents a word, this sentence would buy that *Weird Tales* and return change.

Does this mean that Smith's output was mere hackwork? Far from it! Samuel Johnson, for decades the literary dictator of England, said that no man but a blockhead ever wrote except for money. Charles Dickens, who worked in a factory as a boy, was given a little education and pulled himself out of poverty by writing. Smith's contemporary, Ernest Hemingway, once wrote: "You feel you have to publish crap to make money to live . . . All write [sic] but if you write enough and as well as you can there will be the same amount of masterpiece material . . . " (Letter to F. Scott Fitzgerald 1934)

Smith did not need Hemingway to tell him. He was a poet, with a poet's high, almost satanic, pride. It was not in him to do less than his best, any more than it is in a thoroughbred stallion to race slowly.

At the time he wrote for the pulps, Smith lived in a cabin near an abandoned mine, far from any neighbor. The nearest town was Auburn, northeast of San Francisco; Auburn is not large even today. There can be little doubt that strange lights shone in the windows of that cabin by night, and that strange sounds emanated from it. No source I have found reports these; but when a man like Smith lives in a place like that, he has Visitors.

And that is where this introduction ought to end, but I cannot resist piling on a few more facts that seem to me to illuminate the extraordinary author you will soon begin reading.

The first is that although Smith was locally famous as a poet, he never attained a national reputation. This was undoubtedly because his sort of poetry was utterly out of fashion at the time he wrote it. He was (in Northern California in the nineteen thirties!) a poet of the French decadence. Baudelaire had published *Les Fleurs du mal* in 1857, thirty-six years before Smith was born.

The second is that many of Smith's stories originally included strong sexual elements. These were removed, for the most part, by the editors who bought them. If you are inclined to excoriate the editors for it, as I am, we must remember that the postal inspectors of that day zealously impounded magazines containing material they felt prurient. The slightest nod in the direction of sexual intercourse was dangerous.

The third is that Smith was an amateur painter and sculptor. Those who have examined his work in both media feel that it was in sculpture that he excelled.

As is only to be expected, his sculptures are odd, to say the least. They are largely heads, of which only a few appear human; most might better be called the heads of aliens or demons. Although they are small enough that a man can readily hold them in one hand, they possess an air of massive antiquity. If you were shown a photograph of one without any other object present to provide scale, you might suppose that it would require a truck to move it, and that archaeologists would condemn you for moving it at all. Smith dreamed of antediluvian temples sunk beneath the sea or smothered among triumphant vines, this as he sat alone in the sunshine, carving the soft stone he found in the abandoned mine with a pocket knife.

A few of his carvings he mailed to friends, packing the little heads that loom so large in rags, and stuffing them into empty tins, packing those tins in more rags in cardboard boxes. Most he literally threw away. Since his death, his admirers have combed the area around his cabin, finding a good many.

Earlier I wrote that Smith had come—and gone. That he had been ours only briefly, and now was ours no longer. That is so for me and for many others. If you have yet to read him, it is not so for you. For you solely he is about to live again, whispering of the road between the atoms and the path into far stars.

> "New-born, the mage re-summons stronger spells, and spirits
> With dazzling darkness clad about,
> and fierier flame
> Renewed by æon-curtained slumber.
> All the powers
> Of genii and Solomon the sage inherits;
> And there, to blaze with blinding glory
> the bored hours,
> He calls upon Sham-hamphorash,
> the nameless Name."

THE RETURN OF
THE SORCERER

I had been out of work for several months, and my savings were perilously near the vanishing point. Therefore I was naturally elated when I received from John Carnby a favorable answer inviting me to present my qualifications in person. Carnby had advertised for a secretary, stipulating that all applicants must offer a preliminary statement of their capacities by letter; and I had written in response to the advertisement.

Carnby, no doubt, was a scholarly recluse who felt averse to contact with a long waiting-list of strangers; and he had chosen this manner of weeding out beforehand many, if not all, of those who were ineligible. He had specified his requirements fully and succinctly, and these were of such nature as to bar even the average well-educated person. A knowledge of Arabic was necessary; among other things: and luckily I had acquired a certain degree of scholarship in this unusual tongue.

I found the address, of whose location I had formed only a vague idea, at the end of a hilltop avenue in the suburbs of Oakland. It was a large, two-story house, overshaded by ancient oaks and dark with a mantling of unchecked ivy, among hedges of unpruned privet and shrubbery that had gone wild for many years. It was separated from its neighbors by a vacant, weed-grown lot on one side and a tangle of vines and trees on the other, surrounding the black ruins of a burnt mansion.

Even apart from its air of long neglect, there was something drear and dismal about the place—something that inhered in the ivy-blurred outlines of the house, in the furtive, shadowy windows, and the very forms of the misshapen oaks and oddly sprawling shrubbery. Somehow, my elation became a trifle less exuberant, as I entered the grounds and followed an unswept path to the front door.

When I found myself in the presence of John Carnby, my jubilation was still somewhat further diminished; though I could not have given a tangible reason for the premonitory chill, the dull, somber feeling of alarm that I experienced, and the leaden sinking of my spirits. Perhaps it was the dark library in which he received me as much as the man himself—a room whose musty shadows could never have been wholly dissipated by sun or lamplight. Indeed, it must have been this; for John Carnby himself, in a manner, was very much the sort of person I had pictured him to be.

He had all the earmarks of the lonely scholar who has devoted patient years to some line of erudite research. He was thin and bent, with a massive forehead and a mane of grizzled hair; and the pallor of the library was on his hollow, clean-shaven cheeks. But coupled with this, there was a nerve-shattered air, a fearful shrinking that was more than the normal shyness of a recluse, and an unceasing apprehensiveness that betrayed itself in every glance of his dark-ringed, feverish eyes and every movement of his bony hands. In all likelihood his health had been seriously impaired by over-application; and I could not help but wonder at the nature of the studies that had made him a tremulous wreck. But there was something about him—perhaps the width of his bowed shoulders and the bold aquilinity of his facial outlines—which gave the impression of great former strength and a vigor not yet wholly exhausted.

His voice was unexpectedly deep and sonorous.

"I think you will do, Mr. Ogden," he said, after a few formal questions, most of which related to my linguistic knowledge, and in particular my mastery of Arabic. "Your labors will not be very heavy; but I want someone who can be on hand at any time required.

Therefore you must live with me. I can give you a comfortable room, and I guarantee that my cooking will not poison you. I often work at night; and I hope you will not find the irregular hours too disagreeable."

⁂

No doubt I should have been overjoyed at this assurance that the secretarial position was to be mine. Instead, I was aware of a dim, unreasoning reluctance and an obscure forewarning of evil as I thanked John Carnby and told him that I was ready to move in whenever he desired.

He appeared to be greatly pleased; and the queer apprehensiveness went out of his manner for a moment.

"Come immediately—this very afternoon, if you can," he said. "I shall be very glad to have you, and the sooner the better. I have been living entirely alone for some time; and I must confess that the solitude is beginning to pall upon me. Also, I have been retarded in my labors for lack of the proper help. My brother used to live with me and assist me, but he has gone away on a long trip."

I returned to my downtown lodgings, paid my rent with the last few dollars that remained to me, packed my belongings, and in less than an hour was back at my new employer's home. He assigned me a room on the second floor, which, though unaired and dusty, was more than luxurious in comparison with the hall-bedroom that failing funds had compelled me to inhabit for some time past. Then he took me to his own study, which was on the same floor, at the further end of the hall. Here, he explained to me, most of my future work would be done.

⁂

I could hardly restrain an exclamation of surprise as I viewed the interior of this chamber. It was very much as I should have imagined the den of some old sorcerer to be. There were tables strewn with archaic instruments of doubtful use, with astrological charts, with skulls and alembics and crystals, with censers such as are used in the Catholic Church, and volumes bound in worm-eaten leather with verdigris-mottled clasps. In one corner stood the skeleton of a large ape; in another, a human skeleton; and overhead a stuffed crocodile was suspended.

There were cases overpiled with books, and even a cursory glance at the titles showed me that they formed a singularly comprehensive collection of ancient and modern works on demonology and the black arts. There were some weird paintings and etchings on the walls, dealing with kindred themes; and the whole atmosphere of the room exhaled a medley of half-forgotten superstitions. Ordinarily I would have smiled if confronted with such things; but somehow, in this lonely, dismal house, beside the neurotic, hag-ridden Carnby, it was difficult for me to repress an actual shudder.

On one of the tables, contrasting incongruously with this melange of medievalism and Satanism, there stood a typewriter, surrounded with piles of disorderly manuscript. At one end of the room there was a small, curtained alcove with a bed in which Carnby slept. At the end opposite the alcove, between the human and simian skeletons, I perceived a locked cupboard that was set in the wall.

❧

Carnby had noted my surprise, and was watching me with a keen, analytic expression which I found impossible to fathom. He began to speak, in explanatory tones.

"I have made a life-study of demonism and sorcery," he declared. "It is a fascinating field, and one that is singularly neglected. I am now preparing a monograph, in which I am trying to correlate the magical practices and demon-worship of every known age and people. Your labors, at least for a while, will consist in typing and arranging the voluminous preliminary notes which I have made, and in helping me to track down other references and correspondences. Your knowledge of Arabic will be invaluable to me, for I am none too well-grounded in this language myself, and I am depending for certain essential data on a copy of the *Necronomicon* in the original

Arabic text. I have reason to think that there are certain omissions and erroneous renderings in the Latin version of Olaus Wormius."

I had heard of this rare, well-nigh fabulous volume, but had never seen it. The book was supposed to contain the ultimate secrets of evil and forbidden knowledge; and, moreover, the original text, written by the mad Arab, Abdul Alhazred, was said to be unprocurable. I wondered how it had come into Carnby's possession.

"I'll show you the volume after dinner," Carnby went on. "You will doubtless be able to elucidate one or two passages that have long puzzled me."

The evening meal, cooked and served by my employer himself, was a welcome change from cheap restaurant fare. Carnby seemed to have lost a good deal of his nervousness. He was very talkative, and even began to exhibit a certain scholarly gaiety after we had shared a bottle of mellow Sauterne. Still, with no manifest reason, I was troubled by intimations and forebodings which I could neither analyze nor trace to their rightful source.

We returned to the study, and Carnby brought out from a locked drawer the volume of which he had spoken. It was enormously old, and was bound in ebony covers arabesqued with silver and set with darkly glowing garnets. When I opened the yellowing pages, I drew back with involuntary revulsion at the odor which arose from them— an odor that was more than suggestive of physical decay, as if the book had lain among corpses in some forgotten graveyard and had taken on the taint of dissolution.

Carnby's eyes were burning with a fevered light as he took the old manuscript from my hands and turned to a page near the middle. He indicated a certain passage with his lean forefinger.

"Tell me what you make of this," he said, in a tense, excited whisper.

I deciphered the paragraph, slowly and with some difficulty, and wrote down a rough English version with the pad and pencil which Carnby offered me. Then, at his request, I read it aloud:

"It is verily known by few, but is nevertheless an attestable fact, that the will of a dead sorcerer hath power upon his own body and can raise it up from the tomb and perform therewith whatever action was unfulfilled in life. And such resurrections are invariably for the doing of malevolent deeds and for the detriment of others. Most readily can the corpse be animated if all its members have remained intact; and yet there are cases in which the excelling will of the wizard hath reared up from death the sundered pieces of a body hewn in many fragments, and hath caused them to serve his end, either separately or in a temporary reunion. But in every instance, after the action hath been completed, the body lapseth into its former state."

Of course, all this was errant gibberish. Probably it was the strange, unhealthy look of utter absorption with which my employer listened, more than that damnable passage from the *Necronomicon,* which caused my nervousness and made me start violently when, toward the end of my reading, I heard an indescribable slithering noise in the hall outside. But when I finished the paragraph and looked up at Carnby, I was more than startled by the expression of stark, staring fear which his features had assumed—an expression as of one who is haunted by some hellish phantom. Somehow, I got the feeling that he was listening to that odd noise in the hallway rather than to my translation of Abdul Alhazred.

"The house is full of rats," he explained, as he caught my inquiring glance. "I have never been able to get rid of them, with all my efforts."

The noise, which still continued, was that which a rat might make in dragging some object slowly along the floor. It seemed to draw closer, to approach the door of Carnby's room, and then, after an intermission, it began to move again and receded. My employer's agitation was marked; he listened with fearful intentness and seemed to follow the progress of the sound with a terror that mounted as it drew near and decreased a little with its recession.

"I am very nervous," he said. "I have worked too hard lately, and this is the result. Even a little noise upsets me."

The sound had now died away somewhere in the house. Carnby appeared to recover himself in a measure.

"Will you please re-read your translation?" he requested. "I want to follow it very carefully, word by word."

I obeyed. He listened with the same look of unholy absorption as before, and this time we were not interrupted by any noises in the hallway. Carnby's face grew paler, as if the last remnant of blood had been drained from it, when I read the final sentences; and the fire in his hollow eyes was like phosphorescence in a deep vault.

"That is a most remarkable passage," he commented. "I was doubtful about its meaning, with my imperfect Arabic; and I have found that the passage is wholly omitted in the Latin of Olaus Wormius. Thank you for your scholarly rendering. You have certainly cleared it up for me."

His tone was dry and formal, as if he were repressing himself and holding back a world of unsurmisable thoughts and emotions. Somehow I felt that Carnby was more nervous and upset than ever, and also that my rendering from the *Necronomicon* had in some mysterious manner contributed to his perturbation. He wore a ghastly brooding expression, as if his mind were busy with some unwelcome and forbidden theme.

However, seeming to collect himself, he asked me to translate another passage. This turned out to be a singular incantatory formula for the exorcism of the dead, with a ritual that involved the use of rare Arabian spices and the proper intoning of at least a hundred names of ghouls and demons. I copied it all out for Carnby, who studied it for a long time with a rapt eagerness that was more than scholarly.

"That, too," he observed, "is not in Olaus Wormius." After perusing it again, he folded the paper carefully and put it away in the same drawer from which he had taken the *Necronomicon*.

That evening was one of the strangest I have ever spent. As we sat for hour after hour discussing renditions from that unhallowed volume, I came to know more and more definitely that my employer was mortally afraid of something; that he dreaded being alone and was keeping me with him on this account rather than for any other reason. Always he seemed to be waiting and listening with a painful, tortured expectation, and I saw that he gave only a mechanical awareness to much that was said. Among the weird appurtenances of the room, in that atmosphere of unmanifested evil, of untold horror, the rational part of my mind began to succumb slowly to a recrudescence of dark ancestral fears. A scorner of such things in my normal moments, I was now ready to believe in the most baleful creations of superstitious fancy. No doubt, by some process of mental contagion, I had caught the hidden terror from which Carnby suffered.

By no word or syllable, however, did the man admit the actual feelings that were evident in his demeanor, but he spoke repeatedly of a nervous ailment. More than once, during our discussion, he sought to imply that his interest in the supernatural and the Satanic was wholly intellectual, that he, like myself, was without personal belief in such things. Yet I knew infallibly that his implications were false; that he was driven and obsessed by a real faith in all that he pretended to view with scientific detachment, and had doubtless fallen a victim to some imaginary horror entailed by his occult researches. But my intuition afforded me no clue to the actual nature of this horror.

⁕

There was no repetition of the sounds that had been so disturbing to my employer. We must have sat till after midnight with the writings of the mad Arab open before us. At last Carnby seemed to realize the lateness of the hour.

"I fear I have kept you up too long," he said apologetically. "You must go and get some sleep. I am selfish, and I forget that such hours are not habitual to others, as they are to me."

I made the formal denial of his self-impeachment which courtesy required, said good night, and sought my own chamber with a feeling of intense relief. It seemed to me that I would leave behind me in Carnby's room all the shadowy fear and oppression to which I had been subjected.

Only one light was burning in the long passage. It was near Carnby's door; and my own door at the further end, close to the stair-head, was in deep shadow. As I groped for the knob, I heard a noise behind me, and turned to see in the gloom a small, indistinct body that sprang from the hall-landing to the top stair, disappearing from view. I was horribly startled; for even in that vague, fleeting glimpse, the thing was much too pale for a rat and its form was not at all suggestive of an animal. I could not have sworn what it was, but the outlines had seemed unmentionably monstrous. I stood trembling violently in every limb, and heard on the stairs a singular bumping sound, like the fall of an object rolling downward from step to step. The sound was repeated at regular intervals, and finally ceased.

If the safety of soul and body had depended upon it, I could not have turned on the stair-light; nor could I have gone to the top steps to ascertain the agency of that unnatural bumping. Anyone else, it might seem, would have done this. Instead, after a moment of virtual petrification, I entered my room, locked the door, and went to bed in a turmoil of unresolved doubt and equivocal terror. I left the light burning; and I lay awake for hours, expecting momentarily a recurrence of that abominable sound. But the house was as silent as a morgue, and I heard nothing. At length, in spite of my anticipations to the contrary, I fell asleep and did not awaken till after many sodden, dreamless hours.

※

It was ten o'clock, as my watch informed me. I wondered whether my employer had left me undisturbed through thoughtfulness, or had not arisen himself. I dressed and went downstairs, to find him waiting at the breakfast table. He was paler and more tremulous than ever, as if he had slept badly.

"I hope the rats didn't annoy you too much," he remarked, after a preliminary greeting. "Something really must be done about them."

"I didn't notice them at all," I replied. Somehow, it was utterly impossible for me to mention the queer, ambiguous thing which I had seen and heard on retiring the night before. Doubtless I had been mistaken; doubtless it had been merely a rat after all, dragging something down the stairs. I tried to forget the hideously repeated noise and the momentary flash of unthinkable outlines in the gloom.

My employer eyed me with uncanny sharpness, as if he sought to penetrate my inmost mind. Breakfast was a dismal affair; and the day that followed was no less dreary. Carnby isolated himself till the middle of the afternoon, and I was left to my own devices in the well-supplied but conventional library downstairs. What Carnby was doing alone in his room I could not surmise; but I thought more than once that I heard the faint, monotonous intonations of a solemn voice. Horror-breeding hints and noisome intuitions invaded my brain. More and more the atmosphere of that house enveloped and stifled me with poisonous, miasmal mystery; and I felt everywhere the invisible brooding of malignant incubi.

*

It was almost a relief when my employer summoned me to his study. Entering, I noticed that the air was full of a pungent, aromatic smell and was touched by the vanishing coils of a blue vapor, as if from the burning of Oriental gums and spices in the church censers. An Ispahan rug had been moved from its position near the wall to the center of the room, but was not sufficient to cover entirely a curving violet mark that suggested the drawing of a magic circle on the floor. No doubt Carnby had been performing some sort of incantation; and I thought of the awesome formula I had translated at his request.

However, he did not offer any explanation of what he had been doing. His manner had changed remarkably and was more controlled and confident than at any former time. In a fashion almost businesslike he laid before me a pile of manuscript which he wanted me to type for him. The familiar click of the keys aided me somewhat in dismissing my apprehensions of vague evil, and I could almost smile at the recherché and terrific information comprised in my employer's notes, which dealt mainly with formulae for the acquisition of unlawful power. But still, beneath my reassurance, there was a vague, lingering disquietude.

Evening came; and after our meal we returned again to the study. There was a tenseness in Carnby's manner now, as if he were eagerly awaiting the result of some hidden test. I went on with my work; but some of his emotion communicated itself to me, and ever and anon I caught myself in an attitude of strained listening.

At last, above the click of the keys, I heard the peculiar slithering in the hall. Carnby had heard it, too, and his confident look had utterly vanished, giving place to the most pitiable fear.

The sound drew nearer and was followed by a dull, dragging noise, and then by more sounds of an unidentifiable slithering and scuttling nature that varied in loudness. The hall was seemingly full of them, as if a whole army of rats was hauling some carrion booty along the floor. And yet no rodent or number of rodents could have made such sounds, or could have moved anything so heavy as the object which came behind the rest. There was something in the character of those noises, something without name or definition, which caused a slowly creeping chill to invade my spine.

"Good Lord! What is all that racket?" I cried.

"The rats! I tell you it is only the rats!" Carnby's voice was a high, hysterical shriek.

A moment later, there came an unmistakable knocking on the door, near the sill. At the same time I heard a heavy thudding in the locked cupboard at the further end of the room. Carnby had been standing erect, but now he sank limply into a chair. His features were ashen, and his look was almost maniacal with fright.

The nightmare doubt and tension became unbearable; and I ran to the door and flung it open, in spite of a frantic remonstrance from my employer. I had no idea what I should find as I stepped across the sill into the dim-lit hall.

When I looked down and saw the thing on which I had almost trodden, my feeling was one of sick amazement and actual nausea. It was a human hand which had been severed at the wrist—a bony, bluish hand like that of a week-old corpse, with garden-mold on the fingers and under the long nails. *The damnable thing had moved!* It had drawn back to avoid me, and was crawling along the passage somewhat in the manner of a crab! And following it with my gaze, I saw that there were other things beyond it, one of which I recognized as a man's foot and another as a forearm. I dared not look at the rest. All were moving slowly, hideously away in a charnel procession, and I cannot describe the fashion in which they moved. Their individual vitality was horrifying beyond endurance. It was more than the vitality of life, yet the air was laden with a carrion taint. I averted my eyes and stepped back into Carnby's room, closing the door behind me with a shaking hand. Carnby was at my side with the key, which he turned in the lock with palsy-stricken fingers that had become as feeble as those of an old man.

"You saw them?" he asked in a dry, quavering whisper.

"In God's name, what does it all mean?" I cried.

Carnby went back to his chair, tottering a little with weakness. His lineaments were agonized by the gnawing of some inward horror, and he shook visibly like an ague patient. I sat down in a chair beside him, and he began to stammer forth his unbelievable confession, half incoherently, with inconsequential mouthings and many breaks and pauses:

"He is stronger than I am—even in death, even with his body

dismembered by the surgeon's knife and saw that I used. I thought he could not return after that—after I had buried the portions in a dozen different places, in the cellar, beneath the shrubs, at the foot of the ivy-vines. But the *Necronomicon* is right . . . and Helman Carnby knew it. He warned me before I killed him, he told me he could return—*even in that condition.*

"But I did not believe him. I hated Helman, and he hated me, too. He had attained to higher power and knowledge, and was more favored by the Dark Ones than I. That was why I killed him—my own twin-brother, and my brother in the service of Satan and of Those who were before Satan. We had studied together for many years. We had celebrated the Black Mass together, and we were attended by the same familiars. But Helman Carnby had gone deeper into the occult, into the forbidden, where I could not follow him. I feared him, and I could not endure his supremacy.

⁂

"It is more than a week—it is ten days since I did the deed. But Helman—or some part of him—has returned every night. . . . God! His accursed hands crawling on the floor! His feet, his arms, the segments of his legs, climbing the stairs in some unmentionable way to haunt me! . . . Christ! His awful, bloody torso lying in wait! I tell you, his hands have come even by day to tap and fumble at my door, and I have stumbled over his arms in the dark.

"Oh, God! I shall go mad with the awfulness of it. But he wants me to go mad, he wants to torture me till my brain gives way. That is why he haunts me in this piecemeal fashion. He could end it all at any time, with the demoniacal power that is his. He could re-knit his sundered limbs and body, and slay me as I slew him.

"How carefully I buried the parts, with what infinite forethought! And how useless it was! I buried the saw and knife, too, at the further end of the garden, as far away as possible from his evil, itching hands. But I did not bury the head with the other pieces—I kept it in that cupboard at the end of my room. Sometimes I have heard it moving there, as you heard it a little while ago. . . . But he does not need the head, his will is elsewhere, and can work intelligently through all his members.

"Of course, I locked all the doors and windows at night when I found that he was coming back. . . . But it made no difference. And I have tried to exorcise him with the appropriate incantations—with all those that I knew. To-day I tried that sovereign formula from the *Necronomicon* which you translated for me. I got you here to translate it. Also, I could no longer bear to be alone and I thought that it might help if there were someone else in the house. That formula was my last hope. I thought it would hold him—it is a most ancient and most dreadful incantation. But, as you have seen, it is useless. . . . "

His voice trailed off in a broken mumble, and he sat staring before him with sightless, intolerable eyes in which I saw the beginning flare of madness. I could say nothing—the confession he had made was so ineffably atrocious. The moral shock, and the ghastly supernatural horror, had almost stupefied me. My sensibilities were stunned; and it was not till I had begun to recover myself that I felt the irresistible surge of a flood of loathing for the man beside me.

I rose to my feet. The house had grown very silent, as if the macabre and charnel army of beleaguerment had now retired to its various graves. Carnby had left the key in the lock; and I went to the door and turned it quickly.

"Are you leaving? Don't go." Carnby begged in a voice that was tremulous with alarm, as I stood with my hand on the door-knob.

"Yes, I am going," I said coldly. "I am resigning my position right now; and I intend to pack my belongings and leave your house with as little delay as possible."

I opened the door and went out, refusing to listen to the arguments and pleadings and protestations he had begun to babble. For the nonce, I preferred to face whatever might lurk in the gloomy passage, no matter how loathsome and terrifying, rather than endure any longer the society of John Carnby.

The hall was empty; but I shuddered with repulsion at the memory of what I had seen, as I hastened to my room. I think I should have screamed aloud at the least sound or movement in the shadows.

I began to pack my valise with a feeling of the most frantic urgency and compulsion. It seemed to me that I could not escape soon enough from that house of abominable secrets, over which hung an atmosphere of smothering menace. I made mistakes in my haste, I stumbled over chairs, and my brain and fingers grew numb with a paralyzing dread.

I had almost finished my task, when I heard the sound of slow measured footsteps coming up the stairs. I knew that it was not Carnby, for he had locked himself immediately in his room when I had left; and I felt sure that nothing could have tempted him to emerge. Anyway, he could hardly have gone downstairs without my hearing him.

The footsteps came to the top landing and went past my door along the hall, with that same, dead monotonous repetition, regular as the movement of a machine. Certainly it was not the soft, nervous tread of John Carnby.

Who, then, could it be? My blood stood still in my veins; I dared not finish the speculation that arose in my mind.

⁂

The steps paused; and I knew that they had reached the door of Carnby's room. There followed an interval in which I could scarcely breathe; and then I heard an awful crashing and shattering noise, and above it the soaring scream of a man in the uttermost extremity of fear.

I was powerless to move, as if an unseen iron hand had reached forth to restrain me; and I have no idea how long I waited and listened. The scream had fallen away in a swift silence; and I heard nothing now, except a low, peculiar, recurrent sound which my brain refused to identify.

It was not my own volition, but a stronger will than mine, which drew me forth at last and impelled me down the hall to Carnby's study. I felt the presence of that will as an overpowering, superhuman thing—a demoniac force, a malign mesmerism.

The door of the study had been broken in and was hanging by one hinge. It was splintered as by the impact of more than mortal strength. A light was still burning in the room, and the unmentionable sound I had been hearing ceased as I neared the threshold. It was followed by an evil, utter stillness.

Again I paused, and could go no further. But, this time, it was something other than the hellish, all-pervading magnetism that petrified my limbs and arrested me before the sill. Peering into the room, in the narrow space that was framed by the doorway and lit by an unseen lamp, I saw one end of the Oriental rug, and the gruesome outlines of a monstrous, unmoving shadow that fell beyond it on the floor. Huge, elongated, misshapen, the shadow was seemingly cast by the arms and torso of a naked man who stooped forward with a surgeon's saw in his hand. Its monstrosity lay in this: though the shoulders, chest, abdomen, and arms were all clearly distinguishable, the shadow was headless and appeared to terminate in an abruptly severed neck. It was impossible, considering the relative position, for the head to have been concealed from sight through any manner of foreshortening.

⁂

I waited, powerless to enter or withdraw. The blood had flowed back upon my heart in an ice-thick tide, and thought was frozen in my brain. An interval of termless horror, and then, from the hidden end of Carnby's room, from the direction of the locked cupboard, there came a fearsome and violent crash, and the sound of splintering wood and whining hinges, followed by the sinister, dismal thud of an unknown object striking the floor.

Again there was silence—a silence as of consummated Evil brooding above its unnamable triumph. The shadow had not stirred. There was a hideous contemplation in its attitude, and the saw was still held in its poising hand, as if above a completed task.

Another interval, and then, without warning, I witnessed the awful and unexplainable *disintegration* of the shadow, which seemed to break gently and easily into many different shadows ere it faded from view. I hesitate to describe the manner, or specify the places, in which this singular disruption, this manifold cleavage, occurred. Simultaneously, I heard the muffled clatter of a metallic implement on the Persian rug, and a sound that was not that of a single body but of many bodies falling.

Once more there was silence—a silence as of some nocturnal cemetery, when grave-diggers and ghouls are done with their macabre toil, and the dead alone remain.

⁂

Drawn by that baleful mesmerism, like a somnambulist led by an unseen demon, I entered the room. I knew with a loathly prescience the sight that awaited me beyond the sill—the *double* heap of human segments, some of them fresh and bloody, and others already blue with beginning putrefaction and marked with earth-stains, that were mingled in abhorrent confusion on the rug.

A reddened knife and saw were protruding from the pile; and a little to one side, between the rug and the open cupboard with its shattered door, there reposed a human head that was fronting the other remnants in an upright posture. It was in the same condition of insipid decay as the body to which it had belonged; but I swear that I saw the fading of a malignant exultation from its features as I entered. Even with the marks of corruption upon them, the lineaments bore a manifest likeness to those of John Carnby, and plainly they could belong only to a twin brother.

The frightful inferences that smothered my brain with their black and clammy cloud are not to be written here. The horror which I beheld—and the greater horror which I surmised—would have put to shame Hell's foulest enormities in their frozen pits. There was but one mitigation and one mercy: I was compelled to gaze only for a few instants on that intolerable scene. Then, all at once, I felt that something had withdrawn from the room; the malign spell was broken, the overpowering volition that had held me captive was gone. It had released me now, even as it had released the dismembered corpse of Helman Carnby. I was free to go; and I fled from the ghastly chamber and ran headlong through an unlit house and into the outer darkness of the night.

THE CITY OF SINGING FLAME

FOREWORD

We had been friends for a decade or more, and I knew Giles Angarth as well as anyone could purport to know him. Yet the thing was no less a mystery to me than to others at the time; and it is still a mystery.

Sometimes I think that he and Ebbonly had designed it all between them as a huge, insoluble hoax; that they are still alive somewhere, and are laughing at the world that has been so sorely baffled by their disappearance. And sometimes I make tentative plans to re-visit Crater Ridge and find if I can the two boulders mentioned in Angarth's narrative as having a vague resemblance to broken-down columns.

In the meantime no one has uncovered any trace of the missing men or has heard even the faintest rumor concerning them; and the whole affair, it would seem, is likely to remain a most singular and exasperating riddle.

Angarth, whose fame as a writer of fantastic fiction will probably outlive that of most other modern magazine contributors, had been spending the summer among the Sierras, and had been living alone till the artist Felix Ebbonly went to visit him. Ebbonly, whom I had never met, was well known for his imaginative paintings and drawings; and he had illustrated more than one of Angarth's novels. When neighboring campers became alarmed over the prolonged absence of the two men and the cabin was searched for some possible clue, a package addressed to me was found lying on the table; and I received it in due course of time, after reading many newspaper speculations regarding the double vanishment. The package contained a small, leather-bound notebook. Angarth had written on the flyleaf:

> Dear Hastane:
> You can publish this journal sometime, if you like. People will think it the last and wildest of all my fictions—unless they take it for one of your own. In either case, it will be just as well. Good-bye.
> Faithfully,
> Giles Angarth.

I am now publishing the journal, which will doubtless meet the reception he predicted. But I am not so certain myself, as to whether the tale is truth or fabrication. The only way to make sure will be to locate the two boulders: and anyone who has ever seen Crater Ridge, and has wandered over its miles of rock-strewn desolation, will realize the difficulties of such a task.

THE JOURNAL

JULY 31st, 1930. I have never acquired the diary-keeping habit—mainly, because of my uneventful mode of existence, in which there has seldom been anything to chronicle. But the thing which happened this morning is so extravagantly strange, so remote from mundane laws and parallels, that I feel impelled to write it down to the best of my understanding and ability. Also, I shall keep an account of the possible repetition and continuation of my experience. It will be perfectly safe to do this, for no one who ever reads the record will be likely to believe it.

I had gone for a walk on Crater Ridge, which lies a mile or less to the north of my cabin near Summit. Though differing markedly in its character from the usual landscapes roundabout, it is one of my favorite places. It is exceptionally bare and desolate, with little more in the way of vegetation than mountain sunflowers, wild currant-bushes, and a few sturdy wind-warped pines and supple tamaracks.

Geologists deny it a volcanic origin; yet its outcroppings of rough, nodular stone and enormous rubble-heaps have all the air of scoriac remains—at least, to my non-scientific eye. They look like the slag amid refuse of Cyclopean furnaces, poured out in pre-human years to cool and harden into shapes of limitless grotesquery.

Among them are stones that suggest the fragments of primordial bas-reliefs, or small pre-historic idols and figurines; and others that seem to have been graven with letters of an indecipherable script. Unexpectedly there is a little tarn lying on one end of the long, dry Ridge—a tarn that has never been fathomed. The hill is an odd interlude among the granite sheets and crags, and the fir-clothed ravines and valleys of this region.

It was a clear, windless morning; and I paused often to view the magnificent perspectives of varied scenery that were visible on every hand—the titan battlements of Castle Peak, the rude masses of Don-ner Peak, with its dividing pass of hemlocks, the remote, luminous blue of the Nevada Mountains, and the soft green of willows in the valley at my feet. It was an aloof, silent world; and I heard no sound other than the dry, crackling noise of cicadas among the currant-bushes.

I strolled on in a zig-zag manner for some distance; and coming to one of the rubble fields with which the Ridge is interstrewn, I began to search the ground closely, hoping to find a stone that was sufficiently quaint and grotesque in its form to be worth keeping as a curiosity. I had found several such in my previous wanderings. Suddenly I came to a clear space amid the rubble, in which nothing grew—a space that was round as an artificial ring. In the center were two isolated boul-ders. queerly alike in shape and lying about five feet apart. I paused to examine them. Their substance, a dull, greenish-grey stone, seemed to be different from anything else in the neighborhood; and I conceived at once the weird, unwarrantable fancy that they might be the pedestals of vanished columns, worn away by incalculable years till there remained only these sunken ends.

Certainly the perfect roundness and uniformity of the boulders was peculiar; and though I possess a smattering of geology I could not identify their smooth, soapy material.

My imagination was excited, and I began to indulge in some rather overheated fantasies. But the wildest of these was a homely commonplace in comparison with the thing that happened when I took a single step forward in the vacant space immediately between the two boulders. I shall try to describe it to the utmost of my verbal ability; though human language is naturally wanting in words that are adequate for the delineation of events and sensations beyond the normal scope of human experience.

Nothing is more disconcerting than to miscalculate the degree of descent in taking a step. Imagine then what it was like to step forward on level, open ground, and find utter nothingness underfoot! I seemed to be going down into an empty gulf, and at the same time the landscape before me vanished in a swirl of broken images and everything went blind. There was a feeling of intense, hyperborean cold; and an indescribable sickness and vertigo possessed me, due, no doubt, to the profound disturbance of equilibrium. Also—either from the speed of my descent or for some other reason,—I was totally unable to draw breath.

My thoughts and feelings were unutterably confused, and half the time it seemed to me that I was falling upward rather than downward, or was sliding horizontally or at some oblique angle. At last I had the sensation of turning a complete somersault; and then I found myself standing erect on solid ground once more, without the least shock or jar of impact. The darkness cleared away from my vision, but I was still dizzy, and the optical images I received were altogether meaningless for some moments.

A PLUNGE INTO NOTHINGNESS

When finally I recovered the power of cognizance, and was able to view my surroundings with a measure of perception, I experienced a mental confusion equivalent to that of a man who might find himself cast without warning on the shore of some foreign planet. There was the same sense of utter loss and alienation which would assuredly be felt in such a case—the same vertiginous, overwhelming bewilderment, the same ghastly sense of separation from the familiar environmental details that give color and form and definition to our lives and even determine our very personalities.

I was standing in the midst of a landscape which bore no degree or manner of resemblance to Crater Ridge. A long, gradual slope, covered with violet grass and studded at intervals with stones of monolithic size and shape, ran undulantly away beneath me to a broad plain with sinuous, open meadows and high, stately forests of an unknown vegetation whose predominant hues were purple and yellow. The plain seemed to end in a wall of impenetrable golden-brownish mist, that rose with phantom pinnacles to dissolve on a sky of luminescent amber in which there was no sun.

In the foreground of this amazing scene, not more than two or three miles away, there loomed a city whose massive towers and mountainous ramparts of red stone were such as the Anakim of undiscovered worlds might build. Wall on beetling wall, and spire on giant spire, it soared to confront the heavens, maintaining everywhere the severe and solemn lines of a rectilinear architecture. It seemed to overwhelm and crush down the beholder with its stern and crag-like imminence.

As I viewed this city, I forgot my initial sense of bewildering loss and alienage, in an awe with which something of actual terror was mingled; and, at the same time, I felt an obscure but profound allurement, the cryptic emanation of some enslaving spell. But after I had gazed awhile, the cosmic strangeness and bafflement of my unthinkable position returned upon me; and I felt only a wild desire to escape from the maddeningly oppressive bizarrerie of this region and regain my own world. In an effort to fight down my agitation, I tried to figure out, if possible, what had really happened.

I had read a number of trans-dimensional stories—in fact, I had written one or two myself; and I had often pondered the possibility of other worlds or material planes which may co-exist in the same space with ours, invisible and impalpable to human senses. Of course, I realized at once that I had fallen into some such dimension. Doubtless, when I took that step forward between the boulders, I had been precipitated into some sort of flaw or fissure in space, to emerge at the bottom in this alien sphere—in a totally different kind of space. It sounded simple enough in a way—but not simple enough to make the *modus operandi* anything but a brain-racking mystery.

In a further effort to collect myself, I studied my immediate surroundings with a close attention. This time, I was impressed by the arrangement of the monolithic stones I have spoken of, many of which were disposed at fairly regular intervals in two parallel lines running down the hill, as if to mark the course of some ancient road obliterated by the purple grass.

Turning to follow its ascent, I saw right behind me two columns, standing at precisely the same distance apart as the two odd boulders on Crater Ridge, and formed of the same soapy, greenish-gray stone! The pillars were perhaps nine feet high, and had been taller at one time, since the tops were splintered and broken away. Not far above them, the mounting slope vanished from view in a great bank of the same golden-brown mist that enveloped the remoter plain. But there were no more monoliths—and it seemed as if the road had ended with those pillars.

Inevitably I began to speculate as to the relationship between the columns in this new dimension and the boulders in my own world. Surely the resemblance could not be a matter of mere chance. If I stepped between the columns, could I return to the human sphere by a reversal of my precipitation therefrom? And if so, by what inconceivable beings from foreign time and space had the columns and boulders been established as the portals of a gateway between two worlds? Who could have used the gateway, and for what purpose?

My brain reeled before the infinite vistas of surmise that were opened by such questions.

However, what concerned me most was the problem of getting back to Crater Ridge. The weirdness of it all, the monstrous walls of the nearby town, the unnatural hues and forms of the outlandish scenery, were too much for human nerves; and I felt that I should go mad if forced to remain long in such a milieu. Also, there was no telling what hostile powers or entities I might encounter if I stayed.

The slope and plain were devoid of animate life, as far as I could see; but the great city was presumptive proof of its existence. Unlike the heroes in my own tales, who were wont to visit the fifth dimension or the worlds of Algol with perfect *sang-froid*, I did not feel in the least adventurous; and I shrank back with man's instinctive recoil before the unknown. With one fearful glance at the looming city and the wide plain with its lofty, gorgeous vegetation, I turned and stepped back between the columns.

There was the same instantaneous plunge into blind and freezing gulfs, the same indeterminate falling and twisting, that had marked my descent into this new dimension. At the end I found myself standing, very dizzy and shaken, on the same spot from which I had taken my forward step between the greenish-grey boulders. Crater Ridge was swirling and reeling about me as if in the throes of earthquake; and I had to sit down for a minute or two before I could recover my equilibrium.

I came back to the cabin like a man in a dream. The experience seemed, and still seems, incredible and unreal; and yet it has overshadowed everything else, and has colored and dominated all my thoughts. Perhaps by writing it down I can shake it off a little. It has unsettled me more than any previous experience in my whole life; and the world about me seems hardly less improbable and nightmarish than the one that I have penetrated in a fashion so fortuitous.

AUG. 2nd. I have done a lot of thinking in the past few days—and the more I ponder and puzzle, the more mysterious it all becomes. Granting the flaw in space, which must be an absolute vacuum, impervious to air, ether, light, and matter, how was it possible for me to fall into it? And having fallen in, how could I fall out—particularly into a sphere that has no certifiable relationship with ours?

But, after all, one process would be as easy as the other, in theory. The main objection is, how could one move in a vacuum, either up or down or backward or forward? The whole thing would baffle the comprehension of an Einstein; and I do not feel that I have even approached the true solution.

Also, I have been fighting the temptation to go back, if only to convince myself that the thing really occurred. But, after all, why shouldn't I go back? An opportunity has been vouchsafed to me such as no man may ever have been given before; and the wonders I shall see and the secrets I shall learn are beyond imagining. My nervous trepidation is inexcusably childish under the circumstances.

AUG. 3rd. I went back this morning, armed with a revolver. Somehow, without thinking that it might make a difference, I did not step in the very middle of the space between the boulders. Undoubtedly as a result of this, my descent was more prolonged and impetuous than before, and seemed to consist mainly of a series of spiral somersaults. It must have taken me minutes to recover from the ensuing vertigo; and when I came to, I was lying on the violet grass.

This time, I went boldly down the slope; and keeping as much as I could in the shelter of that bizarre purple and yellow vegetation, I stole toward the looming city. All was very still; and there was no breath of wind in those exotic trees, which appeared to imitate, in their lofty upright boles and horizontal foliage, the severe architectural lines of the Cyclopean buildings.

I had not gone far when I came to a road in the forest—a road paved with stupendous blocks of stone at least twenty feet square. It ran toward the city. I thought for awhile that it was wholly deserted— perhaps disused; and I even dared to walk upon it, till I heard a noise behind me and turning saw the approach of several singular entities. Terrified, I sprang back and hid myself in a thicket, from which I watched the passing of those creatures, wondering fearfully if they had seen me. Apparently my fears were groundless, for they did not even glance at my hiding-place.

It is hard for me to describe or even visualize them now, for they were totally unlike anything that we are accustomed to think of as human or animal. They must have been ten feet tall, and they were moving along with colossal strides that took them from sight in a few instants beyond a turn of the road. Their bodies were bright and shining, as if encased in some sort of armor; and their heads were equipped with high, curving appendages of opalescent hues which nodded above them like fantastic plumes, but may have been antennae or other sense-organs of a novel type.

Trembling with excitement and wonder, I continued my progress through the richly-colored undergrowth. As I went on, I perceived for the first time that there were no shadows anywhere. The light came from all portions of the sunless amber heaven, pervading everything with a soft, uniform luminosity.

All was motionless and silent, as I have said before; and there was no evidence of bird, insect or animal life in all this preternatural landscape. But when I had advanced to within a mile of the city (as well as I could judge the distance in a realm where the very proportions of objects were unfamiliar) I became aware of something which at first was recognizable as a vibration rather than a sound.

There was a queer thrilling in my nerves, the disquieting sense of some unknown force or emanation flowing through my body. This was perceptible for some time before I heard the music; but having heard it, my auditory nerves identified it at once with the vibration.

It was faint and far-off, and seemed to emanate from the very heart of the titan city. The melody was piercingly sweet, and resembled at times the singing of some voluptuous feminine voice. However, no human voice could have possessed the unearthly pitch, the shrill, perpetually sustained notes that somehow suggested the light of remote worlds and stars translated into sound.

Ordinarily I am not very sensitive to music; I have even been reproached for not reacting more strongly to it. But I had not gone much further when I realized the peculiar mental and emotional spell which sound was beginning to exert upon me. There was a siren-like allurement which drew me on, forgetful of the strangeness and potential perils of my situation; and I felt a slow, drug-like intoxication of brain and senses. In some insidious manner, I know not how nor why, the music conveyed the ideas of vast but attainable space and altitude, of superhuman freedom and exultation; and it seemed to promise all the impossible splendors of which my imagination has vaguely dreamt.

⌘

AN AMAZING WORLD

The forest continued almost to the city walls. Peering from behind the final boscage, I saw their overwhelming battlements in the sky above me, and noted the flawless jointure of their prodigious blocks. I was near the great road, which entered an open gate that was large enough to admit the passage of behemoths. There were no guards in sight; and several more of the tall, gleaming entities came striding along and went in as I watched. From where I stood, I was unable to see inside the gate; for the wall was stupendously thick. The music poured from that mysterious entrance in an ever-strengthening flood and sought to draw me on with its weird seduction, eager for unimaginable things.

It was hard to resist, hard to rally my will-power and turn back. I tried to concentrate on the thought of danger—but the thought was tenuously unreal. At last I tore myself away and retraced my footsteps, very slowly and lingeringly, till I was beyond reach of the music. Even then the spell persisted, like the effects of a drug; and all the way home I was tempted to return and follow those shining giants into the city.

Aug. 5th. I have visited the new dimension once more. I thought I could resist that summoning music; and I even took cotton-wadding along with which to stuff my ears if it should affect me too strongly. I began to hear the supernal melody at the same distance as before, and was drawn onward in the same manner. But this time I entered the open gate!

I wonder if I can describe that city. I felt like a crawling ant upon its mammoth pavements, amid the measureless Babel of its buildings, of its streets and arcades. Everywhere there were columns, obelisks. and the perpendicular pylons of fane-like structures that would have dwarfed those of Thebes and Heliopolis.

And the people of the city! How is one to depict them or give them a name! I think that the gleaming entities I first saw are not the true inhabitants, but are only visitors—perhaps from some other world or dimension, like myself. The real people are giants too; but they move slowly, with solemn, hieratic paces. Their bodies are nude and swart; and their limbs are those of caryatides—massive enough, it would seem, to uphold the roofs and lintels of their own buildings. I fear to describe them minutely: for human words would give the idea of something monstrous and uncouth; and these beings are not monstrous but have merely developed in obedience to the laws of another evolution than ours, the environmental forces and conditions of a different world.

Somehow, I was not afraid when I saw them—perhaps the music had drugged me till I was beyond fear. There was a group of them just inside the gate; and they seemed to pay me no attention whatever as I passed them. The opaque, jet-like orbs of their huge eyes were impassive as the carven eyes of andro-sphinxes; and they uttered no sound from their heavy, straight, expressionless lips, perhaps they lack the sense of hearing; for their strange, semi-rectangular heads were devoid of anything in the nature of external ears.

I followed the music, which was still remote and seemed to increase little in loudness. I was soon overtaken by several of those beings whom I had previously seen on the road outside the walls; and they passed me quickly and disappeared in the labyrinth of buildings. After them there came other beings, of a less gigantic kind, and without the bright shards or armor worn by the first-comers. Then, overhead, two creatures with long, translucent, blood-colored wings, intricately veined and ribbed, came flying side by side and vanished behind the others. Their faces, featured with organs of unsurmisable use, were not those of animals; and I felt sure that they were beings of a high order of development.

I saw hundreds of those slow-moving, somber entities whom I have identified as the true inhabitants. None of them appeared to notice me. Doubtless they were accustomed to seeing far weirder and more unusual kinds of life than humanity. As I went on, I was overtaken by dozens of improbable-looking creatures, all going in the same direction as myself, as if drawn by the same siren melody.

⁂

Deeper and deeper I went into the wilderness of colossal architecture, led by that remote, ethereal, opiate music. I soon noticed a sort of gradual ebb and flow in the sound, occupying an interval of ten minutes or more; but by imperceptible degrees it grew sweeter and nearer. I wondered how it could penetrate that manifold maze of builded stone and be heard outside the walls.

I must have walked for miles, in the ceaseless gloom of those rectangular structures that hung above me, tier on tier, at an awful height in the amber zenith. Then, at length, I came to the core and secret of it all. Preceded and followed by a number of those chimerical entities, I emerged on a great square in whose center was a temple-like building more immense than the others. The music poured, imperiously shrill and loud, from its many-columned entrance.

I felt the thrill of one who approaches the sanctum of some hierarchal mystery, when I entered the halls of that building. People who must have come from many different worlds or dimensions, went with me and before me along the titanic colonnades whose pillars were graven with indecipherable runes and enigmatic bas-reliefs.

Also, the dark, colossal inhabitants of the town were standing or roaming about, intent, like all the others, on their own affairs. None of these beings spoke, either to me or to one another; and though several eyed me casually, my presence was evidently taken for granted.

There are no words to convey the incomprehensible wonder of it all. And the music? I have utterly failed to describe that, also. It was as if some marvelous elixir had been turned into sound-waves—an elixir conferring the gift of superhuman life, and the high, magnificent dreams which are dreamt by the immortals. It mounted in my brain like a supernal drunkenness as I approached the hidden source.

I do not know what obscure warning prompted me now to stuff my ears with cotton before I went any further. Though I could still hear it, still feel its peculiar, penetrant vibration, the sound became muted when I had done this; and its influence was less powerful henceforward. There is little doubt that I owe my life to this simple and homely precaution.

The endless rows of columns grew dim for awhile as the interior of a long basaltic cavern; and then, at some distance ahead, I perceived the glimmering of a soft light on the floor and pillars. The light soon became an overflooding radiance, as if gigantic lamps were being lit in the temple's heart; and the vibrations of the hidden music pulsed more strongly in my nerves.

The hall ended in a chamber of immense, indefinite scope, whose walls and roof were doubtful with unremoving shadows. In the center, amid the pavement of mammoth blocks, there was a circular pit above which there seemed to float a fountain of flame that soared in one perpetual, slowly lengthening jet. This flame was the sole illumination; and also it was the source of the wild, unearthly music. Even with my purposely deafened ears, I was wooed by the shrill and starry sweetness of its singing; and I felt the voluptuous lure and the high, vertiginous exaltation.

I knew immediately that the place was a shrine, and that the trans-dimensional beings who accompanied me were visiting pilgrims. There were scores of them—perhaps hundreds; but all were dwarfed in the cosmic immensity of that chamber. They were gathered before the flame in various attitudes of worship; they bowed their exotic heads or made mysterious gestures of adoration with unhuman hands and members. And the voices of several, deep as booming drums, sharp as the stridulation of giant insects, were audible amid the singing of the fountain.

Spell-bound, I went forward and joined them. Enthralled by the music and by the vision of the soaring flame, I paid as little heed to my outlandish companions as they to me.

The fountain rose and rose, till its light flickered on the limbs and features of throned, colossal statues behind it—of heroes or gods or demons from the earlier cycles of alien time, staring in stone from a dusk of illimitable mystery. The fire was green and dazzling; it was pure as the central flame of a star; it blinded me; and when I turned my eyes away, the air was filled with webs of intricate color, with swiftly changing arabesques whose numberless, unwonted hues and patterns were such as no mundane eye had ever beheld. I felt a stimulating warmth that filled my very marrow with intenser life.

THE LURE OF THE FLAME

The music mounted with the flame; and I understood now its recurrent ebb and flow. As I looked and listened, a mad thought was born in my mind—the thought of how marvelous and ecstatical it would be to run forward and leap headlong into the singing fire. The music seemed to tell me that I should find in that moment of flaring dissolution all the delight and triumph, all the splendor and exaltation it had promised from afar. It besought me, it pleaded with tones of supernal melody; and despite the wadding in my ears, the seduction was well-nigh irresistible.

However, it had not robbed me of all sanity. With a sudden start of terror, like one who has been tempted to fling himself from a high precipice, I drew back. Then I saw that the same dreadful impulse was shared by some of my companions. The entities with scarlet wings, whom I previously mentioned, were standing a little apart from the rest of us. Now, with a great fluttering, they rose and flew toward the flame like moths toward a candle. For a brief moment the light shone redly through their half-transparent wings ere they disappeared in the leaping incandescence, which flared briefly and then burned as before.

Then, in rapid succession, a number of other beings who represented the most divergent trends of biology, sprang forward and immolated themselves in the flame. There were creatures with translucent bodies, and some that shone with all the hues of the opal; there were winged colossi, and titans who strode as with seven-league boots; and there was one being with useless, abortive wings, who crawled rather than ran, to seek the same glorious doom as the rest. But among them there were none of the city's people: these merely stood and looked on, impassive and statue-like as ever.

I saw that the fountain had now reached its greatest height and was beginning to decline. It sank steadily but slowly to half its former elevation. During this interval there were no more acts of self-sacrifice; and several of the beings beside me turned abruptly and went away, as if they had overcome the lethal spell.

One of the tall, armored entities, as he left, addressed me in words that were like clarion-notes, with unmistakable accents of warning. By a mighty effort of will, in a turmoil of conflicting emotions, I followed him. At every step the madness and delirium of the music warred with my instincts of self-preservation. More than once I started to go back. My homeward journey was blurred and doubtful as the wanderings of a man in an opium-trance; and the music sang behind me and told me of the rapture I had missed, of the flaming dissolution whose brief instant was better than aeons of mortal life.

AUG. 9th. I have tried to go on with a new story, but have made no progress. Anything that I can imagine, or frame in language, seems flat and puerile beside the world of unsearchable mystery to which I have found admission. The temptation to return is more cogent than ever, the call of that remembered music is sweeter than the voice of a loved woman. And always I am tormented by the problem of it all, and tantalized by the little which I have perceived and understood. What forces are these whose existence and working I have merely apprehended? Who are the inhabitants of the city? And who are the beings that visit the enshrined flame? What rumor or legend has drawn them from outland realms and ulterior planets to that place of blissful danger and destruction? And what is the fountain itself, and what the secret of its lure and its deadly singing? These problems admit of infinite surmise, but no conceivable solution.

I am planning to go back once more—but not alone. Someone must go with me this time, as a witness to the wonder and the peril. It is all too strange for credence—I must have human corroboration of what I have seen and felt and conjectured. Also, another might understand where I have failed to do more than apprehend.

Who shall I take? It will be necessary to invite someone here from the outer world—someone of high intellectual and aesthetic capacity. Shall I ask Philip Hastane, my fellow fiction-writer? Hastane would be too busy, I fear. But there is the Californian artist, Felix Ebbonly, who has illustrated some of my fantastic novels.

Ebbonly would be the man to see and appreciate the new dimension, if he can come. With his bent for the bizarre and the unearthly, the spectacle of that plain and city, the Babelian buildings and arcades, and the temple of the flame, will simply enthrall him. I shall write immediately to his San Francisco address.

AUG. 12th. Ebbonly is here—the mysterious hints in my letter regarding some novel pictorial subjects along his own line, were too provocative for him to resist. Now I have explained fully and have given him a detailed account of my adventures. I can see that he is a little incredulous, for which I hardly blame him. But he will not remain incredulous very long, for tomorrow we shall visit together the city of the singing flame.

AUG. 13th. I must concentrate my disordered faculties, I must choose my words and write with exceeding care. This will be the last entry in my journal, and the last writing I shall ever do. When I have finished, I shall wrap the journal up and address it to Philip Hastane. who can make such disposition of it as he sees fit.

I took Ebbonly into the other dimension today. He was impressed, even as I had been, by the two isolated boulders on Crater Ridge.

"They look like the guttered ends of columns established by pre-human gods," he remarked. "I begin to believe you now."

I told him to go first, and indicated the place where he should step. He obeyed without hesitation, and I had the singular experience of seeing a man melt into utter, instantaneous nothingness. One moment he was there—and the next, there was only bare ground and the far-off tamaracks whose view his body had obstructed. I followed, and found him standing in speechless awe on the violet grass.

"This," he said at last, "is the sort of thing whose existence I have hitherto merely suspected, and have never even been able to hint at in my most imaginative drawings."

We spoke little as we followed the range of monolithic boulders toward the plain. Far in the distance, beyond those high and stately trees with their sumptuous foliage, the golden-brown vapors had parted showing vistas of an immense horizon; and past the horizon were range on range of gleaming orbs and fiery, flying motes in the depth of that amber heaven. It was as if the veil of another universe than ours had been drawn back.

We crossed the plain, and came at length within earshot of the siren music. I warned Ebbonly to stuff his ears with cotton-wadding; but he refused.

"I don't want to deaden any new sensations which I may experience," he observed.

We entered the city. My companion was in a veritable rhapsody of artistic delight when he beheld the enormous buildings and the people. I could see, too, that the music had taken hold upon him: his look soon became fixed and dreamy as that of an opium-eater. At first he made many comments on the architecture and the various beings who passed us, and called my attention to details which I had not perceived heretofore.

However, as we drew nearer to the temple of the flame, his observational interest seemed to flag, and was replaced by more and more of an ecstatic inward absorption. His remarks became fewer and briefer; and he did not even seem to hear my questions. It was evident that the sound had wholly bemused and bewitched him.

Even as on my former visit, there were many pilgrims going toward the shrine—and few that were coming away from it. Most of them belonged to evolutionary types that I had seen before. Among those that were new to me, I recall one gorgeous creature with golden and cerulean wings like those of a giant lepidopter and scintillating, jewel-like eyes that must have been designed to mirror the glories of some Edenic world.

I too felt, as before, the captious thralldom and bewitchment, the insidious, gradual perversion of thought and instinct, as if the music were working in my brain like a subtle alkaloid. Since I had taken my usual precaution, my subjection to the influence was less complete than that of Ebbonly; but nevertheless it was enough to make me forget a number of things—among them, the initial concern which I had felt when my companion refused to employ the same mode of protection as myself. I no longer thought of his danger or my own, except as something very distant and immaterial.

The streets were like the prolonged and bewildering labyrinth of a nightmare. But the music led us forthrightly; and always there were other pilgrims. Like men in the grip of some powerful current, we were drawn to our destination.

As we passed along the hall of gigantic columns and neared the abode of the fiery fountain, a sense of our peril quickened momentarily in my brain, and I sought to warn Ebbonly once more. But all my protests and remonstrances were futile: he was deaf as a machine, and wholly impervious to anything but the lethal music. His expression and his movements were those of a somnambulist. Even when I seized and shook him with such violence as I could muster, he remained oblivious of my presence.

The throng of worshipers was larger than upon my first visit. The jet of pure incandescent flame was mounting steadily as we entered, and it sang with the pure ardor and ecstasy of a star alone in space. Again, with ineffable tones, it told me the rapture of a moth-like death in its lofty soaring, the exultation and triumph of a momentary union with its elemental essence.

The flame rose to its apex; and even for me, the mesmeric lure was well-nigh irresistible. Many of our companions succumbed; and the first to immolate himself was the giant lepidopterous being. Four others, of diverse evolutional types, followed in appallingly swift succession.

In my own partial subjection to the music, my own effort to resist that deadly enslavement, I had almost forgotten the very presence of Ebbonly. It was too late for me to even think of stopping him, when he ran forward in a series of leaps that were both solemn and frenzied, like the beginning of some sacerdotal dance, and hurled himself headlong into the flame. The fire enveloped him, it flared up for an instant with a more dazzling greenness; and that was all.

Slowly, as if from benumbed brain-centers, a horror crept upon my conscious mind, and helped to annul the perilous mesmerism.

I turned, while many others were following Ebbonly's example, and fled from the shrine and from the city. But somehow the horror diminished as I went; and more and more I found myself envying my companion's fate, and wondering as to the sensations he had felt in that moment of fiery dissolution. . . .

Now, as I write this, I am wondering why I came back again to the human world. Words are futile to express what I have beheld and experienced, and the change that has come upon me beneath the play of incalculable forces in a world of which no other mortal is even cognizant.

Literature is nothing more than the shadow; and life, with its drawn-out length of monotonous, reiterative days, is unreal and without meaning now in comparison with the splendid death which I might have had—the glorious doom which is still in store. I have no longer any will to fight the ever-insistent music which I hear in memory. And—there seems to be no reason at all why I should fight it out. Tomorrow I shall return to the city.

BEYOND THE
SINGING FLAME

I

When I, Philip Hastane, gave to the world the journal of my friend
Giles Angarth, I was still doubtful as to whether the incidents related
therein were fiction or verity. The trans-dimensional adventures of
Angarth and Felix Ebbonly, the city of the Flame with its strange
residents and pilgrims, the immolation of Ebbonly, and the hinted
return of the narrator himself for a like purpose after making the
last entry in his diary, were very much the sort of thing that Angarth
might have imagined in one of the fantastic novels for which he had
become so justly famous.

Add to this the seemingly impossible and incredible nature of the
whole tale, and my hesitancy in accepting it as veridical will easily be
understood.

However, on the other hand, there was the unsolved and eternally
recalcitrant enigma offered by the disappearance of the two men.
Both were well known, the one as a writer, the other as an artist; both
were in flourishing circumstances, with no serious cares or troubles;
and their vanishment, all things considered, was difficult to explain
on the ground of any motive less unusual or extraordinary than the
one assigned in the journal.

At first, as I have hinted in my foreword to the published diary,
I thought that the whole affair might well have been devised as a
somewhat elaborate practical joke; but this theory became less and
less tenable as weeks and months went by and linked themselves

slowly into a year, without the reappearance of the presumptive jokers.

Now, at last, I can testify to the truth of all that Angarth wrote— and more. For I too have been in Ydmos, the City of the Singing Flame, and have known also the supernal glories and raptures of the Inner Dimension. And of these I must tell, however falteringly and stumblingly, with mere human words, before the vision fades. For these are things which neither I nor any other shall behold or experience again. Ydmos itself is now a riven ruin, and the temple of the Flame has been blasted to its foundations in the basic rock, and the fountain of singing fire has been stricken at its source. The Inner Dimension has perished like a broken bubble, in the great war that was made upon Ydmos by the rulers of the Outer Lands. . . .

After editing and publishing Angarth's journal, I was unable to forget the peculiar and tantalizing problems it had raised. The vague but infinitely suggestive vistas opened by the tale were such as to haunt my imagination recurrently with a hint of half-revealed or hidden mysteries. I was troubled by the possibility of some great mystic meaning behind it all—some cosmic actuality of which the narrator had perceived merely the external veils and fringes.

As time went on, I found myself pondering it perpetually and more and more I was possessed by an overwhelming wonder, and a sense of something which no mere fiction-weaver would have been likely to invent.

In the early summer of 1931, after finishing a new novel of interplanetary adventure, I felt able for the first time to take the necessary leisure for the execution of a project that had often occurred to me. Putting all my affairs in order, and knitting all the loose ends of my literary labors and personal correspondence in case I should not return, I left Auburn ostensibly for a week's vacation. I went to Summit with the idea of investigating closely the milieu in which Angarth and Ebbonly had disappeared from human ken.

With strange emotions, I visited the forsaken cabin south of Crater

Ridge that had been occupied by Angarth, and saw the rough, home-made table of pine boards upon which my friend had written his journal and had left the sealed package containing it to be forwarded to me after his departure.

⁂

There was a weird and brooding loneliness about the place, as if the non-human infinitudes had already claimed it for their own. The unlocked door had sagged inward from the pressure of high-piled winter snows, and fir-needles had sifted across the sill to strew the unswept floor. Somehow, I know not why, the bizarre narrative became more real and more credible to me, as if an occult intimation of all that had happened to its author still lingered around the cabin.

This mysterious intimation grew stronger when I came to visit Crater Ridge itself, and to search amid its miles of pseudo-volcanic rubble for the two boulders so explicitly described by Angarth as having a likeness to the pedestals of ruined columns.

Many of my readers, no doubt, will remember his description of the Ridge and there is no need to enlarge upon it with reiterative detail, other than that which bears upon my own adventures.

Following the northward path which Angarth must have taken from his cabin, and trying to retrace his wanderings on the long, barren hill, I combed it thoroughly from end to end and from side to side, since he had not specified the location of the boulders. After two mornings spent in this manner without result, I was almost ready to abandon the quest and dismiss the queer, soapy, greenish-grey column-ends as one of Angarth's most provocative and deceptive fictions.

It must have been the formless, haunting intuition of which I have spoken, that made me renew the search on a third morning. This time, after crossing and re-crossing the hill-top for an hour or more, and weaving tortuously to and fro among the cicada-haunted wild currant bushes and sunflowers on the dusty slopes, I came at last to an open, circular, rock-surrounded space that was totally unfamiliar.

I had somehow missed it in all my previous roamings. It was the place of which Angarth had told; and I saw with an inexpressible thrill the two rounded, worn-looking boulders that were situated in the center of the ring.

I believe that I trembled a little with excitement as I went forward to inspect the curious stones. Bending over, but not daring to enter the bare, pebbly space between them, I touched one of them with my hand, and received a sensation of preternatural smoothness, together with a coolness that was inexplicable, considering that the boulders and the soil about them must have lain unshaded from the sultry August sun for many hours.

From that moment, I became fully persuaded that Angarth's account was no mere fable. Just why I should have felt so certain of this, I am powerless to say. But it seemed to me that I stood on the threshold of an ultra-mundane mystery, on the brink of uncharted gulfs. I looked about at the familiar Sierra valleys and mountains, wondering that they still preserved their wonted outlines, and were still unchanged by the contiguity of alien worlds, were still untouched by the luminous glories of arcanic dimensions.

Being convinced that I had indeed found the gateway between the worlds, I was prompted to strange reflections. What, and where, was this other sphere to which my friend had obtained entrance? Was it near at hand, like a secret room in the structure of space? Or was it, in reality, millions or trillions of light-years away by the reckoning of astronomic distance, in a planet of some ulterior galaxy?

After all, we know little or nothing of the actual nature of space; and perhaps, in some way that we cannot imagine, the infinite is doubled upon itself in places, with dimensional folds and tucks, and short-cuts whereby the distance to Algenib or Aldebaran is merely a step. Perhaps, also there is more than one infinity. The spectral "flaw" into which Angarth had fallen might well be a sort of super-dimension, abridging the cosmic intervals and connecting universe with universe.

However, because of this very certitude that I had found the interspheric portals, and could follow Angarth and Ebbonly if I so desired, I hesitated before trying the experiment. I was mindful of the mystic danger and irrefragable lure that had overcome the others. I was consumed by imaginative curiosity, by an avid, well-nigh feverish longing to behold the wonders of this exotic realm; but I did not purpose to become a victim to the opiate power and fascination of the Singing Flame.

I stood for a long time, eyeing the old boulders and the barren, pebble-littered spot that gave admission to the unknown. At length I went away, deciding to defer my venture till the following morn. Visualizing the weird doom to which the others had gone so voluntarily and even gladly, I must confess that I was afraid. On the other hand, I was drawn by the fateful allurement that leads an explorer into far places . . . and perhaps by something more than this.

I slept badly that night, with nerves and brain excited by formless, glowing premonitions, by intimations of half-conceived perils and splendors and vastnesses. Early the next morning, while the sun was still hanging above the Nevada Mountains, I returned to Crater Ridge.

I carried a strong hunting-knife and a Colt revolver, and wore a filled cartridge-belt, and also a knapsack containing sandwiches and a thermos bottle of coffee. Before starting, I had stuffed my ears tightly with cotton soaked in a new anæsthetic fluid, mild but efficacious, which would serve to deafen me completely for many hours. In this way, I felt that I should be immune to the demoralizing music of the fiery fountain.

I peered about on the rugged landscape with its weird and far-flung vistas, wondering if I should ever see it again. Then, resolutely but with the eerie thrilling and shrinking of one who throws himself from a high cliff into some bottomless chasm, I stepped forward into the space between the greyish-green boulders.

My sensations, generally speaking, were similar to those described by Angarth in his diary. Blackness and illimitable emptiness seemed to wrap me round in a dizzy swirl as of rushing wind or milling water, and I went down and down in a spiral descent whose duration I have never been able to estimate. Intolerably stifled, and without even the power to gasp for breath, in the chill, airless vacuum that froze my very muscles and marrow, I felt that I should lose consciousness in another moment, and descend into the greater gulf of death or oblivion.

Something seemed to arrest my fall, and I became aware that I was standing still, though I was troubled for some time by a queer doubt as to whether my position was vertical, horizontal, or upside-down in relation to the solid substance that my feet had encountered.

Then the blackness lifted slowly like a dissolving cloud, and I saw the slope of violet grass, the rows of irregular monoliths running downward from where I stood, and the grey-green columns near at hand. Beyond was the titan, perpendicular city of red stone that was dominant above the high and multi-colored vegetation of the plain.

It was all very much as Angarth had depicted it; but somehow, even then, I became aware of differences that were not immediately or clearly definable, of scenic details and atmospheric elements for which his accounts had not prepared me. And, at the moment, I was too thoroughly disequilibrated and overpowered by the vision of it all to even speculate concerning the character of these differences.

As I gazed at the city with its crowding tiers of battlements and its multitude of overlooming spires, I felt the invisible threads of a secret attraction, was seized by an imperative longing to know the mysteries hidden behind the massive walls and the myriad buildings. Then, a moment later, my gaze was drawn to the remote, opposite horizon of the plain, as if in some conflicting impulse whose nature and origin were undiscoverable.

It must have been because I had formed so clear and definite a picture of the scene from my friend's narrative, that I was surprised and even a little disturbed, as if by something wrong or irrelevant, when I saw in the far distance the shining towers of what seemed to be another city—a city of which Angarth had not spoken. The towers rose in serried lines, reaching for many miles in a curious arc-like formation, and were sharply defined against a blackish mass of cloud that had reared behind them and was spreading out on the luminous amber sky in sullen webs and sinister, crawling filaments.

Subtle disquietude and repulsion seemed to emanate from the far-off, glittering spires, even as attraction emanated from those of the nearer city. I saw them quiver and pulse with an evil light, like living and moving things, through what I assumed to be some refractive trick of the atmosphere. Then for an instant, the black cloud behind them glowed with dull, angry crimson throughout its whole mass, and even its questing webs and tendrils were turned into lurid threads of fire.

The crimson faded, leaving the cloud inert and lumpish as before. But from many of the vanward towers, lines of red and violet flame had leaped like outthrust lances at the bosom of the plain beneath them. They were held thus for at least a minute, moving slowly across a wide area, before they vanished. In the spaces between the towers, I now perceived a multitude of gleaming, restless particles, like armies of militant atoms, and wondered if perchance they were living beings. If the idea had not appeared so fantastical, I could have sworn even then that the far city had already changed its position and was advancing toward the other on the plain.

Apart from the fulguration of the cloud, and the flames that had sprung from the towers, and the quiverings which I deemed a refractive phenomenon, the whole landscape before and about me was unnaturally still. On the strange amber air of the Tyrian-tinted grasses, on the proud, opulent foliage of the unknown trees, there lay the dead calm that precedes the stupendous turmoil of typhonic storm or seismic cataclysm. The brooding sky was permeated with intuitions of cosmic menace, was weighed down by a dim, elemental despair.

II
INTO THE FLAME

Alarmed by this ominous atmosphere, I looked behind me at the two pillars which, according to Angarth, were the gateway of return to the human world. For an instant, I was tempted to go back. Then I turned once more to the nearby city; and the feelings I have just mentioned were lost in an oversurging awesomeness and wonder. I felt the thrill of a deep, supernal exaltation before the magnitude of the mighty buildings; a compelling sorcery was laid upon me by the very lines of their construction, by the harmonies of a solemn architectural music. I forgot my impulse to return to Crater Ridge, and started down the slope toward the city.

Soon the boughs of the purple and yellow forest arched above me like the altitudes of Titan-builded aisles, with leaves that fretted the rich heaven in gorgeous arabesques. Beyond them, ever and anon, I caught glimpses of the piled ramparts of my destination, but looking back, in the direction of that other city on the horizon, I found that its fulgurating towers were now lost to view.

I saw, however, that the masses of the great somber cloud were rising steadily on the sky; and once again they flared to a swart malignant red, as if with some unearthly form of sheet-lightning; and though I could hear nothing with my deadened ears, the ground beneath me trembled with long vibrations as of thunder. There was a queer quality in the vibrations, that seemed to tear my nerves and set my teeth on edge with its throbbing, lancinating discord, painful as broken glass or the torment of a tightened rack.

Like Angarth before me, I came to the paved Cyclopean highway. Following it, in the stillness after the unheard peals of thunder, I felt another and subtler vibration, which I knew to be that of the Singing Flame in the temple at the city's core. It seemed to soothe and exalt and bear me on, to erase with soft caresses the ache that still lingered in my nerves from the torturing pulsations of the thunder.

I met no one on the road, and was not passed by any of the trans-dimensional pilgrims, such as had overtaken Angarth. And when the accumulated ramparts loomed above the highest trees, and I came forth from the wood in their very shadow, I saw that the great gate of the city was closed, leaving no crevice through which a pygmy like myself might obtain entrance.

Feeling a profound and peculiar discomfiture, such as one would experience in a dream that had gone wrong. I stared at the grim, unrelenting blankness of the gate, which seemed to be wrought from one enormous sheet of sombre and lusterless metal. Then I peered upward at the sheerness of the wall, which rose above me like an alpine cliff, and saw that the battlements were seemingly deserted.

Was the city forsaken by its people, by the guardians of the Flame? Was it no longer open to the pilgrims who came from outlying lands to worship the Flame, and to immolate themselves? With curious reluctance, after lingering there for many minutes in a sort of stupor, I turned away to retrace my steps.

In the interim of my journey, the black cloud had drawn immeasurably nearer, and was now blotting half the heaven with two portentous wing-like formations. It was a sinister and terrible sight; and it lightened again with that ominous wrathful flaming, with a detonation that beat upon my deaf ears like waves of disintegrative force, and seemed to lacerate the inmost fibers of my body.

I hesitated, fearing that the storm would burst upon me before I could reach the inter-dimensional portals. I saw that I should be exposed to an elemental disturbance of unfamiliar character and supreme violence.

Then, in mid-air, before the imminent, ever-rising cloud, I perceived two flying creatures, whom I can compare only to gigantic moths. With bright, luminous wings, upon the ebon forefront of the storm, they approached me in level but precipitate flight, and would have crashed headlong against the shut gate, if they had not checked themselves with sudden and easy poise.

With hardly a flutter, they descended and paused on the ground beside me, supporting themselves on queer, delicate legs that branched at the knee-joints in floating antennae and waving tentacles. Their wings were sumptuously mottled webs of pearl and madder and opal and orange, and their heads were circled by a series of convex and concave eyes, and were fringed with coiling, horn-like organs from whose hollow ends there hung aerial filaments.

I was more than startled, more than amazed by their aspect; but somehow, by an obscure telepathy, I felt assured that their intentions toward me were friendly. I knew that they wished to enter the city, and knew also that they understood my predicament.

Nevertheless, I was not prepared for what happened. With movements of utmost celerity and grace, one of the giant moth-like beings stationed himself at my right hand, and the other at my left. Then, before I could even suspect their intention, they enfolded my limbs and body with their long tentacles, wrapping me round and round as if with powerful ropes; and carrying me between them as if my weight were a mere trifle, they rose in the air and soared at the mighty ramparts!

In that swift and effortless ascent, the wall seemed to flow downward beside and beneath us like a wave of molten stone. Dizzily I watched the falling away of the mammoth blocks in endless recession. Then we were level with the broad ramparts, were flying across the unguarded parapets and over a canyon-like space toward the immense rectangular buildings and numberless square towers.

We had hardly crossed the walls, when a weird and flickering glow was cast on the edifices before us by another lightening of the great cloud. The moth-like beings paid no apparent heed, and flew steadily on into the city with their strange faces toward an unseen goal. But, turning my head to peer backward at the storm, I beheld an astounding and appalling spectacle.

Beyond the city ramparts, as if wrought by black magic or the toil of genii, another city had reared, and its high towers were moving swiftly forward beneath the rubescent dome of the burning cloud! A second glance, and I perceived that the towers were identical with those I had beheld afar on the plain. In the interim of my passage through the woods, they had travelled over an expanse of many miles by means of some unknown motive-power, and had closed in on the city of the Flame.

Looking more closely, to determine the manner of their locomotion, I saw that they were not mounted on wheels, but on short, massy legs like jointed columns of metal, that gave them the stride of ungainly colossi. There were six or more of these legs to each tower, and near the tops of the towers were rows of huge eye-like openings, from which issued the bolts of red and violet flame I have mentioned before.

The many-colored forest had been burned away by these flames in a league-wide swath of devastation, even to the walls, and there was nothing but a stretch of black, vaporing desert between the mobile towers and the city. Then, even as I gazed, the long, leaping beams began to assail the craggy ramparts, and the topmost parapets were melting like lava beneath them.

It was a scene of utmost terror and grandeur; but, a moment later, it was blotted from my vision by the buildings among which we had now plunged.

The great lepidopterous creatures who bore me went on with the speed of eyrie-questing eagles. In the course of that flight, I was hardly capable of conscious thought or volition; I lived only in the breathless and giddy freedom of aerial movement, of dream-like levitation above the labyrinthine maze of stone immensitudes and marvels.

Also, I was without conscious cognizance of much that I beheld in that stupendous Babel of architectural imageries; and only afterwards, in the more tranquil light of recollection, could I give coherent form and meaning to many of my impressions. My senses were stunned by the vastness and strangeness of it all; and I realized but dimly the cataclysmic ruin that was being loosed upon the city behind us, and the doom from which we were fleeing. I knew that war was being made with unearthly weapons and engineries, by inimical powers that I could not imagine, for a purpose beyond my conception; but to me, it all had the elemental confusion and vague, impersonal horror of some cosmic catastrophe.

We flew deeper and deeper into the city. Broad, platform roofs and terrace-like tiers of balconies flowed away beneath us, and the pavements raced like darkling streams at some enormous depth. Severe cubicular spires and square monoliths were all about and above us; and we saw on some of the roofs the dark, Atlantean people of the city, moving slowly and statuesquely, or standing in attitudes of cryptic resignation and despair, with their faces toward the flaming cloud. All were weaponless, and I saw no engineries anywhere, such as might be used for purposes of military defense.

Swiftly as we flew, the climbing cloud was swifter, and the darkness of its intermittently glowing dome had overarched the town, its spidery filaments had meshed the further heavens and would soon attach themselves to the opposite horizon. The buildings darkened and lightened with the recurrent fulguration; and I felt in all my tissues the painful pulsing of the thunderous vibrations.

Dully and vaguely, I realized that the winged beings who carried me between them were pilgrims to the temple of the Flame. More and more I became aware of an influence that must have been that of the starry music emanating from the temple's heart. There were soft, soothing vibrations in the air, that seemed to absorb and nullify the tearing discords of the unheard thunder. I felt that we were entering a zone of mystic refuge, of sidereal and celestial security; and my troubled senses were both lulled and exalted.

The gorgeous wings of the giant lepidopters began to slant downward. Before and beneath us, at some distance, I perceived a mammoth pile which I knew at once for the temple of the Flame. Down, still down we went, in the awesome space of the surrounding square; and then I was borne in through the lofty ever-open entrance, and along the high hall with its thousand columns.

It was like some corridor in a Karnak of titan worlds. Pregnant with strange balsams, the dim, mysterious dusk enfolded us; and we seemed to be entering realms of premundane antiquity and transstellar immensity, to be following a pillared cavern that led to the core of some ultimate star.

It seemed that we were the last and only pilgrims and also that the temple was deserted by its guardians for we met no one in the whole extent of that column-crowded gloom. After awhile, the dusk began to lighten, and we plunged into a widening beam of radiance, and then into the vast central chamber in which soared the fountain of green fire.

I remember only the impression of shadowy, flickering space, of a vault that was lost in the azure of infinity, of colossal and Memnonian statues that looked down from Himalaya-like altitudes and, above all, the dazzling jet of flame that aspired from a pit in the pavement and rose in air like the visible rapture of gods.

But all this I saw and knew for an instant only. Then I realized that the beings who bore me were flying straight toward the flame on level wings, without the slightest pause or flutter of hesitation!

⁂

There was no room for fear, no time for alarm, in the dazed and chaotic turmoil of my sensations. I was stupefied by all that I had experienced; and, moreover, the drug-like spell of the Flame was upon me, even though I could not hear its fatal singing. I believe that I struggled a little, by some sort of mechanical muscular revulsion, against the tentacular arms that were wound about me. But the lepidopters gave no heed, and it was plain that they were conscious of nothing but the mounting fire and its seductive music.

I remember, however, that there was no sensation of actual heat, such as might have been expected, when we neared the soaring column. Instead, I felt the most ineffable thrilling in all my fibers, as if I were being permeated by waves of celestial energy and demiurgic ecstasy. Then we entered the Flame.

Like Angarth before me, I had taken it for granted that the fate of all those who flung themselves into the Flame was an instant though blissful destruction. I expected to undergo a briefly flaring dissolution, followed by the nothingness of utter annihilation. The thing which really happened was beyond the boldest reach of speculative thought, and to give even the meagerest idea of my sensations would beggar the resources of language.

The Flame enfolded us like a green curtain, blotting from view the great chamber. Then it seemed to me that I was caught and carried to supercelestial heights in an upward-rushing cataract of quintessential force and deific rapture and all-illuminating light. It seemed that I, and also my companions, had achieved a god-like union with the Flame; that every atom of our bodies had undergone a transcendental expansion, was winged with ethereal lightness; that we no longer existed, except as one divine, indivisible entity, soaring beyond the trammels of matter, beyond the limits of time and space, to attain undreamable shores.

Unspeakable was the joy, and infinite was the freedom of that ascent, in which we seemed to overpass the zenith of the highest star. Then, as if we had risen with the Flame to its culmination, had reached its very apex, we emerged and came to a pause.

My senses were faint with exaltation, my eyes were blind with the glory of the fire; and the world on which I now gazed was a vast arabesque of unfamiliar forms, and bewildering hues from another spectrum than the one to which our eyes are habituated. It swirled before my dizzy eyes like a labyrinth of gigantic jewels, with inter-weaving rays and tangled lusters; and only by slow degrees was I able to establish order and distinguish detail in the surging riot of my perceptions.

All about me were endless avenues of super-prismatic opal and jacinth, arches and pillars of ultra-violet gems, of transcendent sapphire, of unearthly ruby and amethyst, all suffused with a multi-tinted splendor. I appeared to be treading on jewels, and above me was a jeweled sky.

Presently, with recovered equilibrium, with eyes adjusted to a new range of cognition, I began to perceive the actual features of the landscape. With the two moth-like beings still beside me, I was standing on a million-flowered grass, among trees of a paradisal vegetation, with fruit, foliage, blossoms, and trunks whose very forms were beyond the conception of tri-dimensional life. The grace of their drooping boughs, of their fretted fronds, was inexpressible in terms of earthly line and contour; and they seemed to be wrought of pure, ethereal substance, half-translucent to the empyrean light, which accounted for the gem-like impression I had first received.

I breathed a nectar-laden air; and the ground beneath me was ineffably soft and resilient, as if it were composed of some higher form of matter than ours. My physical sensations were those of the utmost buoyancy and well-being, with no trace of fatigue or nervousness, such as might have been looked for after the unparalleled and marvelous events in which I had played a part. I felt no sense of mental dislocation or confusion; and, apart from my ability to recognize unknown colors and non-Euclidean forms, I began to experience a queer alteration and extension of tactility, though which it seemed that I was able to touch remote objects.

III
THE INNER DIMENSION

The radiant sky was filled with many-colored suns, like those that might shine on a world of some multiple solar system. But strangely, as I gazed, their glory became softer and dimmer, and the brilliant luster of the trees and grass was gradually subdued, as if by encroaching twilight.

I was beyond surprise, in the boundless marvel and mystery of it all; and nothing, perhaps, would have seemed incredible. But if anything could have amazed me or defied belief, it was the human face—the face of my vanished friend, Giles Angarth, which now emerged from among the waning jewels of the forest, followed by that of another man whom I recognized from photographs as Felix Ebbonly.

They came out from beneath the gorgeous boughs and paused before me. Both were clad in lustrous fabrics, finer than Oriental silk, and of no earthly cut or pattern. Their look was both joyous and meditative, and their faces had taken on a hint of the same translucency that characterized the ethereal fruits and blossoms.

"We have been looking for you," said Angarth. "It occurred to me that after reading my journal, you might be tempted to try the same experiments, if only to make sure whether the account was truth or fiction. This is Felix Ebbonly, whom I believe you have never met."

It surprised me when I found that I could hear his voice with perfect ease and clearness: and I wondered why the effect of the drug-soaked cotton should have died out so soon in my auditory nerves. Yet such details were trivial, in face of the astounding fact that I had found Angarth and Ebbonly; that they, as well as I, had survived the unearthly rapture of the Flame.

"Where are we?" I asked, after acknowledging his introduction. "I confess that I am totally at a loss to comprehend what has happened."

"We are now in what is called the Inner Dimension," explained Angarth. "It is a higher sphere of space and energy and matter than the one into which we were precipitated from Crater Ridge; and the only entrance is through the Singing Flame in the city of Ydmos. The Inner Dimension is born of the fiery fountain, and sustained by it; and those who fling themselves into the Flame are lifted thereby to this superior plane of vibration. For them, the outer worlds no longer exist. The nature of the Flame itself is not known, except that it is a fountain of pure energy, springing from the central rock beneath Ydmos, and passing beyond mortal ken by virtue of its own ardency."

He paused, and seemed to be peering attentively at the winged entities, who still lingered at my side. Then he continued:

"I haven't been here long enough to learn very much, myself; but I have found out a few things; and Ebbonly and I have established a sort of telepathic communication with the other beings who have passed through the Flame. Many of them have no spoken language, nor organs of speech; and their very methods of thought are basically different from ours, because of their divergent lines of sense-development, and the varying conditions of the worlds from which they come. But we are able to communicate a few images.

"The persons who came with you are trying to tell me something," he went on. "You and they, it seems, are the last pilgrims who will enter Ydmos and attain the Inner Dimension. War is being made on the Flame and its guardians by the rulers of the outer lands, because so many of their people have obeyed the lure of the singing fountain and have vanished into the higher sphere. Even now their armies have closed in upon Ydmos, and are blasting the city's ramparts with the force-bolts of their moving towers."

I told him what I had seen, comprehending now much that had been obscure heretofore. He listened gravely; and then said:

"It has long been feared that such war would be made sooner or later. There are many legends in the Outer Lands, concerning the Flame and the fate of those who succumb to its attraction; but the truth is not known, or is guessed only by a few. Many believe, as I did, that the end is destruction; and even by some who suspect its existence, the Inner Dimension is hated, as a thing that lures idle dreamers away from worldly reality. It is regarded as a lethal and pernicious chimera, or a mere poetic dream, or a sort of opium paradise.

"There are a thousand things to tell you, regarding the inner sphere, and the laws and conditions of being to which we are now subject, after the revibration of all our component atoms and electrons in the Flame. But at present there is no time to speak further, since it is highly probable that we are all in grave danger—that the very existence of the Inner Dimension, as well as our own, is threatened by the inimical forces that are destroying Ydmos.

"There are some who say that the Flame is impregnable, that its pure essence will defy the blasting of all inferior beams, and its source remain impenetrable to the lightnings of the Outer Lords. But most are fearful of disaster, and expect the failure of the fountain itself when Ydmos is riven to the central rock.

"Because of this imminent peril, we must not tarry longer. There is a way which affords egress from the inner sphere to another and remoter cosmos in a second infinity—a cosmos unconceived by mundane astronomers, or by the astronomers of the worlds about Ydmos. The majority of the pilgrims, after a term of sojourn here, have gone on to the worlds of this other universe; and Ebbonly and I have waited only for your coming before following them. We must make haste, and delay no more, or doom will overtake us."

Even as he spoke, the two moth-like entities, seeming to resign me to the care of my human friends, arose on the jewel-tinted air and sailed in long, level flight above the paradisal perspectives whose remoter avenues were lost in glory. Angarth and Ebbonly had now stationed themselves beside me; and one took me by the left arm, and the other by the right.

"Try to imagine that you are flying," said Angarth. "In this sphere, levitation and flight are possible through will-power, and you will soon acquire the ability. We shall support and guide you, however, till you have grown accustomed to the new conditions, and are independent of such help."

I obeyed his injunction, and formed a mental image of myself in the act of flying. I was amazed by the clearness and verisimilitude of the thought-picture, still more by the fact that the picture was becoming an actuality! With little sense of effort, but with exactly the same feeling that characterizes a levitational dream, the three of us were soaring from the jeweled ground, were slanting easily and swiftly upward through the glowing air.

Any effort to describe the experience would be foredoomed to futility; since it seemed that a whole range of new senses had been opened up in me, together with corresponding thought-symbols for which there are no words in human speech. I was no longer Philip Hastane, but a larger and stronger and freer entity, differing as much from my former self as the personality developed beneath the influence of hashish or kava would differ.

The dominant feeling was one of immense joy and liberation, coupled with a sense of imperative haste, of the need to escape into other realms where the joy would endure eternal and unthreatened. My visual perceptions, as we flew above the burning, lucent woods, were marked by intense aesthetic pleasure. It was as far above the normal delight afforded by agreeable imagery as the forms and colors of this world were beyond the cognition of normal eyes. Every changing image was a source of veritable ecstasy: and the ecstasy mounted as the whole landscape began to brighten again and returned to the flashing, scintillating glory it had worn when I first beheld it.

We soared at a lofty elevation, looking down on numberless miles of labyrinthine forest, on long luxurious meadows, on voluptuously folded hills, on palatial buildings, and waters that were clear as the pristine lakes and rivers of Eden. It all seemed to quiver and pulsate like one living, effulgent, ethereal entity; and waves of radiant rapture passed from sun to sun in the splendor-crowded heaven.

As we went on, I noticed again, after an interval, that partial dimming of the light, that somnolent, dreamy saddening of the colors, to be followed by another period of ecstatic brightening. The slow, tidal rhythm of this process appeared to correspond to the rising and falling of the Flame, as Angarth had described it in his journal; and I suspected immediately that there was some connection.

No sooner had I formulated this thought, when I became aware that Angarth was speaking. And yet I am not sure whether he spoke, or whether his worded thought was perceptible to me through another sense than that of physical audition. At any rate, I was cognizant of his comment: "You are right. The waning and waxing of the fountain and its music is perceived in the Inner Dimension as a clouding and lightening of all visual images."

Our flight began to swiften, and I realized that my companions were employing all their psychic energies in an effort to redouble our speed. The lands below us blurred to a cataract of streaming color, a sea of flowing luminosity; and we seemed to be hurtling onward like stars through the fiery air.

The ecstasy of that endless soaring, the anxiety of that precipitate flight from an unknown doom, are incommunicable. But I shall never forget them, and never forget the state of ineffable communion and understanding that existed between the three of us. The memory of it all is housed in the deepest and most abiding cells of my brain.

Others were flying beside and above and beneath us now, in the fluctuant glory: pilgrims of hidden worlds and occult dimensions, proceeding as we ourselves toward that other cosmos of which the Inner Sphere was the ante-chamber. These beings were strange and outré beyond belief in their corporeal forms and attributes; and yet I took no thought of their strangeness, but felt toward them the same conviction of fraternity that I felt toward Angarth and Ebbonly.

⁘

Now, as we still went on, it appeared to me that my two companions were telling me many things; were communicating, by what means I am not sure, much that they had learned in their new existence. With a grave urgency, as if perhaps the time for imparting this information might well be brief, ideas were expressed and conveyed which I could never have understood amid terrestrial circumstances. Things that were inconceivable in terms of the five senses, or in abstract symbols of philosophic or mathematic thought, were made plain to me as the letters of the alphabet.

Certain of these data, however, are roughly conveyable or suggestible in language. I was told of the gradual process of initiation into the life of the new dimension, of the powers gained by the neophyte during his term of adaptation; of the various recondite aesthetic joys experienced through a mingling and multiplying of all the perceptions; of the control acquired over natural forces and over matter itself, so that raiment could be woven and buildings reared solely through an act of volition.

I learned also of the laws that would control our passage to the further cosmos, and the fact that such passage was difficult and dangerous for anyone who had not lived a certain length of time in the Inner Dimension. Likewise, I was told that no one could return to our present plane from the higher cosmos, even as no one could go backward through the Flame into Ydmos.

Angarth and Ebbonly had dwelt long enough in the Inner Dimension (they said) to be eligible for entrance to the worlds beyond; and they thought that I too could escape through their assistance, even though I had not yet developed the faculty of spatial equilibrium necessary to sustain those who dared the interspheric path and its dreadful subjacent gulfs alone.

There were boundless, unforeseeable realms, planet on planet, universe on universe, to which we might attain, and among whose prodigies and marvels we could dwell or wander indefinitely. In these worlds, our brains would be attuned to the comprehension or apprehension of vaster and higher scientific laws, and states of entity beyond those of our present dimensional milieu.

I have no idea of the duration of our flight; since, like everything else, my sense of time was completely altered and transfigured. Relatively speaking, we may have gone on for hours; but it seemed to me that we had crossed an area of that supernal terrain for whose transit many years or centuries might well have been required.

Even before we came within sight of it, a clear pictorial image of our destination had arisen in my mind, doubtless through some sort of thought-transference. I seemed to envision a stupendous mountain range, with alp on celestial alp, higher than the summer cumuli of earth; and above them all the horn of an ultra-violet peak whose head was enfolded in a hueless and spiral cloud, touched with the sense of invisible chromatic overtones, that seemed to come down upon it from skies beyond the zenith. I knew that the way to the outer cosmos was hidden in the high cloud.

On, on, we soared; and at length the mountain-range appeared on the far horizon, and I saw the paramount peak of ultra-violet with its dazzling crown of cumulus. Nearer still we came, till the strange volutes of cloud were almost above us, towering to the heavens and vanishing among the vari-colored suns. We saw the gleaming forms of pilgrims who preceded us, as they entered the swirling folds.

At this moment, the sky and the landscape had flamed again to their culminating brilliance, they burned with a thousand hues and lusters; so that the sudden, unlooked-for eclipse which now occurred was all the more complete and terrible.

Before I was conscious of anything amiss, I seemed to hear a despairing cry from my friends, who must have felt the oncoming calamity through a subtler sense than any of which I was yet capable.

Then, beyond the high and luminescent alp of our destination, I saw the mounting of a wall of darkness, dreadful and instant and positive and palpable, that rose everywhere and toppled like some Atlantean wave upon the irised suns and the fiery-colored vistas of the Inner Dimension.

We hung irresolute in the shadowed air, powerless and hopeless before the impending catastrophe, and saw that the darkness had surrounded the entire world and was rushing upon us from all sides. It ate the heavens, it blotted the outer suns; and the vast perspectives over which we had flown appeared to shrink and shrivel like a blackened paper. We seemed to wait alone for one terrible instant, in a center of dwindling light, on which the cyclonic forces of night and destruction were impinging with torrential rapidity.

The center shrank to a mere point—and then the darkness was upon us like an overwhelming maelstrom—like the falling and crashing of cyclopean walls. I seemed to go down with the wreck of shattered worlds in a roaring sea of vortical space and force, to descend into some intra-stellar pit, some ultimate limbo to which the shards of forgotten suns and systems are flung. Then, after a measureless interval, there came the sensation of violent impact, as if I had fallen among these shards, at the bottom of the universal night.

*

I struggled back to consciousness with slow, prodigious effort, as if I were crushed beneath some irremovable weight, beneath the lightless and inert debris of galaxies. It seemed to require the labors of a Titan to lift my lids; and my body and limbs were heavy as if they had been turned to some denser element than human flesh; or had been subjected to the gravitation of a grosser planet than the earth.

My mental processes were benumbed and painful and confused to the last degree; but at length I realized that I was lying on a riven and tilted pavement, among gigantic blocks of fallen stone. Above me, the light of a livid heaven came down among overturned and jagged walls that no longer supported their colossal dome. Close beside me, I saw a fuming pit, from which a ragged rift extended through the floor, like the chasm wrought by an earthquake.

I could not recognize my surroundings for a time; but at last, with a toilsome groping of thought, I understood that I was lying in the ruined temple of Ydmos. The pit whose grey and acrid vapors rose beside me was that from which the fountain of singing flame had issued.

It was a scene of stupendous havoc and devastation. The wrath that had been visited upon Ydmos had left no wall nor pylon of the temple standing. I stared at the blighted heavens from an architectural ruin in which the remains of On and Angkor would have been mere rubble-heaps.

With herculean effort, I turned my head away from the smoking pit, whose thin, sluggish fumes curled upward in fantasmal coils where the green ardor of the Flame had soared and sung. Not until then did I perceive my companions. Angarth, still insensible, was lying near at hand; and just beyond him I saw the contorted face of Ebbonly, whose lower limbs and body were pinned down by the rough and broken pediment of a fallen pillar.

Striving as in some eternal nightmare to throw off the leaden-clinging weight of my inertia, and able to bestir myself only with the most painful slowness and laboriousness, I got somehow to my feet and went over to Ebbonly. Angarth, I saw at a glance, was uninjured, and would presently regain consciousness; but Ebbonly, crushed by the monolithic mass of stone, was dying swiftly; and even with the help of a dozen men, I could not have released him from his imprisonment nor could I have done anything to palliate his agony.

He tried to smile, with gallant and piteous courage as I stooped above him.

"It's no use—I'm going in a moment," he whispered. "Good-bye, Hastane—and tell Angarth good-bye for me, too." His tortured lips relaxed, his eyelids dropped, and his head fell back on the temple pavement. With an unreal, dream-like horror, almost without emotion, I saw that he was dead. The exhaustion that still beset me was too profound to permit of thought or feeling; it was like the first reaction that follows the awakening from a drug-debauch. My nerves were like burnt-out wires, my muscles were dead and unresponsive as clay, my brain was ashen and gutted as if a great fire burned within it and had gone out.

Somehow, after an interval of whose length my memory is uncertain, I managed to revive Angarth, and he sat up dully and dazedly. When I told him that Ebbonly was dead, my words appeared to make no impression upon him and I wondered for awhile if he understood. Finally, rousing himself a little with evident difficulty, he peered at the body of our friend, and seemed to realize in some measure the horror of the situation. But I think he would have remained there for hours, or perhaps for all time, in his utter despair and lassitude, if I had not taken the initiative.

"Come," I said, with an attempt at firmness. "We must get out of this."

"Where to?" he queried, dully. "The Flame has failed at its source; and the Inner Dimension is no more. I wish I were dead, like Ebbonly—I might as well be, judging from the way I feel."

"We must find our way back to Crater Ridge," I said. "Surely we can do it, if the inter-dimensional portals have not been destroyed."

Angarth did not seem to hear me; but he followed obediently when I took him by the arm and began to seek an exit from the temple's heart among the roofless halls and overturned columns.

My recollections of our return are dim and confused, and are full of the tediousness of some interminable delirium. I remember looking back at Ebbonly, lying white and still beneath the massive pillar that would serve as an eternal monument; and I recall the mountainous ruins of the city, in which it seemed that we were the only living beings. It was a wilderness of chaotic stone, of fused, obsidian-like blocks, where streams of molten lava still ran in the mighty chasms, or poured like torrents adown unfathomable pits that had opened in the ground. And I remember seeing amid the wreckage the charred bodies of those dark colossi who were the people of Ydmos and the warders of the Flame.

Like pygmies lost in some shattered fortalice of the giants, we stumbled onward, strangling in mephitic and metallic vapors, reeling with weariness, dizzy with the heat that emanated everywhere to surge upon us in buffeting waves. The way was blocked by overthrown buildings, by toppled towers and battlements, over which we climbed precariously and toilsomely; and often we were compelled to divagate from our direct course by enormous rifts that seemed to cleave the foundations of the world.

The moving towers of the wrathful Outer Lords had withdrawn, their armies had disappeared on the plain beyond Ydmos, when we staggered over the riven and shapeless and scoriac crags that had formed the city's ramparts. Before us there was nothing but desolation—a fire-blackened and vapor-vaulted expanse in which no tree or blade of grass remained.

Across this waste we found our way to the slope of violet grass above the plain, which had lain beyond the path of the invaders' bolts. There the guiding monoliths, reared by a people of whom we were never to learn even the name, still looked down on the fuming desert and the mounded wrack of Ydmos. And there, at length, we came once more to the greyish-green columns that were the gateway between the worlds.

THE VAULTS OF
YOH-VOMBIS

If the doctors are correct in their prognostication, I have only a few Martian hours of life remaining to me. In those hours I shall endeavor to relate, as a warning to others who might follow in our footsteps, the singular and frightful happenings that terminated our researches among the ruins of Yoh-Vombis. If my story will only serve to prevent future explorations, the telling will not have been in vain.

There were eight of us, professional archæologists with more or less terrene and interplanetary experience, who set forth with native guides from Ignarh, the commercial metropolis of Mars, to inspect that ancient, eon-deserted city. Octave, our official leader, held his primacy by knowing more about Martian archæology than any other Terrestrial on the planet, and others of the party, such as William Harper and Jonas Halgren, had been associated with him in many of his previous researches. I, Rodney Severn, was more of a newcomer, having spent a few months on Mars; and the greater part of my own ultra-terrene delvings had been confined to Venus.

The nude, sponge-chested Aihais had spoken deterringly of vast deserts filled with ever-swirling sandstorms, through which we must pass to reach Yoh-Vombis; and in spite of our munificent offers of payment, it had been difficult to secure guides for the journey. Therefore we were surprised as well as pleased when we came to the ruins after seven hours of plodding across the flat, treeless, orange-yellow desolation to the southwest of Ignarh.

We beheld our destination, for the first time, in the setting of the small, remote sun. For a little, we thought that the domeless, three-angled towers and broken-down monoliths were those of some unlegended city, other than the one we sought. But the disposition of the ruins, which lay in a sort of arc for almost the entire extent of a low, gneissic, league-long elevation of bare, eroded stone, together with the type of architecture, soon convinced us that we had found our goal. No other ancient city on Mars had been laid out in that manner; and the strange, many-terraced buttresses, like the stairways of forgotten Anakim, were peculiar to the prehistoric race that had built Yoh-Vombis.

I have seen the hoary, sky-confronting walls of Machu Picchu amid the desolate Andes; and the frozen, giant-builded battlements of Uogam on the glacial tundras of the nightward hemisphere of Venus. But these were as things of yesteryear compared to the walls upon which we gazed. The whole region was far from the life-giving canals beyond whose environs even the more noxious flora and fauna are seldom found; and we had seen no living thing since our departure from Ignarh. But here, in this place of petrified sterility, of eternal bareness and solitude, it seemed that life could never have been.

I think we all received the same impression as we stood staring in silence while the pale, sanies-like sunset fell on the dark and megalithic ruins. I remember gasping a little, in an air that seemed to have been touched by the irrespirable chill of death; and I heard the same sharp, laborious intake of breath from others of our party.

"That place is deader than an Egyptian morgue," observed Harper.

"Certainly it is far more ancient," Octave assented. "According to the most reliable legends, the Yorhis, who built Yoh-Vombis, were wiped out by the present ruling race at least forty thousand years ago."

"There's a story, isn't there," said Harper, "that the last remnant of the Yorhis was destroyed by some unknown agency—something too horrible and outré to be mentioned even in a myth?"

"Of course, I've heard that legend," agreed Octave. "Maybe we'll find evidence among the ruins to prove or disprove it. The Yorhis may have been cleaned out by some terrible epidemic, such as the Yashta pestilence, which was a kind of green mold that ate all the bones of the body, starting with the teeth. But we needn't be afraid of getting it, if there are any mummies in Yoh-Vombis—the bacteria will all be dead as their victims, after so many cycles of planetary desiccation."

The sun had gone down with uncanny swiftness, as if it had disappeared through some sort of prestidigitation rather than the normal process of setting. We felt the instant chill of the blue-green twilight; and the ether above us was like a huge, transparent dome of sunless ice, shot with a million bleak sparklings that were the stars. We donned the coats and helmets of Martian fur, which must always be worn at night; and going on to westward of the walls, we established our camp in their lee, so that we might be sheltered a little from the *jaar*, that cruel desert wind that always blows from the east before dawn. Then, lighting the alcohol lamps that had been brought along for cooking purposes, we huddled around them while the evening meal was prepared and eaten.

Afterward, for comfort rather than because of weariness, we retired early to our sleeping-bags; and the two Aihais, our guides, wrapped themselves in the cerement-like folds of *bassa*-cloth which are all the protection their leathery skins appear to require even in sub-zero temperatures.

Even in my thick, double-lined bag, I still felt the rigor of the night air; and I am sure it was this, rather than anything else, which kept me awake for a long while and rendered my eventual slumber some- what restless and broken. At any rate, I was not troubled by even the least presentiment of alarm or danger; and I should have laughed at the idea that anything of peril could lurk in Yoh-Vombis, amid whose undreamable and stupefying antiquities the very phantoms of its dead must long since have faded into nothingness.

I must have drowsed again and again, with starts of semi-wakefulness. At last, in one of these, I knew vaguely that the small twin moons, Phobos and Deimos, had risen and were making huge and far-flung shadows with the domeless towers; shadows that almost touched the glimmering, shrouded forms of my companions.

The whole scene was locked in a petrific stillness; and none of the sleepers stirred. Then, as my lids were about to close, I received an impression of movement in the frozen gloom; and it seemed to me that a portion of the foremost shadow had detached itself and was crawling toward Octave, who lay nearer to the ruins than we others.

Even through my heavy lethargy, I was disturbed by a warning of something unnatural and perhaps ominous. I started to sit up; and even as I moved, the shadowy object, whatever it was, drew back and became merged once more in the greater shadow. Its vanishment startled me into full wakefulness; and yet I could not be sure that I had actually seen the thing. In that brief, final glimpse, it had seemed like a roughly circular piece of cloth or leather, dark and crumpled, and twelve or fourteen inches in diameter, that ran along the ground with the doubling movement of an inch-worm, causing it to fold and unfold in a startling manner as it went.

I did not go to sleep again for nearly an hour; and if it had not been for the extreme cold, I should doubtless have gotten up to investigate and make sure whether I had really beheld an object of such bizarre nature or had merely dreamt it. But more and more I began to convince myself that the thing was too unlikely and fantastical to have been anything but the figment of a dream. And at last I nodded off into light slumber.

The chill, demoniac sighing of the *jaar* across the jagged walls awoke me, and I saw that the faint moonlight had received the hueless accession of early dawn. We all arose, and prepared our breakfast with fingers that grew numb in spite of the spirit-lamps.

My queer visual experience during the night had taken on more than ever a fantasmagoric unreality; and I gave it no more than a passing thought and did not speak of it to the others. We were all eager to begin our explorations; and shortly after sunrise we started on a preliminary tour of examination.

Strangely, as it seemed, the two Martians refused to accompany us. Stolid and taciturn, they gave no explicit reason; but evidently nothing would induce them to enter Yoh-Vombis. Whether or not they were afraid of the ruins, we were unable to determine: their enigmatic faces, with the small oblique eyes and huge, flaring nostrils, betrayed neither fear nor any other emotion intelligible to man. In reply to our questions, they merely said that no Aihai had set foot among the ruins for ages. Apparently there was some mysterious taboo in connection with the place.

For equipment in that preliminary tour we took along only our electric torches and a crowbar. Our other tools, and some cartridges of high explosives, we left at our camp, to be used later if necessary, after we had surveyed the ground. One or two of us owned automatics; but these also were left behind; for it seemed absurd to imagine that any form of life would be encountered among the ruins.

Octave was visibly excited as we began our inspection, and maintained a running fire of exclamatory comment. The rest of us were subdued and silent: it was impossible to shake off the somber awe and wonder that fell upon us from those megalithic stones.

We went on for some distance among the triangular, terraced buildings, following the zigzag streets that conformed to this peculiar architecture. Most of the towers were more or less dilapidated; and everywhere we saw the deep erosion wrought by cycles of blowing wind and sand, which, in many cases, had worn into roundness the sharp angles of the mighty walls. We entered some of the towers, but found utter emptiness within. Whatever they had contained in the way of furnishings must long ago have crumbled into dust; and the dust had been blown away by the searching desert gales.

At length we came to the wall of a vast terrace, hewn from the plateau itself. On this terrace, the central buildings were grouped like a sort of acropolis. A flight of time-eaten steps, designed for longer limbs than those of men or even the gangling modern Martians, afforded access to the hewn summit.

Pausing, we decided to defer our investigation of the higher buildings, which, being more exposed than the others, were doubly ruinous and dilapidated, and in all likelihood would offer little for our trouble. Octave had begun to voice his disappointment over our failure to find anything in the nature of artifacts or carvings that would throw light on the history of Yoh-Vombis.

Then, a little to the right of the stairway, we perceived an entrance in the main wall, half choked with ancient debris. Behind the heap of detritus, we found the beginning of a downward flight of steps. Darkness poured from the opening, noisome and musty with primordial stagnancies of decay; and we could see nothing below the first steps, which gave the appearance of being suspended over a black gulf.

Throwing his torch-beam into the abyss, Octave began to descend the stairs. His eager voice called us to follow.

At the bottom of the high, awkward steps, we found ourselves in a long and roomy vault, like a subterranean hallway. Its floor was deep with siftings of immemorial dust. The air was singularly heavy, as if the lees of an ancient atmosphere, less tenuous than that of Mars today, had settled down and remained in that stagnant darkness. It was harder to breathe than the outer air: it was filled with unknown effluvia; and the light dust arose before us at every step, diffusing a faintness of bygone corruption, like the dust of powdered mummies.

At the end of the vault, before a strait and lofty doorway, our torches revealed an immense, shallow urn or pan, supported on short cube-shaped legs, and wrought from a dull, blackish-green material. In its bottom, we perceived a deposit of dark and cinder-like fragments, which gave off a slight but disagreeable pungence like the phantom of some more powerful odor. Octave, bending over the rim, began to cough and sneeze as he inhaled it.

"That stuff, whatever it was, must have been a pretty strong fumigant," he observed. "The people of Yoh-Vombis may have used it to disinfect the vaults."

The doorway beyond the shallow urn admitted us to a larger chamber, whose floor was comparatively free of dust. We found that the dark stone beneath our feet was marked off in multiform geometric patterns, traced with ochreous ore, amid which, as in Egyptian cartouches, hieroglyphics and highly formalized drawings were enclosed. We could make little from most of them; but the figures in many were doubtless designed to represent the Yorhis themselves. Like the Aihais, they were tall and angular, with great, bellows-like chests. The ears and nostrils, as far as we could judge, were not so huge and flaring as those of the modern Martians. All of these Yorhis were depicted as being nude; but in one of the cartouches, done in a far hastier style than the others, we perceived two figures whose high, conical craniums were wrapped in what seemed to be a sort of turban, which they were about to remove or adjust. The artist seemed to have laid a peculiar emphasis on the odd gesture with which the sinuous, four-jointed fingers were plucking at these head-dresses; and the whole posture was unexplainably contorted.

From the second vault, passages ramified in all directions, leading to a veritable warren of catacombs. Here, enormous pot-bellied urns of the same material as the fumigating-pan, but taller than a man's head and fitted with angular-handled stoppers, were ranged in solemn rows along the walls, leaving scant room for two of us to walk abreast. When we succeeded in removing one of the huge stoppers, we saw that the jar was filled to the rim with ashes and charred fragments of bone. Doubtless (as is still the Martian custom) the Yorhis had stored the cremated remains of whole families in single urns.

Even Octave became silent as we went on; and a sort of meditative awe seemed to replace his former excitement. We others, I think, were utterly weighed down to a man by the solid gloom of a concept-defying antiquity, into which it seemed that we were going farther and farther at every step.

The shadows fluttered before us like the monstrous and misshapen wings of phantom bats. There was nothing anywhere but the atom-like dust of ages, and the jars that held the ashes of a long-extinct people. But, clinging to the high roof in one of the farther vaults, I saw a dark and corrugated patch of circular form, like a withered fungus. It was impossible to reach the thing; and we went on after peering at it with many futile conjectures. Oddly enough, I failed to remember at that moment the crumpled shadowy object I had seen or dreamt of the night before.

I have no idea how far we had gone, when we came to the last vault; but it seemed that we had been wandering for ages in that forgotten underworld. The air was growing fouler and more irrespirable, with a thick, sodden quality, as if from a sediment of material rottenness; and we had about decided to turn back. Then, without warning, at the end of a long, urn-lined catacomb, we found ourselves confronted by a blank wall.

Here we came upon one of the strangest and most mystifying of our discoveries: a mummified and incredibly desiccated figure, standing erect against the wall. It was more than seven feet in height, of a brown, bituminous color, and was wholly nude except for a sort of black cowl that covered the upper head and drooped down at the sides in wrinkled folds. From the size and general contour, it was plainly one of the ancient Yorhis—perhaps the sole member of this race whose body had remained intact.

We all felt an inexpressible thrill at the sheer age of this shrivelled thing, which, in the dry air of the vault, had endured through all the historic and geologic vicissitudes of the planet, to provide a visible link with lost cycles.

Then, as we peered closer with our torches, we saw *why* the mummy had maintained an upright position. At ankles, knees, waist, shoulders, and neck it was shackled to the wall by heavy metal bands, so deeply eaten and embrowned with a sort of rust that we had failed to distinguish them at first sight in the shadow. The strange cowl on the head, when closelier studied, continued to baffle us. It was covered with a fine, mold-like pile, unclean and dusty as ancient cobwebs. Something about it, I know not what, was abhorrent and revolting.

"By Jove! This is a real find!" ejaculated Octave, as he thrust his torch into the mummified face, where shadows moved like living things in the pit-deep hollows of the eyes and the huge triple nostrils and wide ears that flared upward beneath the cowl.

Still lifting the torch, he put out his free hand and touched the body very lightly. Tentative as the touch had been, the lower part of the barrel-like torso, the legs, the hands and forearms all seemed to dissolve into powder, leaving the head and upper body and arms still hanging in their metal fetters. The progress of decay had been queerly unequal, for the remnant portions gave no sign of disintegration.

Octave cried out in dismay, and then began to cough and sneeze, as the cloud of brown powder, floating with airy lightness, enveloped him. We others all stepped back to avoid the powder. Then, above the spreading cloud, I saw an unbelievable thing. The black cowl on the mummy's head began to curl and twitch upward at the corners, it writhed with a verminous motion, it fell from the withered cranium, seeming to fold and unfold convulsively in midair as it fell. Then it dropped on the bare head of Octave who, in his disconcertment at the crumbling of the mummy, had remained standing close to the wall. At that instant, in a start of profound terror, I remembered the thing that had inched itself from the shadows of Yoh-Vombis in the light of the twin moons, and had drawn back like a figment of slumber at my first waking movement.

Cleaving closely as a tightened cloth, the thing enfolded Octave's hair and brow and eyes, and he shrieked wildly, with incoherent pleas for help, and tore with frantic fingers at the cowl, but failed to loosen it. Then his cries began to mount in a mad crescendo of agony, as beneath some instrument of infernal torture; and he danced and capered blindly about the vault, eluding us with strange celerity as we all sprang forward in an effort to reach him and release him from his weird incumbrance. The whole happening was mysterious as a nightmare; but the thing that had fallen on his head was plainly some unclassified form of Martian life, which, contrary to all the known laws of science, had survived in those primordial catacombs. We must rescue him from its clutches if we could.

We tried to close in on the frenzied figure of our chief—which, in the far from roomy space between the last urns and the wall, should have been an easy matter. But, darting away, in a manner doubly incomprehensible because of his blindfolded condition, he circled about us and ran past, to disappear among the urns toward the outer labyrinth of intersecting catacombs.

"My God! What has happened to him?" cried Harper. "The man acts as if he were possessed."

There was obviously no time for a discussion of the enigma, and we all followed Octave as speedily as our astonishment would permit. We had lost sight of him in the darkness; and when we came to the first division of the vaults, we were doubtful as to which passage he had taken, till we heard a shrill scream, several times repeated, in a catacomb on the extreme left. There was a shrill, unearthly quality in those screams, which may have been due to the long-stagnant air or the peculiar acoustics of the ramifying caverns. But somehow I could not imagine them as issuing from human lips—at least not from those of a living man. They seemed to contain a soulless, mechanical agony, as if they had been wrung from a devil-driven corpse.

Thrusting our torches before us into the lurching, fleeing shadows, we raced along between rows of mighty urns. The screaming had died away in sepulchral silence; but far off we heard the light and muffled thud of running feet. We followed in headlong pursuit; but, gasping painfully in the vitiated, miasmal air, we were soon compelled to slacken our pace without coming in sight of Octave. Very faintly, and farther away than ever, like the tomb-swallowed steps of a phantom, we heard his vanishing footfalls. Then they ceased; and we heard nothing, except our own convulsive breathing, and the blood that throbbed in our temple-veins like steadily beaten drums of alarm.

We went on, dividing our party into three contingents when we came to a triple branching of the caverns. Harper and Halgren and I took the middle passage, and after we had gone on for an endless interval without finding any trace of Octave, and had threaded our way through recesses piled to the roof with colossal urns that must have held the ashes of a hundred generations, we came out in the huge chamber with the geometric floor-designs. Here, very shortly, we were joined by the others, who had likewise failed to locate our missing leader.

It would be useless to detail our renewed and hour-long search of the myriad vaults, many of which we had not hitherto explored. All were empty, as far as any sign of life was concerned. I remember passing once more through the vault in which I had seen the dark, rounded patch on the ceiling, and noting with a shudder that the patch was gone. It was a miracle that we did not lose ourselves in that underworld maze; but at last we came back again to the final catacomb, in which we had found the shackled mummy.

We heard a measured and recurrent clangor as we neared the place—a most alarming and mystifying sound under the circumstances. It was like the hammering of ghouls on some forgotten mausoleum. When we drew nearer, the beams of our torches revealed a sight that was no less unexplainable than unexpected. A human figure, with its back toward us and the head concealed by a swollen black object that had the size and form of a sofa cushion, was standing near the remains of the mummy and was striking at the wall with a pointed metal bar. How long Octave had been there, and where he had found the bar, we could not know. But the blank wall had crumbled away beneath his furious blows, leaving on the floor a pile of comet-like fragments; and a small, narrow door, of the same ambiguous material as the cinerary urns and the fumigating-pan, had been laid bare.

Amazed, uncertain, inexpressibly bewildered, we were all incapable of action or volition at that moment. The whole business was too fantastic and too horrifying, and it was plain that Octave had been overcome by some sort of madness. I, for one, felt the violent upsurge of sudden nausea when I had identified the loathsomely bloated thing that clung to Octave's head and drooped in obscene tumescence on his neck. I did not dare to surmise the causation of its bloating.

⁂

Before any of us could recover our faculties, Octave flung aside the metal bar and began to fumble for something in the wall. It must have been a hidden spring; though how he could have known its location or existence is beyond all legitimate conjecture. With a dull, hideous grating, the uncovered door swung inward, thick and ponderous as a mausolean slab, leaving an aperture from which the nether midnight seemed to well like a flood of eon-buried foulness. Somehow, at that instant, our electric torches appeared to flicker and grow dim; and we all breathed a suffocating fœtor, like a draft from inner worlds of immemorial putrescence.

Octave had turned toward us now, and he stood in an idle posture before the open door, like one who has finished some ordained task. I was the first of our party to throw off the paralyzing spell; and pulling out a clasp-knife—the only semblance of a weapon which I carried—I ran over to him. He moved back, but not quickly enough to evade me, when I stabbed with the four-inch blade at the black, turgescent mass that enveloped his whole upper head and hung down upon his eyes.

What the thing was, I should prefer not to imagine—if it were possible to imagine. It was formless as a great slug, with neither head nor tail nor apparent organs—an unclean, puffy, leathery thing covered with that fine, mold-like fur of which I have spoken. The knife tore into it as if through rotten parchment, making a long gash, and the horror appeared to collapse like a broken bladder. Out of it, there gushed a sickening torrent of human blood, mingled with dark, filiated masses that may have been half-dissolved hair, and floating gelatinous lumps like molten bone, and shreds of a curdy white substance. At the same time, Octave began to stagger, and went down at full length on the floor. Disturbed by his fall, the mummy-dust arose about him in a curling cloud, beneath which he lay mortally still.

Conquering my revulsion, and choking with the dust, I bent over him and tore the flaccid, oozing horror from his head. It came with unexpected ease, as if I had removed a limp rag: but I wish to God that I had let it remain. Beneath, there was no longer a human cranium, for all had been eaten away, even to the eyebrows, and the half-devoured brain was laid bare as I lifted the cowl-like object. I dropped the unnameable thing from fingers that had grown suddenly nerveless, and it turned over as it fell, revealing on the nether side many rows of pinkish suckers, arranged in circles about a pallid disk that was covered with nervelike filaments, suggesting a sort of plexus.

My companions had pressed forward behind me; but, for an appreciable interval, no one spoke.

"How long do you suppose he has been dead?" It was Halgren who whispered the awful question, which we had all been asking ourselves. Apparently no one felt able or willing to answer it; and we could only stare in horrible, timeless fascination at Octave.

At length I made an effort to avert my gaze; and turning at random, I saw the remnants of the shackled mummy, and noted for the first time, with mechanical, unreal horror, the half-eaten condition of the withered head. From this, my gaze was diverted to the newly opened door at one side, without perceiving for a moment what had drawn my attention. Then, startled, I beheld beneath my torch, far down beyond the door, as if in some nether pit, a seething, multitudinous, worm-like movement of crawling shadows. They seemed to boil up in the darkness; and then, over the broad threshold of the vault, there poured the verminous vanguard of a countless army: things that were kindred to the monstrous, diabolic leech I had torn from Octave's eaten head. Some were thin and flat, like writhing, doubling disks of cloth or leather, and others were more or less poddy, and crawled with glutted slowness. What they had found to feed on in the sealed, eternal midnight I do not know; and I pray that I never shall know.

I sprang back and away from them, electrified with terror, sick with loathing; and the black army inched itself unendingly with nightmare swiftness from the unsealed abyss, like the nauseous vomit of horror-sated hells. As it poured toward us, burying Octave's body from sight in a writhing wave, I saw a stir of life from the seemingly dead thing I had cast aside, and saw the loathly struggle which it made to right itself and join the others.

But neither I nor my companions could endure to look longer. We turned and ran between the mighty rows of urns, with the slithering mass of demon leeches close upon us, and scattered in blind panic when we came to the first division of the vaults. Heedless of each other or of anything but the urgency of flight, we plunged into the ramifying passages at random. Behind me, I heard someone stumble and go down, with a curse that mounted to an insane shrieking; but I knew that if I halted and went back, it would be only to invite the same baleful doom that had overtaken the hindmost of our party.

Still clutching the electric torch and my open clasp-knife, I ran along a minor passage which, I seemed to remember, would conduct with more or less directness upon the large outer vault with the painted floor. Here I found myself alone. The others had kept to the main catacombs; and I heard far off a muffled babel of mad cries, as if several of them had been seized by their pursuers.

❧

It seemed that I must have been mistaken about the direction of the passage; for it turned and twisted in an unfamiliar manner, with many intersections, and I soon found that I was lost in the black labyrinth, where the dust had lain unstirred by living feet for inestimable generations. The cinerary warren had grown still once more; and I heard my own frenzied panting, loud and stertorous as that of a Titan in the dead silence.

Suddenly, as I went on, my torch disclosed a human figure coming toward me in the gloom. Before I could master my startlement, the figure had passed me with long, machine-like strides, as if returning to the inner vaults. I think it was Harper, since the height and build were about right for him; but I am not altogether sure, for the eyes and upper head were muffled by a dark, inflated cowl, and the pale lips were locked as if in a silence of tetanic torture—or death. Whoever he was, he had dropped his torch; and he was running blindfold, in utter darkness, beneath the impulsion of that unearthly vampirism, to seek the very fountain-head of the unloosed horror. I knew that he was beyond human help; and I did not even dream of trying to stop him.

Trembling violently, I resumed my flight, and was passed by two more of our party, stalking by with mechanical swiftness and sureness, and cowled with those Satanic leeches. The others must have returned by way of the main passages; for I did not meet them; and I was never to see them again.

The remainder of my flight is a blur of pandemonian terror. Once more, after thinking that I was near the outer cavern, I found myself astray, and fled through a ranged eternity of monstrous urns, in vaults that must have extended for an unknown distance beyond our explorations. It seemed that I had gone on for years; and my lungs were choking with the eon-dead air, and my legs were ready to crumble beneath me, when I saw far off a tiny point of blessed daylight. I ran toward it with all the terrors of the alien darkness crowding behind me, and accursed shadows flittering before, and saw that the vault ended in a low, ruinous entrance, littered by rubble on which there fell an arc of thin sunshine.

It was another entrance than the one by which we had penetrated this lethal underworld. I was within a dozen feet of the opening when, without sound or other intimation, something dropped upon my head from the roof above, blinding me instantly and closing upon me like a tautened net. My brow and scalp, at the same time, were shot through with a million needle-like pangs—a manifold, ever-growing agony that seemed to pierce the very bone and converge from all sides upon my inmost brain.

The terror and suffering of that moment were worse than aught which the hells of earthly madness or delirium could ever contain. I felt the foul, vampiric clutch of an atrocious death—and of more than death.

I believe that I dropped the torch; but the fingers of my right hand had still retained the open knife. Instinctively—since I was hardly capable of conscious volition—I raised the knife and slashed blindly, again and again, many times, at the thing that had fastened its deadly folds upon me. The blade must have gone through and through the clinging monstrosity, to gash my own flesh in a score of places; but I did not feel the pain of those wounds in the million-throbbing torment that possessed me.

At last I saw light, and saw that a black strip, loosened from above my eyes and dripping with my own blood, was hanging down my cheek. It writhed a little, even as it hung, and I ripped it away, and ripped the other remnants of the thing, tatter by oozing, bloody tatter, from off my brow and head. Then I staggered toward the entrance; and the wan light turned to a far, receding, dancing flame before me as I lurched and fell outside the cavern—a flame that fled like the last star of creation above the yawning, sliding chaos and oblivion into which I descended. . . .

❧

I am told that my unconsciousness was of brief duration. I came to myself, with the cryptic faces of the two Martian guides bending over me. My head was full of lancinating pains, and half-remembered terrors closed upon my mind like the shadows of mustering harpies. I rolled over, and looked back toward the cavern-mouth, from which the Martians, after finding me, had seemingly dragged me for some little distance. The mouth was under the terraced angle of an outer building, and within sight of our camp.

I stared at the black opening with hideous fascination, and descried a shadowy stirring in the gloom—the writhing, verminous movement of things that pressed forward from the darkness but did not emerge into the light. Doubtless they could not endure the sun, those creatures of ultramundane night and cycle-sealed corruption.

It was then that the ultimate horror, the beginning madness, came upon me. Amid my crawling revulsion, my nausea-prompted desire to flee from that seething cavern-mouth, there rose an abhorrently conflicting impulse to return; to thread my backward way through all the catacombs, as the others had done; to go down where never men save they, the inconceivably doomed and accursed, had ever gone; to seek beneath that damnable compulsion a nether world that human thought can never picture. There was a black light, a soundless calling, in the vaults of my brain: the implanted summons of the Thing, like a permeating and sorcerous poison. It lured me to the subterranean door that was walled up by the dying people of Yoh-Vombis, to immure those hellish and immortal leeches, those dark parasites that engraft their own abominable life on the half-eaten brains of the dead. It called me to the depths beyond, where dwell the noisome, necromantic Ones, of whom the leeches, with all their powers of vampirism and diabolism, are but the merest minions . . .

It was only the two Aihais who prevented me from going back. I struggled, I fought them insanely as they strove to retard me with their spongy arms; but I must have been pretty thoroughly exhausted from all the superhuman adventures of the day; and I went down once more, after a little, into fathomless nothingness, from which I floated out at long intervals, to realize that I was being carried across the desert toward Ignarh.

Well, that is all my story. I have tried to tell it fully and coherently, at a cost that would be unimaginable to the sane . . . to tell it before the madness falls upon me again, as it will very soon—as it is doing now . . . Yes, I have told my story . . . and you have written it all out, haven't you? Now I must go back to Yoh-Vombis—back across the desert and down through all the catacombs to the vaster vaults beneath. Something is in my brain, that commands me and will direct me . . . I tell you, I must go . . .

POSTSCRIPT

As an intern in the territorial hospital at Ignarh, I had charge of the singular case of Rodney Severn, the one surviving member of the Octave Expedition to Yoh-Vombis, and took down the above story from his dictation. Severn had been brought to the hospital by the Martian guides of the Expedition. He was suffering from a horribly lacerated and inflamed condition of the scalp and brow, and was wildly delirious part of the time, and had to be held down in his bed during recurrent seizures of a mania whose violence was doubly inexplicable in view of his extreme debility.

The lacerations, as will have been learned from the story, were mainly self-inflicted. They were mingled with numerous small round wounds, easily distinguished from the knife-slashes, and arranged in regular circles, through which an unknown poison had been injected into Severn's scalp. The causation of these wounds was difficult to explain; unless one were to believe that Severn's story was true, and was no mere figment of his illness. Speaking for myself, in the light of what afterward occurred, I feel that I have no other resource than to believe it. There are strange things on the red planet; and I can only second the wish that was expressed by the doomed archæologist in regard to future explorations.

The night after he had finished telling me his story, while another doctor than myself was supposedly on duty, Severn managed to escape from the hospital, doubtless in one of the strange seizures at which I have hinted: a most astonishing thing, for he had seemed weaker than ever after the long strain of his terrible narrative, and his demise had been hourly expected. More astonishing still, his bare footsteps were found in the desert, going toward Yoh-Vombis, till they vanished in the path of a light sandstorm; but no trace of Severn himself has yet been discovered.

THE DOUBLE SHADOW

My name is Pharpetron, among those who have known me in Poseidonis; but even I, the last and most forward pupil of the wise Avyctes, know not the name of that which I am fated to become ere tomorrow. Therefore, by the ebbing silver lamps, in my master's marble house above the loud, ever-ravening sea, I write this tale with a hasty hand, scrawling an ink of wizard virtue on the grey, priceless, antique parchment of dragons. And having written, I shall enclose the pages in a sealed cylinder of orichalchum, and shall cast the cylinder from a high window into the sea, lest that which I am doomed to become should haply destroy the writing. And it may be that mariners from Lephara, passing to Umb and Pneor in their tall triremes, will find the cylinder; or fishers will draw it from the wave in their seines of byssus; and having read my story, men will learn the truth and take warning; and no man's feet, henceforward, will approach the pale and demon-haunted house of Avyctes.

For six years, I have dwelt apart with the aged master, forgetting youth and its wonted desires in the study of arcanic things. Together, we have delved more deeply than all others before us in an interdicted lore; we have solved the keyless hieroglyphs that guard ante-human formulae; we have talked with the prehistoric dead; we have called up the dwellers in sealed crypts, in fearful abysses beyond space. Few are the sons of mankind who have cared to seek us out among the desolate, wind-worn crags; and many, but nameless, are the visitants who have come to us from further bourns of place and time.

Stern and white as a tomb, older than the memory of the dead, and built by men or devils beyond the recording of myth, is the mansion in which we dwell. Far below, on black, naked reefs, the northern sea climbs and roars indomitably, or ebbs with a ceaseless murmur as of armies of baffled demons; and the house is filled evermore, like a hollow-sounding sepulcher, with the drear echo of its tumultuous voices; and the winds wail in dismal wrath around the high towers, but shake them not. On the seaward side, the mansion rises sheerly from the straight-falling cliff; but on the other sides there are narrow terraces, grown with dwarfish, crooked cedars that bow always beneath the gale. Giant marble monsters guard the landward portals; and huge marble women ward the strait porticoes above the sea; and mighty statues and mummies stand everywhere in the chambers and along the halls. But, saving these, and the spirits we have summoned, there is none to companion us; and liches and shadows have been the servitors of our daily needs.

All men have heard the fame of Avyctes, the sole surviving pupil of that Malygris who tyrannized in his necromancy over Susran from a tower of sable stone; Malygris, who lay dead for years while men believed him living; who, lying thus, still uttered potent spells and dire oracles with decaying lips. But Avyctes lusted not for temporal power in the manner of Malygris; and having learned all that the elder sorcerer could teach him, withdrew from the cities of Poseidonis to seek another and vaster dominion; and I, the youth Pharpetron, in the latter years of Avyctes, was permitted to join him in this solitude; and since then, I have shared his austerities and vigils and evocations . . . and now, likewise, I must share the weird doom that has come in answer to his summoning.

Not without terror (since man is but mortal) did I, the neophyte, behold at first the abhorrent and tremendous faces of them that obeyed Avyctes: the genii of the sea and earth, of the stars and the heavens, who passed to and fro in his marmorean halls. I shuddered at the black writhing of submundane things from the many-volumed smoke of the braziers; I cried in horror at the grey foulnesses, colossal, without form, that crowded malignly about the drawn circle of seven colors, threatening unspeakable trespass on us that stood at the center. Not without revulsion did I drink wine that was poured by cadavers, and eat bread that was purveyed by phantoms. But use and custom dulled the strangeness, destroyed the fear; and in time I believed implicitly that Avyctes was the lord of all incantations and exorcisms, with infallible power to dismiss the beings he evoked.

Well had it been for Avyctes—and for me—if the master had contented himself with the lore preserved from Atlantis and Thule, or brought over from Mu and Mayapan. Surely this should have been enough: for in the ivory-sheeted books of Thule there were blood-writ runes that would call the demons of the fifth and seventh planets, if spoken aloud at the hour of their ascent; and the sorcerers of Mu had left record of a process whereby the doors of far-future time could be unlocked; and our fathers, the Atlanteans, had known the road between the atoms and the path into far stars, and had held speech with the spirits of the sun. But Avyctes thirsted for a darker knowledge, a deeper empery; and into his hands, in the third year of my novitiate, there came the mirror-bright tablet of the lost serpent-people.

Strange, and apparently fortuitous, was our finding of the tablet. At certain hours, when the tide had fallen from the steep rocks, we were wont to descend by cavern-hidden stairs to a cliff-walled crescent beach behind the promontory on which stood the house of Avyctes. There, on the dun, wet sands, beyond the foamy tongues of the surf, would lie the worn and curious driftage of alien shores, and trove that hurricanes had cast up from unsounded deeps. And there we had found the purple and sanguine volutes of great shells, and rude lumps of ambergris, and white flowers of perpetually blooming coral; and once, the barbaric idol of green brass that had been the figurehead of a galley from far hyperborean isles.

There had been a great storm, such as must have riven the sea to its nethermost profound; but the tempest had gone by with morning, and the heavens were cloudless on that fatal day when we found the tablet, and the demon winds were hushed among the high crags and chasms; and the sea lisped with a low whisper, like the rustle of gowns of samite trailed by fleeing maidens on the sand. And just beyond the ebbing wave, in a tangle of russet seaweed, we beheld a thing that glittered with blinding sun-like brilliance. And running forward, I plucked it from the wrack before the wave's return, and bore it to Avyctes.

The tablet was wrought of some nameless metal, like never-rusting iron, but heavier. It had the form of a triangle and was broader at the widest than a man's heart. On one side it was wholly blank; and Avyctes and I, in turn, beheld our features mirrored strangely, like the drawn, pallid features of the dead, in its burnished surface. On the other side many rows of small crooked ciphers were incised deeply in the metal, as if by the action of some mordant acid; and these ciphers were not the pictorial symbols or alphabetic characters of any language known to the master or to me.

Of the tablet's age and origin, likewise, we could form no conjecture; and our erudition was altogether baffled. For many days thereafter we studied the writing and held argument that came to no issue. And night by night, in a high chamber closed against the perennial winds, we pondered over the dazzling triangle by the tall straight flames of silver lamps. For Avyctes deemed that knowledge of rare value (or haply some secret of an alien or elder magic) was holden by the clueless crooked ciphers. Then, since all our scholarship was in vain, the master sought another divination, and had recourse to wizardy and necromancy. But at first, among the devils and phantoms that answered our interrogation, none could tell us aught concerning the tablet. And any other than Avyctes would have despaired in the end . . . and well would it have been if he had despaired, and had sought no longer to decipher the writing . . .

The months and years went by with a slow thundering of seas on the dark rocks, and a headlong clamor of winds around the white towers. Still we continued our delvings and evocations; and further, always further we went into lampless realms of space and spirit; learning, perchance, to unlock the hithermost of the manifold infinities. And at whiles, Avyctes would resume his pondering of the sea-found tablet; or would question some visitant from other spheres of time and place regarding its interpretation.

At last, by the use of a chance formula, in idle experiment, he summoned up the dim, tenuous ghost of a sorcerer from prehistoric years; and the ghost, in a thin whisper of uncouth, forgotten speech, informed us that the letters on the tablet were those of a language of the serpent-men, whose primordial continent had sunk aeons before the lifting of Hyperborea from the ooze. But the ghost could tell us naught of their significance; for, even in his time, the serpent-people had become a dubious legend; and their deep, ante-human lore and sorcery were things irretrievable by man.

Now, in all the books of conjuration owned by Avyctes, there was no spell whereby we could call the lost serpent-men from their fabulous epoch. But there was an old Lemurian formula, recondite and uncertain, by which the shadow of a dead man could be sent into years posterior to those of his own life-time, and could be recalled after an interim by the wizard. And the shade, being wholly insubstantial, would suffer no harm from the temporal transition, and would remember, for the information of the wizard, that which he had been instructed to learn during the journey.

So, having called again the ghost of the prehistoric sorcerer, whose name was Ybith, Avyctes made a singular use of several very ardent gums and combustible fragments of fossil wood; and he and I, reciting the responses to the formula, sent the thin spirit of Ybith into the far ages of the serpent-men. And after a time which the master deemed sufficient, we performed the curious rites of incantation that would recall Ybith from his alienage. And the rites were successful; and Ybith stood before us again, like a blown vapor that is nigh to vanishing. And in words that were faint as the last echo of perishing memories, the specter told us the key to the meaning of the letters, which he had learned in the primeval past; and after this, we questioned Ybith no more, but suffered him to return unto slumber and oblivion.

Then, knowing the import of the tiny, twisted ciphers, we read the writing on the tablet and made thereof a transliteration, though not without labor and difficulty, since the very phonetics of the serpent tongue, and the symbols and ideas expressed in the writing, were somewhat alien to those of mankind. And when we had mastered the inscription, we found that it contained the formula for a certain evocation which, no doubt, had been used by the serpent sorcerers. But the object of the evocation was not named; nor was there any clue to the nature or identity of that which would come in answer to the rites. And moreover there was no corresponding rite of exorcism nor spell of dismissal.

Great was the jubilation of Avyctes, deeming that we had learned a lore beyond the memory or prevision of man. And though I sought to dissuade him, he resolved to employ the evocation, arguing that our discovery was no chance thing but was fatefully predestined from the beginning. And he seemed to think lightly of the menace that might be brought upon us by the conjuration of things whose nativity and attributes were wholly obscure. "For," said Avyctes, "I have called up, in all the years of my sorcery, no god or devil, no demon or lich or shadow, which I could not control and dismiss at will. And I am loath to believe that any power or spirit beyond the subversion of my spells could have been summoned by a race of serpents, whatever their skill in demonism and necromancy."

So, seeing that he was obstinate, and acknowledging him for my master in all ways, I consented to aid Avyctes in the experiment, though not without dire misgivings. And then we gathered together, in the chamber of conjuration, at the specified hour and configuration of the stars, the equivalents of sundry rare materials that the tablet had instructed us to use in the ritual.

Of much that we did, and of certain agents that we employed, it were better not to tell; nor shall I record the shrill, sibilant words, difficult for beings not born of serpents to articulate, whose intonation formed a signal part of the ceremony. Toward the last, we drew a triangle on the marble floor with the fresh blood of birds; and Avyctes stood at one angle, and I at another; and the gaunt umber mummy of an Atlantean warrior, whose name had been Oigos, was stationed at the third angle. And standing thus, Avyctes and I held tapers of corpse-tallow in our hands, till the tapers had burned down between our fingers as into a socket. And in the outstretched palms of the mummy of Oigos, as if in shallow thuribles, talc and asbestos burned, ignited by a strange fire whereof we knew the secret. At one side we had traced on the floor an infrangible ellipse, made by an endless linked repetition of the twelve unspeakable Signs of Oumor, to which we could retire if the visitant should prove inimical or rebellious. We waited while the pole-circling stars went over, as had been prescribed. Then, when the tapers had gone out between our seared fingers, and the talc and asbestos were wholly consumed in the mummy's eaten palms, Avyctes uttered a single word whose sense was obscure to us; and Oigos, being animated by sorcery and subject to our will, repeated the word after a given interval, in tones that were hollow as a tomb-born echo; and I in my turn also repeated it.

Now, in the chamber of evocation, before beginning the ritual, we had opened a small window giving upon the sea, and had likewise left open a high door on the hall to landward, lest that which came in answer to us should require a spatial mode of entrance. And during the ceremony, the sea became still and there was no wind, and it seemed that all things were hushed in awful expectation of the nameless visitor. But after all was done, and the last word had been repeated by Oigos and me, we stood and waited vainly for a visible sign or other manifestation. The lamps burned stilly in the midnight room; and no shadows fell, other than were cast by ourselves and Oigos and by the great marble women along the walls. And in the magic mirrors we had placed cunningly, to reflect those that were otherwise unseen, we beheld no breath or trace of any image.

At this, after a reasonable interim, Avyctes was sorely disappointed, deeming that the evocation had failed of its purpose; and I, having the same thought, was secretly relieved. And we questioned the mummy of Oigos, to learn if he had perceived in the room, with such senses as are peculiar to the dead, the sure token or doubtful proof of a presence undescried by us the living. And the mummy gave a necromantic answer, saying that there was nothing.

"Verily," said Avyctes, "it were useless to wait longer. For surely in some way we have misunderstood the purport of the writing, or have failed to duplicate the matters used in the evocation, or the correct intonement of the words. Or it may be that in the lapse of so many aeons, the thing that was formerly wont to respond has long ceased to exist, or has altered in its attributes so that the spell is now void and valueless." To this I assented readily, hoping that the matter was at an end. So, after erasing the blood-marked triangle and the sacred ellipse of the linked Signs of Oumor, and after dismissing Oigos to his wonted place among other mummies, we retired to sleep. And in the days that followed, we resumed our habitual studies, but made no mention to each other of the strange triangular tablet or the vain formula.

Even as before, our days went on; and the sea climbed and roared in white fury on the cliffs, and the winds wailed by in their unseen, sullen wrath, bowing the dark cedars as witches are bowed by the breath of Taaran, god of evil. Almost, in the marvel of new tests and cantrips, I forgot the ineffectual conjuration, and I deemed that Avyctes had also forgotten it.

All things were as of yore, to our sorcerous perception; and there was naught to trouble us in our wisdom and power and serenity, which we deemed secure above the sovereignty of kings. Reading the horoscopic stars, we found no future ill in their aspect; nor was any shadow of bale foreshown to us through geomancy, or other modes of divination such as we employed. And our familiars, though grisly and dreadful to mortal gaze, were wholly obedient to us the masters.

Then, on a clear summer afternoon, we walked, as was often our custom, on the marble terrace behind the house. In robes of ocean-purple, we paced among the windy trees with their blown, crooked shadows; and there, following us as we went to and fro, I saw the blue shadow of Avyctes and my own shadow on the marble; and between them, an adumbration that was not wrought by any of the cedars. And I was greatly startled, but spoke not of the matter to Avyctes, and observed the unknown shadow with covert care.

I saw that it followed closely the shadow of Avyctes, keeping ever the same distance. And it fluttered not in the wind, but moved with a flowing as of some heavy, thick, putrescent liquid; and its color was not blue nor purple nor black, nor any other hue to which man's eyes are habituated, but a hue as of some unearthly purulence; and its form was altogether monstrous, having a squat head and a long, undulant body, without similitude to beast or devil.

Avyctes heeded not the shadow; and still I feared to speak, though I thought it an ill thing for the master to be companioned thus. And I moved closer to him, in order to detect by touch or other perception the invisible presence that had cast the adumbration. But the air was void to sunward of the shadow; and I found nothing opposite the sun nor in any oblique direction, though I searched closely, knowing that certain beings cast their shadows thus.

After a while, at the customary hour, we returned by the coiling stairs and monster-flanked portals into the high house. And I saw that the strange adumbration moved ever behind the shadow of Avyctes, falling horrible and unbroken on the steps and passing clearly separate and distinct amid the long umbrages of the towering monsters. And in the dim halls beyond the sun, where shadows should not have been, I beheld with terror the distorted loathly blot, having a pestilent, unnamable hue, that followed Avyctes as if in lieu of his own extinguished shadow. And all that day, everywhere that we went, at the table served by specters, or in the mummy-warded room of volumes and books, the thing pursued Avyctes, clinging to him even as leprosy to the leper. And still the master had perceived it not; and still I forbore to warn him, hoping that the visitant would withdraw in its own time, going obscurely as it had come.

But at midnight, when we sat together by the silver lamps, pondering the blood-writ runes of Hyperborea, I saw that the shadow had drawn closer to the shadow of Avyctes, towering behind his chair on the wall between the huge sculptured women and the mummies. And the thing was a streaming ooze of charnel pollution, a foulness beyond the black leprosies of Hell; and I could bear it no more; and I cried out in my fear and loathing, and informed the master of its presence.

Beholding now the shadow, Avyctes considered it closely and in silence; and there was neither fear nor awe nor abhorrence in the deep, graven wrinkles of his visage. And he said to me at last:

"This thing is a mystery beyond my lore; but never, in all the practice of my art, has any shadow come to me unbidden. And since all others of our evocations have found answer ere this, I must deem that the shadow is a veritable entity, or the sign of an entity, that has come in belated response to the formula of the serpent-sorcerers, which we thought powerless and void. And I think it well that we should now repair to the chamber of conjuration, and interrogate the shadow in such manner as we may, to inquire its nativity and purpose."

We went forthwith into the chamber of conjuration, and made such preparations as were both necessary and possible. And when we were prepared to question it, the unknown shadow had drawn closer still to the shadow of Avyctes, so that the clear space between the two was no wider than the thickness of a necromancer's rod.

Now, in all ways that were feasible, we interrogated the shadow, speaking through our own lips and the lips of mummies and statues.

But there was no determinable answer; and calling certain of the devils and phantoms that were our familiars, we made question through the mouths of these, but without result. And all the while, our magic mirrors were void of any reflection of a presence that might have cast the shadow; and they that had been our spokesmen could detect nothing in the room. And there was no spell, it seemed, that had power upon the visitant. So Avyctes became troubled; and drawing on the floor with blood and ashes the ellipse of Oumor, wherein no demon nor spirit may intrude, he retired to its center. But still within the ellipse, like a flowing taint of liquid corruption, the shadow followed his shadow; and the space between the two was no wider than the thickness of a wizard's pen.

Now, on the face of Avyctes, horror had graven new wrinkles; and his brow was beaded with a deathly sweat. For he knew, even as I, that this was a thing beyond all laws, and foreboding naught but disaster and evil. And he cried to me in a shaken voice, and said:

"I have no knowledge of this thing nor its intention toward me, and no power to stay its progress. Go forth and leave me now; for I would not that any man should witness the defeat of my sorcery and the doom that may follow thereupon. Also, it were well to depart while there is time, lest you too should become the quarry of the shadow and be compelled to share its menace."

Though terror had fastened upon my inmost soul, I was loath to leave Avyctes. But I had sworn to obey his will at all times and in every respect; and moreover I knew myself doubly powerless against the adumbration, since Avyctes himself was impotent.

So, bidding him farewell, I went forth with trembling limbs from the haunted chamber; and peering back from the threshold, I saw that the alien umbrage, creeping like a noisome blotch on the floor, had touched the shadow of Avyctes. And at that moment the master shrieked aloud like one in nightmare; and his face was no longer the face of Avyctes but was contorted and convulsed like that of some helpless madman who wrestles with an unseen incubus. And I looked no more, but fled along the dim outer hall and through the high portals giving upon the terrace.

A red moon, ominous and gibbous, had declined above the terrace and the crags; and the shadows of the cedars were elongated in the moon; and they wavered in the gale like the blown cloaks of enchanters. And stooping against the gale, I fled across the terrace toward the outer stairs that led to a steep path in the riven waste of rocks and chasms behind Avyctes's house. I neared the terrace edge, running with the speed of fear; but I could not reach the topmost outer stair; for at every step the marble flowed beneath me, fleeing like a pale horizon before the seeker. And though I raced and panted without pause, I could draw no nearer to the terrace edge.

At length I desisted, seeing that an unknown spell had altered the very space about the house of Avyctes, so that none could escape therefrom to landward. So, resigning myself in despair to whatever might befall, I returned toward the house. And climbing the white stairs in the low, level beams of the crag-caught moon, I saw a figure that awaited me in the portals. And I knew by the trailing robe of sea-purple, but by no other token, that the figure was Avyctes. For the face was no longer in its entirety the face of man, but was become a loathly fluid amalgam of human features with a thing not to be identified on earth. The transfiguration was ghastlier than death or the changes of decay; and the face was already hued with the nameless, corrupt, and purulent color of the strange shadow, and had taken on, in respect to its outlines, a partial likeness to the squat profile of the shadow. The hands of the figure were not those of any terrene being; and the shape beneath the robe had lengthened with a nauseous undulant pliancy; and the face and fingers seemed to drip in the moonlight with a deliquescent corruption. And the pursuing umbrage, like a thickly flowing blight, had corroded and distorted the very shadow of Avyctes, which was now double in a manner not to be narrated here.

Fain would I have cried or spoken aloud; but horror had dried up the fount of speech. And the thing that had been Avyctes beckoned me in silence, uttering no word from its living and putrescent lips. And with eyes that were no longer eyes, but had become an oozing abomination, it peered steadily upon me. And it clutched my shoulder closely with the soft leprosy of its fingers, and led me half-swooning with revulsion along the hall, and into that room where the mummy of Oigos, who had assisted us in the threefold incantation of the serpent-men, was stationed with several of his fellows.

By the lamps which illumed the chamber, burning with pale, still, perpetual flames, I saw that the mummies stood erect along the wall in their exanimate repose, each in his wonted place with his tall shadow beside him. But the great, gaunt shadow of Oigos on the marble wall was companioned by an adumbration similar in all respects to the evil thing that had followed the master and was now incorporate with him. I remembered that Oigos had performed his share of the ritual, and had repeated an unknown stated word in turn after Avyctes; and so I knew that the horror had come to Oigos in turn, and would wreak itself upon the dead even as on the living. For the foul, anonymous thing that we had called in our presumption could manifest itself to mortal ken in no other way than this. We had drawn it from unfathomable depths of time and space, using ignorantly a dire formula; and the thing had come at its own chosen hour, to stamp itself in abomination uttermost on the evocators.

Since then, the night has ebbed away, and a second day has gone by like a sluggish ooze of horror . . . I have seen the complete identification of the shadow with the flesh and the shadow of Avyctes . . . and also I have seen the slow encroachment of that other umbrage, mingling itself with the lank shadow and the sere, bituminous body of Oigos, and turning them to a similitude of the thing which Avyctes has become. And I have heard the mummy cry out like a living man in great pain and fear, as with the throes of a second dissolution, at the impingement of the shadow. And long since it has grown silent, like the other horror, and I know not its thoughts or its intent . . . And verily I know not if the thing that has come to us be one or several;

nor if its avatar will rest complete with the three that summoned it forth into time, or be extended to others.

But these things, and much else, I shall soon know; for now, in turn, there is a shadow that follows mine, drawing ever closer. The air congeals and curdles with an unseen fear; and they that were our familiars have fled from the mansion; and the great marble women seem to tremble where they stand along the walls. But the horror that was Avyctes, and the second horror that was Oigos, have left me not, and neither do they tremble. And with eyes that are not eyes, they seem to brood and watch, waiting till I too shall become as they. And their stillness is more terrible than if they had rended me limb from limb. And there are strange voices in the wind, and alien roarings upon the sea; and the walls quiver like a thin veil in the black breath of remote abysses.

So, knowing that the time is brief, I have shut myself in the room of volumes and books, and have written this account. And I have taken the bright triangular tablet, whose solution was our undoing, and have cast it from the window into the sea, hoping that none will find it after us. And now I must make an end, and enclose this writing in the sealed cylinder of orichalchum, and fling it forth to drift upon the wave. For the space between my shadow and the shadow of the horror is straitened momentarily . . . and the space is no wider than the thickness of a wizard's pen.

THE MONSTER OF
THE PROPHECY

I

A dismal, fog-dank afternoon was turning into a murky twilight when Theophilus Alvor paused on Brooklyn Bridge to peer down at the dim river with a shudder of sinister surmise. He was wondering how it would feel to cast himself into the chill, turbid waters, and whether he could summon up the necessary courage for an act which, he had persuaded himself, was now becoming inevitable as well as laudable. He felt that he was too weary, sick and disheartened to go on with the evil dream of existence.

From any human standpoint, there was doubtless abundant reason for Alvor's depression. Young, and full of unquenched visions and desires, he had come to Brooklyn from an up-state village three months before, hoping to find a publisher for his writings; but his old-fashioned classic verses, in spite (or because) of their high imaginative fire, had been unanimously rejected both by magazines and book-firms. Though Alvor had lived frugally and had chosen lodgings so humble as almost to constitute the proverbial poetic garret, the small sum of his savings was now exhausted. He was not only quite penniless, but his clothes were so worn as to be no longer presentable in editorial offices, and the soles of his shoes were becoming rapidly non-existent from the tramping he had done. He had not eaten for days, and his last meal, like the several preceding ones, had been at the expense of his soft-hearted Irish landlady.

For more reasons than one, Alvor would have preferred another death than that of drowning. The foul and icy waters were not inviting from an esthetic point; and in spite of all he had heard to the contrary, he did not believe that such a death could be anything but painful and disagreeable. By choice he would have selected a sovereign Oriental opiate, whose insidious slumber would have led through a realm of gorgeous dreams to the gentle night of an ultimate oblivion; or, failing this, a deadly poison of merciful swiftness. But such Lethean media are not readily obtainable by a man with an empty purse.

Damning his own lack of forethought in not reserving enough money for such an eventuation, Alvor shuddered on the twilight bridge, and looked at the dismal waters, and then at the no less dismal fog through which the troubled lights of the city had begun to break. And then, through the instinctive habit of a country-bred person who is also imaginative and beauty-seeking, he looked at the heavens above the city to see if any stars were visible. He thought of his recent *Ode to Antares,* which, unlike his earlier productions, was written in *vers libre* and had a strong modernistic irony mingled with its planturous lyricism. It had, however, proved as unsalable as the rest of his poems. Now, with a sense of irony far more bitter than that which he had put into his ode, he looked for the ruddy spark of Antares itself, but was unable to find it in the sodden sky. His gaze and his thoughts returned to the river.

"There is no need for that, my young friend," said a voice at his elbow. Alvor was startled not only by the words and by the clairvoyance they betrayed, but also by something that was unanalyzably strange in the tones of the voice that uttered them. The tones were both refined and authoritative, but in them there was a quality which, for lack of more precise words or imagery, he could think of only as metallic and unhuman. While his mind wrestled with swift-born unseizable fantasies, he turned to look at the stranger who had accosted him.

The man was neither uncommonly nor disproportionately tall; and he was modishly dressed, with a long overcoat and top hat. His features were not unusual, from what could be seen of them in the dusk, except for his full-lidded and burning eyes, like those of some nyctalopic animal. But from him there emanated a palpable sense of things that were inconceivably strange and terrifying and remote—a sense that was more patent, more insistent than any impression of mere form and odor and sound could have been, and which was well-nigh tactual in its intensity.

"I repeat," continued the man, "that there is no necessity for you to drown yourself in that river. A vastly different fate can be yours, if you choose. . . . In the meanwhile, I shall be honored and delighted if you will accompany me to my house, which is not far away."

In a daze of astonishment preclusive of all analytical thought, or even of any clear cognizance of where he was going or what was happening, Alvor followed the stranger for several blocks in the swirling fog. Hardly knowing how he had come there, he found himself in the library of an old house which must in its time have had considerable pretensions to aristocratic dignity, for the paneling, carpet and furniture were all antique and were both rare and luxurious.

The poet was left alone for a few minutes in the library. Then his host re-appeared and led him to a dining-room where an excellent meal for two had been brought in from a neighboring restaurant. Alvor, who was faint with inanition, ate with no attempt to conceal his ravening appetite, but noticed that the stranger made scarcely even a pretense of touching his own food. With a manner preoccupied and distrait, the man sat opposite Alvor, giving no more ostensible heed to his guest than the ordinary courtesies of a host required.

"We will talk now," said the stranger, when Alvor had finished. The poet, whose energies and mental faculties had been revived by the food, became bold enough to survey his host with a frank attempt at appraisal. He saw a man of indefinite age, whose lineaments and complexion were Caucasian, but whose nationality he was unable to determine. The eyes had lost something of their weird luminosity beneath the electric light, but nevertheless they were most remarkable, and from them there poured a sense of unearthly knowledge and power and strangeness not to be formulated by human thought or conveyed in human speech. Under his scrutiny, vague, dazzling, intricate, unshapable images rose on the dim borders of the poet's mind and fell back into oblivion ere he could confront them. Apparently without rime or reason, some lines of his *Ode to Antares* returned to him, and he found that he was repeating them over and over beneath his breath:

> "Star of strange hope,
> Pharos beyond our desperate mire.
> Lord of unscalable gulfs,
> Lamp of unknowable life."

The hopeless, half-satiric yearning for another sphere which he had expressed in this poem, haunted his thoughts with a weird insistence.

"Of course, you have no idea who or what I am," said the stranger, "though your poetic intuitions are groping darkly toward the secret of my identity. On my part, there is no need for me to ask you anything, since I have already learned all that there is to learn about your life, your personality, and the dismal predicament from which I am now able to offer you a means of escape. Your name is Theophilus Alvor, and you are a poet whose classic style and romantic genius are not likely to win adequate recognition in this age and land. With an inspiration more prophetic than you dream, you have written, among other masterpieces, a quite admirable *Ode to Antares*."

"How do you know all this?" cried Alvor.

"To those who have the sensory apparatus with which to perceive them, thoughts are no less audible than spoken words. I can hear your thoughts, so you will readily understand that there is nothing surprising in my possession of more or less knowledge concerning you."

"But who are you?" exclaimed Alvor. "I have heard of people who could read the minds of others; but I did not believe that there was any human being who actually possessed such powers."

"I am not a human being," rejoined the stranger, "even though I have found it convenient to don the semblance of one for a while, just as you or another of your race might wear a masquerade costume. Permit me to introduce myself: my name, as nearly as can be conveyed in the phonetics of your world, is Vizaphmal, and I have come from a planet of the far-off mighty sun that is known to you as Antares. In my own world, I am a scientist, though the more ignorant classes look upon me as a wizard. In the course of profound experiments and researches, I have invented a device which enables me at will to visit other planets, no matter how remote in space. I have sojourned for varying intervals in more than one solar system; and I have found your world and its inhabitants so quaint and curious and monstrous that I have lingered here a little longer than I intended, because of my taste for the bizarre—a taste which is ineradicable, though no doubt reprehensible. It is now time for me to return: urgent duties call me, and I can not tarry. But there are reasons why I should like to take with me to my world a member of your race; and when I saw you on the bridge tonight, it occurred to me that you might be willing to undertake such an adventure. You are, I believe, utterly weary of the sphere in which you find yourself, since a little while ago you were ready to depart from it into the unknown dimension that you call death. I can offer you something much more agreeable and diversified than death, with a scope of sensation, a potentiality of experience beyond anything of which you have had even the faintest intimation in the poetic reveries looked upon as extravagant by your fellows."

Again and again, while listening to this long and singular address, Alvor seemed to catch in the tones of the voice that uttered it a supervening resonance, a vibration of overtones beyond the compass of a mortal throat. Though perfectly clear and correct in all details of enunciation, there was a hint of vowels and consonants not to be found in any terrestrial alphabet. However, the logical part of his mind refused to accept entirely these intimations of the supermundane; and he was now seized by the idea that the man before him was some new type of lunatic.

"Your thought is natural enough, considering the limitations of your experience," observed the stranger calmly. "However, I can easily convince you of its error by revealing myself to you in my true shape."

He made the gesture of one who throws off a garment. Alvor was blinded by an insufferable blaze of light, whose white glare, emanating in huge beams from an orb-like center, filled the entire room and seemed to pass illimitably beyond through dissolving walls. When his eyes became accustomed to the light, he saw before him a being who had no conceivable likeness to his host. This being was more than seven feet in height, and had no less than five intricately jointed arms and three legs that were equally elaborate. His head, on a long, swan-like neck, was equipped not only with visual, auditory, nasal, and oral organs of unfamiliar types, but had several appendages whose use was not readily to be determined. His three eyes, obliquely set and with oval pupils, rayed forth a green phosphorescence; the mouth, or what appeared to be such, was very small and had the lines of a downward-curving crescent; the nose was rudimentary, though with finely wrought nostrils; in lieu of eyebrows, he had a triple series of semicircular markings on his forehead, each of a different hue; and above his intellectually shapen head, above the tiny drooping ears with their complex lobes, there towered a gorgeous comb of crimson, not dissimilar in form to the crest on the helmet of a Grecian warrior. The head, the limbs, and the whole body were mottled with interchanging lunes and moons of opalescent colors, never the same for a moment in their unresting flux and reflux.

Alvor had the sensation of standing on the rim of prodigious gulfs, on a new earth beneath new heavens; and the vistas of illimitable horizons, fraught with the multitudinous terror and manifold beauty of an imagery no human eye had ever seen, hovered and wavered and flashed upon him with the same unstable fluorescence as the lunar variegations of the body at which he stared with such stupefaction. Then, in a little while, the strange light seemed to withdraw upon itself, retracting all its beams to a common center, and faded in a whirl of darkness. When this darkness had cleared away, he saw once more the form of his host, in conventional garb. with a slight ironic smile about his lips.

"Do you believe me now?" Vizaphmal queried.

"Yes, I believe you."

"Are you willing to accept my offer?"

"I accept it." A thousand questions were forming in Alvor's mind, but he dared not ask them, Divining these questions, the stranger spoke as follows:

"You wonder how it is possible for me to assume a human shape. I assure you, it is merely a matter of taking thought. My mental images are infinitely clearer and stronger than those of any earth-being, and by conceiving myself as a man, I can appear to you and your fellows as such.

"You wonder also as to the modus operandi of my arrival on earth. This I shall now show and explain to you, if you will follow me."

He led the way to an upper story of the old mansion. Here, in a sort of attic, beneath a large skylight in the southward-sloping roof, there stood a curious mechanism, wrought of a dark metal which Alvor could not identify. It was a tall, complicated framework with many transverse bars and two stout upright rods terminating at each end in a single heavy disk. These disks seemed to form the main portions of the top and bottom.

"Put your hand between the bars," commanded Alvor's host.

Alvor tried to obey this command, but his fingers met with an adamantine obstruction, and he realized that the intervals of the bars were filled with an unknown material clearer than glass or crystal.

"You behold here," said Vizaphmal, "an invention which, I flatter myself, is quite unique anywhere this side of the galactic suns. The disks at top and bottom are a vibratory device with a twofold use; and no other material than that of which they are wrought would have the same properties, the same achievable rates of vibration. When you and I have locked ourselves within the framework, as we shall do anon, a few revolutions of the lower disk will have the effect of isolating us from our present environment, and we shall find ourselves in the midst of what is known to you as space, or ether. The vibrations of the upper disk, which we shall then employ, are of such potency as to annihilate space itself in any direction desired. Space, like everything else in the atomic universe, is subject to laws of integration and dissolution. It was merely a matter of finding the vibrational power that would effect this dissolution; and, by untiring research, by ceaseless experimentation, I located and isolated the rare metallic elements which, in a state of union, are capable of this power."

While the poet was pondering all he had seen and heard, Vizaphmal touched a tiny knob, and one side of the framework swung open. He then turned off the electric light in the garret, and simultaneously with its extinction, a ruddy glow was visible in the interior of the machine, serving to illumine all the parts, but leaving the room around it in darkness. Standing beside his invention, Vizaphmal looked at the skylight, and Alvor followed his gaze. The fog had cleared away; and many stars were out, including the red gleam of Antares, now high in the south. The stranger was evidently making certain preliminary calculations, for he moved the machine a little after peering at the star, and adjusted a number of fine wires in the interior, as if he were tuning some stringed instrument.

At last he turned to Alvor.

"Everything is now in readiness," he announced. "If you are still prepared to accompany me, we will take our departure."

Alvor was conscious of an unexpected coolness and fortitude as he answered: "I am at your service." The unparalleled occurrences and disclosures of the evening, the well-nigh undreamable imminence of a plunge across untold immensitude, such as no man had been privileged to dare before, had really benumbed his imagination, and he was unable at the moment to conceive the true awesomeness of what he had undertaken.

Vizaphmal indicated the place where Alvor was to stand in the machine. The poet entered, and assumed a position between one of the upright rods and the side, opposite Vizaphmal. He found that a layer of the transparent material was interposed between his feet and the large disk in which the rods were based. No sooner had he stationed himself, than, with a celerity and an utter silence that were uncanny, the framework closed upon itself with hermetic tightness, till the jointure where it had opened was no longer detectable.

"We are now in a sealed compartment," explained the Antarean, "into which nothing can penetrate. Both the dark metal and the crystalline are substances that refuse the passage of heat and cold, of air and ether, or of any known cosmic ray, with the one exception of light itself, which is admitted by the clear metal."

When he ceased, Alvor realized that they were walled about with an insulating silence utter and absolute as that of some intersidereal void. The traffic in the streets without, the rumbling and roaring and jarring of the great city, so loud a minute before, might have been a million miles away in some other world for all that he could hear or feel of its vibration.

In the red glow that pervaded the machine, emanating from a source he could not discover, the poet gazed at his companion. Vizaphmal had now resumed his Antarean form, as if all necessity for a human disguise were at an end, and he towered above Alvor, glorious with intermerging zones of fluctuant colors, where hues the poet had not seen in any spectrum were simultaneous or intermittent with flaming blues and coruscating emeralds and amethysts and fulgurant purples and vermilions and saffrons. Lifting one of his five arms, which terminated in two finger-like appendages with many joints all capable of bending in any direction, the Antarean touched a thin wire that was stretched overhead between the two rods. He plucked at this wire like a musician at a lute-string, and from it there emanated a single clear note higher in pitch than anything Alvor had ever heard. Its sheer unearthly acuity caused a shudder of anguish to run through the poet, and he could scarcely have borne a prolongation of the sound, which, however, ceased in a moment and was followed by a much more endurable humming and singing noise which seemed to arise at his feet. Looking down, he saw that the large disk at the bottom of the medial rods had begun to revolve. This revolution was slow at first, but rapidly increased in its rate, till he could no longer see the movement; and the singing sound became agonizingly sweet and high till it pierced his senses like a knife.

Vizaphmal touched a second wire, and the revolution of the disk was brought abruptly to an end. Alvor felt an unspeakable relief at the cessation of the torturing music.

"We are now in etheric space," the Antarean declared. "Look out, if you so desire."

Alvor peered through the interstices of the dark metal, and saw around and above and below them the unlimited blackness of cosmic night and the teeming of uncountable trillions of stars. He had a sensation of frightful and deadly vertigo, and staggered like a drunken man as he tried to keep himself from falling against the side of the machine.

Vizaphmal plucked at a third wire, but this time Alvor was not aware of any sound. Something that was like an electric shock, and also like the crushing impact of a heavy blow, descended upon his head and shook him to the soles of his feet. Then he felt as if his tissues were being stabbed by innumerable needles of fire, and then that he was being torn apart in a thousand thousand fragments, bone by bone, muscle by muscle, vein by vein, and nerve by nerve, on some invisible rack. He swooned and fell huddled in a corner of the machine, but his unconsciousness was not altogether complete. He seemed to be drowning beneath an infinite sea of darkness, beneath the accumulation of shoreless gulfs, and above this sea, so far away that he lost it again and again, there thrilled a supernal melody, sweet as the singing of sirens or the fabled music of the spheres, together with an insupportable dissonance like the shattering of all the battlements of time. He thought that all his nerves had been elongated to an enormous distance, where the outlying parts of himself were being tortured in the oubliettes of fantastic inquisitions by the use of instruments of percussion, diabolically vibrant, that were somehow identified with certain of his own body-cells. Once he thought that he saw Vizaphmal standing a million leagues remote on the shore of an alien planet, with a sky of soaring many-colored flame behind him and the night of all the universe rippling gently at his feet like a submissive ocean. Then he lost the vision, and the intervals of the far unearthly music became more prolonged, and at last he could not hear it at all, nor could he feel any longer the torturing of his remote nerve-ends. The gulf deepened above him, and he sank through eons of darkness and emptiness to the very nadir of oblivion.

II

Alvor's return to consciousness was even more slow and gradual than his descent into Lethe had been. Still lying at the bottom of a shoreless and boundless night, he became aware of an unidentifiable odor with which in some way the sense of ardent warmth was associated. This odor changed incessantly, as if it were composed of many diverse ingredients, each of which predominated in turn. Myrrh-like and mystic in the beginning as the fumes of an antique altar, it assumed the heavy languor of unimaginable flowers, the sharp sting of vaporizing chemicals unknown to science, the smell of exotic water and exotic earth, and then a medley of other elements that conveyed no suggestion of anything whatever, except of evolutionary realms and ranges that were beyond all human experience or calculation. For a while he lived and was awake only in his sensory response to this potpourri of odors; then the awareness of his own corporeal being came back to him through tactual sensations of an unusual order, which he did not at first recognize as being within himself, but which seemed to be those of a foreign entity in some other dimension, with whom he was connected across unbridgeable gulfs by a nexus of gossamer tenuity. This entity, he thought, was reclining on a material of great softness, into which he sank with a supreme and leaden indolence and a feeling of sheer bodily weight that held him utterly motionless. Then, floating along the ebon cycles of the void, this being came with ineffable slowness toward Alvor, and at last, by no perceptible transition, by no breath of physical logic or mental congruity, was incorporate with him. Then a tiny light, like a star burning all alone in the center of infinitude, began to dawn far off; and it drew nearer and nearer, and grew larger and larger till it turned the black void to a dazzling luminescence, to a many-tinted glory that smote full upon Alvor.

He found that he was lying with wide-open eyes on a huge couch, in a sort of pavilion consisting of a low and elliptical dome support-ed on double rows of diagonally fluted pillars. He was quite naked, though a sheet of some thin and pale yellow fabric had been thrown across his lower limbs. He saw at a glance, even though his brain-centers were still half benumbed as by the action of some opiate, that this fabric was not the product of any terrestrial loom. Beneath his body, the couch was covered with gray and purple stuffs, but whether they were made of feathers, fur or cloth he was altogether uncertain, for they suggested all three of these materials. They were very thick and resilient, and accounted for the sense of extreme softness underneath him that had marked his return from the swoon. The couch itself stood higher above the floor than an ordinary bed, and was also longer, and in his half-narcotized condition this troubled Alvor even more than other aspects of his situation which were far less normal and explicable.

Amazement grew upon him as he looked about with reviving faculties, for all that he saw and smelt and touched was totally foreign and unaccountable. The floor of the pavilion was wrought in a geometric marquetry of ovals, rhomboids, and equilaterals, in white, black, and yellow metal that no earthly mine had ever disclosed, and the pillars were of the same three metals, regularly alternating. The dome alone was entirely of yellow. Not far from the couch, there stood on a squat tripod a dark and wide-mouthed vessel from which poured an opalescent vapor. Someone standing behind it, invisible through the cloud of gorgeous fumes, was fanning the vapor toward Alvor. He recognized it as the source of the myrrh-like odor that had first troubled his reanimating senses. It was quite agreeable but was borne away from him again and again by gusts of hot wind which brought into the pavilion a mixture of perfumes that were both sweet and acrid, and were altogether novel. Looking between the pillars, he saw the monstrous heads of towering blossoms with pagoda-like tiers of sultry, sullen petals, and beyond them a terraced landscape of low hills of mauve and nacarat soil, extending toward a horizon incredibly remote, till they rose and rose against the heavens. Above all this was a whitish sky, filled with a blinding radiation of intense light from a sun that was now hidden by the dome. Alvor's eyes began to ache, the odors disturbed and oppressed him, and he was possessed by a terrible dubiety and perplexity, amid which he remembered vaguely his meeting with Vizaphmal, and the events preceding his swoon. He was unbearably nervous, and for some time all his ideas and sensations took on the painful disorder and irrational fears of incipient delirium.

A figure stepped from behind the veering vapors and approached the couch. It was Vizaphmal, who bore in one of his five hands the large thin circular fan of bluish metal he had been using. He was holding in another hand a tubular cup, half full of an erubescent liquid.

"Drink this," he ordered, as he put the cup to Alvor's lips. The liquid was so bitter and fiery that Alvor could swallow it only in sips, between periods of gasping and coughing. But once he had gotten it down, his brain cleared with celerity and all his sensations were soon comparatively normal.

"Where am I?" he asked. His voice sounded very strange and unfamiliar to him, and its effect bordered upon ventriloquism— which, as he afterward learned, was due to certain peculiarities of the atmospheric medium.

"You are on my country estate, in Ulphalor, a kingdom which occupies the whole northern hemisphere of Satabbor, the inmost planet of Sanarda, that sun which is called Antares in your world. You have been unconscious for three of our days, a result which I anticipated, knowing the profound shock your nervous system would receive from the experience through which you have passed. However, I do not think you will suffer any permanent illness or inconvenience; and I have just now administered to you a sovereign drug which will aid in the adjustment of your nerves and your corporeal functions to the novel conditions under which you are to live henceforward. I employed the opalescent vapor to arouse you from your swoon, when I deemed that it had become safe and wise to do this. The vapor is produced by the burning of an aromatic seaweed, and is magisterial in its restorative effect."

Alvor tried to grasp the full meaning of this information, but his brain was still unable to receive anything more than a melange of impressions that were totally new and obscure and outlandish. As he pondered the words of Vizaphmal, he saw that rays of bright light had fallen between the columns and were creeping across the floor. Then the rim of a vast ember-colored sun descended below the rim of the dome; and he felt an overwhelming, but somehow not insupportable, warmth. His eyes no longer ached, not even in the direct beams of this luminary; nor did the perfumes irritate him, as they had done for a while.

"I think," said Vizaphmal, "that you may now arise. It is afternoon, and there is much for you to learn, and much to be done."

Alvor threw off the thin covering of yellow cloth, and sat up, with his legs hanging over the edge of the couch.

"But my clothing?" he queried.

"You will need none in our climate. No one has ever worn anything of the sort in Satabbor."

Alvor digested this idea, and though he was slightly disconcerted, he made up his mind that he would accustom himself to whatever should be required of him. Anyway, the lack of his usual habiliments was far from disagreeable in the dry, sultry air of this new world.

He slid from the couch to the floor, which was nearly five feet below him, and took several steps. He was not weak or dizzy, as he had half expected, but all his movements were characterized by the same sense of extreme bodily weight of which he had been dimly aware while still in a semi-conscious condition.

"The world in which you now dwell is somewhat larger than your own," explained Vizaphmal, "and the force of gravity is proportionately greater. Your weight has been increased by no less than a third; but I think you will soon become habituated to this, as well as to the other novelties of your situation."

Motioning the poet to follow him, he led the way through that portion of the pavilion which had been behind Alvor's head as he lay on the couch. A spiral bridge of ascending stairs ran from this pavilion to a much larger pile where numerous wings and annexes of the same aerial architecture of domes and columns flared from a central edifice with a circular wall and many thin spires. Below the bridge, about the pavilion, and around the whole edifice above, were gardens of trees and flowers that caused Alvor to recall the things he had seen during his one experiment with hashish. The foliation of the trees was either very fine and hair-like, or else it consisted of huge, semi-globular, and discoid forms depending from horizontal branches and suggesting a novel union of fruit and leaf. Almost all colors, even green, were shown in the bark and foliage of these trees. The flowers were mainly similar to those Alvor had seen from the pavilion, but there were others of a short, puffy-stemmed variety, with no trace of leaves, and with malignant purple-black heads full of crimson mouths, which swayed a little even when there was no wind. There were oval pools and meandering streams of a dark water with irisated glints all through this garden, which, with the columnar edifice, occupied the middle of a small plateau.

As Alvor followed his guide along the bridge, a perspective of hills and plains all marked out in geometric diamonds and squares and triangles, with a large lake or island sea in their midst, was revealed momently. Far in the distance, more than a hundred leagues away, were the gleaming domes and towers of some baroque city, toward which the enormous orb of the sun was now declining. When he looked at this sun and saw the whole extent of its diameter for the first time, he felt an overpowering thrill of imaginative awe and wonder and exaltation at the thought that it was identical with the red star to which he had addressed in another world the half-lyric, half-ironic lines of his ode.

At the end of the spiral bridge, they came to a second and more spacious pavilion, in which stood a high table with many seats attached to it by means of curving rods. Table and chairs were of the same material, a light, grayish metal. As they entered this pavilion, two strange beings appeared and bowed before Vizaphmal. They were like the scientist in their organic structure, but were not so tall, and their coloring was very drab and dark, with no hint of opalescence. By certain bizarre indications Alvor surmised that the two beings were of different sexes.

"You are right," said Vizaphmal, reading his thought. "These persons are a male and female of the two inferior sexes called Abbars, who constitute the workers, as well as the breeders, of our world. There are two superior sexes, who are sterile, and who form the intellectual, esthetic, and ruling classes, to whom I belong. We call ourselves the Alphads. The Abbars are more numerous, but we hold them in close subjection; and even though they are our parents as well as our slaves, the ideas of filial piety which prevail in your world would be regarded as truly singular by us. We supervise their breeding, so that the due proportion of Abbars and Alphads may be maintained, and the character of the progeny is determined by the injection of certain serums at the time of conceiving. We ourselves, though sterile, are capable of what you call love, and our amorous delights are more complex than yours in their nature."

He now turned and addressed the two Abbars. The phonetic forms and combinations that issued from his lips were unbelievably different from those of the scholarly English in which he had spoken to Alvor. There were strange gutturals and linguals and oddly prolonged vowels which Alvor, for all his subsequent attempts to learn the language, could never quite approximate and which argued a basic divergence in the structure of the vocal organs of Vizaphmal from that of his own.

Bowing till their heads almost touched the floor, the two Abbars disappeared among the columns in a wing of the building and soon returned, carrying long trays on which were unknown foods and beverages in utensils of unearthly forms.

"Be seated," said Vizaphmal. The meal that followed was far from unpleasant, and the foodstuffs were quite palatable, though Alvor was not sure whether they were meats or vegetables. He learned that they were really both, for his host explained that they were the prepared fruits of plants which were half animal in their cellular composition and characteristics. These plants grew wild, and were hunted with the same care that would be required in hunting dangerous beasts, on account of their mobile branches and the poisonous darts with which they were armed. The two beverages were a pale, colorless wine with an acrid flavor, made from a root, and a dusky, sweetish liquid, the natural water of this world. Alvor noticed that the water had a saline after-taste.

"The time has now come," announced Vizaphmal at the end of the meal, "to explain frankly the reason why I have brought you here. We will now adjourn to that portion of my home which you would term a laboratory, or workshop, and which also includes my library."

They passed through several pavilions and winding colonnades, and reached the circular wall at the core of the edifice. Here a high narrow door, engraved with heteroclitic ciphers, gave admission to a huge room without windows, lit by a yellow glow whose cause was not ascertainable.

"The walls and ceiling are lined with a radioactive substance," said Vizaphmal, "which affords this illumination. The vibrations of this substance are also highly stimulating to the processes of thought."

Alvor looked about him at the room, which was filled with alembics and cupels and retorts and sundry other scientific mechanisms, all of unfamiliar types and materials. He could not even surmise their use. Beyond them, in a corner, he saw the apparatus of intersecting bars, with the two heavy disks, in which he and Vizaphmal had made their passage through etheric space. Around the walls there were a number of deep shelves, laden with great rolls that were like the volumes of the ancients.

Vizaphmal selected one of these rolls, and started to unfurl it. It was four feet wide, was gray in color, and was closely written with many rows of dark violet and maroon characters that ran horizontally instead of up and down.

"It will be necessary," said Vizaphmal, "to tell you a few facts regarding the history, religion, and intellectual temper of our world, before I read to you the singular prophecy contained in one of the columns of this ancient chronicle.

"We are a very old people, and the beginnings, or even the first maturity of our civilization, antedate the appearance of the lowliest forms of life on your earth. Religious sentiment and the veneration of the past have always been dominant factors among us, and have shaped our history to an amazing extent. Even today, the whole mass of the Abbars and the majority of the Alphads are immersed in superstition, and the veriest details of quotidian life are regulated by sacerdotal law. A few scientists and thinkers, like myself, are above all such puerilities; but, strictly between you and me, the Alphads, for all their superior and highly aristocratic traits, are mainly the victims of arrested development in this regard. They have cultivated the epicurean and esthetic side of life to a high degree, they are accomplished artists, sybarites, and able administrators or politicians; but, intellectually, they have not freed themselves from the chains of a sterile pantheism and an all-too-prolific hierarchy.

"Several cycles ago, in what might be called an early period of our history, the worship of all our sundry deities was at its height. There was at this time a veritable eruption, a universal plague of prophets, who termed themselves the voices of the gods, even as similarly-minded persons have done in your world. Each of these prophets made his own especial job-lot of predictions, often quite minutely worked out and elaborate, and sometimes far from lacking in imaginative quality. A number of these prophecies have since been fulfilled to the letter, which, as you may well surmise, has helped enormously in confirming the hold of religion. However, between ourselves, I suspect that their fulfillment has had behind it more or less of a shrewd instrumentality, supplied by those who could profit therefrom in one way or another.

"There was one vates, Abbolechiolor by name, who was even more fertile-minded and long-winded than his fellows. I shall now translate to you, from the volumen I have just unrolled, a prediction that he made in the year 299 of the cycle of Sargholoth, the third of the seven epochs into which our known history has been subdivided. It runs thus:

" 'When, for the second time following this prediction, the two outmost moons of Satabbor shall be simultaneously darkened in a total eclipse by the third and innermost moon, and when the dim night of this occultation shall have worn away in the dawn, a mighty wizard shall appear in the city of Sarpoulom, before the palace of the kings of Ulphalor, accompanied by a most unique and unheard-of monster with two arms, two legs, two eyes, and a white skin. And he that then rules in Ulphalor shall be deposed ere noon of this day, and the wizard shall be enthroned in his place, to reign as long as the white monster shall abide with him.' "

Vizaphmal paused, as if to give Alvor a chance to cogitate the matters that had been presented to him. Then, while his three eyes assumed a look of quizzical sharpness and shrewdness, he continued:

"Since the promulgation of this prophecy, there has already been one total eclipse of our two outer moons by the inner one. And, according to all the calculations of our astronomers, in which I can find no possible flaw, a second similar eclipse is now about to take place—in fact, it is due this very night. If Abbolechiolor was truly inspired, tomorrow morn is the time when the prophecy will be fulfilled. However, I decided some while ago that its fulfillment should not be left to chance; and one of my purposes in designing the mechanism with which I visited your world, was to find a monster who would meet the specifications of Abbolechiolor. No creature of this anomalous kind has ever been known, or even fabled, to exist in Satabbor; and I made a thorough search of many remote and outlying planets without being able to obtain what I required. In some of these worlds there were monsters of very uncommon types, with an almost unlimited number of visual organs and limbs; but the variety to which you belong, with only two eyes, two arms, and two legs, must indeed be rare throughout the infra-galactic universe, since I have not discovered it in any other planet than your own.

"I am sure that you now conceive the project I have long nurtured. You and I will appear at dawn in Sarpoulom, the capital of Ulphalor, whose domes and towers you saw this afternoon far off on the plain. Because of the celebrated prophecy, and the publicly known calculations regarding the imminence of a second two-fold eclipse, a great crowd will doubtless be gathered before the palace of the kings to await whatever shall occur. Akkiel, the present king, is by no means popular, and your advent in company with me, who am widely famed as a wizard, will be the signal for his dethronement. I shall then be ruler in his place, even as Abbolechiolor has so thoughtfully predicted. The holding of supreme temporal power in Ulphalor is not undesirable, even for one who is wise and learned and above most of the vanities of life, as I am. When this honor has devolved upon my unworthy shoulders, I shall be able to offer you, as a reward for your miraculous aid, an existence of rare and sybaritic luxury, of rich and varied sensation, such as you can hardly have imagined. It is true, no doubt, that you will be doomed to a certain loneliness among us: you will always be looked upon as a monster, a portentous anomaly; but such, I believe, was your lot in the world where I found you and where you were about to cast yourself into a most unpleasant river. There, as you have learned, all poets are regarded as no less anomalous than double-headed snakes or five-legged calves."

Alvor had listened to this speech in manifold and ever-increasing amazement. Toward the end, when there was no longer any doubt concerning Vizaphmal's intention, he felt the sting of a bitter and curious irony at the thought of the rôle he was destined to play. However, he could do no less than admit the cogency of Vizaphmal's final argument.

"I trust," said Vizaphmal, "that I have not injured your feelings by my frankness, or by the position in which I am about to place you."

"Oh, no, not at all," Alvor hastened to assure him.

"In that case, we shall soon begin our journey to Sarpoulom, which will take all night. Of course, we could make the trip in the flash of an instant with my space-annihilator, or in a few minutes with one of the air-machines that have long been employed among us. But I intend to use a very old-fashioned mode of conveyance for the occasion, so that we will arrive in the proper style, at the proper time, and also that you may enjoy our scenery and view the double eclipse at leisure."

When they emerged from the windowless room, the colonnades and pavilions without were full of a rosy light, though the sun was still an hour above the horizon. This, Alvor learned, was the usual prelude of a Satabborian sunset. He and Vizaphmal watched while the whole landscape before them became steeped in the ruddy glow, which deepened through shades of cinnabar and ruby to a rich garnet by the time Antares had begun to sink from sight. When the huge orb had disappeared, the intervening lands took on a fiery amethyst, and tall auroral flames of a hundred hues shot upward to the zenith from the sunken sun. Alvor was spellbound by the glory of the spectacle.

Turning from this magnificent display at an unfamiliar sound, he saw that a singular vehicle had been brought by the Abbars to the steps of the pavilion in which they stood. It was more like a chariot than anything else, and was drawn by three animals undreamt of in human fable or heraldry. These animals were black and hairless, their bodies were extremely long, each of them had eight legs and a forked tail; and their whole aspect, including their flat, venomous, triangular heads, was uncomfortably serpentine. A series of green and scarlet wattles hung from their throats and bellies, and semi-translucent membranes, erigible at will, were attached to their sides.

"You behold," Vizaphmal informed Alvor, "the traditional conveyance that has been used since time immemorial by all orthodox wizards in Ulphalor. These creatures are called *orpods,* and they are among the swiftest of our mammalian serpents."

He and Alvor seated themselves in the vehicle. Then the three *orpods,* who had no reins in all their complicated harness, started off at a word of command on a spiral road that ran from Vizaphmal's home to the plain beneath. As they went, they erected the membranes at their sides and soon attained an amazing speed.

Now, for the first time, Alvor saw the three moons of Satabbor, which had risen opposite the afterglow. They were all large, especially the innermost one; a perceptible warmth was shed by their pink rays; and their combined illumination was nearly as clear and bright as that of a terrestrial day.

The land through which Vizaphmal and the poet now passed was uninhabited, in spite of its nearness to Sarpoulom, and they met no one. Alvor learned that the terraces he had seen upon awaking were not the work of intelligent beings, as he had thought, but were a natural formation of the hills. Vizaphmal had chosen this location for his home because of the solitude and privacy, so desirable for the scientific experiments to which he had devoted himself.

After they had traversed many leagues, they began to pass occasional houses, of a like structure to that of Vizaphmal's. Then the road meandered along the rim of cultivated fields, which Alvor recognized as the source of the geometric divisions he had seen from afar during the day. He was told that these fields were given mainly to the growing of root-vegetables, of a gigantic truffle, and a kind of succulent cactus, which formed the chief foods of the Abbars. The Alphads ate by choice only the meat of animals and the fruits of wild, half-animal plants, such as those with which Alvor had been served.

By midnight, the three moons had drawn very close together and the second moon had begun to occlude the outermost. Then the inner moon came slowly across the others, till in an hour's time the eclipse was complete. The diminution of light was very marked, and the whole effect was now similar to that of a moonlit night on earth.

"It will be morning in a little more than two hours," said Vizaphmal, "since our nights are extremely short at this time of year. The eclipse will be over before then. But there is no need for us to hurry."

He spoke to the *orpods,* who folded their membranes and settled to a sort of trot.

Sarpoulom was now visible in the heart of the plain, and its outlines were rendered more distinct as the two hidden moons began to draw forth from the adumbration of the other. When to this triple light the ruby rays of earliest morn were added, the city loomed upon the travelers with fantastic many-storied piles of that same open type of metal architecture which the home of Vizaphmal had displayed. This architecture, Alvor found, was general throughout the land, though an older type with closed walls was occasionally to be met with, and was used altogether in the building of prisons and the inquisitions maintained by the priesthoods of the various deities.

It was an incredible vision that Alvor saw—a vision of high domes upborne on slender elongated columns, tier above tier, of airy colonnades and bridges and hanging gardens loftier than Babylon or than Babel, all tinged by the ever-changing red that accompanied and followed the Satabborian dawn, even as it had preceded the sunset. Into this vision, along streets that were paven with the same metal as that of the buildings, Alvor and Vizaphmal were drawn by the three *orpods.*

The poet was overcome by the sense of an unimaginably old and alien and diverse life which descended upon him from these buildings. He was surprised to find that the streets were nearly deserted and that little sign of activity was manifest anywhere. A few Abbars, now and then, scuttled away in alleys or entrances at the approach of the *orpods,* and two beings of a coloration similar to that of Vizaphmal, one of whom Alvor took to be a female, issued from a colonnade and stood staring at the travelers in evident stupefaction.

When they had followed a sort of winding avenue for more than a mile, Alvor saw, between and above the edifices in front of them, the domes and upper tiers of a building that surpassed all the others in its extent.

"You now behold the palace of the kings of Ulphalor," his companion told him.

In a little while they emerged upon a great square that surrounded the palace. This square was crowded with the people of the city, who, as Vizaphmal had surmised, were all gathered to await the fulfillment or non-fulfillment of the prophecy of Abbolechiolor. The open galleries and arcades of the huge edifice, which rose to a height of ten stories, were also laden with watching figures. Abbars were the most plentiful element in this throng, but there were also multitudes of the gaily colored Alphads among them.

At sight of Alvor and his companion, a perceptible movement, a sort of communal shuddering which soon grew convulsive, ran through the whole assemblage in the square and along the galleries of the edifice above. Loud cries of a peculiar shrillness and harshness arose, there was a strident sound of beaten metal in the heart of the palace, like the gongs of an alarm, and mysterious lights glowed out and were extinguished in the higher stories. Clangors of unknown machines, the moan and roar and shriek of strange instruments, were audible above the clamor of the crowd, which grew more tumultuous and agitated in its motion. A way was opened for the car drawn by the three *orpods,* and Vizaphmal and Alvor were soon at the entrance of the palace.

There was an unreality about it all to Alvor, and the discomfiture he had felt in drawing upon himself the weird phosphoric gaze of ten thousand eyes, all of whom were now intent with a fearsome uncanny curiosity on every detail of his physique, was like the discomfiture of some absurd and terrible dream. The movement of the crowd had ceased, while the car was passing along the unhuman lane that had been made for it, and there was an interval of silence. Then, once more, there were babble and debate, and cries that had the accent of martial orders or summonses were caught up and repeated. The throng began to move, with a new and more concentric swirling, and the foremost ranks of Abbars and Alphads swelled like a dark and tinted wave into the colonnades of the palace. They climbed the pillars with a dreadful swift agility to the stories above, they thronged the courts and pavilions and arcades, and though a weak resistance was apparently put up by those within, there was nothing that could stem them.

Through all this clangor and clamor and tumult, Vizaphmal stood in the car with an imperturbable mien beside the poet. Soon a number of Alphads, evidently a delegation, issued from the palace and made obeisance to the wizard, whom they addressed in humble and supplicative tones.

"A revolution has been precipitated by our advent," explained Vizaphmal, "and Akkiel the king has fled. The chamberlains of the court and the high priests of all our local deities are now offering me the throne of Ulphalor. Thus the prophecy is being fulfilled to the letter. You must agree with me that the great Abbolechiolor was happily inspired."

III

The ceremony of Vizaphmal's enthronement was held almost immediately, in a huge hall at the core of the palace, open like all the rest of the structure, and with columns of colossal size. The throne was a great globe of azure metal, with a seat hollowed out near the top, accessible by means of a serpentine flight of stairs. Alvor, at an order issued by the wizard, was allowed to stand at the base of this globe with some of the Alphads.

The enthronement itself was quite simple. The wizard mounted the stairs, amid the silence of a multitude that had thronged the hall, and seated himself in the hollow of the great globe. Then a very tall and distinguished-looking Alphad also climbed the steps, carrying a heavy rod, one half of which was green, and the other a swart, sullen crimson, and placed this rod in the hands of Vizaphmal. Later, Alvor was told that the crimson end of this rod could emit a death-dealing ray, and the green a vibration that cured almost all the kinds of illness to which the Satabborians were subject. Thus it was more than symbolical of the twofold power of life and death with which the king had been invested.

The ceremony was now at an end, and the gathering quickly dispersed. Alvor, at the command of Vizaphmal, was installed in a suite of open apartments on the third story of the palace, at the end of many labyrinthine stairs. A dozen Abbars, who were made his personal retainers, soon came in, each carrying a different food or drink. The foods were beyond belief in their strangeness, for they included the eggs of a moth-like insect large as a plover, and the apples of a fungoid tree that grew in the craters of dead volcanoes. They were served in ewers of a white and shining mineral upborne on legs of fantastic length, and wrought with a cunning artistry. Likewise he was given, in shallow bowls, liquor made from the blood-like juice of living plants, and a wine in which the narcotic pollen of some night-blooming flower had been dissolved.

The days and weeks that now followed were, for the poet, an experience beyond the visionary resources of any terrestrial drug. Step by step, he was initiated, as much as possible for one so radically alien, into the complexities and singularities of life in a new world. Gradually his nerves and his mind, by the aid of the erubescent liquid which Vizaphmal continued to administer to him at intervals, became habituated to the strong light and heat, the intense radiative properties of a soil and atmosphere with unearthly chemical constituents, the strange foods and beverages, and the people themselves with their queer anatomy and queerer customs. Tutors were engaged to teach him the language, and, in spite of the difficulties presented by certain unmanageable consonants, certain weird ululative vowels, he learned enough of it to make his simpler ideas and wants understood.

He saw Vizaphmal every day, and the new king seemed to cherish a real gratitude toward him for his indispensable aid in the fulfilment of the prophecy. Vizaphmal took pains to instruct him in regard to all that it was necessary to know, and kept him well-informed as to the progress of public events in Ulphalor. He was told, among other things, that no news had been heard concerning the whereabouts of Akkiel, the late ruler. Also, Vizaphmal had reason to be aware of more or less opposition toward himself on the part of the various priesthoods, who, in spite of his life-long discretion, had somehow learned of his free-thinking propensities.

For all the attention, kindness, and service that he received, and the unique luxury with which he was surrounded, Alvor felt that these people, even as the wizard had forewarned him, looked upon him merely as a kind of unnatural curiosity or anomaly. He was no less monstrous to them than they were to him, and the gulf created by the laws of a diverse biology, by an alien trend of evolution, seemed impossible to bridge in any manner. He was questioned by many of them, and, in especial, by more than one delegation of noted scientists, who desired to know as much as he could tell them about himself. But the queries were so patronizing, so rude and narrow-minded and scornful and smug, that he was soon wont to feign a total ignorance of the language on such occasions. Indeed, there was a gulf; and he was rendered even more acutely conscious of it whenever he met any of the female Abbars or Alphads of the court, who eyed him with disdainful inquisitiveness, and among whom a sort of tittering usually arose when he passed. His naked members, so limited in number, were obviously as great a source of astonishment to them as their own somewhat intricate and puzzling charms were to him. All of them were quite nude; indeed, nothing, not even a string of jewels or a single gem, was ever worn by any of the Satabborians. The female Alphads, like the males, were extremely tall and were gorgeous with epidermic hues that would have outdone the plumage of any peacock; and their anatomical structure was most peculiar ... Alvor began to feel the loneliness of which Vizaphmal had spoken, and he was overcome at times by a great nostalgia for his own world, by a planetary homesickness. He became atrociously nervous, even if not actually ill.

While he was still in this condition, Vizaphmal took him on a tour of Ulphalor that had become necessary for political reasons. More or less incredulity concerning the real existence of such a monstrosity as Alvor had been expressed by the folk of outlying provinces, of the polar realms, and the antipodes; and the new ruler felt that a visual demonstration of the two-armed, two-legged, and two-eyed phenomenon would be far from inadvisable, to establish beyond dispute the legitimacy of his own claim to the throne. In the course of this tour, they visited many unique cities, and rural and urban centers of industries peculiar to Satabbor; and Alvor saw the mines from which the countless minerals and metals used in Ulphalor were extracted by the toil of millions of Abbars. These metals were found in a pure state, and were of inexhaustible extent. Also, he saw the huge oceans, which, with certain inland seas and lakes that were fed from underground sources, formed the sole water-supply of the aging planet, where no rain had even been rumored to fall for centuries. The seawater, after undergoing a treatment that purged it of a number of undesirable elements, was carried all through the land by a system of conduits. Moreover, he saw the marshlands at the north pole, with their vicious tangle of animate vegetation, into which no one had ever tried to penetrate.

They met many outland peoples in the course of this tour; but the general characteristics were the same throughout Ulphalor, except in one or two races of the lowest aborigines, among whom there were no Alphads. Everywhere the poet was eyed with the same cruel and ignorant curiosity that had been shown in Sarpoulom. However, he became gradually inured to this; and the varying spectacles of bizarre interest and the unheard-of scenes that he saw daily, helped to divert him a little from his nostalgia for the lost earth.

When he and Vizaphmal returned to Sarpoulom, after an absence of many weeks, they found that much discontent and revolutionary sentiment had been sown among the multitude by the hierarchies of the Satabborian gods and goddesses, particularly by the priesthood of Cunthamosi, the Cosmic Mother, a female deity in high favor among the two reproductive sexes, from whom the lower ranks of her hierophants were recruited. Cunthamosi was worshipped as the source of all things: her maternal organs were believed to have given birth to the sun, the moon, the world, the stars, the planets, and even the meteors which often fell in Satabbor. But it was argued by her priests that such a monstrosity as Alvor could not possibly have issued from her womb, and that therefore his very existence was a kind of blasphemy, and that the rule of the heretic wizard, Vizaphmal, based on the advent of this abnormality, was likewise a flagrant insult to the Cosmic Mother. They did not deny the apparently miraculous fulfilment of the prophecy of Abbolechiolor, but it was maintained that this fulfilment was no assurance of the perpetuity of Vizaphmal's reign, and no proof that his reign was countenanced by any of the gods.

"I can not conceal from you," said Vizaphmal to Alvor, "that the position in which we both stand is now slightly parlous. I intend to bring the space-annihilator from my country home to the court, since it is not impossible that I may have need for it, and that some foreign sphere will soon become more salubrious for me than my native one."

However, it would seem that this able scientist, alert wizard, and competent king had not altogether grasped the real imminence of the danger that threatened his reign; or else he spoke, as was sometimes his wont, with sardonic moderation. He showed no further concern, beyond setting a strong guard about Alvor to attend him at all times, lest an attempt should be made to kidnap the poet in consideration of the last clause of the prophecy.

Three days after the return to Sarpoulom, while Alvor was standing in one of his private balconies looking out over the roofs of the town, with his guards chattering idly in the rooms behind, he saw that the streets were dark with a horde of people, mainly Abbars, who were streaming silently toward the palace. A few Alphads, distinguishable even at a distance by their gaudy hues, were at the head of this throng. Alarmed at the spectacle, and remembering what the king had told him, he went to find Vizaphmal and climbed the eternal tortuous series of complicated stairs that led to the king's personal suite. Others among the inmates of the court had seen the advancing crowd, and there were agitation, terror and frantic hurry everywhere. Mounting the last flight of steps to the king's threshold, Alvor was astounded to find that many of the Abbars, who had gained ingress from the other side of the palace and had scaled the successive rows of columns and stairs with ape-like celerity, were already pouring into the room. Vizaphmal himself was standing before the open framework of the space-annihilator, which had now been installed beside his couch. The rod of royal investiture was in his hand, and he was leveling the crimson end at the foremost of the invading Abbars. As this creature leapt toward him, waving an atrocious weapon lined by a score of hooked blades, Vizaphmal tightened his hold on the rod, thus pressing a secret spring, and a thin rose-colored ray of light was emitted from the end, causing the Abbar to crumple and fall. Others, in nowise deterred, ran forward to succeed him, and the king turned his lethal beam upon them with the calm air of one who is conducting a scientific experiment, till the floor was piled with dead Abbars. Still others took their place, and some began to cast their hooked weapons at the king. None of these touched him, but he seemed to weary of the sport, and stepping within the framework, he closed it upon himself. A moment more, and then there was a roar as of a thousand thunders; and the mechanism and Vizaphmal were no longer to be seen. Never, at any future time, was the poet to learn what had become of him, nor in what stranger world than Satabbor he was now indulging his scientific fancies and curiosities.

Alvor had no time to feel, as he might conceivably have done, that he had been basely deserted by the king. All the nether and upper stories of the great edifice were now a-swarm with the invading crowd, who were no longer silent, but were uttering shrill, ferocious cries as they bore down the opposition of the courtiers and slaves. The whole place was inundated by an ever-mounting sea, in which there were now myriads of Alphads as well as of Abbars; and no escape was possible. In a few instants, Alvor himself was seized by a group of the Abbars, who seemed to have been enraged rather than terrified or discomforted by the vanishing of Vizaphmal. He recognized them as priests of Cunthamosi by an odd oval and vertical marking of red pigments on their swart bodies. They bound him viciously with cords that were made from the intestines of a dragon-like animal, and carried him away from the palace, along streets that were lined by a staring and gibbering mob, to a building on the southern outskirts of Sarpoulom, which Vizaphmal had once pointed out to him as the Inquisition of the Cosmic Mother.

This edifice, unlike most of the buildings in Sarpoulom, was walled on all sides and was constructed entirely of enormous gray bricks, made from the local soil, and bigger and harder than blocks of granite. In a long five-sided chamber illumined only by narrow slits in the roof, Alvor found himself arraigned before a jury of the priests, presided over by a swollen and pontifical-looking Alphad, the Grand Inquisitor.

The place was filled with ingenious and grotesque implements of torture, and the very walls were hung to the ceiling with contrivances that would have put Torquemada to shame. Some of them were very small, and were designed for the treatment of special and separate nerves; and others were intended to harrow the entire epidermic area of the body at a single twist of their screw-like mechanism.

Alvor could understand little of the charges that were preferred against him, but gathered that they were the same, or included the same, of which Vizaphmal had spoken: to wit, that he, Alvor, was a monstrosity that could never have been conceived or brought forth by Cunthamosi, and whose very existence, past, present, and future, was a dire affront to this divinity. The entire scene—the dark and lurid room with its array of hellish instruments, the diabolic faces of the inquisitors, and the high unhuman drone of their voices as they intoned the charges and brought judgment against Alvor—was laden with a horror beyond the horror of dreams.

Presently the Grand Inquisitor focussed the malign gleam of his three unblinking orbs upon the poet, and began to pronounce an interminable sentence, pausing a little at quite regular intervals which seemed to mark the clauses of the punishment that was to be inflicted. These clauses were well-nigh innumerable, but Alvor could comprehend almost nothing of what was said; and doubtless it was as well that he did not comprehend.

When the voice of the swollen Alphad had ceased, the poet was led away through endless corridors and down a stairway that seemed to descend into the bowels of Satabbor. These corridors, and also the stairway, were luminous with self-emitted light that resembled the phosphorescence of decaying matter in tombs and catacombs. As Alvor went downward with his guards, who were all Abbars of the lowest type, he could hear somewhere in sealed unknowable vaults the moan and shriek of beings who endured the ordeals imposed by the inquisitors of Cunthamosi.

They came to the final step of the stairway, where, in a vast vault, an abyss whose bottom was not discernible yawned in the center of the floor. On its edge there stood a fantastic sort of windlass on which was wound an immense coil of blackish rope.

The end of this rope was now tied about Alvor's ankles, and he was lowered head downward into the gulf by the inquisitors. The sides were not luminous like those of the stairway, and he could see nothing. But, as he descended into the gulf, the terrible discomfort of his position was increased by sensations of an ulterior origin. He felt that he was passing through a kind of hairy material with numberless filaments that clung to his head and body and limbs like minute tentacles, and whose contact gave rise to an immediate itching.

The substance impeded him more and more, till at last he was held immovably suspended as in a net, and all the while the separate hairs seemed to be biting into his flesh with a million microscopic teeth, till the initial itching was followed by a burning and a deep convulsive throbbing more exquisitely painful than the flames of an *auto da fé*. The poet learned long afterward that the material into which he had been lowered was a subterranean organism, half vegetable, half animal, which grew from the side of the gulf, with long mobile feelers that were extremely poisonous to the touch. But at the time, not the least of the horrors he underwent was the uncertainty as to its precise nature.

After he had hung for quite a while in this agonizing web, and had become almost unconscious from the pain and the unnatural position, Alvor felt that he was being drawn upward. A thousand of the fine thread-like tentacles clung to him, and his whole body was encircled with a mesh of insufferable pangs as he broke loose from them. He swooned with the intensity of this pain, and when he recovered, he was lying on the floor at the edge of the gulf, and one of the priests was prodding him with a many-pointed weapon.

Alvor gazed for a moment at the cruel visages of his tormenters, in the luminous glow from the sides of the vault, and wondered dimly what infernal torture was next to follow, in the carrying-out of the interminable sentence that had been pronounced. He surmised, of course, that the one he had just undergone was mild in comparison to the many that would succeed it. But he never knew, for at that instant there came a crashing sound like the fall and shattering of the universe; the walls, the floor, and the stairway rocked to and fro in a veritable convulsion; and the vault above was riven asunder, letting through a rain of fragments of all sizes, some of which struck several of the inquisitors and swept them into the gulf. Others of the priests leapt over the edge in their terror, and the two who remained were in no condition to continue their official duties. Both of them were lying beside Alvor with broken heads from which, in lieu of blood, there issued a glutinous light-green liquid.

Alvor could not imagine what had happened, but knew only that he himself was unhurt, as far as the results of the cataclysm were concerned. His mental state was not one to admit of scientific surmise: he was sick and dizzy from the ordeal he had suffered, and his whole body was swollen, was blood-red and violently burning from the touch of the organisms in the gulf. He had, however, enough strength and presence of mind to grope with his bound hands for the weapon that had been dropped by one of the inquisitors. By much patience, by untiring ingenuity, he was able to cut the thongs about his wrists and ankles on the sharp blade of one of the five points.

Carrying this weapon, which he knew that he might need, he began the ascent of the subterranean stairway. The steps were half blocked by fallen masses of stone, and some of the landings and stairs, as well as the sides of the wall, were cloven with enormous rents; and his egress was by no means an easy matter. When he reached the top, he found that the whole edifice was a pile of shattered walls, with a great pit in its center from which a cloud of vapors issued. An immense meteor had fallen, and had struck the Inquisition of the Cosmic Mother.

Alvor was in no condition to appreciate the irony of this event, but at least he was able to comprehend his chance of freedom. The only inquisitors now visible were lying with squashed bodies whose heads or feet protruded from beneath the large squares of overthrown brick, and Alvor lost no time in quitting the vicinity.

It was now night, and only one of the three moons had arisen. Alvor struck off through the level arid country to the south of Sarpoulom, where no one dwelt, with the idea of crossing the boundaries of Ulphalor into one of the independent kingdoms that lay below the equator. He remembered Vizaphmal telling him once that the people of these kingdoms were more enlightened and less priest-ridden than those of Ulphalor.

All night he wandered, in a sort of daze that was at times delirium. The pain of his swollen limbs increased, and he grew feverish. The moonlit plain seemed to shift and waver before him, but was interminable as the landscape of a hashish-dream. Presently the other two moons arose, and in the overtaxed condition of his mind and nerves, he was never quite sure as to their actual number. Usually, there appeared to be more than three, and this troubled him prodigiously. He tried to resolve the problem for hours, as he staggered on, and at last, a little before dawn, he became altogether delirious.

He was unable afterward to recall anything about his subsequent journey. Something impelled him to go on even when his thews were dead and his brain an utter blank: he knew nothing of the waste and terrible lands through which he roamed in the hour-long ruby-red of morn and beneath a furnace-like sun; nor did he know when he crossed the equator at sunset and entered Omanorion, the realm of the empress Ambiala, still carrying in his hand the five-pointed weapon of one of the dead inquisitors.

IV

It was night when Alvor awoke, but he had no means of surmising that it was not the same night in which he had fled from the Inquisition of the Cosmic Mother; and that many Satabborian days had gone by since he had fallen totally exhausted and unconscious within the boundary-line of Omanorion. The warm, rosy beams of the three moons were full in his face, but he could not know whether they were ascending or declining. Anyhow, he was lying on a very comfortable couch that was not quite so disconcertingly long and high as the one upon which he had first awakened in Ulphalor. He was in an open pavilion, and this pavilion was also a bower of multitudinous blossoms which leaned toward him with faces that were both grotesque and weirdly beautiful, from vines that had scaled the columns, or from the many curious metal pots that stood upon the floor. The air that he breathed was a medley of perfumes more exotic than frangipani; they were extravagantly sweet and spicy, but somehow he did not find them oppressive. Rather, they served to augment the deep, delightful languor of all his sensations.

As he opened his eyes and turned a little on the couch, a female Alphad, not so tall as those of Ulphalor and really quite of his own stature, came out from behind the flower-pots and addressed him. Her language was not that of the Ulphalorians, it was softer and less utterly unhuman, and though he could not understand a word, he was immediately aware of a sympathetic note or undertone which, so far, he had never heard on the lips of any one in this world, not even Vizaphmal.

He replied in the language of Ulphalor, and found that he was understood. He and the female Alphad now carried on as much of a conversation as Alvor's linguistic abilities would permit. He learned that he was talking to the empress Ambiala, the sole and supreme ruler of Omanorion, a quite extensive realm contiguous to Ulphalor. She told him that some of her servitors, while out hunting the wild, ferocious, half-animal fruits of the region, had found him lying unconscious near a thicket of the deadly plants that bore these fruits, and had brought him to her palace in Lompior, the chief city of Omanorion. There, while he still lay in a week-long stupor, he had been treated with medicaments that had now almost cured the painful swellings resultant from his plunge among the hair-like organism in the Inquisition.

With genuine courtesy, the empress forbore to question the poet regarding himself, nor did she express any surprise at his anatomical peculiarities. However, her whole manner gave evidence of an eager and even fascinated interest, for she did not take her eyes away from him at any time. He was a little embarrassed by her intent scrutiny, and to cover this embarrassment, as well as to afford her the explanations due to so kind a hostess, he tried to tell her as much as he could of his own history and adventures.

It was doubtful if she understood more than half of what he said, but even this half obviously lent him an increasingly portentous attraction in her eyes. All of her three orbs grew round with wonder at the tale related by this fantastic Ulysses, and whenever he stopped she would beg him to go on. The garnet and ruby and cinnabar gradations of the dawn found Alvor still talking and the empress Ambiala still listening.

In the full light of Antares, Alvor saw that his hostess was, from a Satabborian viewpoint, a really beautiful and exquisite creature. The iridescence of her coloring was very soft and subtle; her arms and legs, though of the usual number, were all voluptuously rounded; and the features of her face were capable of a wide range of expression. Her usual look, however, was one of a sad and wistful yearning. This look Alvor came to understand, when, with a growing knowledge of her language, he learned that she too was a poet, that she had always been troubled by vague desires for the exotic and the far-off, and that she was thoroughly bored with everything in Omanorion, and especially with the male Alphads of that region, none of whom could rightfully boast of having been her lover even a day. Alvor's biological difference from these males was evidently the secret of his initial fascination for her.

The poet's life in the palace of Ambiala, where he found that he was looked upon as a permanent guest, was from the beginning much more agreeable than his existence in Ulphalor had been. For one thing, there was Ambiala herself, who impressed him as being infinitely more intelligent than the females of Sarpoulom, and whose attitude was so thoughtful and sympathetic and admiring, in contradistinction to the attitude of these aforesaid females. Also, the servitors of the palace and the people of Lompior, though they doubtless regarded Alvor as a quite singular sort of being, were at least more tolerant than the Ulphalorians; and he met with no manner of rudeness among them at any time. Moreover, if there were any priesthoods in Omanorion, they were not of the uncompromising type he had met north of the equator, and it would seem that nothing was to be feared from them. No one ever spoke of religion to Alvor in this ideal realm, and somehow he never actually learned whether or not Omanorion possessed any gods or hierarchies. Remembering his ordeal in the Inquisition of the Cosmic Mother, he was quite willing not to broach the subject, anyway.

Alvor made rapid progress in the language of Omanorion, since the empress herself was his teacher. He soon learned more and more about her ideas and tastes, about her romantic love for the triple moonlight, and the odd flowers that she cultivated with so much care and so much delectation. These blossoms were rare anywhere in Satabbor: some of them were anemones that came from the tops of almost inaccessible mountains many leagues in height, and others were forms inconceivably more bizarre than orchids, mainly from terrific jungles near the southern pole. He was soon privileged to hear her play on a certain musical instrument of the country, in which were combined the characters of the flute and the lute. And at last, one day, when he knew enough of the tongue to appreciate a few of its subtleties, she read to him from a scroll of vegetable vellum one of her poems, an ode to a star known as Atana by the people of Omanorion. This ode was truly exquisite, was replete with poetic fancies of a high order, and expressed a half-ironic yearning, sadly conscious of its own impossibility, for the ultra-sidereal realms of Atana. Ending, she added:

"I have always loved Atana, because it is so little and so far away."

On questioning her, Alvor learned to his overwhelming amazement, that Atana was identical with a minute star called Arot in Ulphalor, which Vizaphmal had once pointed out to him as the sun of his own earth. This star was visible only in the rare interlunar dark, and it was considered a test of good eyesight to see it even then.

When the poet had communicated this bit of astronomical information to Ambiala, that the star Atana was his own native sun, and had also told her of his *Ode to Antares*, a most affecting scene occurred, for the empress encircled him with her five arms and cried out:

"Do you not feel, as I do, that we were destined for each other?"

Though he was a little discomposed by Ambiala's display of affection, Alvor could do no less than assent. The two beings, so dissimilar in external ways, were absolutely overcome by the rapport revealed in this comparing of poetic notes; and a real understanding, rare even with persons of the same evolutionary type, was established between them henceforward. Also, Alvor soon developed a new appreciation of the outward charms of Ambiala, which, to tell the truth, had not altogether intrigued him heretofore. He reflected that after all her five arms and three legs and three eyes were merely a superabundance of anatomical features upon which human love was wont to set a by no means lowly value. As for her opalescent coloring, it was, he thought, much more lovely than the agglomeration of outlandish hues with which the human female figure had been adorned in many modernistic paintings.

When it became known in Lompior that Alvor was the lover of Ambiala, no surprise or censure was expressed by any one. Doubtless the people, especially the male Alphads who had vainly wooed the empress, thought that her tastes were queer, not to say eccentric. But anyway, no comment was made; it was her own amour after all, and no one else could carry it on for her. It would seem, from this, that the people of Omanorion had mastered the ultra-civilized art of minding their own business.

THE HUNTERS FROM BEYOND

I have seldom been able to resist the allurement of a book store, particularly one that is well supplied with rare and exotic items. Therefore I turned in at Toleman's to browse around for a few minutes. I had come to San Francisco for one of my brief, biannual visits, and had started early that idle forenoon to an appointment with Cyprian Sincaul, the sculptor, a second or third cousin of mine, whom I had not seen for several years.

His studio was only a block from Toleman's, and there seemed to be no especial object in reaching it ahead of time. Cyprian had offered to show me his collection of recent sculptures; but, remembering the smooth mediocrity of his former work, amid which were a few banal efforts to achieve horror and grotesquerie, I did not anticipate anything more than an hour or two of dismal boredom.

The little shop was empty of customers. Knowing my proclivities, the owner and his one assistant became tacitly non-attentive after a word of recognition, and left me to rummage at will among the curiously laden shelves. Wedged in between other but less alluring titles, I found a deluxe edition of Goya's "Proverbes." I began to turn the heavy pages, and was soon engrossed in the diabolic art of these nightmare-nurtured drawings.

It has always been incomprehensible to me that I did not shriek aloud with mindless, overmastering terror, when I happened to look up from the volume, and saw the thing that was crouching in a corner of the book-shelves before me. I could not have been more hideously startled if some hellish conception of Goya had suddenly come to life and emerged from one of the pictures in the folio.

What I saw was a forward slouching, vermin-gray figure, wholly devoid of hair or down or bristles, but marked with faint, etiolated rings like those of a serpent that has lived in darkness. It possessed the head and brow of an anthropoid ape, a semi-canine mouth and jaw, and arms ending in twisted hands whose black hyena talons nearly scraped the floor. The thing was infinitely bestial, and, at same time, macabre; for its parchment skin was shriveled, corpselike, mummified, in a manner impossible to convey; and from eye sockets well-nigh deep as those of a skull, there glimmered evil slits of yellowish phosphorescence, like burning sulphur. Fangs that were stained as if with poison or gangrene, issued from the slavering, half-open mouth; and the whole attitude of the creature was that of some maleficent monster in readiness to spring.

Though I had been for years a professional writer of stories that often dealt with occult phenomena, with the weird and the spectral, I was not at this time possessed of any clear and settled belief regarding such phenomena. I had never before seen anything that I could identify as a phantom, nor even an hallucination; and I should hardly have said offhand that a bookstore on a busy street, in full summer daylight, was the likeliest of places in which to see one. But the thing before me was assuredly nothing that could ever exist among the permissible forms of a sane world. It was too horrific, too atrocious, to be anything but a creation of unreality.

Even as I stared across the Goya, sick with a half-incredulous fear, the apparition moved toward me. I say that it moved, but its change of position was so instantaneous, so utterly without effort or visible transition, that the verb is hopelessly inadequate. The foul specter had seemed five or six feet away. But now it was stooping directly above the volume that I still held in my hands, with its loathesomely lambent eyes peering upward at my face, and a gray-green slime drooling from its mouth on the broad pages. At the same time I breathed an insupportable fœtor, like a mingling of rancid serpent-stench with the moldiness of antique charnels and the fearsome reek of newly decaying carrion.

In a frozen timelessness that was perhaps no more than a second or two, my heart appeared to suspend its beating, while I beheld the ghastly face. Gasping, I let the Goya drop with a resonant bang on the floor, and even as it fell, I saw that the vision had vanished.

Toleman, a tonsured gnome with shell-rimmed goggles, rushed forward to retrieve the fallen volume, exclaiming: "What is wrong, Mr. Hastane? Are you ill?" From the meticulousness with which he examined the binding in search of possible damage, I knew that his chief solicitude was concerning the Goya. It was plain that neither he nor his clerk had seen the phantom; nor could I detect aught in their demeanor to indicate that they had noticed the mephitic odor that still lingered in the air like an exhalation from broken graves. And, as far as I could tell, they did not even perceive the grayish slime that still polluted the open folio.

I do not remember how I managed to make my exit from the shop. My mind had become a seething blur of muddled horror, of crawling, sick revulsion from the supernatural vileness I had beheld, together with the direst apprehension for my own sanity and safety. I recall only that I found myself on the street above Toleman's, walking with feverish rapidity toward my cousin's studio, with a neat parcel containing the Goya volume under my arm. Evidently, in an effort to atone for my clumsiness, I must have bought and paid for the book by a sort of automatic impulse, without any real awareness of what I was doing.

I came to the building in which was my destination, but went on around the block several times before entering. All the while I fought desperately to regain my self-control and equipoise. I remember how difficult it was even to moderate the pace at which I was walking, or refrain from breaking into a run; for it seemed to me that I was fleeing all the time from an invisible pursuer. I tried to argue with myself, to convince the rational part of my mind that the apparition had been the product of some evanescent trick of light and shade, or a temporary dimming of eyesight. But such sophistries were useless; for I had seen the gargoylish terror all too distinctly, in an unforgettable fullness of grisly detail.

What could the thing mean? I had never used narcotic drugs or abused alcohol. My nerves, as far as I knew, were in sound condition. But either I had suffered a visual hallucination that might mark the beginning of some obscure cerebral disorder, or had been visited by a spectral phenomenon, by something from realms and dimensions that are past the normal scope of human perception. It was a problem either for the alienist or the occultist.

Though I was still damnably upset, I contrived to regain a nominal composure of my faculties. Also, it occurred to me that the unimaginative portrait busts and tamely symbolic figure-groups of Cyprian Sincaul might serve admirably to soothe my shaken nerves. Even his grotesques would seem sane and ordinary by comparison with the blasphemous gargoyle that had drooled before me in the book shop.

I entered the studio building, and climbed a worn stairway to the second floor, where Cyprian had established himself in a somewhat capacious suite of rooms. As I went up the stairs, I had the peculiar feeling that somebody was climbing them just ahead of me; but I could neither see nor hear anyone, and the hall above was no less silent and empty than the stairs.

⁂

Cyprian was in his atelier when I knocked. After an interval which seemed unduly long, I heard him call out, telling me to enter. I found him wiping his hands on an old cloth, and surmised that he had been modeling. A sheet of light burlap had been thrown over what was plainly an ambitious but unfinished group of figures, which occupied the center of the long room. All around were other sculptures, in clay, bronze, marble, and even the terra-cotta and steatite which he sometimes employed for his less conventional conceptions. At one end of the room there stood a heavy Chinese screen.

At a single glance I realized that a great change had occurred, both in Cyprian Sincaul and his work. I remembered him as an amiable, somewhat flabby-looking youth, always dapperly dressed, with no trace of the dreamer or visionary. It was hard to recognize him now, for he had become lean, harsh, vehement, with an air of pride and penetration that was almost Luciferian. His unkempt mane of hair was already shot with white, and his eyes were electrically brilliant with a strange knowledge, and yet somehow were vaguely furtive, as if there dwelt behind them a morbid and macabre fear.

The change in his sculpture was no less striking. The respectable tameness and polished mediocrity were gone, and in their place, incredibly, was something little short of genius. More unbelievable still, in view of the laboriously ordinary grotesques of his earlier phase, was the trend that his art had now taken. All around me were frenetic, murderous demons, satyrs mad with nympholepsy, ghouls that seemed to sniff the odors of the charnel, lamias voluptuously coiled about their victims, and less namable things that belonged to the outland realms of evil myth and malign superstition.

Sin, horror, blasphemy, diablerie—the lust and malice of pandemonium—all had been caught with impeccable art. The potent nightmarishness of these creations was not calculated to reassure my trembling nerves; and all at once I felt an imperative desire to escape from the studio, to flee from the baleful throng of frozen cacodemons and chiseled chimeras.

My expression must have betrayed my feelings to some extent.

"Pretty strong work, aren't they?" said Cyprian, in a loud, vibrant voice, with a note of harsh pride and triumph. "I can see that you are surprised—you didn't look for anything of the sort, I dare say."

"No, candidly, I didn't," I admitted. "Good Lord, man, you will become the Michelangelo of diabolism if you go on at this rate. Where on earth do you get such stuff?"

"Yes, I've gone pretty far," said Cyprian, seeming to disregard my question. "Further even than you think, probably. If you could know what I know, could see what I have seen, you might make something really worth-while out of your weird fiction, Philip. You are very clever and imaginative, of course. But you've never had any experience."

I was startled and puzzled. "Experience? What do you mean?"

"Precisely that. You try to depict the occult and the supernatural without even the most rudimentary first-hand knowledge of them. I tried to do something of the same sort in sculpture, years ago, without knowledge; and doubtless you recall the mediocre mess that I made of it. But I've learned a thing or two since then."

"Sounds as if you had made the traditional bond with the devil, or something of that sort," I observed, with a feeble and perfunctory levity.

Cyprian's eyes narrowed slightly, with a strange, secret look.

"I know what I know. Never mind how or why. The world in which we live isn't the only world; and some of the others lie closer at hand than you think. The boundaries of the seen and the unseen are sometimes interchangeable."

※

Recalling the malevolent phantom, I felt a peculiar disquietude as I listened to his words. An hour before, his statement would have impressed me as mere theorizing, but now it assumed an ominous and terrifying significance.

"What makes you think I have had no experience of the occult?" I asked.

"Your stories hardly show anything of the kind—anything factual or personal. They are all palpably made up. When you've argued with a ghost, or watched the ghouls at mealtime, or fought with an incubus, or suckled a vampire, you may achieve some genius characterization and color along such lines."

For reasons that should be fairly obvious, I had not intended to tell anyone of the unbelievable thing at Toleman's. Now, with a singular mixture of emotions, of compulsive, eerie terrors and desire to refute the animal versions of Cyprian, I found myself describing the phantom.

He listened with an inexpressive look, as if his thoughts were occupied with other matters than my story. Then, when I had finished:

"You are becoming more psychic than I imagined. Was your apparition anything like one of these?"

With the last words, he lifted the sheet of burlap from the muffled group of figures beside which he had been standing.

❦

I cried out involuntarily with the shock of that appalling revelation, and almost tottered as I stepped back.

Before me, in a monstrous semicircle, were seven creatures who might all have been modeled from the gargoyle that had confronted me across the folio of Goya drawings. Even in several that were still amorphous or incomplete, Cyprian had conveyed with a damnable art the peculiar mingling of primal bestiality and mortuary putrescence that had signalized the phantom. The seven monsters had closed in on a cowering, naked girl, and were all clutching foully toward her with their hyena claws. The stark, frantic, insane terror on the face of the girl, and the slavering hunger of her assailants, were alike unbearable. The group was a masterpiece, in its consummate power of technique—but a masterpiece that inspired loathing rather than admiration. And following my recent experience, the sight of it affected me with indescribable alarm. It seemed to me that I had gone astray from the normal, familiar world into a land of detestable mystery, of prodigious and unnatural menace.

Held by an abhorrent fascination, it was hard for me to wrench my eyes away from the figure-piece. At last I turned from it to Cyprian himself. He was regarding me with a cryptic air, beneath which I suspected a covert gloating.

"How do you like my little pets?" he inquired. "I am going to call the composition 'The Hunters from Beyond.'"

Before I could answer, a woman suddenly appeared from behind the Chinese screen. I saw that she was the model for the girl in the unfinished group. Evidently she had been dressing, and she was now ready to leave, for she wore a tailored suit and a smart toque. She was beautiful, in a dark, semi-Latin fashion; but her mouth was sullen and reluctant; and her wide, liquid eyes were wells of strange terror as she gazed at Cyprian, myself, and the uncovered statue-piece.

Cyprian did not introduce me. He and the girl talked together in low tones for a minute or two, and I was unable to overhear more than half of what they said. I gathered, however, that an appointment was being made for the next sitting. There was a pleading, frightened note in the girl's voice, together with an almost maternal concern; and Cyprian seemed to be arguing with her or trying to reassure her about something. At last she went out, with a queer, supplicative glance at me—a glance whose meaning I could only surmise and could not wholly fathom.

"That was Marta," said Cyprian. "She is half Irish, half Italian. A good model; but my new sculptures seem to be making her a little nervous." He laughed abruptly, with a mirthless, jarring note that was like the cachinnation of a sorcerer.

"In God's name, what are you trying to do here?" I burst out. "What does it all mean? Do such abominations really exist, on earth or in any hell?"

He laughed again, with an evil subtlety, and became evasive all at once. "Anything may exist, in a boundless universe with multiple dimensions. Anything may be real—or unreal. Who knows? It is not for me to say. Figure it out for yourself, if you can—there's a vast field for speculation—and perhaps for more than speculation."

With this, he began immediately to talk of other topics. Baffled, mystified, with a sorely troubled mind and nerves that were more unstrung than ever by the black enigma of it all, I ceased to question him. Simultaneously, my desire to leave the studio became almost overwhelming—a mindless, whirlwind panic that prompted me to run pell-mell from the room and down the stairs into the wholesome normality of the common, Twentieth Century streets. It seemed to me that the rays which fell through the skylight were not those of the sun, but of some darker orb; that the room was touched with unclean webs of shadows where shadow should not have been; that the stone Satans, the bronze lamias, the terra-cotta satyrs and the clay gargoyles had somehow increased in number and might spring to malignant life at any instant.

Hardly knowing what I said, I continued to converse for a while with Cyprian. Then, excusing myself on the score of a nonexistent luncheon appointment, and promising vaguely to return for another visit before my departure from the city, I took my leave.

I was surprised to find my cousin's model in the lower hall, at the foot of the stairway. From her manner, and her first words, it was plain that she had been waiting.

"You are Mr. Philip Hastane, aren't you?" she said, in an eager, agitated voice. "I am Marta Fitzgerald. Cyprian has often mentioned you, and I believe that he admires you a lot.

"Maybe you'll think me crazy," she went on, "but I had to speak to you. I can't stand the way that things are going here, and I'd refuse to come to the place any more, if it wasn't that I like Cyprian so well.

"I don't know what he has done—or what has been done to him—but he is altogether different from what he used to be. His new work is so horrible—you can't imagine how it frightens me. The sculptures he does are more hideous, more hellish all the time. Ugh! those drooling, dead-gray monsters in that new group of his—I can hardly bear to be in the studio with them. It isn't right for anyone to depict such things. Don't you think they are awful, Mr. Hastane? They look as if they had broken loose from Hell—and make you think that Hell can't be very far away. It is wrong and wicked for anyone to—even imagine them; and I wish that Cyprian would stop. I am afraid that something will happen to him—to his mind—if he goes on. And I'll go mad, too, if I have to see those monsters many more times. My God! No one could keep sane in that studio."

She paused, and appeared to hesitate. Then:

"Can't you do something, Mr. Hastane? Can't you talk to him, and tell him how wrong it is, and how dangerous to his mental health? You must have a lot of influence with Cyprian—you are his cousin, aren't you? And he thinks you are very clever, too. I wouldn't ask you, if I hadn't been forced to notice so many things that aren't as they should be.

"I wouldn't bother you, either, if I knew anyone else to ask. He has shut himself up in that awful studio for the past year, and he hardly ever sees anybody. You are the first person that he has invited to see his new sculptures. He wants them to be a complete surprise for the critics and the public, when he holds his next exhibition.

"But you'll speak to Cyprian, won't you, Mr. Hastane? I can't do anything to stop him—he seems to exult in the mad horrors he creates. And he merely laughs at me when I try to tell him the danger. However, I think that those things are making him a little nervous sometimes—that he is growing afraid of his own morbid imagination. Perhaps he will listen to you."

If I had needed anything more to unnerve me, the desperate pleading of the girl and her dark, obscurely baleful hintings would have been enough. I could see that she loved Cyprian, that she was frantically anxious concerning him, and hysterically afraid; otherwise, she would not have approached an utter stranger in this fashion.

"But I haven't any influence with Cyprian," I protested, feeling a queer embarrassment. "And what am I to say to him, anyway? Whatever he is doing is his own affair, not mine. His new sculptures are magnificent—I have never seen any thing more powerful of the kind. And how could I advise him to stop doing them? There would be no legitimate reason; he would simply laugh me out of the studio. An artist has the right to choose his own subject-matter, even if he takes it from the nether pits of Limbo and Erebus."

The girl must have pleaded and argued with me for many minutes in that deserted hall. Listening to her, and trying to convince her of my inability to fulfill her request, was like a dialog in some futile and tedious nightmare. During the course of it, she told me a few details that I am unwilling to record in this narrative; details that were too morbid and too shocking for belief, regarding the mental alteration of Cyprian, and his new subject matter and method of work. There were direct and oblique hints of a growing perversion; but somehow it seemed that much more was being held back; that even in her most horrifying disclosures she was not wholly frank with me. At last, with some sort of hazy promise that I would speak to Cyprian, would remonstrate with him, I succeeded in getting away from her, and returned to my hotel.

The afternoon and evening that followed were tinged as by the tyrannous adumbration of an ill dream. I felt that I had stepped from the solid earth into a gulf of seething, menacing, madness-haunted shadow, and was lost henceforward to all rightful sense of location or direction. It was all too hideous—and too doubtful and unreal. The change in Cyprian himself was no less bewildering, and hardly less horrifying, than the vile phantom of the bookshop, and the demon sculptures that displayed a magisterial art. It was as if the man had become possessed by some satanic energy or entity.

Everywhere that I went, I was powerless to shake off the feeling of an intangible pursuit, of a frightful, unseen vigilance. It seemed to me that the worm-gray face and sulphurous eyes would reappear at any moment; that the semi-canine mouth with its gangrene-dripping fangs might come to slaver above the restaurant table at which I ate, or upon the pillow of my bed. I did not dare to reopen the purchased Goya volume, for fear of finding that certain pages were still defiled with a spectral slime.

I went out and spent the evening in cafés, in theaters, wherever people thronged and lights were bright. It was after midnight when I finally ventured to brave the solitude of my hotel bedroom. Then there were endless hours of nerve-wrung insomnia, of shivering, sweating apprehension beneath the electric bulb that I had left burning. Finally, a little before dawn, by no conscious transition and with no premonitory drowsiness, I fell asleep.

I remember no dreams—only the vast, incubus-like oppression that persisted even in the depth of slumber, as if to drag me down with its formless, ever-clinging weight into gulfs beyond the reach of created light or the fathoming of organized entity.

It was almost noon when I awoke, and found myself staring into the verminous, apish, mummy-dead face and hell-illumined eyes of the gargoyle that had crouched before me in the corner at Toleman's. The thing was standing at the foot of my bed; and behind it as I stared, the wall of the room, which was covered with a floral paper, dissolved in an infinite vista of grayness, teeming with ghoulish forms that emerged like monstrous, misshapen bubbles from plains of undulant ooze and skies of serpentine vapor. It was another world, and my very sense of equilibrium was disturbed by an evil vertigo as I gazed. It seemed to me that my bed was heaving dizzily, was turning slowly, deliriously toward the gulf; that the feculent vista and the vile apparition were swimming beneath me; that I would fall toward them in another moment and be precipitated forever into that world of abysmal monstrosity and obscenity.

In a start of profound alarm, I fought my vertigo, fought the sense that another will than mine was drawing me, that the unclean gargoyle was luring me by some unspeakable mesmeric spell, as a serpent is said to lure its prey. I seemed to read a nameless purpose in its yellow-slitted eyes, in the soundless moving of its oozy lips: and my very soul recoiled with nausea and revulsion as I breathed its pestilential fœtor.

Apparently, the mere effort of mental resistance was enough. The vista and the face receded; they went out in a swirl of daylight. I saw the design of tea roses on the wallpaper beyond; and the bed beneath me was sanely horizontal once more. I lay sweating with my terror, all adrift on a sea of nightmare surmise, of unearthly threat and whirlpool madness, till the ringing of the telephone bell recalled me automatically to the known world.

I sprang to answer the call. It was Cyprian, though I should hardly have recognized the dead, hopeless tones of his voice, from which the mad pride and self-assurance of the previous day had wholly vanished.

"I must see you at once," he said. "Can you come to the studio?"

I was about to refuse, to tell him that I had been called home suddenly, that there was no time, that I must catch the noon train— any thing to avert the ordeal of another visit to that place of mephitic evil—when I heard his voice again.

"You simply must come, Philip. I can't tell you about it over the phone, but a dreadful thing has happened: Marta has disappeared."

I consented, telling him that I would start for the studio as soon as I had dressed. The whole nightmare had closed in, had deepened immeasurably with his last words; but, remembering the haunted face of the girl, her hysteric fears, her frantic plea, and my vague promise, I could not very well decline to go.

I dressed and went out with my mind in a turmoil of abominable conjecture, of ghastly doubt, and apprehension all the more hideous because I was unsure of its object. I tried to imagine what had happened, tried to piece together the frightful, evasive, half-admitted hints of unknown terror into a tangible coherent fabric, but found myself involved in a chaos of shadowy menace.

I could not have eaten any breakfast, even if I had taken the necessary time. I went at once to the studio, and found Cyprian standing aimlessly amid his baleful statuary. His look was that of a man who has been stunned by the blow of some crushing weapon, or has gazed on the very face of Medusa. He greeted me in a vacant manner, with dull, toneless words. Then, like a charged machine, as if his body rather than his mind were speaking, he began at once to pour forth the atrocious narrative.

⁂

"They took her," he said, simply. "Maybe you didn't know it, or weren't sure of it; but I've been doing all my new sculptures from life—even that last group. Marta was posing for me this forenoon—only an hour ago—or less. I had hoped to finish her part of the modeling to-day; and she wouldn't have had to come again for this particular piece. I hadn't called the Things this time, since I knew she was beginning to fear them more and more. I think she feared them on my account more than her own—and they were making me a little uneasy too, by the boldness with which they sometimes lingered when I had ordered them to leave, and the way they would sometimes appear when I didn't want them.

"I was busy with some of the final touches on the girl-figure, and wasn't even looking at Marta, when suddenly I knew that the Things were there. The smell told me, if nothing else—I guess you know what the smell is like. I looked up, and found that the studio was full of them—they had never before appeared in such numbers. They were surrounding Marta, were crowding and jostling each other, were all reaching toward her with their filthy talons; but even then, I didn't think that they could harm her. They aren't material beings, in the sense that we are, and they really have no physical power outside their own plane. All that they do have is a sort of snaky mesmerism, and they'll always try to drag you down to their own dimension by means of it. God help anyone who yields to them; but you don't have to go, unless you are weak, or willing. I've never had any doubt of my power to resist them, and I didn't really dream they could do anything to Marta.

"It startled me, though, when I saw the whole crowding hell-pack, and I ordered them to go pretty sharply. I was angry—and somewhat alarmed, too. But they merely grimaced and slavered, with that slow, twisting movement of their lips that is like a voiceless gibbering, and then they closed in on Marta, just as I represented them doing in that accursed group of sculpture. Only there were scores of them now, instead of merely seven.

※

"I can't describe how it happened, but all at once their foul talons had reached the girl; they were pawing her, were pulling at her hands, her arms, her body. She screamed—and I hope I'll never hear another scream so full of black agony and soul-unhinging fright. Then I knew that she had yielded to them—either from choice, or from excess of terror—and knew that they were taking her away.

"For a moment, the studio wasn't there at all—only a long, gray, oozing plain, beneath skies where the fumes of Hell were writhing like a million ghostly and distorted dragons. Marta was sinking into that ooze, and the Things were all about her, gathering in fresh hundreds from every side, fighting each other for place, sinking with her like bloated, misshaped fen-creatures into their native slime. Then everything vanished—and I was standing here in the studio, all alone with these damned sculptures."

He paused for a little, and stared with dreary, desolate eyes at the floor. Then:

"It was awful, Philip, and I'll never forgive myself for having anything to do with those monsters. I must have been a little mad, but I've always had a strong ambition to create some real stuff in the field of the grotesque and visionary and macabre. I don't suppose you ever suspected, back in my stodgy phase, that I had a veritable appetence for such things. I wanted to do in sculpture what Poe and Lovecraft and Baudelaire have done in literature, what Rops and Goya did in pictorial art.

"That was what led me into the occult, when I realized my limitations. I knew that I had to see the dwellers of the invisible worlds before I could depict them. I wanted to do it. I longed for this power of vision and representation more than anything else. And then, all at once, I found that I had the power of summoning the unseen.

"There was no magic involved, in the usual sense of the word—no spells and circles, no pentacles and burning gums from old sorcery books. At bottom, it was just will-power, I guess—a will to divine the satanic, to summon the innumerable malignities and grotesqueries that people other planes than ours, or mingle unperceived with humanity.

"You've no idea what I have beheld, Philip. These statues of mine—these devils, vampires, lamias, satyrs—were all done from life, or at least from recent memory. The originals are what the occultists would call elementals, I suppose. There are endless worlds, contiguous to our own, or coexisting with it, that such beings inhabit. All the creations of myth and fantasy, all the familiar spirits that sorcerers have evoked, are resident in these worlds.

"I made myself their master, I levied upon them at will. Then, from a dimension that must be a little lower than all others, a little nearer the ultimate nadir of Hell, I called the innominate beings who posed for this new figure-piece.

"I don't know what they are, but I have surmised a good deal. They are hateful as the worms of the Pit, they are malevolent as harpies, they drool with a poisonous hunger not to be named or imagined. But I believed that they were powerless to do anything outside their own sphere, and I've always laughed at them when they tried to entice me—even though that snakish mental pull of theirs was rather creepy at times. It was as if soft, invisible, gelatinous arms were trying to drag you down from the firm shore into a bottomless bog.

"They are hunters—I am sure of that—the hunters from Beyond. God knows what they will do to Marta now that they have her at their mercy. That vast, viscid, miasma-haunted place to which they took her is awful beyond the imagining of a Satan. Perhaps—even there—they couldn't harm her body. But bodies aren't what they want—it isn't for human flesh that they grope with those ghoulish claws, and gape and slaver with those gangrenous mouths. The brain itself—and the soul, too—is their food: they are the creatures who prey on the minds of madmen and mad women, who devour the disembodied spirits that have fallen from the cycles of incarnation, have gone down beyond the possibility of rebirth.

"To think of Marta in their power—it is worse than Hell or madness. Marta loved me, and I loved her, too, though I didn't have the sense to realize it, wrapped as I was in my dark, baleful ambition and impious egotism. She was afraid for me, and I believe she surrendered voluntarily to the Things. She must have thought that they would leave me alone if they secured another victim in my place."

He ceased, and began to pace idly and feverishly about. I saw that his hollow eyes were alight with torment, as if the mechanical telling of his horrible story had in some manner served to re-quicken his crushed mind. Utterly and starkly appalled by his hideous revelations, I could say nothing, but could only stand and watch his torture-twisted face.

Incredibly, his expression changed, with a wild, startled look that was instantly transfigured into joy. Turning to follow his gaze, I saw that Marta was standing in the center of the room. She was nude, except for a Spanish shawl that she must have worn while posing. Her face was bloodless as the marble of a tomb, and her eyes were wide and blank, as if she had been drained of all life, of all thought or emotion or memory, as if even the knowledge of horror had been taken away from her. It was the face of the living dead, the soulless mask of ultimate idiocy; and the joy faded from Cyprian's eyes as he stepped toward her.

He took her in his arms, he spoke to her with a desperate, loving tenderness, with cajoling and caressing words. She made no answer, however, no movement of recognition or awareness, but stared beyond him with her blank eyes, to which the daylight and the darkness, the void air and her lover's face, would henceforward be the same. He and I both knew, in that instant, that she would never again respond to any human voice, or to human love or terror; that she was like an empty cerement, retaining the outward form of that which the worms have eaten in their mausolean darkness. Of the noisome pits wherein she had been, of that bournless realm and its pullulating phantoms, she could tell us nothing: her agony had ended with the terrible mercy of complete forgetfulness.

Like one who confronts the Gorgon, I was frozen by her wide and sightless gaze. Then, behind her, where stood an array of carven Satans and lamias, the room seemed to recede, the walls and floor dissolved in a seething, unfathomable gulf, amid whose pestilential vapors the statues were mingled in momentary and loathsome ambiguity with the ravening faces, the hunger-contorted forms that swirled toward us from their ultra-dimensional limbo like a devil-laden hurricane from Malebolge. Outlined against that boiling, measureless cauldron of malignant storm, Marta stood like an image of glacial death and silence in the arms of Cyprian. Then, once more, after a little, the abhorrent vision faded, leaving only the diabolic statuary.

I think that I alone had beheld it; that Cyprian had seen nothing but the dead face of Marta. He drew her close, he repeated his hopeless words of tenderness and cajolery. Then, suddenly, he released her with a vehement sob of despair. Turning away, while she stood and still looked on with unseeing eyes, he snatched a heavy sculptor's mallet from the table on which it was lying, and proceeded to smash with furious blows the newly-modeled group of gargoyles, till nothing was left but the figure of the terror-maddened girl, crouching above a mass of cloddish fragments and formless, half-dried clay.

THE ISLE OF
THE TORTURERS

Between the sun's departure and return, the Silver Death had fallen upon Yoros. Its advent, however, had been foretold in many prophecies, both immemorial and recent. Astrologers had said that this mysterious malady, heretofore unknown on earth, would descend from the great star, Achernar, which presided balefully over all the lands of the southern continent of Zothique; and having sealed the flesh of a myriad men with its bright, metallic pallor, the plague would still go on in time and space, borne by the dim currents of ether to other worlds.

Dire was the Silver Death; and none knew the secret of its contagion or the cure. Swift as the desert wind, it came into Yoros from the devastated realm of Tasuun, overtaking the very messengers who ran by night to give warning of its nearness. Those who were smitten felt an icy, freezing cold, an instant rigor, as if the outermost gulf had breathed upon them. Their faces and bodies whitened strangely, gleaming with a wan luster, and became stiff as long-dead corpses, all in an interim of minutes.

In the streets of Silpon and Siloar, and in Faraad, the capital of Yoros, the plague passed like an eerie, glittering light from countenance to countenance under the golden lamps; and the victims fell where they were stricken; and the deathly brightness remained upon them.

The loud, tumultuous public carnivals were stilled by its passing, and the merrymakers were frozen in frolic attitudes. In proud mansions, the wine-flushed revelers grew pale amid their garish feasts, and reclined in their opulent chairs, still holding the half-emptied cups with rigid fingers. Merchants lay in their counting-houses on the heaped coins they had begun to reckon; and thieves, entering later, were unable to depart with their booty. Diggers died in the half-completed graves they had dug for others; but no one came to dispute their possession.

There was no time to flee from the strange, inevitable scourge. Dreadfully and quickly, beneath the clear stars, it breathed upon Yoros; and few were they who awakened from slumber at dawn. Fulbra, the young king of Yoros, who had but newly succeeded to the throne, was virtually a ruler without a people.

※

Fulbra had spent the night of the plague's advent on a high tower of his palace above Faraad: an observatory tower, equipped with astronomical appliances. A great heaviness had lain on his heart, and his thoughts were dulled with an opiate despair; but sleep was remote from his eyelids. He knew the many predictions that foretold the Silver Death; and moreover, he had read its imminent coming in the stars, with the aid of the old astrologer and sorcerer, Vemdeez. This latter knowledge he and Vemdeez had not cared to promulgate, knowing full well that the doom of Yoros was a thing decreed from all time by infinite destiny; and that no man could evade the doom, unless it were written that he should die in another way than this.

Now Vemdeez had cast the horoscope of Fulbra; and, though he found therein certain ambiguities that his science could not resolve, it was nevertheless written plainly that the king would not die in Yoros. Where he would die, and in what manner, were alike doubtful. But Vemdeez, who had served Altath the father of Fulbra, and was no less devoted to the new ruler, had wrought by means of his magical art an enchanted ring that would protect Fulbra from the Silver Death in all times and places.

The ring was made of a strange red metal, darker than ruddy gold or copper, and was set with a black and oblong gem, not known to terrestrial lapidaries, that gave forth eternally a strong, aromatic perfume. The sorcerer told Fulbra never to remove the ring from the middle finger on which he wore it—not even in lands afar from Yoros and in days after the passing of the Silver Death: for if once the plague had breathed upon Fulbra, he would bear its subtle contagion always in his flesh; and the contagion would assume its wonted virulence with the ring's removal. But Vemdeez did not tell the origin of the red metal and the dark gem, nor the price at which the protective magic had been purchased.

With a sad heart, Fulbra had accepted the ring and had worn it; and so it was that the Silver Death blew over him in the night and harmed him not. But waiting anxiously on the high tower, and watching the golden lights of Faraad rather than the white, implacable stars, he felt a light, passing chillness that belonged not to the summer air. And even as it passed the gay noises of the city ceased; and the moaning lutes faltered strangely and expired. A stillness crept on the carnival; and some of the lamps went out and were not relit. In the palace beneath him there was also silence; and he heard no more the laughter of his courtiers and chamberlains. And Vemdeez came not, as was his custom, to join Fulbra on the tower at midnight. So Fulbra knew himself for a realmless king; and the grief that he still felt for the noble Altath was swollen by a great sorrow for his perished people.

Hour by hour he sat motionless, too sorrowful for tears. The stars changed above him; and Achernar glared down perpetually like the bright, cruel eye of a mocking demon; and the heavy balsam of the black-jeweled ring arose to his nostrils and seemed to stifle him. And once the thought occurred to Fulbra, to cast the ring away and die as his people had died. But his despair was too heavy upon him even for this; and so, at length, the dawn came slowly in heavens pale as the Silver Death, and found him still on the tower.

In the dawn, King Fulbra rose and descended the coiled stairs of porphyry into his palace. And midway on the stairs he saw the fallen corpse of the old sorcerer Vemdeez, who had died even as he climbed to join his master. The wrinkled face of Vemdeez was like polished metal, and was whiter than his beard and hair; and his open eyes, which had been dark as sapphires, were frosted with the plague. Then, grieving greatly for the death of Vemdeez, whom he had loved as a foster father, the king went slowly on. And in the suites and halls below, he found the bodies of his courtiers and servants and guardsmen. And none remained alive, excepting three slaves who warded the green, brazen portals of the lower vaults, far beneath the palace.

Now Fulbra bethought him of the counsel of Vemdeez, who had urged him to flee from Yoros and to seek shelter in the southern isle of Cyntrom, which paid tribute to the kings of Yoros. And though he had no heart for this, nor for any course of action, Fulbra bade the three remaining slaves to gather food and such other supplies as were necessary for a voyage of some length, and to carry them aboard a royal barge of ebony that was moored at the palace porticoes on the river Voum.

Then, embarking with the slaves, he took the helm of the barge, and directed the slaves to unfurl the broad amber sail. And past the stately city of Faraad, whose streets were thronged with the silvery dead, they sailed on the widening jasper estuary of the Voum, and into the amaranth-colored gulf of the Indaskian Sea.

A favorable wind was behind them, blowing from the north over desolate Tasuun and Yoros, even as the Silver Death had blown in the night. And idly beside them, on the Voum, there floated seaward many vessels whose crews and captains had all died of the plague. And Faraad was still as a necropolis of old time; and nothing stirred on the estuary shores, excepting the plumy, fan-shapen palms that swayed southward in the freshening wind. And soon the green strand of Yoros receded, gathering to itself the blueness and the dreams of distance.

Creaming with a winy foam, full of strange murmurous voices and vague tales of exotic things, the halcyon sea was about the voyagers now beneath the high-lifting summer sun. But the sea's enchanted voices and its long, languorous, immeasurable cradling could not soothe the sorrow of Fulbra; and in his heart a despair abided, black as the gem that was set in the red ring of Vemdeez.

Howbeit, he held the great helm of the ebon barge, and steered as straightly as he could by the sun toward Cyntrom. The amber sail was taut with the favoring wind; and the barge sped onward all that day, cleaving the amaranth waters with its dark prow that reared in the carven form of an ebony goddess. And when the night came with familiar austral stars, Fulbra was able to correct such errors as he had made in reckoning the course.

For many days they flew southward; and the sun lowered a little in its circling behind them; and new stars climbed and clustered at evening about the black goddess of the prow. And Fulbra, who had once sailed to the isle of Cyntrom in boyhood days with his father Altath, thought to see ere long the lifting of its shores of camphor and sandalwood from the winy deep. But in his heart there was no gladness; and often now he was blinded by wild tears, remembering that other voyage with Altath.

Then, suddenly and at high noon, there fell an airless calm; and the waters became as purple glass about the barge. The sky changed to a dome of beaten copper, arching close and low; and, as if by some evil wizardry, the dome darkened with untimely night; and a tempest rose like the gathered breath of mighty devils and shaped the sea into vast ridges of abysmal valleys. The mast of ebony snapped like a reed in the wind, and the sail was torn asunder, and the helpless vessel pitched headlong in the dark troughs and was hurled upward through veils of blinding foam to the giddy summits of the billows.

Fulbra clung to the useless helm, and the slaves, at his command, took shelter in the forward cabin. For countless hours they were borne onward at the will of the mad hurricane; and Fulbra could see naught in the lowering gloom, except the pale crests of the beetling waves; and he could tell no longer the direction of their course.

Then, in that lurid dusk, he beheld at intervals another vessel that rode the storm-driven sea, not far from the barge. He thought that the vessel was a galley such as might be used by merchants that voyaged among the southern isles, trading for incense and plumes and vermilion; but its oars were mostly broken, and the toppled mast hung forward on the prow.

For a time the ships drove on together; till Fulbra saw, in a rifting of the gloom, the sharp and somber crags of an unknown shore, with sharper towers that lifted palely above them. He could not turn the helm; and the barge and its companion vessel were carried toward the looming rocks, till Fulbra thought that they would crash thereon. But, as if by some enchantment, even as it had risen, the sea fell abruptly in a windless calm; and quiet sunlight poured from a clearing sky; and the barge was left on a broad crescent of ocher-yellow sand between the crags and the lulling waters, with the galley beside it.

Dazed and marveling, Fulbra leaned on the helm, while his slaves crept timidly forth from the cabin, and men began to appear on the decks of the galley. And the king was about to hail these men, some of whom were dressed as humble sailors and others in the fashion of rich merchants. But he heard a laughter of strange voices, high and shrill and somehow evil, that seemed to fall from above; and looking up he saw that many people were descending a sort of stairway in the cliffs that enclosed the beach.

The people drew near, thronging about the barge and the galley. They wore fantastic turbans of blood-red, and were clad in closely-fitting robes of vulturine black. Their faces and hands were yellow as saffron; their small and slaty eyes were set obliquely beneath lashless lids; and their thin lips, which smiled eternally, were crooked as the blades of scimitars.

They bore sinister and wicked-looking weapons, in the form of saw-toothed swords and double-headed spears. Some of them bowed low before Fulbra and addressed him obsequiously, staring upon him all the while with an unblinking gaze that he could not fathom. Their speech was no less alien than their aspect; it was full of sharp and hissing sounds; and neither the king nor his slaves could comprehend it. But Fulbra bespoke the people courteously, in the mild and mellow-flowing tongue of Yoros, and inquired the name of this land whereon the barge had been cast by the tempest.

Certain of the people seemed to understand him, for a light came in their slaty eyes at his question; and one of them answered brokenly in the language of Yoros, saying that the land was the Isle of Ucca-strog. Then, with something of covert evil in his smile, this person added that all shipwrecked mariners and seafarers would receive a goodly welcome from Ildrac, the king of the Isle.

At this, the heart of Fulbra sank within him; for he had heard numerous tales of Uccastrog in bygone years; and the tales were not such as would reassure a stranded traveler. Uccastrog, which lay far to the east of Cyntrom, was commonly known as the Isle of the Torturers; and men said that all who landed upon it unaware, or were cast thither by the seas, were imprisoned by the inhabitants and were subjected later to unending curious tortures whose infliction formed the chief delight of these cruel beings. No man, it was rumored, had ever escaped from Uccastrog; but many had lingered for years in its dungeons and hellish torture-chambers, kept alive for the pleasure of King Ildrac and his followers. Also, it was believed that the Torturers were great magicians who could raise mighty storms with their enchantments, and could cause vessels to be carried far from the maritime routes, and then fling them ashore upon Uccastrog.

Seeing that the yellow people were all about the barge, and that no escape was possible, Fulbra asked them to take him at once before King Ildrac. To Ildrac he would announce his name and royal rank; and it seemed to him, in his simplicity, that one king, even though cruel-hearted, would scarcely torture another or keep him captive. Also, it might be that the inhabitants of Uccastrog had been some-what maligned by the tales of travelers.

So Fulbra and his slaves were surrounded by certain of the throng and were led toward the palace of Ildrac, whose high, sharp towers crowned the crags beyond the beach, rising above those clustered abodes in which the island people dwelt. And while they were climbing the hewn steps in the cliff, Fulbra heard a loud outcry below and a clashing as of steel against steel; and looking back, he saw that the crew of the stranded galley had drawn their swords and were fighting the islanders. But being outnumbered greatly, their resistance was borne down by the swarming Torturers; and most of them were taken alive. And Fulbra's heart misgave him sorely at this sight; and more and more did he mistrust the yellow people.

Soon he came into the presence of Ildrac, who sat on a lofty brazen chair in a vast hall of the palace. Ildrac was taller by half a head than any of his followers; and his features were like a mask of evil wrought from some pale, gilded metal; and he was clad in vestments of a strange hue, like sea-purple brightened with fresh-flowing blood. About him were many guardsmen, armed with terrible scythe-like weapons; and the sullen, slant-eyed girls of the palace, in skirts of vermilion and breast-cups of lazuli, went to and fro among huge basaltic columns. About the hall stood numerous engines of wood and stone and metal such as Fulbra had never beheld, and having a formidable aspect with their heavy chains, their beds of iron teeth, and their cords and pulleys of fish-skin.

❧

The young king of Yoros went forward with a royal and fearless bearing, and addressed Ildrac, who sat motionless and eyed him with a level, unwinking gaze. And Fulbra told Ildrac his name and station, and the calamity that had caused him to flee from Yoros; and he mentioned also his urgent desire to reach the Isle of Cyntrom.

"It is a long voyage to Cyntrom," said Ildrac, with a subtle smile. "Also, it is not our custom to permit guests to depart without having fully tasted the hospitality of the Isle of Uccastrog. Therefore, King

Fulbra, I must beg you to curb your impatience. We have much to show you here, and many diversions to offer. My chamberlains will now conduct you to a room befitting your royal rank. But first I must ask you to leave with me the sword that you carry at your side; for swords are often sharp—and I do not wish my guests to suffer injury by their own hands."

So Fulbra's sword was taken from him by one of the palace guardsmen; and a small ruby-hilted dagger that he carried was also removed. Then several of the guards, hemming him in with their scythed weapons, led him from the hall and by many corridors and downward flights of stairs into the solid rock beneath the palace. And he knew not whither his three slaves were taken, or what disposition was made of the captured crew of the galley. And soon he passed from the daylight into cavernous halls illumed by sulphur-colored flames in copper cressets; and all around him, in hidden chambers, he heard the sound of dismal moans and loud, maniacal howlings that seemed to beat and die upon adamantine doors.

In one of these halls, Fulbra and his guardsmen met a young girl, fairer and less sullen of aspect than the others; and Fulbra thought that the girl smiled upon him compassionately as he went by; and it seemed that she murmured faintly in the language of Yoros: "Take heart, King Fulbra, for there is one who would help you." And her words, apparently, were not heeded or understood by the guards, who knew only the harsh and hissing tongue of Uccastrog.

After descending many stairs, they came to a ponderous door of bronze; and the door was unlocked by one of the guards, and Fulbra was compelled to enter; and the door clanged dolorously behind him.

The chamber into which he had been thrust was walled on three sides with the dark stone of the island, and was walled on the fourth with heavy, unbreakable glass. Beyond the glass he saw the blue-green, glimmering waters of the undersea, lit by the hanging cressets of the chamber; and in the waters were great devil-fish whose tentacles writhed along the wall; and huge pythonomorphs with fabulous golden coils receding in the gloom; and the floating corpses of men that stared in upon him with eyeballs from which the lids had been excised.

There was a couch in one corner of the dungeon, close to the wall of glass; and food and drink had been supplied for Fulbra in vessels of wood. The king laid himself down, weary and hopeless, without tasting the food. Then, lying with close-shut eyes while the dead men and the sea-monsters peered in upon him by the glare of the cressets, he strove to forget his griefs and the dolorous doom that impended. And through his clouding terror and sorrow, he seemed to see the comely face of the girl who had smiled upon him compassionately, and who, alone of all that he had met in Uccastrog, had spoken to him with words of kindness. The face returned ever and anon, with a soft haunting, a gentle sorcery; and Fulbra felt, for the first time in many suns, the dim stirring of his buried youth and the vague, obscure desire of life. So, after a while he slept; and the face of the girl came still before him in his dreams.

The cressets burned above him with undiminished flames when he awakened; and the sea beyond the wall of glass was thronged with the same monsters as before, or with others of like kind. But amid the floating corpses he now beheld the flayed bodies of his own slaves, who, after being tortured by the island people, had been cast forth into the submarine cavern that adjoined his dungeon, so that he might see them on awakening.

He sickened with new horror at the sight; but even as he stared at the dead faces, the door of bronze swung open with a sullen grinding, and his guards entered. Seeing that he had not consumed the food and water provided for him, they forced him to eat and drink a little, menacing him with their broad, crooked blades till he complied. And then they led him from the dungeon and took him before King Ildrac, in the great hall of tortures.

Fulbra saw, by the level golden light through the palace windows and the long shadows of the columns and machines of torment, that the time was early dawn. The hall was crowded with the Torturers and their women; and many seemed to look on while others, of both sexes, busied themselves with ominous preparations. And Fulbra saw that a tall brazen statue, with cruel and demonian visage, like some implacable god of the underworld, was now standing at the right hand of Ildrac where he sat aloft on his brazen chair.

⁓※⁓

Fulbra was thrust forward by his guards, and Ildrac greeted him briefly, with a wily smile that preceded the words and lingered after them. And when Ildrac had spoken, the brazen image also began to speak, addressing Fulbra in the language of Yoros, with strident and metallic tones, and telling him with full and minute circumstance the various infernal tortures to which he was to be subjected on that day.

When the statue had done speaking, Fulbra heard a soft whisper in his ear, and saw beside him the fair girl whom he had previously met in the nether corridors. And the girl, seemingly unheeded by the Torturers, said to him: "Be courageous, and endure bravely all that is inflicted; for I shall effect your release before another day, if this be possible."

Fulbra was cheered by the girl's assurance; and it seemed to him that she was fairer to look upon than before; and he thought that her eyes regarded him tenderly; and the twin desires of love and life were strangely resurrected in his heart, to fortify him against the tortures of Ildrac.

Of that which was done to Fulbra for the wicked pleasure of King Ildrac and his people, it were not well to speak fully. For the islanders of Uccastrog had designed innumerable torments, curious and subtle, wherewith to harry and excruciate the five senses; and they could harry the brain itself, driving it to extremes more terrible than madness; and could take away the dearest treasures of memory and leave unutterable foulness in their place.

On that day, however, they did not torture Fulbra to the uttermost. But they racked his ears with cacophonous sounds; with evil flutes that chilled the blood and curdled it upon his heart; with deep drums that seemed to ache in all his tissues; and thin tabors that wrenched his very bones. Then they compelled him to breathe the mounting fumes of braziers wherein the dried gall of dragons and the adipocere of dead cannibals were burned together with a fœtid wood. Then, when the fire had died down, they freshened it with the oil of vampire-bats; and Fulbra swooned, unable to bear the fœtor any longer.

Later, they stripped away his kingly vestments and fastened about his body a silken girdle that had been freshly dipped in an acid corrosive only to human flesh; and the acid ate slowly, fretting his skin with infinite fiery pangs.

Then, after removing the girdle lest it slay him, the Torturers brought in certain creatures that had the shape of ell-long serpents, but were covered from head to tail with sable hairs like those of a caterpillar. And these creatures twined themselves tightly about the arms and legs of Fulbra; and though he fought wildly in his revulsion, he could not loosen them with his hands; and the hairs that covered their constringent coils began to pierce his limbs like a million tiny needles, till he screamed with the agony. And when his breath failed him and he could scream no longer, the hairy serpents were induced to relinquish their hold by a languorous piping of which the islanders knew the secret. They dropped away and left him; but the mark of their coils was imprinted redly about his limbs; and around his body there burned the raw branding of the girdle.

King Ildrac and his people looked on with a dreadful gloating; for in such things they took their joy, and strove to pacify an implacable obscure desire. But seeing now that Fulbra could endure no more, and wishing to wreak their will upon him for many future days, they took him back to his dungeon.

Lying sick with remembered horror, feverish with pain, he longed not for the clemency of death but hoped for the coming of the girl to release him as she had promised. The long hours passed with a half-delirious tedium; and the cressets, whose flames had been changed to crimson, appeared to fill his eyes with flowing blood; and the dead men and the sea-monsters swam as if in blood beyond the wall of glass. And the girl came not; and Fulbra had begun to despair. Then, at last, he heard the door open gently and not with the harsh clangor that had proclaimed the entrance of his guards.

Turning, he saw the girl, who stole swiftly to his couch with a lifted finger-tip, enjoining silence. She told him with soft whispers that her plan had failed; but surely on the following night she would be able to drug the guards and obtain the keys of the outer gates; and Fulbra could escape from the palace to a hidden cove in which a boat with water and provisions lay ready for his use. She prayed him to endure for another day the torments of Ildrac; and to this, perforce, he consented. And he thought that the girl loved him; for tenderly she caressed his feverous brow, and rubbed his torture-burning limbs with a soothing ointment. He deemed that her eyes were soft with a compassion that was more than pity. So Fulbra believed the girl and trusted her, and took heart against the horror of the coming day. Her name, it seemed, was Ilvaa; and her mother was a woman of Yoros who had married one of the evil islanders, choosing this repugnant union as an alternative to the flaying-knives of Ildrac.

Too soon the girl went away, pleading the great danger of discovery, and closed the door softly upon Fulbra. And after a while the king slept; and Ilvaa returned to him amid the delirious abominations of his dreams, and sustained him against the terror of strange hells.

At dawn the guards came with their hooked weapons and led him again before Ildrac. And again the brazen, demoniac statue, in a strident voice, announced the fearful ordeals that he was to undergo. And this time he saw that other captives, including the crew and merchants of the galley, were also awaiting the malefic ministrations of the Torturers in the vast hall.

Once more in the throng of watchers the girl Ilvaa pressed close to him, unreprimanded by his guards, and murmured words of comfort;

so that Fulbra was enheartened against the enormities foretold by the brazen oracular image. And indeed a bold and hopeful heart was required to endure the ordeals of that day . . .

Among other things less goodly to be mentioned, the Torturers held before Fulbra a mirror of strange wizardry, wherein his own face was reflected as if seen after death. The rigid features, as he gazed upon them, became marked with the green and bluish marbling of corruption; and the withering flesh fell in on the sharp bones and displayed the visible fretting of the worm. Hearing meanwhile the dolorous groans and agonizing cries of his fellow-captives all about the hall, he beheld other faces, dead, swollen, lidless, and flayed, that seemed to approach from behind and to throng about his own face in the mirror. Their locks were dank and dripping, like the hair of corpses recovered from the sea; and sea-weed was mingled with the locks. Then, turning at a cold and clammy touch, he found that these faces were no illusion but the actual reflection of cadavers drawn from the under-sea by a malign sorcery, that had entered the hall of Ildrac like living men and were peering over his shoulder.

His own slaves, with flesh that the sea-things had gnawed even to the bone, were among them. And the slaves came toward him with glaring eyes that saw only the voidness of death. And beneath the sorcerous control of Ildrac, their evilly animated corpses began to assail Fulbra, clawing at his face and raiment with half-eaten fingers. And Fulbra, faint with loathing, struggled against his dead slaves, who knew not the voice of their master and were deaf as the wheels and racks of torment used by Ildrac.

Anon the drowned and dripping corpses went away; and Fulbra was stripped by the Torturers and was laid supine on the palace floor, with iron rings that bound him closely to the flags at knee and wrist, at elbow and ankle. Then they brought in the disinterred body of a woman, nearly eaten, in which a myriad maggots swarmed on the uncovered bones and tatters of dark corruption; and this body they placed on the right hand of Fulbra. And also they fetched the carrion of a black goat that was newly touched with beginning decay; and they laid it down beside him on the left hand. Then, across Fulbra, from right to left, the hungry maggots crawled in a long and undulant wave . . .

After the consummation of this torture, there came many others that were equally ingenious and atrocious, and were well designed for the delectation of King Ildrac and his people. And Fulbra endured the tortures valiantly, upheld by the thought of Ilvaa.

Vainly, however, on the night that followed this day, he waited in his dungeon for the girl. The cressets burned with a bloodier crimson; and new corpses were among the flayed and floating dead in the sea cavern; and strange, double-bodied serpents of the nether deep arose with an endless squirming; and their horned heads appeared to bloat immeasurably against the crystal wall. Yet the girl Ilvaa came not to free him as she had promised; and the night passed. But, though despair resumed its old dominion in the heart of Fulbra, and terror came with talons steeped in fresh venom, he refused to doubt Ilvaa, telling himself that she had been delayed or prevented by some unforeseen mishap.

At dawn of the third day, he was again taken before Ildrac. The brazen image, announcing the ordeals of the day, told him that he was to be bound on a wheel of adamant; and, lying on the wheel, was to drink a drugged wine that would steal away his royal memories for ever, and would conduct his naked soul on a long pilgrimage through monstrous and infamous hells before bringing it back to the hall of Ildrac and the broken body on the wheel.

Then certain women of the Torturers, laughing obscenely, came forward and bound King Fulbra to the adamantine wheel with thongs of dragon-gut. And after they had done this, the girl Ilvaa, smiling with the shameless exultation of open cruelty, appeared before Fulbra and stood close beside him, holding a golden cup that contained the drugged wine. She mocked him for his folly and credulity in trusting her promises; and the other women and the male Torturers, even to

Ildrac on his brazen seat, laughed loudly and evilly at Fulbra, and praised Ilvaa for the perfidy she had practiced upon him.

So Fulbra's heart grew sick with a darker despair than any he had yet known. The brief, piteous love that had been born amid sorrow and agony perished within him, leaving but ashes steeped in gall. Yet, gazing at Ilvaa with sad eyes, he uttered no word of reproach. He wished to live no longer; and, yearning for swift death, he bethought him of the wizard ring of Vemdeez and of that which Vemdeez had said would follow its removal from his finger. He still wore the ring, which the Torturers had deemed a bauble of small value. But his hands were bound tightly to the wheel, and he could not remove it. So, with a bitter cunning, knowing full well that the islanders would not take away the ring if he should offer it to them, he feigned a sudden madness and cried wildly:

"Steal my memories, if ye will, with your accursed wine—and send me through a thousand hells and bring me back again to Uccastrog; but take not the ring that I wear on my middle finger; for it is more precious to me than many kingdoms or the pale breasts of love."

Hearing this, King Ildrac rose from his brazen seat; and, bidding Ilvaa to delay the administration of the wine, he came forward and inspected curiously the ring of Vemdeez, which gleamed darkly, set with its rayless gem, on Fulbra's finger. And all the while, Fulbra cried out against him in a frenzy, as if fearing that he would take the ring.

So Ildrac, deeming that he could plague the prisoner thereby and could heighten his suffering a little, did the very thing for which Fulbra had planned. And the ring came easily from the shrunken finger; and Ildrac, wishing to mock the royal captive, placed it on his own middle digit.

Then, while Ildrac regarded the captive with a more deeply graven smile of evil on the pale, gilded mask of his face, there came to King Fulbra of Yoros the dreadful and longed-for thing. The Silver Death, that had slept so long in his body beneath the magical abeyance of the ring of Vemdeez, was made manifest even as he hung on the adamantine wheel. His limbs stiffened with another rigor than that of agony; and his face shone brightly with the coming of the Death; and so he died.

Then, to Ilvaa and to many of the Torturers who stood wondering about the wheel, the chill and instant contagion of the Silver Death was communicated. They fell even where they had stood; and the pestilence remained like a glittering light on the faces and hands of the men, and shone forth from the nude bodies of the women. And the plague passed along the immense hall; and the other captives of King Ildrac were released thereby from their various torments; and the Torturers found surcease from the dire longing that they could assuage only through the pain of their fellow men. And through all the palace, and throughout the Isle of Uccastrog, the Death flew swiftly, visible in those upon whom it had breathed, but otherwise unseen and impalpable.

But Ildrac, wearing the ring of Vemdeez, was immune. And, guessing not the reason of his immunity, he beheld with consternation the doom that had overtaken his followers, and watched in stupefaction the freezing of his victims. Then, fearful of some inimic sorcery, he rushed from the hall; and, standing in the early sun on a palace terrace above the sea, he tore the ring of Vemdeez from his finger and hurled it to the foamy billows far below, deeming in his terror that the ring was perhaps the source or agent of the unknown hostile magic.

So Ildrac, in his turn, when all the others had fallen, was smitten by the Silver Death; and its peace descended upon him where he lay in his robes of blood-brightened purple, with features shining palely to the unclouded sun. And oblivion claimed the Isle of Uccastrog; and the Torturers were one with the tortured.

A NIGHT
IN MALNÉANT

My sojourn in the city of Malnéant occurred during a period of my life no less dim and dubious than that city itself and the misty regions lying thereabout. I have no precise recollection of its locality, nor can I remember exactly when and how I came to visit it. But I had heard vaguely that such a place was situated along my route; and when I came to the fog-enfolded river that flows beside its walls, and heard beyond the river the mortuary tolling of many bells, I surmised that I was approaching Malnéant.

On reaching the gray, colossal bridge that crosses the river, I could have continued at will on other roads leading to remoter cities: but it seemed to me that I might as well enter Malnéant as any other place. And so it was that I set foot on the bridge of shadowy arches, under which the black waters flowed in stealthy division and were joined again in a silence as of Styx and Acheron.

That period of my life, I have said, was dim and dubious: all the more so, mayhap, because of my need for forgetfulness, my persistent and at times partially rewarded search for oblivion. And that which I needed to forget above all was the death of the lady Mariel, and the fact that I myself had slain her as surely as if I had done the deed with my own hand. For she had loved me with an affection deeper and purer and more stable than mine; and my changeable temper, my fits of cruel indifference or ferocious irritability, had broken her gentle heart. So it was that she had sought the anodyne of a lethal poison; and after she was laid to rest in the somber vaults of her ancestors, I had become a wanderer, followed and forever tortured by a belated remorse. For months, or years, I am uncertain which, I roamed from old-world city to city, heeding little where I went if only wine and the other agents of oblivion were available . . . And thus I came, some while in my indefinite journeying, to the dim environs of Malnéant.

The sun (if ever there was a sun above this region) had been lost for I knew not how long in a sky of leaden vapors; the day was drear and sullen at best. But now, by the thickening of the shadows and the mist, I felt that evening must be near; and the bells I had heard, however heavy and sepulchral their tolling, gave at least the assurance of prospective shelter for the night. So I crossed the long bridge and entered the grimly yawning gate with a quickening of my footsteps even if with no alacrity of spirit.

The dusk had gathered behind the gray walls, but there were few lights in the city. Few people were abroad, and these went upon their way with a sort of solemn haste, as if on some funereal errand that would permit no delay. The streets were narrow, the houses high, with overhanging balconies and heavily curtained or shuttered windows. All was very silent, except for the bells, which tolled recurrently, sometimes faint and far off, and sometimes with a loud and startling clangor that seemed to come almost from overhead.

As I plunged among the shadowy mansions, along the streets from which a visible twilight issued to envelop me, it seemed that I was going farther and farther away from my memories at every step. For this reason I did not at once inquire my way to a tavern but was content to lose myself more and more in the gray labyrinth of buildings, which grew vaguer and vaguer amid the ever-mounting darkness and fog, as if they were about to dissolve in oblivion.

I think that my soul would have been almost at peace with itself, if it had not been for the re-iterant ringing of the bells, which were like all bells that toll for the repose of the dead, and therefore set me to remembering those that had rung for Mariel. But whenever they ceased, my thoughts would drift back with an indolent ease, a recovered security, to the all-surrounding vagueness . . .

I had no idea how far I had gone in Malnéant, nor how long I had roamed among those houses that hardly seemed as if they could be peopled by any but the sleeping or the dead. At last, however, I became aware that I was very tired, and bethought me of food and wine and a lodging for the night. But nowhere in my wanderings had I noticed the sign-board of an inn; so I resolved to ask the next passer-by for the desired direction.

As I have said before, there were few people abroad. Now, when I made up my mind to address one of them, it appeared that there was no one at all; and I walked onward through street after street in my futile search for a living face.

At length I met two women, clothed in gray that was cold and dim as the folds of the fog, and veiled withal, who were hurrying along with the same funereal intentness I had perceived in all other denizens of that city. I made bold to accost them, asking if they could direct me to an inn.

Scarcely pausing or even turning their heads, they answered: "We cannot tell you. We are shroud-weavers, and we have been busy making a shroud for the lady Mariel."

Now, at that name, which of all names in the world was the one I should least have expected or cared to hear, an unspeakable chill invaded my heart, and a dreadful dismay smote me like the breath of the tomb. It was indeed strange that in this dim city, so far in time and space from all I had fled to escape, a woman should have recently died who was also named Mariel. The coincidence appeared so sinister that an odd fear of the streets through which I had wandered was born suddenly in my soul. The name had evoked, with a more irrevocable fatality than the tolling of the bells, all that I had vainly wished to forget; and my memories were like living coals in my heart.

As I went onward, with paces that had become more hurried, more feverish than those of the people of Malnéant, I met two men, who were likewise dressed from head to foot in gray; and I asked of them the same question I had asked of the shroud-weavers.

"We cannot tell you," they replied. "We are coffin-makers, and we have been busy making a coffin for the lady Mariel."

As they spoke, and hastened on, the bells rang out again, this time very near at hand, with a more dismal and sepulchral menace in their leaden tolling. And everything about me, the tall and misty houses, the dark, indefinite streets, the rare and wraith-like figures, became as if part of the obscure confusion and fear and bafflement of a nightmare. Moment by moment, the coincidence on which I had stumbled appeared all too bizarre for belief, and I was troubled now by the monstrous and absurd idea that the Mariel I knew had only just died, and that this fantastic city was in some unsurmisable manner connected with her death. But this, of course, my reason rejected summarily, and I kept repeating to myself: "The Mariel of whom they speak is another Mariel." And it irritated me beyond all measure that a thought so enormous and ludicrous should return when my logic had dismissed it.

I met no more people of whom to inquire my way. But at length, as I fought with my shadowy perplexity and my burning memories, I found that I had paused beneath the weather-beaten sign of an inn, on which the lettering had been half effaced by time and the brown lichens. The building was obviously very old, like all the houses in Malnéant; its upper stories were lost in the swirling fog, except for a few furtive lights that glowed obscurely down; and a vague and musty odor of antiquity came forth to greet me as I mounted the steps and tried to open the ponderous door. But the door had been locked or bolted; so I began to pound upon it with my fists to attract the attention of those within.

After much delay, the door was opened slowly and grudgingly, and a cadaverous-looking individual peered forth, frowning with portentous gravity as he saw me.

"What do you desire?" he queried, in tones that were both brusk and solemn.

"A room for the night, and wine," I requested.

"We cannot accommodate you. All the rooms are occupied by people who have come to attend the obsequies of the lady Mariel; and all the wine in the house has been requisitioned for their use. You will have to go elsewhere."

He closed the door quickly upon me with the last words. I turned to resume my wanderings, and all that had troubled me before was now intensified a hundredfold. The gray mists and the grayer houses were full of the menace of memory: they were like traitorous tombs from which the cadavers of dead hours poured forth to assail me with envenomed fangs and talons. I cursed the hour when I had entered Malnéant, for it seemed to me now that in so doing I had merely completed a funereal, sinister circle through time, and had returned to the day of Mariel's death. And certainly, all my recollections of Mariel, of her final agony and her entombment, had assumed the frightful vitality of present things. But my reason still maintained, of course, that the Mariel who lay dead somewhere in Malnéant, and for whom all these obsequial preparations were being made, was not the lady whom I had loved, but another.

After threading streets that were even darker and narrower than those before traversed, I found a second inn, bearing a similar weather-beaten sign, and in all other respects very much like the first. The door was barred, and I knocked thereon with trepidation and was in no manner surprised when a second individual with a cadaverous face informed me in tones of sepulchral solemnity:

"We cannot accommodate you. All the rooms have been taken by musicians and mourners who will serve at the obsequies of the lady Mariel; and all the wine has been reserved for their use."

Now I began to dread the city about me with a manifold fear: for apparently the whole business of the people in Malnéant consisted of preparations for the funeral of this lady Mariel. And it began to be obvious that I must walk the streets of the city all night because of these same preparations. All at once, an overwhelming weariness was mingled with my nightmare terror and perplexity.

I had not long continued my peregrinations, after leaving the second inn, when the bells were tolled once more. For the first time, I found it possible to identify their source: they were in the spires of a great cathedral which loomed immediately before me through the fog. Some people were entering the cathedral, and a curiosity, which I knew to be both morbid and perilous, prompted me to follow them. Here, I somehow felt, I should be able to learn more regarding the mystery that tormented me.

All was dim within, and the light of many tapers scarcely served to illumine the vast nave and altar. Masses were being said by priests in black whose faces I could not see distinctly; and to me, their chanting was like words in a dream; and I could hear nothing, and nothing was plainly visible in all the place, except a bier of opulent fabrics on which there lay a motionless form in white. Flowers of many hues had been strewn upon the bier, and their fragrance filled the air with a drowsy languor, with an anodyne that seemed to drug my heart and brain. Such flowers had been cast on the bier of Mariel; and even thus, at her funeral, I had been overcome by a momentary dulling of the senses because of their perfume.

Dimly I became aware that someone was at my elbow. With eyes still intent on the bier, I asked:

"Who is it that lies yonder, for whom these masses are being said and these bells are rung?" And a slow, sepulchral voice replied:

"It is the lady Mariel, who died yesterday and who will be interred tomorrow in the vaults of her ancestors. If you wish, you may go forward and gaze upon her."

So I went down the cathedral aisle, even to the side of the bier, whose opulent fabrics trailed on the cold flags. And the face of her who lay thereon, with a tranquil smile upon the lips, and tender shadows upon the shut eyelids, was the face of the Mariel I had loved and of none other. The tides of time were frozen in their flowing;

and all that was or had been or could be, all of the world that existed aside from her, became as fading shadows; and even as once before (was it eons or instants ago?) my soul was locked in the marble hell of its supreme grief and regret. I could not move, I could not cry out nor even weep, for my very tears were turned to ice. And now I knew with a terrible certitude that this one event, the death of the lady Mariel, had drawn apart from all other happenings, had broken away from the sequence of time, and had found for itself a setting of appropriate gloom and solemnity; or perhaps had even built around itself the whole enormous maze of that spectral city, in which to abide my destined return among the mists of a deceptive oblivion.

At length, with an awful effort of will, I turned my eyes away; and leaving the cathedral with steps that were both hurried and leaden, I sought to find an egress from the dismal labyrinth of Malnéant to the gate by which I had entered. But this was by no means easy, and I must have roamed for hours in alleys blind and stifling as tombs, and along the tortuous, self-reverting thoroughfares, ere I came to a familiar street and was able henceforward to direct my paces with something of surety. And a dull and sunless daylight was dawning behind the mists when I crossed the bridge and came again to the road that would lead me away from that fatal city.

Since then, I have wandered long and in many places. But never again have I cared to revisit those old-world realms of fog and mist, for fear that I should come once more to Malnéant, and find that its people are still busied with their preparations for the obsequies of the lady Mariel.

THE CHAIN
OF AFORGOMON

It is indeed strange that John Milwarp and his writings should have fallen so speedily into semi-oblivion. His books, treating of Oriental life in a somewhat flowery, romantic style, were popular a few months ago. But now, in spite of their range and penetration, their pervasive verbal sorcery, they are seldom mentioned; and they seem to have vanished unaccountably from the shelves of bookstores and libraries.

Even the mystery of Milwarp's death, baffling to both law and science, has evoked but a passing interest, an excitement quickly lulled and forgotten.

I was well acquainted with Milwarp over a term of years. But my recollection of the man is becoming strangely blurred, like an image in a misted mirror. His dark, half-alien personality, his preoccupation with the occult, his immense knowledge of Eastern life and lore, are things I remember with such effort and vagueness as attends the recovery of a dream. Sometimes I almost doubt that he ever existed. It is as if the man, and all that pertains to him, were being erased from human record by some mysterious acceleration of the common process of obliteration.

In his will, he appointed me his executor. I have vainly tried to interest publishers in the novel he left among his papers: a novel surely not inferior to anything he ever wrote. They say that his vogue has passed. Now I am publishing as a magazine story the contents of the diary kept by Milwarp for a period preceding his demise.

Perhaps, for the open-minded, this diary will explain the enigma of his death. It would seem that the circumstances of that death are virtually forgotten, and I repeat them here as part of my endeavor to revive and perpetuate Milwarp's memory.

Milwarp had returned to his house in San Francisco after a long sojourn in Indo-China. We who knew him gathered that he had gone into places seldom visited by Occidentals. At the time of his demise he had just finished correcting the typescript of a novel which dealt with the more romantic and mysterious aspects of Burma.

On the morning of April 2nd, 1933, his housekeeper, a middle-aged woman, was startled by a glare of brilliant light which issued from the half-open door of Milwarp's study. It was as if the whole room were in flames. Horrified, the woman hastened to investigate. Entering the study, she saw her master sitting in an armchair at the table, wearing the rich, somber robes of Chinese brocade which he affected as a dressing-gown. He sat stiffly erect, a pen clutched unmoving in his fingers on the open pages of a manuscript volume. About him, in a sort of nimbus, glowed and flickered the strange light; and her only thought was that his garments were on fire.

She ran toward him, crying out a warning. At that moment the weird nimbus brightened intolerably, and the wan early dayshine, the electric bulbs that still burned to attest the night's labor, were alike blotted out. It seemed to the housekeeper that something had gone wrong with the room itself; for the walls and table vanished, and a great, luminous gulf opened before her; and on the verge of the gulf, in a seat that was not his cushioned armchair but a huge and roughhewn seat of stone, she beheld her master stark and rigid. His heavy brocaded robes were gone, and about him, from head to foot, were blinding coils of pure white fire, in the form of linked chains. She could not endure the brilliance of the chains, and cowering back, she shielded her eyes with her hands. When she dared to look again, the weird glowing had faded, the room was as usual; and Milwarp's motionless figure was seated at the table in the posture of writing.

Shaken and terrified as she was, the woman found courage to approach her master. A hideous smell of burnt flesh arose from beneath his garments, which were wholly intact and without visible trace of fire. He was dead, his fingers clenched on the pen, and his features frozen in a stare of tetanic agony. His neck and wrists were completely encircled by frightful burns that had charred them deeply. The coroner, in his examination, found that these burns, preserving an outline as of heavy links, were extended in long unbroken spirals around the arms and legs and torso. The burning was apparently the cause of Milwarp's death: it was as if iron chains, heated to incandescence, had been wrapped about him.

Small credit was given to the housekeeper's story of what she had seen. No one, however, could suggest an acceptable explanation of the bizarre mystery. There was, at the time, much aimless discussion; but, as I have hinted, people soon turned to other matters. The efforts made to solve the riddle were somewhat perfunctory. Chemists tried to determine the nature of a queer drug, in the form of a gray powder with pearly granules, to which use Milwarp had become addicted. But their tests merely revealed the presence of an alkaloid whose source and attributes were obscure to Western science.

Day by day, the whole incredible business lapsed from public attention; and those who had known Milwarp began to display the forgetfulness that was no less unaccountable than his weird doom. The housekeeper, who had held steadfastly in the beginning to her story, came at length to share the common dubiety. Her account, with repetition, became vague and contradictory; detail by detail, she seemed to forget the abnormal circumstances that she had witnessed with overwhelming horror.

The manuscript volume, in which Milwarp had apparently been writing at the time of death, was given into my charge with his other papers. It proved to be a diary, its last entry breaking off abruptly. Since reading the diary, I have hastened to transcribe it in my own hand, because, for some mysterious reason, the ink of the original is already fading and has become almost illegible in places.

The reader will note certain lacunae, due to passages written in an alphabet which neither I nor any scholar of my acquaintance can transliterate. These passages seem to form an integral part of the narrative, and they occur mainly toward the end, as if the writer had turned more and more to a language remembered from his ancient avatar. To the same mental reversion one must attribute the singular dating, in which Milwarp, still employing English script, appears to pass from our contemporary notation to that of some premundane world.

I give hereunder the entire diary, which begins with an undated footnote:

❦

This book, unless I have been misinformed concerning the qualities of the drug *souvara,* will be the record of my former life in a lost cycle. I have had the drug in my possession for seven months, but fear has prevented me from using it. Now, by certain tokens, I perceive that the longing for knowledge will soon overcome the fear.

Ever since my earliest childhood I have been troubled by intimations, dim, unplaceable, that seemed to argue a forgotten existence. These intimations partook of the nature of feelings rather than ideas or images: they were like the wraiths of dead memories. In the background of my mind there has lurked a sentiment of formless, melancholy desire for some nameless beauty long perished out of time. And, coincidentally, I have been haunted by an equally formless dread, an apprehension as of some bygone but still imminent doom.

Such feelings have persisted, undiminished, throughout my youth and maturity, but nowhere have I found any clue to their causation. My travels in the mystic Orient, my delvings into occultism, have merely convinced me that these shadowy intuitions pertain to some incarnation buried under the wreck of remotest cycles.

Many times, in my wanderings through Buddhistic lands, I had heard of the drug *souvara,* which is believed to restore, even for the uninitiate, the memory of other lives. And at last, after many vain efforts, I managed to procure a supply of the drug. The manner in which I obtained it is a tale sufficiently remarkable in itself, but of no special relevance here. So far—perhaps because of that apprehension which I have hinted—I have not dared to use the drug.

꽃

March 9th, 1933. This morning I took *souvara* for the first time, dissolving the proper amount in pure distilled water as I had been instructed to do. Afterward I leaned back easily in my chair, breathing with a slow, regular rhythm. I had no preconceived idea of the sensations that would mark the drug's initial effect, since these were said to vary prodigiously with the temperament of the users; but I composed myself to await them with tranquillity, after formulating clearly in my mind the purpose of the experiment.

For a while there was no change in awareness. I noticed a slight quickening of the pulse, and modulated my breathing in conformity with this. Then, by slow degrees, I experienced a sharpening of visual perception. The Chinese rugs on the floor, the backs of the serried volumes in my bookcases, the very wood of chairs, table, and shelves, began to exhibit new and unimagined colors. At the same time there were curious alterations of outline, every object seeming to extend itself in a hitherto unsuspected fashion. Following this, my surroundings became semi-transparent, like molded shapes of mist. I found that I could see through the marbled cover the illustrations in a volume of John Martin's edition of *Paradise Lost,* which lay before me on the table.

All this, I knew, was a mere extension of ordinary physical vision. It was only a prelude to those apperceptions of occult realms which I sought through *souvara.* Fixing my mind once more on the goal of the experiment, I became aware that the misty walls had vanished like a drawn arras. About me, like reflections in rippled water, dim sceneries wavered and shifted, erasing one another from instant to instant. I seemed to hear a vague but ever-present sound, more musical than the murmurs of air, water or fire, which was a property of the unknown element that environed me.

With a sense of troublous familiarity, I beheld the blurred unstable pictures which flowed past me upon this never-resting medium. Orient temples, flashing with sun-struck bronze and gold; the sharp, crowded gables and spires of medieval cities; tropic and northern forests; the costumes and physiognomies of the Levant, of Persia, of old Rome and Carthage, went by like blown, flying mirages. Each succeeding tableau belonged to a more ancient period than the one before it—and I knew that each was a scene from some former existence of my own.

Still tethered, as it were, to my present self, I reviewed these visible memories, which took on tri-dimensional depth and clarity. I saw myself as warrior and troubadour, as noble and merchant and mendicant. I trembled with dead fears, I thrilled with lost hopes and raptures, and was drawn by ties that death and Lethe had broken. Yet never did I fully identify myself with those other avatars: for I knew well that the memory I sought pertained to some incarnation of older epochs.

Still the fantasmagoria streamed on, and I turned giddy with vertigo ineffable before the vastness and diuturnity of the cycles of being. It seemed that I, the watcher, was lost in a gray land where the homeless ghosts of all dead ages went fleeing from oblivion to oblivion.

The walls of Nineveh, the columns and towers of unnamed cities, rose before me and were swept away. I saw the luxuriant plains that are now the Gobi desert. The sea-lost capitals of Atlantis were drawn to the light in unquenched glory. I gazed on lush and cloudy scenes from the first continents of Earth. Briefly I relived the beginnings of terrestrial man—and knew that the secret I would learn was ancienter even than these.

My visions faded into black voidness—and yet, in that void, through fathomless eons, it seemed that I existed still like a blind atom in the space between the worlds. About me was the darkness and repose of that night which antedated the Earth's creation. Time flowed backward with the silence of dreamless sleep.

❦

The illumination, when it came, was instant and complete. I stood in the full, fervid blaze of day amid royally towering blossoms in a deep garden, beyond whose lofty, vine-clad walls I heard the confused murmuring of the great city called Kalood. Above me, at their vernal zenith, were the four small suns that illumed the planet Hestan. Jewel-colored insects fluttered about me, lighting without fear on the rich habiliments of gold and black, enwrought with astronomic symbols, in which I was attired. Beside me was a dial-shaped altar of zoned agate, carved with the same symbols, which were those of the dreadful omnipotent time-god, Aforgomon, whom I served as a priest.

I had not even the slightest memory of myself as John Milwarp, and the long pageant of my terrestrial lives was as something that had never been—or was yet to be. Sorrow and desolation choked my heart as ashes fill some urn consecrated to the dead; and all the hues and perfumes of the garden about me were redolent only of the bitterness of death. Gazing darkly upon the altar, I muttered blasphemy against Aforgomon, who, in his inexorable course, had taken away my beloved and had sent no solace for my grief. Separately I cursed the signs upon the altar: the stars, the worlds, the suns, the moons, that meted and fulfilled the processes of time. Belthoris, my betrothed, had died at the end of the previous autumn: and so, with double maledictions, I cursed the stars and planets presiding over that season.

I became aware that a shadow had fallen beside my own on the altar, and knew that the dark sage and sorcerer Atmox had obeyed my summons. Fearfully but not without hope I turned toward him, noting first of all that he bore under his arm a heavy, sinister-looking volume with covers of black steel and hasps of adamant. Only when I had made sure of this did I lift my eyes to his face, which was little less somber and forbidding than the tome he carried.

"Greeting, O Calaspa," he said harshly. "I have come against my own will and judgment. The lore that you request is in this volume; and since you saved me in former years from the inquisitorial wrath of the time-god's priests, I cannot refuse to share it with you. But understand well that even I, who have called upon names that are dreadful to utter, and have evoked forbidden presences, shall never dare to assist you in this conjuration. Gladly would I help you to hold converse with the shadow of Belthoris, or to animate her still unwithered body and draw it forth from the tomb. But that which you purpose is another matter. You alone must perform the ordained rites, must speak the necessary words: for the consequences of this thing will be direr than you deem."

"I care not for the consequences," I replied eagerly, "if it be possible to bring back the lost hours which I shared with Belthoris. Think you that I could content myself with her shadow, wandering thinly back from the Borderland? Or that I could take pleasure in the fair clay that the breath of necromancy has troubled and has made to arise and walk without mind or soul? Nay, the Belthoris I would summon is she on whom the shadow of death has never yet fallen!"

It seemed that Atmox, the master of doubtful arts, the vassal of umbrageous powers, recoiled and blenched before my vehement declaration.

"Bethink you," he said with minatory sternness, "that this thing will constitute a breach of the sacred logic of time and a blasphemy against Aforgomon, god of the minutes and the cycles. Moreover, there is little to be gained: for not in its entirety may you bring back the season of your love, but only one single hour, torn with infinite violence from its rightful period in time . . . Refrain, I adjure you, and content yourself with a lesser sorcery."

"Give me the book," I demanded. "My service to Aforgomon is forfeit. With due reverence and devotion I have worshipped the time-god, and have done in his honor the rites ordained from eternity; and for all this the god has betrayed me."

Then, in that high-climbing, luxuriant garden beneath the four suns, Atmox opened the adamantine clasps of the steel-bound volume; and, turning to a certain page, he laid the book reluctantly in my hands. The page, like its fellows, was of some unholy parchment streaked with musty discolorations and blackening at the margin with sheer antiquity; but upon it shone unquenchably the dread characters a primal archimage had written with an ink bright as the new-shod ichor of demons. Above this page I bent in my madness, conning it over and over till I was dazzled by the fiery runes; and, shutting my eyes, I saw them burn on a red darkness, still legible, and writhing like hellish worms.

Hollowly, like the sound of a far bell, I heard the voice of Atmox: "You have learned, O Calaspa, the unutterable name of that One whose assistance can alone restore the fled hours. And you have learned the incantation that will rouse that hidden power, and the sacrifice needed for its propitiation. Knowing these things, is your heart still strong and your purpose firm?"

The name I had read in the wizard volume was that of the chief cosmic power antagonistic to Aforgomon; the incantation and the required offering were those of a foul demonolatry. Nevertheless, I did not hesitate, but gave resolute affirmative answer to the somber query of Atmox.

※

Perceiving that I was inflexible, he bowed his head, trying no more to dissuade me. Then, as the flame-runed volume had bade me do, I defiled the altar of Aforgomon, blotting certain of its prime symbols with dust and spittle. While Atmox looked on in silence, I wounded my right arm to its deepest vein on the sharp-tipped gnomon of the dial; and, letting the blood drip from zone to zone, from orb to orb on the graven agate, I made unlawful sacrifice, and intoned aloud, in the name of the Lurking Chaos, Xexanoth, an abominable ritual composed by a backward repetition and jumbling of litanies sacred to the time-god.

Even as I chanted the incantation, it seemed that webs of shadow were woven foully athwart the suns; and the ground shook a little, as if colossal demons trod the world's rim, striding stupendously from abysses beyond. The garden walls and trees wavered like a wind-blown reflection in a pool; and I grew faint with the loss of that life-blood I had poured out in demonolatrous offering. Then, in my flesh and in my brain, I felt the intolerable racking of a vibration like the long-drawn shock of cities riven by earthquake, and coasts crumbling before some chaotic sea; and my flesh was torn and harrowed, and my brain shuddered with the toneless discords sweeping through me from deep to deep.

I faltered, and confusion gnawed at my inmost being. Dimly I heard the prompting of Atmox, and dimmer still was the sound of my own voice that made answer to Xexanoth, naming the impious necromancy which was to be effected only through its power. Madly I implored from Xexanoth, in despite of time and its ordered seasons, one hour of that bygone autumn which I had shared with Belthoris; and imploring this, I named no special hour: for all, in memory, had seemed of an equal joy and gladness.

As the words ceased upon my lips, I thought that darkness fluttered in the air like a great wing; and the four suns went out, and my heart was stilled as if in death. Then the light returned, falling obliquely from suns mellow with full-tided autumn; and nowhere beside me was there any shadow of Atmox; and the altar of zoned agate was bloodless and undefiled. I, the lover of Belthoris, witting not of the doom and sorrow to come, stood happily with my beloved before the altar, and saw her young hands crown its ancient dial with the flowers we had plucked from the garden.

Dreadful beyond all fathoming are the mysteries of time. Even I, the priest and initiate, though wise in the secret doctrines of Aforgomon, know little enough of that elusive, ineluctable process whereby the present becomes the past and the future resolves itself into the present. All men have pondered the riddles of duration and transience; have wondered, vainly, to what bourn the lost days and the sped cycles are consigned. Some have dreamt that the past abides unchanged, becoming eternity as it slips from our mortal ken; and others have deemed that time is a stairway whose steps crumble one by one behind the climber, falling into a gulf of nothing.

Howsoever this may be, I know that she who stood beside me was the Belthoris on whom no shadow of mortality had yet descended. The hour was one new-born in a golden season; and the minutes to come were pregnant with all wonder and surprise belonging to the untried future.

Taller was my beloved than the frail, unbowed lilies of the garden. In her eyes was the sapphire of moonless evenings sown with small golden stars. Her lips were strangely curved, but only blitheness and joy had gone to their shaping. She and I had been betrothed from our childhood, and the time of the marriage-rites was now approaching. Our intercourse was wholly free, according to the custom of that world. Often she came to walk with me in my garden and to decorate the altar of that god whose revolving moons and suns would soon bring the season of our felicity.

The moths that flew about us, winged with aerial cloth-of-gold, were no lighter than our hearts. Making blithe holiday, we fanned our frolic mood to a high flame of rapture. We were akin to the full-hued, climbing flowers, the swift-darting insects, and our spirits blended and soared with the perfumes that were drawn skyward in the warm air. Unheard by us was the loud murmuring of the mighty city of Kalood lying beyond my garden walls; for us the many-peopled planet known as Hestan no longer existed; and we dwelt alone in a universe of light, in a blossomed heaven. Exalted by love in the high harmony of those moments, we seemed to touch eternity; and even I, the priest of Aforgomon, forgot the blossom-fretting days, the system-devouring cycles.

In the sublime folly of passion, I swore then that death or discord could never mar the perfect communion of our hearts. After we had wreathed the altar, I sought the rarest, the most delectable flowers: frail-curving cups of wine-washed pearl, of moony azure and white with scrolled purple lips; and these I twined, between kisses and laughter, in the black maze of Belthoris's hair; saying that another shrine than that of time should receive its due offering.

Tenderly, with a lover's delay, I lingered over the wreathing; and, ere I had finished, there fluttered to the ground beside us a great, crimson-spotted moth whose wing had somehow been broken in its airy voyaging through the garden. And Belthoris, ever tender of heart and pitiful, turned from me and took up the moth in her hands; and some of the bright blossoms dropped from her hair unheeded. Tears welled from her deep blue eyes; and seeing that the moth was sorely hurt and would never fly again, she refused to be comforted; and no longer would she respond to my passionate wooing. I, who grieved less for the moth than she, was somewhat vexed; and between her sadness and my vexation, there grew between us some tiny, temporary rift . . .

Then, ere love had mended the misunderstanding; then, while we stood before the dread altar of time with sundered hands, with eyes averted from each other, it seemed that a shroud of darkness descended upon the garden. I heard the crash and crumbling of shattered worlds, and a black flowing of ruinous things that went past me through the darkness. The dead leaves of winter were blown about me, and there was a falling of tears or rain . . . Then the vernal suns came back, high-stationed in cruel splendor; and with them came the knowledge of all that had been, of Belthoris's death and my sorrow, and the madness that had led to forbidden sorcery. Vain now, like all other hours, was the resummoned hour; and doubly irredeemable was my loss. My blood dripped heavily on the dishallowed altar, my faintness grew deathly, and I saw through murky mist the face of Atmox beside me; and the face was like that of some comminatory demon.

March 13th, I, John Milwarp, write this date and my name with an odd dubiety. My visionary experience under the drug *souvara* ended with that rilling of my blood on the symboled dial, that glimpse of the terror-distorted face of Atmox. All this was in another world, in a life removed from the present by births and deaths without number; and yet, it seems, not wholly have I returned from the twice-ancient past. Memories, broken but strangely vivid and living, press upon me from the existence of which my vision was a fragment; and portions of the lore of Hestan, and scraps of its history, and words from its lost language, arise unbidden in my mind.

Above all, my heart is still shadowed by the sorrow of Calaspa. His desperate necromancy, which would seem to others no more than a dream within a dream, is stamped as with fire on the black page of recollection. I know the awfulness of the god he had blasphemed, and the foulness of the demonolatry he had done, and the sense of guilt and despair under which he swooned. It is *this* that I have striven all my life to remember, this which I have been doomed to re-experience. And I fear with a great fear the farther knowledge which a second experiment with the drug will reveal to me.

⚶

The next entry of Milwarp's diary begins with a strange dating in English script: "The second day of the moon Occalat, in the thousand-and-ninth year of the Red Eon." This dating, perhaps, is repeated in the language of Hestan: for, directly beneath it, a line of unknown ciphers is set apart. Several lines of the subsequent text are in the alien tongue; and then, as if by an unconscious reversion, Milwarp continues the diary in English. There is no reference to another experiment with *souvara,* but apparently such had been made, with a continued revival of his lost memories.

⚶

. . . What genius of the nadir gulf had tempted me to this thing and had caused me to overlook the consequences? Verily, when I called up for myself and Belthoris an hour of former autumn, with all that was attendant upon the hour, *that bygone interim was likewise evoked and repeated for the whole world Hestan, and the four suns of Hestan.* From the full midst of spring, all men had stepped backward into autumn, keeping only the memory of things prior to the hour thus resurrected, and knowing not the events future to the hour. But, returning to the present, they recalled with amazement the unnatural necromancy; and fear and bewilderment were upon them; and none could interpret the meaning.

For a brief period, the dead had lived again; the fallen leaves had returned to the bough; the heavenly bodies had stood at a long-abandoned station; the flower had gone back into the seed, the plant into the root. Then, with eternal disorder set among all its cycles, time had resumed its delayed course.

No movement of any cosmic body, no year or instant of the future, would be precisely as it should have been. The error and discrepancy I had wrought would bear fruit in ways innumerable. The suns would find themselves at fault; the worlds and atoms would go always a little astray from their appointed bourn.

It was of these matters that Atmox spoke, warning me, after he had stanched my bleeding wound. For he too, in that relumined hour, had gone back and had lived again through a past happening. For him the hour was one in which he had descended into the nether vaults of his house. There, standing in a many-pentacled circle, with burning of unholy incense and uttering of accurst formulae, he had called upon a malign spirit from the bowels of Hestan and had questioned it concerning the future. But the spirit, black and voluminous as the fumes of pitch, refused to answer him directly and pressed furiously with its clawed members against the confines of the circle. It said only: "Thou hast summoned me at thy peril. Potent are the spells thou hast used, and strong is the circle to withstand me, and I am restrained by time and space from the wreaking of my anger upon thee. *But haply thou shalt summon me again, albeit in the same hour of the same autumn;* and in that summoning the laws of time shall be broken, and a rift shall be made in space; and through the rift, though with some delay and divagation, I will yet win to thee."

Saying no more, it prowled restlessly about the circle; and its eyes burned down upon Atmox like embers in a high-lifted sooty brazier; and ever and anon its fanged mouth was flattened on the spell-defended air. And in the end he could dismiss it only after a double repetition of the form of exorcism.

As he told me this tale in the garden, Atmox trembled; and his eyes searched the narrow shadows wrought by the high suns; and he seemed to listen for the noise of some evil thing that burrowed toward him beneath the earth.

Fourth day of the moon Occalat. Stricken with terrors beyond those of Atmox, I kept apart in my mansion amid the city of Kalood. I was still weak with the loss of blood I had yielded to Xexanoth; my senses were full of strange shadows; my servitors, coming and going after me, were as phantoms; and scarcely I heeded the pale fear in their eyes or heard the dreadful things they whispered. . . . Madness and chaos, they told me, were abroad in Kalood; the divinity of Aforgomon was angered. All men thought that some baleful doom impended because of that unnatural confusion which had been wrought among the hours of time.

This afternoon they brought me the story of Atmox's death. In bated tones they told me how his neophytes had heard a roaring as of a loosed tempest in the chamber where he sat alone with his wizard volumes and paraphernalia. Above the roaring, for a little, human screams had sounded, together with a clashing as of hurled censers and braziers, a crashing as of overthrown tables and tomes. Blood rilled from under the shut door of the chamber, and, rilling, it took from instant to instant the form of dire ciphers that spelt an unspeakable name. After the noises had ceased, the neophytes waited a long while ere they dared to open the door. Entering at last, they saw the floor and the walls heavily bespattered with blood, and rags of the sorcerer's raiment mingled everywhere with the sheets of his torn volumes of magic, and the shreds and manglings of his flesh strewn amid broken furniture, and his brains daubed in a horrible paste on the high ceiling.

Hearing this tale, I knew that the earthly demon feared by Atmox had found him somehow and had wreaked its wrath upon him. In ways unguessáble, it had reached him through the chasm made in ordered time and space by one hour repeated through necromancy. And because of that lawless chasm, the magician's power and lore had utterly failed to defend him from the demon . . .

⁂

Fifth day of the moon Occalat. Atmox, I am sure, had not betrayed me: for in so doing, he must have betrayed his own implicit share in my crime . . . Howbeit, this evening the priests came to my house ere the setting of the westernmost sun: silent, grim, with eyes averted as if from a foulness innominable. Me, their fellow, they enjoined with loth gestures to accompany them . . .

Thus they took me from my house and along the thoroughfares of Kalood toward the lowering suns. The streets were empty of all other passers, and it seemed that no man desired to meet or behold the blasphemer . . .

Down the avenue of gnomon-shaped pillars, I was led to the portals of Aforgomon's fane: those awfully gaping portals arched in the likeness of some devouring chimera's mouth . . .

⁂

SIXTH day of the moon Occalat. They had thrust me into an oubliette beneath the temple, dark, noisome, and soundless except for the maddening, measured drip of water beside me. There I lay and knew not when the night passed and the morning came. Light was admitted only when my captors opened the iron door, coming to lead me before the tribunal . . .

. . . Thus the priests condemned me, speaking with one voice in whose dreadful volume the tones of all were indistinguishably blended. Then the aged high-priest Helpenor called aloud upon Afor-gomon, offering himself as a mouthpiece to the god, and asking the god to pronounce through him the doom that was adequate for such enormities as those of which I had been judged guilty by my fellows.

Instantly, it seemed, the god descended into Helpenor; and the figure of the high priest appeared to dilate prodigiously beneath his mufflings; and the accents that issued from his mouth were like thunders of the upper heaven:

"O Calaspa, thou hast set disorder amid all future hours and eons through this evil necromancy. Thereby, moreover, thou hast wrought thine own doom: fettered art thou for ever to the hour thus unlawfully repeated, apart from its due place in time. According to hieratic rule, thou shalt meet the death of the fiery chains: but deem not that this death is more than the symbol of thy true punishment. Thou shalt pass hereafter through other lives in Hestan, and shalt climb midway in the cycles of the world subsequent to Hestan in time and space. But through all thine incarnations the chaos thou hast invoked will attend thee, widening ever like a rift. And always, in all thy lives, the rift will bar thee from reunion with the soul of Belthoris; and always, though merely by an hour, thou shalt miss the love that should otherwise have been oftentimes regained.

"At last, when the chasm has widened overmuch, thy soul shall fare no farther in the onward cycles of incarnation. At that time it shall be given thee to remember clearly thine ancient sin; and remembering, thou shalt perish out of time. Upon the body of that latter life shall be found the charred imprint of the chains, as the final token of thy bondage. But they that knew thee will soon forget, and thou shalt belong wholly to the cycles limited for thee by thy sin."

❧

March 29th. I write this date with infinite desperation, trying to convince myself that there is a John Milwarp who exists on Earth, in the Twentieth Century. For two days running, I have not taken the drug *souvara:* and yet I have returned twice to that oubliette of

Aforgomon's temple, in which the priest Calaspa awaits his doom. Twice I have been immersed in its stagnant darkness, hearing the slow drip of water beside me, like a clepsydra that tells the black ages of the damned.

Even as I write this at my library table, it seems that an ancient midnight plucks at the lamp. The bookcases turn to walls of oozing, nighted stone. There is no longer a table . . . nor one who writes . . . and I breathe the noisome dankness of a dungeon lying unfathomed by any sun, in a lost world.

Eighteenth day of the moon Occalat. Today, for the last time, they took me from my prison. Helpenor, together with three others, came and led me to the adytum of the god. Far beneath the outer temple we went, through spacious crypts unknown to the common worshipers. There was no word spoken, no glance exchanged between the others and me; and it seemed that they already regarded me as one cast out from time and claimed by oblivion.

We came ultimately to that sheer-falling gulf in which the spirit of Aforgomon is said to dwell. Lights, feeble and far-scattered, shone around it like stars on the rim of cosmic vastness, shedding no ray into the depths. There, in a seat of hewn stone overhanging the frightful verge, I was placed by the executioners; and a ponderous chain of black unrusted metal, stapled in the solid rock, was wound about and about me, circling my naked body and separate limbs, from head to foot.

To this doom, others had been condemned for heresy or impiety . . . though never for a sin such as mine. After the chaining of the victim, he was left for a stated interim, to ponder his crime—and haply to confront the dark divinity of Aforgomon. At length, from the abyss into which his position forced him to peer, a light would dawn, and a bolt of strange flame would leap upward, striking the many-coiled chain about him and heating it instantly to the whiteness of candescent iron. The source and nature of the flame were mysterious, and many ascribed it to the god himself rather than to mortal agency . . .

Even thus they have left me, and have gone away. Long since the burden of the massy links, cutting deeper and deeper into my flesh, has become an agony. I am dizzy from gazing downward into the abyss—and yet I cannot fall. Beneath, immeasurably beneath, at recurrent intervals, I hear a hollow and solemn sound. Perhaps it is the sigh of sunken waters . . . of cavern-straying winds . . . or the respiration of One that abides in the darkness, meting with his breath the slow minutes, the hours, the days, the ages . . . My terror has become heavier than the chain, my vertigo is born of a two-fold gulf . . .

Eons have passed by and all the worlds have ebbed into nothingness, like wreckage borne on a chasm-falling stream, taking with them the lost face of Belthoris. I am poised above the gaping maw of the Shadow . . . Somehow, in another world, an exile phantom has written these words . . . a phantom who must fade utterly from time and place, even as I, the doomed priest Calaspa. I cannot remember the name of the phantom.

Beneath me, in the black depths, there is an awful brightening . . .

THE DARK EIDOLON

Thasaidon, lord of seven hells
Wherein the single Serpent dwells,
With volumes drawn from pit to pit
Through fire and darkness infinite—
Thasaidon, sun of nether skies,
Thine ancient evil never dies,
For aye thy somber fulgors flame
On sunken worlds that have no name,
Man's heart enthrones thee, still supreme,
Though the false sorcerers blaspheme.
—The Song of Xeethra

On Zothique, the last continent of Earth, the sun no longer shone with the whiteness of its prime, but was dim and tarnished as if with a vapor of blood. New stars without number had declared themselves in the heavens, and the shadows of the infinite had fallen closer. And out of the shadows, the older gods had returned to man: the gods forgotten since Hyperborea, since Mu and Poseidonis, bearing other names but the same attributes. And the elder demons had also returned, battening on the fumes of evil sacrifice, and fostering again the primordial sorceries.

Many were the necromancers and magicians of Zothique, and the infamy and marvel of their doings were legended everywhere in the latter days. But among them all there was none greater than

Namirrha, who imposed his black yoke on the cities of Xylac, and later, in a proud delirium, deemed himself the veritable peer of Thasaidon, lord of Evil.

Namirrha had built his abode in Ummaos, the chief town of Xylac, to which he came from the desert realm of Tasuun with the dark renown of his thaumaturgies like a cloud of desert storm behind him. And no man knew that in coming to Ummaos he returned to the city of his birth; for all deemed him a native of Tasuun. Indeed, none could have dreamt that the great sorcerer was one with the beggar-boy, Narthos, an orphan of questionable parentage, who had begged his daily bread in the streets and bazaars of Ummaos. Wretchedly had he lived, alone and despised; and a hatred of the cruel, opulent city grew in his heart like a smothered flame that feeds in secret, biding the time when it shall become a conflagration consuming all things.

Bitterer always, through his boyhood and early youth, was the spleen and rancor of Narthos toward men. And one day the prince Zotulla, a boy but little older than he, riding a restive palfrey, came upon him in the square before the imperial palace; and Narthos implored an alms. But Zotulla, scorning his plea, rode arrogantly forward, spurring the palfrey; and Narthos was ridden down and trampled under its hooves. And afterward, nigh to death from the trampling, he lay senseless for many hours, while the people passed him by unheeding. And at last, regaining his senses, he dragged himself to his hovel; but he limped a little thereafter all his days, and the mark of one hoof remained like a brand on his body, fading never. Later, he left Ummaos and was forgotten quickly by its people. Going southward into Tasuun, he lost his way in the great desert, and was near to perishing. But finally he came to a small oasis, where dwelt the wizard Ouphaloc, a hermit who preferred the company of honest jackals and hyenas to that of men. And Ouphaloc, seeing the great craft and evil in the starveling boy, gave succor to Narthos and sheltered him. He dwelt for years with Ouphaloc, becoming the wizard's pupil and the heir of his demon-wrested lore. Strange things he learned in that hermitage, being fed on fruits and grain that had sprung not from the watered earth, and wine that was not the juice of terrene grapes. And like Ouphaloc, he became a master in devildom and drove his own bond with the archfiend Thasaidon. When Ouphaloc died, the boy Narthos took the name of Namirrha, and went forth as a mighty sorcerer among the wandering peoples and the deep-buried mummies of Tasuun. But never could he forget the miseries of his boyhood in Ummaos and the wrong he had endured from Zotulla; and year by year he spun over in his thoughts the black web of revenge. And his fame grew ever darker and vaster, and men feared him in remote lands beyond Tasuun. With bated whispers they spoke of his deeds in the cities of Yoros, and in Zul-Bha-Sair, the abode of the ghoulish deity Mordiggian. And long before the coming of Namirrha himself, the people of Ummaos knew him as a fabled scourge that was direr than simoom or pestilence.

Now, in the years that followed the going-forth of the boy Narthos from Ummaos, Pithaim, the father of Prince Zotulla, was slain by the sting of a small adder that had crept into his bed for warmth on an autumn night. Some said that the adder had been purveyed by Zotulla, but this was a thing that no man could verily affirm. After the death of Pithaim, Zotulla, being his only son, was emperor of Xylac, and ruled evilly from his throne in Ummaos. Indolent he was, and tyrannic, and full of strange luxuries and cruelties; but the people, who were also evil, acclaimed him in his turpitude. So he prospered, and the lords of Hell and Heaven smote him not. And the red suns and ashen moons went westward over Xylac, falling into that seldom-voyaged sea, which, if the mariners' tales were true, poured evermore like a swiftening river past the infamous isle of Naat, and fell in a worldwide cataract upon nether space from the far, sheer edge of Earth.

Grosser still he grew, and his sins were as overswollen fruits that ripen above a deep abyss. But the winds of time blew softly; and the fruits fell not. And Zotulla laughed amid his fools and his eunuchs and his lemans; and the tale of his luxuries was borne afar, and was told by dim outland peoples, as a twin marvel with the bruited necromancies of Namirrha.

It came to pass, in the year of the Hyena and the month of the star Canicule, that a great feast was given by Zotulla to the inhabitants of Ummaos. Meats that had been cooked in exotic spices from Sotar, isle of the east, were spread everywhere; and the ardent wines of Yoros and Xylac, filled as with subterranean fires, were poured inexhaustibly from huge urns for all. The wines awoke a furious mirth and a royal madness; and afterward they brought a slumber no less profound than the Lethe of the tomb. And one by one, as they drank, the revelers fell down in the streets, the houses and gardens, as if a plague had struck them; and Zotulla slept in his banquet-hall of gold and ebony, with his odalisques and chamberlains about him. So, in all Ummaos, there was no man or woman wakeful at the hour when Sirius began to fall toward the west.

Thus it was that none saw or heard the coming of Namirrha. But awakening heavily in the latter forenoon, the emperor Zotulla heard a confused babble, a troublous clamor of voices from such of his eunuchs and women as had awakened before him. Inquiring the cause, he was told that a strange prodigy had occurred during the night; but, being still bemused with wine and slumber, he comprehended little enough of its nature, till his favorite concubine, Obexah, led him to the eastern portico of the palace, from which he could behold the marvel with his own eyes.

Now the palace stood alone at the center of Ummaos, and to north, west, and south, for wide intervals of distance, there stretched the imperial gardens, full of superbly arching palms and loftily spiring fountains. But to eastward was a broad open area, used as a sort of common, between the palace and the mansions of high optimates. And in this space, which had lain wholly vacant at eve, a building towered colossal and lordly beneath the full-risen sun, with domes like monstrous fungi of stone that had come up in the night. And the domes, rearing level with those of Zotulla, were builded of death-white marble; and the huge façade, with multi-columned porticoes and deep balconies, was wrought in alternate zones of night-black onyx and porphyry hued as with dragons'-blood. And Zotulla swore lewdly, calling with hoarse blasphemies on the gods and devils of Xylac; and great was his dumbfoundment, deeming the marvel a work of wizardry. The women gathered about him, crying out with shrill cries of awe and terror; and more and more of his courtiers, awakening, came to swell the hubbub; and the fat castradoes diddered in their cloth-of-gold like immense black jellies in golden basins. But Zotulla, mindful of his dominion as emperor of all Xylac, sought to conceal his own trepidation, saying:

"Now who is this that has presumed to enter Ummaos like a jackal in the dark, and has made his impious den in proximity and coun-terview with my palace? Go forth, and inquire the miscreant's name; but, ere you go, instruct the imperial headsman to make sharp his double-handed sword."

Then, fearing the emperor's wrath if they tarried, certain of the chamberlains went forth unwillingly and approached the portals of the strange edifice. It seemed that the portals were deserted till they drew near, and then, on the threshold, there appeared a titanic skeleton, taller than any man of earth; and it strode forward to meet them with ell-long strides. The skeleton was swathed in a loin-cloth of scarlet silk with a buckle of jet, and it wore a black turban, starred with diamonds, whose topmost foldings nearly touched the lofty lintel. Eyes like flickering marsh-fires burned in its deep eye-sockets; and a blackened tongue like that of a long-dead man protruded between its teeth; but otherwise it was clean of flesh, and the bones glittered whitely in the sun as it came onward.

The chamberlains were mute before it, and there was no sound except the golden creaking of their girdles, the shrill rustling of their silks, as they shook and trembled. And the foot-bones of the skeleton clicked sharply on the pavement of black onyx as it paused; and the putrefying tongue began to quiver between its teeth; and it uttered these words in an unctuous, nauseous voice:

"Return, and tell the emperor Zotulla that Namirrha, seer and magician, has come to dwell beside him."

Hearing the skeleton speak as if it had been a living man, and hearing the dread name of Namirrha as men hear the tocsin of doom in some fallen city, the chamberlains could stand before it no longer, and they fled with ungainly swiftness and bore the message to Zotulla.

Now, learning who it was that had come to neighbor with him in Ummaos, the emperor's wrath died out like a feeble and blustering flame on which the wind of darkness has blown; and the vinous purple of his cheeks was mottled with a strange pallor; and he said nothing, but his lips mumbled loosely as if in prayer or malediction. And the news of Namirrha's coming passed like the flight of evil night-birds through all the palace: and throughout the city, leaving a noisome terror that abode in Ummaos thereafter till the end. For Namirrha, through the black renown of his thaumaturgies and the frightful entities who served him, had become a power that no secular sovereign dared dispute; and men feared him everywhere, even as they feared the gigantic, shadowy lords of Hell and of outer space. And in Ummaos, people said that he had come on the desert wind from Tasuun with his underlings, even as the pestilence comes, and had reared his house in an hour with the aid of devils beside Zotulla's palace. And they said that the foundations of the house were laid on the adamantine cope of Hell; and in its floors were pits at whose bottom burned the nether fires, or stars could be seen as they passed under in lowermost night. And the followers of Namirrha were the dead of strange kingdoms, the demons of sky and earth and the abyss, and mad, impious, hybrid things that the sorcerer himself had created from forbidden unions.

Men shunned the neighborhood of his lordly house; and in the palace of Zotulla few cared to approach the windows and balconies that gave thereon; and the emperor himself spoke not of Namirrha, pretending to ignore the intruder; and the women of the harem babbled evermore with an evil gossip concerning Namirrha and his concubines. But the sorcerer himself was not beheld by the people of the city, though some believed that he walked forth at will, clad with invisibility. His servitors likewise were not seen; but a howling as of the damned was sometimes heard to issue from his portals; and sometimes there came a stony cachinnation, as if some adamantine image had laughed aloud; and sometimes there was a chuckling like the sound of shattered ice in a frozen hell. Dim shadows moved in the porticoes when there was neither sunlight nor lamp to cast them; and red, eerie lights appeared and vanished in the windows at eve, like a blinking of demoniac eyes. And slowly the ember-colored suns went over Xylac, and were quenched in far seas; and the ashy moons were blackened as they fell nightly toward the hidden gulf. Then, seeing that the wizard had wrought no open evil, and that none had endured palpable harm from his presence, the people took heart; and Zotulla drank deeply, and feasted in oblivious luxury as before; and dark Thasaidon, prince of all turpitudes, was the true but never-acknowledged lord of Xylac. And in time the men of Ummaos bragged a little of Namirrha and his dread thaumaturgies, even as they had boasted of the purple sins of Zotulla.

But Namirrha, still unbeheld by living men and living women, sat in the inner halls of that house which his devils had reared for him, and spun over and over in his thoughts the black web of revenge. And in all Ummaos there was none, even among his fellow-beggars, who recalled the beggar-boy Narthos. And the wrong done by Zotulla to Narthos in old time was the least of those cruelties which the emperor had forgotten.

Now, when the fears of Zotulla were somewhat lulled, and his women gossiped less often of the neighboring wizard, there occurred a new wonder and a fresh terror. For, sitting one eve at his banquet-table with his courtiers about him, the emperor heard a noise as of myriad iron-shod hooves that came trampling through the palace-gardens. And the courtiers also heard the sound, and were startled amid their mounting drunkenness; and the emperor was angered, and he sent certain of his guards to examine into the cause of the trampling. But peering forth upon the moon-bright lawns and parterres, the guards beheld no visible shape, though the loud sounds of trampling still went to and fro. It seemed as if a rout of wild stallions passed and re-passed before the façade of the palace with tumultuous gallopings and capricoles. And a fear came upon the guards as they looked and listened, and they dared not venture forth, but returned to Zotulla. And the emperor himself grew sober when he heard their tale; and he went forth with high blusterings to view the prodigy. And all night the unseen hooves rang out sonorously on the pavements of onyx, and ran with deep thuddings over the grasses and flowers. The palm-fronds waved on the windless air as if parted by racing steeds; and visibly the tall-stemmed lilies and broad-petaled exotic blossoms were trodden under. And rage and terror nested together in Zotulla's heart as he stood in a balcony above the garden, hearing the spectral tumult, and beholding the harm done to his rarest flowerbeds. The women, the courtiers, and the eunuchs cowered behind him, and there was no slumber for any occupant of the palace; but toward dawn the clamor of hooves departed, going toward Namirrha's house.

When the dawn was full-grown above Ummaos, the emperor walked forth with his guards about him, and saw that the crushed grasses and broken-down stems were blackened as if by fire where the hooves had fallen. Plainly were the marks imprinted, like the tracks of a great company of horses, in all the lawns and parterres; but they ceased at the verge of the gardens. And though every one believed that the visitation had come from Namirrha, there was no proof of this in the grounds that fronted the sorcerer's abode; for here the turf was untrodden.

"A pox upon Namirrha, if he has done this!" cried Zotulla. "For what harm have I ever done to him? Verily, I shall set my heel on the dog's neck; and the torture-wheel shall serve him even as these horses from Hell have served my blood-red lilies of Sotar and my vein-colored irises of Naat and my orchids from Uccastrog which were purple as the bruises of love. Yea, though he stand the viceroy of Thasaidon above Earth, and overlord of ten thousand devils, my wheel shall break him and fire shall heat the wheel white-hot in its turning, till he withers black as the seared blossoms." Thus did Zotulla make his brag; but he issued no orders for the execution of the threat; and no man stirred from the palace toward Namirrha's house. And from the portals of the wizard none came forth; or if any came, there was no visible sign or sound.

So the day went over, and the night rose, bringing later a moon that was slightly darkened at the rim. And the night was silent; and Zotulla, sitting long at the banquet-table, drained his wine-cup often and wrathfully, muttering new threats against Namirrha. And the night wore on, and it seemed that the visitation would not be repeated. But at midnight, lying in his chamber with Obexah, and fathom-deep in slumber from his wine, Zotulla was awakened by a monstrous clangor of hooves that raced and capered in the palace porticoes and in the long balconies. All night the hooves thundered back and forth, echoing awfully in the vaulted stone, while Zotulla and Obexah, listening, huddled close amid their cushions and coverlets; and all the occupants of the palace, wakeful and fearful, heard the noise but stirred not from their chambers. A little before dawn the hooves departed suddenly; and afterward, by day, their marks were found on the marble flags of the porches and balconies; and the marks were countless, deep-graven, and black as if branded there by flame.

Like mottled marble were the emperor's cheeks when he saw the hoof-printed floors; and terror stayed with him hence forward, following him to the depths of his inebriety, since he knew not where the haunting would cease. His women murmured and some wished to flee from Ummaos, and it seemed that the revels of the day and the evening were shadowed by ill wings that left their umbrage in the yellow wine and bedimmed the aureate lamps. And again, toward midnight, the slumber of Zotulla was broken by the hooves, which came galloping and pacing on the palace-roof and through all the corridors and halls. Thereafter, till dawn, the hooves filled the palace with their iron clatterings, and they rang hollowly on the topmost domes, as if the coursers of gods had trodden there, passing from heaven to heaven in tumultuous cavalcade.

Zotulla and Obexah, lying together while the terrible hooves went to and fro in the hall outside their chamber, had no heart or thought for sin, nor could they find any comfort in their nearness. In the gray hour before dawn they heard a great thundering high on the barred brazen door of the room, as if some mighty stallion, rearing, had drummed there with his forefeet. And soon after this, the hooves went away, leaving a silence like an interlude in some gathering storm of doom. Later, the marks of the hooves were found everywhere in the halls, marring the bright mosaics. Black holes were burnt in the golden-threaded rugs and the rugs of silver and scarlet; and the high white domes were pitted pox-wise with the marks; and far up on the brazen door of Zotulla's chamber the prints of a horse's forefeet were incised deeply.

Now, in Ummaos, and throughout Xylac, the tale of this haunting became known, and the thing was deemed an ominous prodigy, though people differed in their interpretations. Some held that the sending came from Namirrha, and was meant as a token of his supremacy above all kings and emperors; and some thought that it came from a new wizard who had risen in Tinarath, far to the east, and who wished to supplant Namirrha. And the priests of the gods of Xylac held that their various deities had dispatched the haunting, as a sign that more sacrifices were required in the temples.

Then, in his hall of audience, whose floor of sard and jasper had been grievously pocked by the unseen hooves, Zotulla called together many priests and magicians and soothsayers, and asked them to declare the cause of the sending and to devise a mode of exorcism. But, seeing that there was no agreement among them, Zotulla provided the several priestly sects with the wherewithal of sacrifice to their sundry gods, and sent them away; and the wizards and prophets, under threat of decapitation if they refused, were enjoined to visit Namirrha in his mansion of sorcery and learn his will, if haply the sending were his and not the work of another.

Loth were the wizards and the soothsayers, fearing Namirrha, and caring not to intrude upon the frightful mysteries of his obscure mansion. But the swordsmen of the emperor drave them forth, lifting great crescent blades against them when they tarried; so one by one, in a straggling order, the delegation went toward Namirrha's portals and vanished into the devil-built house.

Pale, muttering, and distraught, like men who have looked upon Hell and have seen their doom, they returned before sunset to the emperor. And they said that Namirrha had received them courteously and had sent them back with this message:

"Be it known to Zotulla that the haunting is a sign of that which he has long forgotten; and the reason of the haunting will be revealed to him at the hour prepared and set apart by destiny. And the hour draws near: for Namirrha bids the emperor and all his court to a great feast on the afternoon of the morrow."

Having delivered this message, to the wonder and consternation of Zotulla, the delegation begged his leave to depart. And though the emperor questioned them minutely, they seemed unwilling to relate the circumstances of their visit to Namirrha; nor would they describe the sorcerer's fabled house, except in a vague manner, each contradicting the other as to what he had seen. So, after a little, Zotulla bade them go, and when they had gone he sat musing for a long while on the invitation of Namirrha, which was a thing that he cared not to accept but feared to decline. That evening he drank even more liberally than was his wont; and he slept a Lethean slumber, nor was there any noise of trampling hooves about the palace to awaken him. And silently, during the night, the prophets and the magicians passed like furtive shadows from Ummaos; and no man saw them depart; and at morning they were gone from Xylac into other lands, never to return . . .

Now, on that same evening, in the great hall of his house, Namirrha sat alone, having dismissed the mummies, the monsters, the skeletons, and the familiars who attended him ordinarily. Before him, on an altar of jet, was the dark, gigantic statue of Thasaidon which a devil-begotten sculptor had wrought in ancient days for an evil king of Tasuun, called Pharnoc. The archdemon was depicted in the guise of a full-armored warrior, lifting a spiky mace as if in heroic battle. Long had the statue lain in the desert-sunken palace of Pharnoc, whose very site was disputed by the nomads; and Namirrha, by his divination, had found it and had reared up the infernal image to abide with him always thereafter. And often, through the mouth of the statue, Thasaidon would utter oracles to Namirrha, or would answer interrogations.

Before the black-armored image there hung seven silver lamps, wrought in the form of horses' skulls, with flames issuing changeably in blue and purple and crimson from their eye-sockets. Wild and lurid was their light, and the face of the demon, peering from under his crested helmet, was filled with malign, equivocal shadows that shifted and changed eternally. And sitting in his serpent-carven chair, Namirrha regarded the statue grimly, with a deep-furrowed frown between his eyes: for he had asked a certain thing of Thasaidon, and the fiend, replying through the statue, had refused him. And rebellion was in the heart of Namirrha, grown mad with pride, and deeming himself the lord of all sorcerers and a ruler by his own right among the princes of devildom. So, after long pondering, he repeated his request in a bold and haughty voice, like one who addresses an equal rather than the all-formidable suzerain to whom he has sworn a fatal fealty.

"I have helped you heretofore in all things," said the image, with stony and sonorous accents that were echoed metallically in the seven silver lamps. "Yea, the undying worms of fire and darkness have come forth like an army at your summons, and the wings of nether genii have risen to occlude the sun when you called them. But, verily, I will not aid you in this vengeance you have planned; for the emperor Zotulla has done me no wrong and has served me well though unwittingly; and the people of Xylac, by reason of their turpitudes, are not the least of my terrestrial worshipers. Therefore, Namirrha, it were well for you to live in peace with Zotulla, and well to forget this olden wrong that was done to the beggar-boy Narthos. For the ways of destiny are strange, and the workings of its laws are sometimes hidden; and truly, if the hooves of Zotulla's palfrey had not spurned you and trodden you under, your life had been otherwise, and the name and renown of Namirrha had still slept in oblivion as a dream undreamed. Yea, you would tarry still as a beggar in Ummaos, content with a beggar's guerdon, and would never have fared forth to become the pupil of the wise and learned Ouphaloc; and I, Thasaidon, would have lost the lordliest of all necromancers who have accepted my service and my bond. Think well, Namirrha, and ponder these matters: for both of us, it would seem, are indebted to Zotulla in all gratitude for the trampling that he gave you."

"Yea, there is a debt," Namirrha growled implacably. "And truly, I will pay the debt tomorrow, even as I have planned . . . There are Those who will aid me, Those who will answer my summoning in your despite."

"It is an ill thing to affront me," said the image, after an interval. "And also, it is not well to call upon Those that you designate. However, I perceive clearly that such is your intent. You are proud and stubborn and revengeful. Do, then, as you will, but blame me not for the outcome."

So, after this, there was silence in the hall where Namirrha sat before the eidolon; and the flames burned darkly, with changeable colors, in the skull-shapen lamps; and the shadows fled and returned, unresting, on the face of the statue and the face of Namirrha. Then, toward midnight, the necromancer rose and went upward by many spiral stairs to a high dome of his house in which was a single small round window that looked forth on the constellations. The window was set in the top of the dome; but Namirrha had contrived, by means of his magic, that one entering by the last spiral of the stairs would suddenly seem to descend rather than climb, and, reaching the final step, would peer *downward* through the window while stars passed under him in a giddying gulf. There, kneeling, Namirrha touched a secret spring in the marble, and the circular pane slid back without sound. Then, lying prone on the curved interior of the dome, with his face over the abyss, and his long beard trailing stiffly into space, he whispered a pre-human rune, and held speech with certain entities who belonged neither to Hell nor the mundane elements, and were more fearsome to invoke than the infernal genii or the devils of earth, air, water and flame. With them he made his compact, defying Thasaidon's will, while the air curled about him with their voices, and rime gathered palely on his sable beard from the cold that was wrought by their breathing as they leaned earthward.

Laggard and loth was the awakening of Zotulla from his wine; and quickly, ere he opened his eyes, the daylight was poisoned for him by the thought of that invitation which he feared to accept or decline. But he spoke to Obexah, saying:

"Who, after all, is this wizardly dog, that I should obey his summons like a beggar called in from the street by some haughty lord?"

Obexah, a golden-skinned and oblique-eyed girl from Uccastrog, Isle of the Torturers, eyed the emperor subtly, and said:

"O Zotulla, it is yours to accept or refuse, as you deem fitting. And truly, it is a small matter for the lord of Ummaos and all Xylac, whether to go or stay, since naught can impugn your sovereignty. Therefore, were it not as well to go?" For Obexah, though fearful of the wizard, was curious regarding that devil-built house of which so little was known; and likewise, in the manner of women, she wished to behold the famed Namirrha, whose mien and appearance were still but a far-brought legend in Ummaos.

"There is something in what you say," admitted Zotulla. "But an emperor, in his conduct, must always consider the public good; and there are matters of state involved, which a woman can scarcely be expected to understand."

So, later in the forenoon, after an ample and well-irrigated breakfast, he called his chamberlains and courtiers about him and took counsel with them. And some advised him to ignore the invitation of Namirrha; and others held that the invitation should be accepted, lest a graver evil than the trampling of ghostly hooves should be sent upon the palace and the city.

Then Zotulla called the many priesthoods before him in a body, and sought to resummon those wizards and soothsayers who had fled privily in the night. Among all the latter, there was none who answered the crying of his name through Ummaos; and this aroused a certain wonder. But the priests came in greater number than before, and thronged the hall of audience so that the paunches of the foremost were straitened against the imperial dais and the buttocks of the hindmost were flattened on the rear walls and pillars. And Zotulla debated with them the matter of acceptance or refusal. And the priests argued, as before, that Namirrha was nowise concerned with the sending; and his invitation, they said, portended no harm nor bale to the emperor; and it was plain, from the terms of the message, that an oracle would be imparted to Zotulla by the wizard; and this oracle, if Namirrha were a true archimage, would confirm their own holy wisdom and re-establish the divine source of the sending; and the gods of Xylac would again be glorified.

Then, having heard the pronouncement of the priests, the emperor instructed his treasurers to load them down with new offerings; and, calling unctuously upon Zotulla and all his household the vicarious blessings of their several gods, the priests departed. And the day wore on, and the sun passed its meridian, falling slowly beyond Ummaos through the spaces of afternoon that were floored with sea-ending deserts. And still Zotulla was irresolute; and he called his wine-bearers, bidding them pour for him the strongest and most magistral of their vintages; but in the wine he found neither certitude nor decision.

Sitting still on his throne in the hall of audience, he heard, toward middle afternoon, a mighty and clamorous outcry that arose at the palace-portals. There were deep wailings of men and the shrillings of eunuchs and women, as if terror passed from tongue to tongue, invading the halls and apartments. And the fearful clamor spread throughout all the palace, and Zotulla, rousing from the lethargy of wine, was about to send his attendants to inquire the cause.

Then, into the hall, there filed an array of tall mummies, clad in royal cerements of purple and scarlet, and wearing gold crowns on their withered craniums. And after them, like servitors, came gigantic skeletons who wore loin-cloths of nacarat orange and about whose upper skulls from brow to crown, live serpents of banded saffron and ebon had wrapped themselves for head-dresses. And the mummies bowed before Zotulla, saying with thin, sere voices:

"We, who were kings of the wide realm of Tasuun aforetime, have been sent as a guard of honor for the emperor Zotulla, to attend him as is befitting when he goes forth to the feast prepared by Namirrha."

Then, with dry clickings of their teeth, and whistlings as of air through screens of fretted ivory, the skeletons spoke:

"We, who were giant warriors of a race forgotten, have also been sent by Namirrha, so that the emperor's household, following him to the feast, should be guarded from all peril and should fare forth in such pageantry as is meet and proper."

Witnessing these prodigies, the wine-bearers and other attendants cowered about the imperial dais or hid behind the pillars, while Zotulla, with pupils swimming starkly in a bloodshot white, with face bloated and ghastly pale, sat frozen on his throne and could utter no word in reply to the ministers of Namirrha.

Then, coming forward, the mummies said in dusty accents: "All is made ready, and the feast awaits the arrival of Zotulla." And the cerements of the mummies stirred and fell open at the bosom, and small rodent monsters, brown as bitumen, eyed as with accursed rubies, reared forth from the eaten hearts of the mummies like rats from their holes and chittered shrilly in human speech, repeating the words. The skeletons in turn took up the solemn sentence; and the black and saffron serpents hissed it from their skulls; and the words were repeated lastly in baleful rumblings by certain furry creatures of dubious form, hitherto unseen by Zotulla, who sat behind the ribs of the skeletons as if in cages of white wicker.

Like a dreamer who obeys the doom of dreams, the emperor rose from his throne and went forward, and the mummies surrounded him like an escort. And each of the skeletons drew from the reddish-yellow folds of his loin-cloth a curiously pierced archaic flute of silver; and all began a sweet and evil and deathly fluting as the emperor went out through the halls of the palace. A fatal spell was in the music: for the chamberlains, the women, the guards, the eunuchs, and all members of Zotulla's household even to the cooks and scullions, were drawn like a procession of night-walkers from the rooms and alcoves in which they had vainly hidden themselves; and, marshaled by the flutists, they followed after Zotulla. A strange thing it was to behold this mighty company of people, going forth in the slanted sunlight toward Namirrha's house, with a cortège of dead kings about them, and the blown breath of skeletons thrilling eldritchly in the silver flutes. And little was Zotulla comforted when he found the girl Obexah at his side, moving, as he, in a thralldom of involitient horror, with the rest of his women close behind.

Coming to the open portals of Namirrha's house, the emperor saw that they were guarded by great crimson-wattled things, half dragon, half man, who bowed before him, sweeping their wattles like bloody besoms on the flags of dark onyx. And the emperor passed with Obexah between the louting monsters, with the mummies, the skeletons and his own people behind him in strange pageant, and entered a vast and multi-columned hall, where the daylight, following timidly, was drowned by the baleful arrogant blaze of a thousand lamps.

Even amid his horror, Zotulla marveled at the vastness of the chamber, which he could hardly reconcile with the mansion's outer length and height and breadth, though these indeed were of most palatial amplitude. For it seemed that he gazed down great avenues of topless pillars, and vistas of tables laden with piled-up viands and thronged urns of wine, that stretched away before him into luminous distance and gloom as of starless night.

In the wide intervals between the tables, the familiars of Namirrha and his other servants went to and fro incessantly, as if a fantasmagoria of ill dreams were embodied before the emperor. Kingly cadavers in robes of time-rotten brocade, with worms seething in their eye-pits, poured a blood-like wine into cups of the opalescent horn of unicorns. Lamias, trident-tailed, and four-breasted chimeras, came in with fuming platters lifted high by their brazen claws. Dog-headed devils, tongued with lolling flames, ran forward to offer themselves as ushers for the company. And before Zotulla and Obexah, there appeared a curious being with the full-fleshed lower limbs and hips of a great black woman and the clean-picked bones of some titanic ape from there-upward. And this monster signified by certain indescribable becks of its finger-bones that the emperor and his favorite odalisque were to follow it.

Verily, it seemed to Zotulla that they had gone a long way into some malignly litten cavern of Hell, when they came to the end of that perspective of tables and columns down which the monster had led them. Here, at the room's end, apart from the rest, was a table at which Namirrha sat alone, with the flames of the seven horse-skull lamps burning restlessly behind him, and the mailed black image of Thasaidon towering from the altar of jet at his right hand. And a little aside from the altar, a diamond mirror was upborne by the claws of iron basilisks.

Namirrha rose to greet them, observing a solemn and funereal courtesy. His eyes were bleak and cold as distant stars in the hollows wrought by strange fearful vigils. His lips were like a pale-red seal on a shut parchment of doom. His beard flowed stiffly in black anointed banded locks across the bosom of his vermilion robe, like a mass of straight black serpents. Zotulla felt the blood pause and thicken about his heart, as if congealing into ice. And Obexah, peering beneath lowered lids, was abashed and frightened by the visible horror that invested this man and hung upon him even as royalty upon a king. But amid her fear, she found room to wonder what manner of man he was in his intercourse with women.

"I bid you welcome, O Zotulla, to such hospitality as is mine to offer," said Namirrha, with the iron ringing of some hidden mortuary bell deep down in his hollow voice. "Prithee, be seated at my table."

Zotulla saw that a chair of ebony had been placed for him opposite Namirrha; and another chair, less stately and imperial, had been placed at the left hand for Obexah. And the twain seated themselves; and Zotulla saw that his people were sitting likewise at other tables throughout the huge hall, with the frightful servitors of Namirrha waiting upon them busily, like devils attending the damned.

Then Zotulla perceived that a dark and corpse-like hand was pouring wine for him in a crystal cup; and upon the hand was the signet-ring of the emperors of Xylac, set with a monstrous fire-opal in the mouth of a golden bat: even such a ring as Zotulla himself wore perpetually on his index-finger. And, turning, he beheld at his right hand a figure that bore the likeness of his father, Pithaim, after the poison of the adder, spreading through all his limbs, had left behind it the purple bloating of death. And Zotulla, who had caused the adder to be placed in the bed of Pithaim, cowered in his seat and trembled with a guilty fear. And the thing that wore the similitude of Pithaim, whether corpse or ghost or an image wrought by Namirrha's enchantment, came and went at Zotulla's elbow waiting upon him with stark, black, swollen fingers that never fumbled. Horribly he was aware of its bulging, unregarding eyes, and its livid purple mouth that was locked in a rigor of mortal silence, and the spotted adder that peered at intervals with chill orbs from its heavy-folded sleeve as it leaned beside him to replenish his cup or to serve him with meat. And dimly, through the icy mist of his terror, the emperor beheld the shadowy armored shape, like a moving replica of the still, grim statue of Thasaidon, which Namirrha had reared up in his blasphemy to perform the same office for himself. And vaguely, without comprehension, he saw the dreadful ministrant that hovered beside Obexah: a flayed and eyeless corpse in the image of her first lover, a boy from Cyntrom who had been cast ashore in shipwreck on the Isle of the Torturers. There Obexah had found him, lying beyond the ebbing wave; and reviving the boy, she had hidden him awhile in a secret cave for her own pleasure, and had brought him food and drink. Later, wearying, she had betrayed him to the Torturers, and had taken a new delight in the various pangs and ordeals inflicted upon him before death by that cruel, pernicious people.

"Drink," said Namirrha, quaffing a strange wine that was red and dark as if with disastrous sunsets of lost years. And Zotulla and Obexah drank the wine, feeling no warmth in their veins thereafter, but a chill as of hemlock mounting slowly toward the heart.

"Verily, 'tis a good wine," said Namirrha, "and a proper one in which to toast the furthering of our acquaintance: for it was buried long ago with the royal dead, in amphorae of somber jasper shapen like funeral urns; and my ghouls found it, whenas they came to dig in Tasuun."

Now it seemed that the tongue of Zotulla froze in his mouth, as a mandrake freezes in the rime-bound soil of winter; and he found no reply to Namirrha's courtesy.

"Prithee, make trial of this meat," quoth Namirrha, "for it is very choice, being the flesh of that boar which the Torturers of Uccastrog are wont to pasture on the well-minced leavings of their wheels and racks; and, moreover, my cooks have spiced it with the powerful balsams of the tomb, and have farced it with the hearts of adders and the tongues of black cobras."

Naught could the emperor say; and even Obexah was silent, being sorely troubled in her turpitude by the presence of that flayed and piteous thing which had the likeness of her lover from Cyntrom. And her dread of the necromancer grew prodigiously; for his knowledge of this old, forgotten crime, and the raising of the fantasm, appeared to her a more baleful magic than all else.

"Now, I fear," said Namirrha, "that you find the meat devoid of savor, and the wine without fire. So, to enliven our feasting, I shall call forth my singers and my musicians."

He spoke a word unknown to Zotulla or Obexah, which sounded throughout the mighty hall as if a thousand voices in turn had taken it up and prolonged it. Anon there appeared the singers, who were she-ghouls with shaven bodies and hairy shanks, and long yellow tushes full of shredded carrion curving across their chaps from mouths that fawned hyena-wise on the company. Behind them entered the musicians, some of whom were male devils pacing erect on the hind-quarters of sable stallions and plucking with the fingers of white apes at lyres of the bone and sinew of cannibals from Naat; and others were pied satyrs pulling their goatish cheeks at hautboys made from the femora of young witches, or bagpipes formed from the bosom-skin of negro queens and the horn of rhinoceri.

They bowed before Namirrha with grotesque ceremony. Then, without delay, the she-ghouls began a most dolorous and execrable howling, as of jackals that have sniffed their carrion; and the satyrs and devils played a lament that was like the moaning of desert-born winds through forsaken palace harems. And Zotulla shivered, for the singing filled his marrow with ice, and the music left in his heart a desolation as of empires fallen and trod under by the iron-shod hooves of time. Ever, amid that evil music, he seemed to hear the sifting of sand across withered gardens, and the windy rustling of rotted silks upon couches of bygone luxury, and the hissing of coiled serpents from the low fusts of shattered columns. And the glory that had been Ummaos seemed to pass away like the blown pillars of the simoom.

"Now that was a brave tune," said Namirrha when the music ceased and the she-ghouls no longer howled. "But verily I fear that you find my entertainment somewhat dull. Therefore, my dancers shall dance for you."

He turned toward the great hall, and described in the air an enigmatic sign with the fingers of his right hand. In answer to the sign, a hueless mist came down from the high roof and hid the room like a fallen curtain for a brief interim. There was a babel of sounds, confused and muffled, beyond the curtain, and a crying of voices faint as if with distance.

Then, dreadfully, the vapor rolled away, and Zotulla saw that the laden tables were gone. In the wide interspaces of the columns, his palace-inmates, the chamberlains, the eunuchs, the courtiers and odalisques and all the others, lay trussed with thongs on the floor, like so many fowls of gorgeous plumage. Above them, in time to a music made by the lyrists and flutists of the necromancer, a troupe of skeletons pirouetted with light clickings of their toe-bones; and a rout of mummies bounded stiffly; and others of Namirrha's creatures moved with monstrous caperings. To and fro they leapt on the bodies of the emperor's people, in the paces of an evil saraband. At every step they grew taller and heavier, till the saltant mummies were as the mummies of Anakim, and the skeletons were boned like colossi; and louder the music rose, drowning the faint cries of Zotulla's people. And huger still became the dancers, towering far into vaulted shadow among the vast columns, with thudding feet that wrought thunder in the room; and those whereon they danced were as grapes trampled for a vintage in autumn; and the floor ran deep with a sanguine must.

As a man drowning in a noisome, night-bound fen, the emperor heard the voice of Namirrha:

"It would seem that my dancers please you not. So now I shall present you a most royal spectacle. Arise and follow me, for the spectacle is one that requires an empire for its stage."

Zotulla and Obexah rose from their chairs in the fashion of night-walkers. Giving no backward glance at their ministering phantoms, or the hall where the dancers bounded, they followed Namirrha to an alcove beyond the altar of Thasaidon. Thence, by the upward-coiling stairways, they came at length to a broad high balcony that faced Zotulla's palace and looked forth above the city roofs toward the bourn of sunset.

It seemed that several hours had gone by in that hellish feasting and entertainment; for the day was near to its close, and the sun, which had fallen from sight behind the imperial palace, was barring the vast heavens with bloody rays.

"Behold," said Namirrha, adding a strange vocable to which the stone of the edifice resounded like a beaten gong.

The balcony pitched a little, and Zotulla, looking over the balustrade, beheld the roofs of Ummaos lessen and sink beneath him. It seemed that the balcony flew skyward to a prodigious height, and he peered down across the domes of his own palace, upon the houses, the tilled fields, and the desert beyond, and the huge sun brought low on the desert's verge. And Zotulla grew giddy; and the chill airs of the upper heavens blew upon him. But Namirrha spoke another word, and the balcony ceased to ascend.

"Look well," said the necromancer, "on the empire that was yours, but shall be yours no longer." Then, with arms outstretched toward the sunset, and the gulfs beyond the sunset, he called aloud the twelve names that were perdition to utter, and after them the tremendous invocation: *Gna padambis devompra thungis furidor avoragomon.*

Instantly, it seemed that great ebon clouds of thunder beetled against the sun. Lining the horizon, the clouds took the form of colossal monsters with heads and members somewhat resembling those of stallions. Rearing terribly, they trod down the sun like an extinguished ember; and racing as in some hippodrome of Titans, they rose higher and vaster, coming toward Ummaos. Deep, calamitous rumblings preceded them, and the earth shook visibly, till Zotulla saw that these were not immaterial clouds, but actual living forms that had come forth to tread the world in macrocosmic vastness. Throwing their shadows for many leagues before them, the coursers charged as if devil-ridden into Xylac, and their feet descended like falling mountain crags upon far oases and towns of the outer waste.

Like a many-turreted storm they came, and it seemed that the world sank gulfward, tilting beneath the weight. Still as a man enchanted into marble, Zotulla stood and beheld the ruining that was wrought on his empire. And closer drew the gigantic stallions, racing with inconceivable speed, and louder was the thundering of their footfalls, that now began to blot the green fields and fruited orchards lying for many miles to the west of Ummaos. And the shadow of the stallions climbed like an evil gloom of eclipse, till it covered Ummaos; and looking up, the emperor saw their eyes half way between earth and zenith, like baleful suns that glare down from soaring cumuli.

Then, in the thickening gloom, above that insupportable thunder, he heard the voice of Namirrha, crying in mad triumph:

"Know, Zotulla, that I have called up the coursers of Thamorgorgos, lord of the abyss. And the coursers will tread your empire down, even as your palfrey trod and trampled in former time a beggar-boy named Narthos. And learn also that I, Namirrha, was that boy." And the eyes of Namirrha, filled with a vainglory of madness and bale, burned like malign, disastrous stars at the hour of their culmination.

To Zotulla, wholly mazed with the horror and tumult, the necromancer's words were no more than shrill, shrieked overtones of the tempest of doom; and he understood them not. Tremendously, with a rending of staunch-built roofs, and an instant cleavage and crumbling down of mighty masonries, the hooves descended upon Ummaos. Fair temple-domes were pashed like shells of the haliotis, and haughty mansions were broken and stamped into the ground even as gourds; and house by house the city was trampled flat with a crashing as of worlds beaten into chaos. Far below, in the darkened streets, men and camels fled like scurrying emmets but could not escape. And implacably the hooves rose and fell, till ruin was upon half the city, and night was over all. The palace of Zotulla was trodden under, and now the forelegs of the coursers loomed level with Namirrha's balcony, and their heads towered awfully above. It seemed that they would rear and trample down the necromancer's house; but at that moment they parted to left and right, and a dolorous glimmering came from the low sunset; and the coursers went on, treading under them that portion of Ummaos which lay to the eastward. And Zotulla and Obexah and Namirrha looked down on the city's fragments as on a shard-strewn midden, and heard the cataclysmic clamor of the hooves departing toward eastern Xylac.

"Now that was a goodly spectacle," quoth Namirrha. Then, turning to the emperor, he added malignly: "Think not that I have done with thee, however, or that doom is yet consummate."

It seemed that the balcony had fallen to its former elevation, which was still a lofty vantage above the sharded ruins. And Namirrha plucked the emperor by the arm and led him from the balcony to an inner chamber, while Obexah followed mutely. The emperor's heart was crushed within him by the trampling of such calamities, and despair weighed upon him like a foul incubus on the shoulders of a man lost in some land of accursed night. And he knew not that he had been parted from Obexah on the threshold of the chamber; and that certain of Namirrha's creatures, appearing like shadows, had compelled the girl to go downward with them by the stairs and had stifled her outcries with their rotten cerements as they went.

⁘

The chamber was one that Namirrha used for his most unhallowed rites and alchemies. The rays of the lamps that illumed it were saffron-red like the spilt ichor of devils, and they flowed on aludels and crucibles and black athanors and alembics whereof the purpose was hardly to be named by mortal man. The sorcerer heated in one of the alembics a dark liquid full of star-cold lights, while Zotulla looked on unheeding. And when the liquid bubbled and sent forth a spiral vapor, Namirrha distilled it into goblets of gold-rimmed iron, and gave one of the goblets to Zotulla and retained the other himself. And he said to Zotulla with a stern imperative voice: "I bid thee quaff this liquor."

Zotulla, fearing that the draft was poison, hesitated. And the necromancer regarded him with a lethal gaze, and cried loudly: "Fearest thou to do as I?" and therewith he set the goblet to his lips.

So the emperor drank the draft, constrained as if by the bidding of some angel of death, and a darkness fell upon his senses. But, ere the darkness grew complete, he saw that Namirrha had drained his own goblet. Then, with unspeakable agonies, it seemed that the emperor died; and his soul floated free; and again he saw the chamber, though with bodiless eyes. And discarnate he stood in the saffron-crimson light, with his body lying as if dead on the floor beside him, and near it the prone body of Namirrha and the two fallen goblets.

Standing thus, he beheld a strange thing: for anon his own body stirred and arose, while that of the necromancer remained still as death. And Zotulla looked on his own lineaments and his figure in its short cloak of azure samite sewn with black pearls and balas-rubies; and the body lived before him, though with eyes that held a darker fire and a deeper evil than was their wont. Then, without corporeal ears, Zotulla heard the figure speak, and the voice was the strong, arrogant voice of Namirrha, saying:

"Follow me, O houseless phantom, and do in all things as I enjoin thee."

Like an unseen shadow, Zotulla followed the wizard, and the twain went downward by the stairs to the great banquet hall. They came to the altar of Thasaidon and the mailed image, with the seven horse-skull lamps burning before it as formerly. Upon the altar, Zotulla's beloved leman Obexah, who alone of women had power to stir his sated heart, was lying bound with thongs at Thasaidon's feet. But the hall beyond was deserted, and nothing remained of that Saturnalia of doom except the fruit of the treading, which had flowed together in dark pools among the columns.

Namirrha, using the emperor's body in all ways for his own, paused before the dark eidolon; and he said to the spirit of Zotulla: "Be imprisoned in this image, without power to free thyself or to stir in any wise."

Being wholly obedient to the will of the necromancer, the soul of Zotulla was embodied in the statue, and he felt its cold, gigantic armor about him like a strait sarcophagus, and he peered forth immovably from the bleak eyes that were overhung by its carven helmet.

Gazing thus, he beheld the change that had come on his own body through the sorcerous possession of Namirrha: for below the short azure cloak, the legs had turned suddenly to the hind legs of a black stallion, with hooves that glowed redly as if heated by infernal fires. And even as Zotulla watched this prodigy, the hooves glowed white and incandescent, and fumes mounted from the floor beneath them.

Then, on the black altar, the hybrid abomination came pacing haughtily toward Obexah, and smoking hoofprints appeared behind it as it came. Pausing beside the girl, who lay supine and helpless regarding it with eyes that were pools of frozen horror, it raised one glowing hoof and set the hoof on her naked bosom between the small breast-cups of golden filigree begemmed with rubies. And the girl screamed beneath that atrocious treading as the soul of one newly damned might scream in Hell; and the hoof glared with intolerable brilliance, as if freshly plucked from a furnace wherein the weapons of demons were forged.

At that moment, in the cowed and crushed and sodden shade of the emperor Zotulla, close-locked within the adamantine image, there awoke the manhood that had slumbered unaroused before the ruining of his empire and the trampling under of his retinue. Immediately a great abhorrence and a high wrath were alive in his soul, and mightily he longed for his own right arm to serve him, and a sword in his right hand.

Then it seemed that a voice spoke within him, chill and bleak and awful, and as if uttered inwardly by the statue itself. And the voice said: "I am Thasaidon, lord of the seven hells beneath the earth, and the hells of man's heart above the earth, which are seven times seven. For the moment, O Zotulla, my power is become thine for the sake of a mutual vengeance. Be one in all ways with the statue that has my likeness, even as the soul is one with the flesh. Behold! there is a mace of adamant in thy right hand. Lift up the mace, and smite."

Zotulla was aware of a great power within him, and giant thews about him that thrilled with the power and responded agilely to his will. He felt in his mailed right hand the haft of the huge spiky-headed mace; and though the mace was beyond the lifting of any man in mortal flesh, it seemed no more than a goodly weight to Zotulla. Then, rearing the mace like a warrior in battle, he struck down with one crashing blow the impious thing that wore his own rightful flesh united with the legs and hooves of a demon courser. And the thing crumpled swiftly down and lay with the brain spreading pulpily from its shattered skull on the shining jet. And the legs twitched a little and then grew still; and the hooves glowed from a fiery, blinding white to the redness of red-hot iron, cooling slowly.

❧

For a space there was no sound, other than the shrill screaming of the girl Obexah, mad with pain and the terror of those prodigies which she had beheld. Then, in the soul of Zotulla, grown sick with that screaming, the chill, awful voice of Thasaidon spoke again:

"Go free, for there is nothing more for thee to do." So the spirit of Zotulla passed from the image of Thasaidon and found in the wide air the freedom of utter nothingness and oblivion.

But the end was not yet for Namirrha, whose mad, arrogant soul had been loosened from Zotulla's body by the blow, and had returned darkly, not in the manner planned by the magician, to its own body lying in the room of accursed rites and forbidden transmigrations. There Namirrha woke anon, with a dire confusion in his mind, and a partial forgetfulness: for the curse of Thasaidon was upon him now because of his blasphemies.

Nothing was clear in his thought except a malign, exorbitant longing for revenge; but the reason thereof, and the object, were as doubtful shadows. And still prompted by that obscure animus, he arose; and girding to his side an enchanted sword with runic sapphires and opals in its hilt, he descended the stair and came again to the altar of Thasaidon, where the mailed statue stood impassive, as before, with the poised mace in its immovable right hand, and below it, on the altar, the double sacrifice.

A veil of weird darkness was upon the senses of Namirrha, and he saw not the stallion-legged horror that lay dead with slowly blackening hooves; and he heard not the moaning of the girl Obexah, who still lived beside it. But his eyes were drawn by the diamond mirror that was upheld in the claws of black iron basilisks beyond the altar; and going to the mirror, he saw therein a face that he knew no longer for his own. And because his eyes were shadowed and his brain filled with shifting webs of delusion, he took the face for that of the emperor Zotulla. Insatiable as Hell's own flame, his old hatred rose within him; and he drew the enchanted sword and began to hew therewith at the reflection. Sometimes, because of the curse laid upon him, and the impious transmigration which he had performed, he thought himself Zotulla warring with the necromancer; and again, in the shiftings of his madness, he was Namirrha smiting at the emperor; and then, without name, he fought a nameless foe. And soon the sorcerous blade, though tempered with formidable spells, was broken close to the hilt, and Namirrha beheld the image still unharmed. Then, howling aloud the half-forgotten runes of a most tremendous curse, made invalid through his forgettings, he hammered still with the heavy sword-hilt on the mirror, till the runic sapphires and opals cracked in the hilt and fell away at his feet in little fragments.

Obexah, dying on the altar, saw Namirrha battling with his image, and the spectacle moved her to mad laughter like the pealing of bells of ruined crystal. And above her laughter, and above the cursings of Namirrha, there came anon like a rumbling of swift-risen storm the thunder made by the macrocosmic stallions of Thamorgorgos, returning gulfward through Xylac over Ummaos, to trample down the one house that they had spared aforetime.

THE SEVEN GEASES

The Lord Ralibar Vooz, high magistrate of Commoriom and third cousin to King Homquat, had gone forth with six-and-twenty of his most valorous retainers in quest of such game as was afforded by the black Eiglophian Mountains. Leaving to lesser sportsmen the great sloths and vampire-bats of the intermediate jungle, as well as the small but noxious dinosauria, Ralibar Vooz and his followers had pushed rapidly ahead and had covered the distance between the Hyperborean capital and their objective in a day's march. The glassy scaurs and grim ramparts of Mount Voormithadreth, highest and most formidable of the Eiglophians, had beetled above them, wedging the sun with dark scoriac peaks at midafternoon, and walling the blazonries of sunset wholly from view. They had spent the night beneath its lowermost crags, keeping a ceaseless watch, piling dead branches on their fires, and hearing on the grisly heights above them the wild and dog-like ululations of those subhuman savages, the Voormis for which the mountain was named. Also, they heard the bellowing of an alpine catoblepas pursued by the Voormis, and the mad snarling of a saber-toothed tiger assailed and dragged down; and Ralibar Vooz had deemed that these noises boded well for the morrow's hunting.

He and his men rose betimes; and, having breakfasted on their provisions of dried bear-meat and a dark sour wine that was noted for its invigorative qualities, they began immediately the ascent of the mountain, whose upper precipices were hollow with caves occupied by the Voormis. Ralibar Vooz had hunted these creatures before; and a certain room of his house in Commoriom was arrased with their thick and shaggy pelts. They were usually deemed the most dangerous of the Hyperborean fauna; and the mere climbing of Voormithadreth, even without the facing of its inhabitants, would have been a feat attended by more than sufficient peril: but Ralibar Vooz, having tasted of such sport, could now satisfy himself with nothing tamer.

He and his followers were well armed and accoutered. Some of the men bore coils of rope and grappling-hooks to be deployed in the escalade of the steeper crags. Some carried heavy crossbows; and many were equipped with long-handled and saber-bladed bills which, from experience, had proved the most effective weapons in close-range fighting with the Voormis. The whole party was variously studded with auxiliary knives, throwing darts, two-handed scimitars, maces, bodkins, and saw-toothed axes. The men were all clad in jerkins and hose of dinosaur-leather, and were shod with brazen-spiked buskins. Ralibar Vooz himself wore a light suiting of copper chain-mail, which, flexible as cloth, in no wise impeded his movements. In addition he carried a buckler of mammoth-hide with a long bronze spike in its center that could be used as a thrusting-sword; and, being a man of huge stature and strength, his shoulders and baldric were hung with a whole arsenal of weaponries.

The mountain was of volcanic origin, though its four craters were supposedly all extinct. For hours the climbers toiled upward on the fearsome scarps of black lava and obsidian, seeing the sheerer heights above them recede interminably into a cloudless zenith, as if not to be approached by man. Far faster than they the sun climbed, blazing torridly upon them and heating the rocks till their hands were scorched as if by the walls of a furnace. But Ralibar Vooz, eager to flesh his weapons, would permit no halting in the shady chasms nor under the scant umbrage of rare junipers.

That day, however, it seemed that the Voormis were not abroad upon Mount Voormithadreth. No doubt they had feasted too well during the night, when their hunting cries had been heard by the

Commorians. Perhaps it would be necessary to invade the warren of caves in the loftier crags: a procedure none too palatable even for a sportsman of such hardihood as Ralibar Vooz. Few of these caverns could be reached by men without the use of ropes; and the Voormis, who were possessed of quasi-human cunning, would hurl blocks and rubble upon the heads of the assailants. Most of the caves were narrow and darksome, thus putting at a grave disadvantage the hunters who entered them; and the Voormis would fight redoubtably in defense of their young and their females, who dwelt in the inner recesses; and the females were fiercer and more pernicious, if possible, than the males.

Such matters as these were debated by Ralibar Vooz and his henchmen as the escalade became more arduous and hazardous, and they saw far above them the pitted mouths of the lower dens. Tales were told of brave hunters who had gone into those dens and had not returned; and much was said of the vile feeding habits of the Voormis and the uses to which their captives were put before death and after it. Also, much was said regarding the genesis of the Voormis, who were popularly believed to be the offspring of women and certain atrocious creatures that had come forth in primal days from a tenebrous cavern-world in the bowels of Voormithadreth. Somewhere beneath that four-coned mountain, the sluggish and baleful god Tsathoggua, come down from Saturn in years immediately following the Earth's creation, was fabled to reside; and during the rite of worship at his black altars the devotees were always careful to orient themselves toward Voormithadreth. Other and more doubtful beings than Tsathoggua slept below the extinct volcanoes, or ranged and ravened throughout that hidden underworld; but of these beings few men, other than the more adept or abandoned wizards, professed to know anything at all.

❦

Ralibar Vooz, who had a thoroughly modern disdain of the supernatural, avowed his skepticism in no equivocal terms when he heard his henchmen regaling each other with these antique legendries. He swore with many ribald blasphemies that there were no gods anywhere, above or under Voormithadreth. As for the Voormis themselves, they were indeed a misbegotten species; but it was hardly necessary, in explaining their generation, to go beyond the familiar laws of nature. They were merely the remnant of a low and degraded tribe of aborigines, who, sinking further into brutehood, had sought refuge in those volcanic fastnesses after the coming of the true Hyperboreans.

Certain grizzled veterans of the party shook their heads and muttered at these heresies; but because of their respect for the high rank and prowess of Ralibar Vooz, they did not venture to gainsay him openly.

After several hours of heroic climbing, the hunters came within measurable distance of those nether caves. Below them now, in a vast and dizzying prospect, were the wooded hills and fair, fertile plains of Hyperborea. They were alone in a world of black, riven rock, with innumerable precipices and chasms above, beneath and on all sides. Directly overhead, in the face of an almost perpendicular cliff, were three of the cavern mouths, which had the aspect of volcanic fumaroles. Much of the cliff was glazed with obsidian, and there were few ledges or hand-grips. It seemed that even Voormis, agile as apes, could scarcely climb that wall; and Ralibar Vooz, studying it with a strategic eye, decided that the only feasible approach to the dens was from above. A diagonal crack, running from a shelf just below them to the summit, no doubt afforded an egress to their occupants.

First, however, it was necessary to gain the precipice above: a difficult and precarious feat in itself. At one side of the long talus on which the hunters were standing, there was a chimney that wound upward in the wall, ceasing thirty feet from the top and leaving a sheer, smooth surface. Working along the chimney to its upper end, a good alpinist could hurl his rope and grappling-hook to the summit-edge.

The advisability of bettering their present vantage was now emphasized by a shower of stones and offal from the caverns. They noted certain human relics, well-gnawed and decayed, amid the offal. Ralibar Vooz, animated by wrath against these miscreants, as well as by the fervor of the huntsman, led his six-and-twenty followers in the escalade. He soon reached the chimney's termination, where a slanting ledge offered bare foothold at one side. After the third cast, his rope held; and he went up hand over hand to the precipice.

He found himself on a broad and comparatively level-topped buttress of the lowest cone of Voormithadreth, which still rose for two thousand feet above him like a steep pyramid. Before him on the buttress, the black lava-stone was gnarled into numberless low ridges and strange masses like the pedestals of gigantic columns. Dry, scanty grasses and withered alpine flowers grew here and there in shallow basins of darkish soil; and a few cedars, levin-struck or stunted, had taken root in the fissured rock. Amid the black ridges, and seemingly close at hand, a thread of pale smoke ascended, serpenting oddly in the still air of noon and reaching an unbelievable height ere it vanished. Ralibar Vooz inferred that the buttress was inhabited by some person nearer to civilized humanity than the Voormis, who were quite ignorant of the use of fire. Surprised by this discovery, he did not wait for his men to join him, but started off at once to investigate the source of the curling smoke-thread.

He had deemed it merely a few steps away, behind the first of those grotesque furrows of lava. But evidently he had been deceived in this: for he climbed ridge after ridge and rounded many broad and curious dolmens and great dolomites which rose inexplicably before him where, an instant previous, he had thought there were only ordinary boulders; and still the pale, sinuous wisp went skyward at the same seeming interval.

Ralibar Vooz, high magistrate and redoubtable hunter, was both puzzled and irritated by this behavior of the smoke. Likewise, the aspect of the rocks around him was disconcertingly and unpleasantly deceitful. He was wasting too much time in an exploration idle and quite foreign to the real business of the day; but it was not his nature to abandon any enterprise, no matter how trivial, without reaching the set goal. Halloing loudly to his men, who must have climbed the cliff by now, he went on toward the elusive smoke.

It seemed to him, once or twice, that he heard the answering shouts of his followers, very faint and indistinct, as if across some mile-wide chasm. Again he called lustily, but this time there was no audible reply. Going a little farther, he began to detect among the rocks beside him a peculiar conversational droning and muttering in which four or five different voices appeared to take part. Seemingly they were much nearer at hand than the smoke, which had now receded like a mirage. One of the voices was clearly that of a Hyperborean; but the others possessed a timbre and accent which Ralibar Vooz, in spite of his varied ethnic knowledge, could not associate with any branch or sub-division of mankind. They affected his ears in a most unpleasant fashion, suggesting by turns the hum of great insects, the murmurs of fire and water, and the rasping of metal.

Ralibar Vooz emitted a hearty and somewhat ireful bellow to announce his coming to whatever persons were convened amid the rocks. His weapons and accouterments clattering loudly, he scrambled over a sharp lava-ridge toward the voices.

⁂

Topping the ridge, he looked down on a scene that was both mysterious and unexpected. Below him, in a circular hollow, there stood a rude hut of boulders and stone fragments roofed with cedar boughs. In front of this hovel, on a large flat block of obsidian, a fire burned with flames alternately blue, green, and white; and from it rose the pale thin spiral of smoke whose situation had eluded him so strangely.

An old man, withered and disreputable-looking, in a robe that appeared no less antique and unsavory than himself, was standing near to the fire. He was not engaged in any visible culinary operations; and, in view of the torrid sun, it hardly seemed that he required the warmth given by the queer-colored blaze. Aside from this individual, Ralibar Vooz looked in vain for the participants of the muttered conversation he had just overheard. He thought there was an evanescent fluttering of dim, grotesque shadows around the obsidian block; but the shadows faded and vanished in an instant; and, since there were no objects or beings that could have cast them, Ralibar Vooz deemed that he had been victimized by another of those highly disagreeable optic illusions in which that part of the mountain Voormithadreth seemed to abound.

The old man eyed the hunter with a fiery gaze and began to curse him in fluent but somewhat archaic diction as he descended into the hollow. At the same time, a lizard-tailed and sooty-feathered bird, which seemed to belong to some night-flying species of archæopteryx, began to snap its toothed beak and flap its digited wings on the objectionably shapen stela that served it for a perch. This stela, standing on the lee side of the fire and very close to it, had not been perceived by Ralibar Vooz at first glance.

"May the ordure of demons bemire you from heel to crown!" cried the venomous ancient. "O lumbering, bawling idiot! You have ruined a most promising and important evocation. How you came here I can not imagine. I have surrounded this place with twelve circles of illusion, whose effect is multiplied by their myriad intersections; and the chance that any intruder would ever find his way to my abode was mathematically small and insignificant. Ill was that chance which brought you here: for They that you have frightened away will not return until the high stars repeat a certain rare and quickly passing conjunction; and much wisdom is lost to me in the interim."

"How now, varlet!" said Ralibar Vooz, astonished and angered by this greeting, of which he understood little save that his presence was unwelcome to the old man. "Who are you that speak so churlishly to a magistrate of Commoriom and a cousin of King Homquat? I advise you to curb such insolence: for, if so I wish, it lies in my power to serve you even as I serve the Voormis. Though methinks," he added, "your pelt is far too filthy and verminous to merit room amid my trophies of the chase."

"Know that I am the sorcerer Ezdagor," proclaimed the ancient, his voice echoing among the rocks with dreadful sonority. "By choice I have lived remote from cities and men; nor have the Voormis of the mountain troubled me in my magical seclusion. I care not if you are the magistrate of all swinedom or a cousin to the king of dogs. In retribution for the charm you have shattered, the business you have undone by this oafish trespass, I shall put upon you a most dire and calamitous and bitter geas."

"You speak in terms of outmoded superstition," said Ralibar Vooz, who was impressed against his will by the weighty oratorical style in which Ezdagor had delivered these periods.

The old man seemed not to hear him.

"Harken then to your geas, O Ralibar Vooz," he fulminated. "For this is the geas, that you must cast aside all your weapons and go unarmed into the dens of the Voormis; and fighting bare-handed against the Voormis and against their females and their young, you must win to that secret cave in the bowels of Voormithadreth, beyond the dens, wherein abides from eldermost eons the god Tsathoggua. You shall know Tsathoggua by his great girth and his bat-like furriness and the look of a sleepy black toad which he has eternally. He will rise not from his place, even in the ravening of hunger, but will wait in divine slothfulness for the sacrifice. And, going close to Lord Tsathoggua, you must say to him: 'I am the blood-offering sent by the sorcerer Ezdagor.' Then, if it be his pleasure, Tsathoggua will avail himself of the offering.

"In order that you may not go astray, the bird Raphtontis, who is my familiar, will guide you in your wanderings on the mountain-side and through the caverns." He indicated with a peculiar gesture the night-flying archæopteryx on the foully symbolic stela, and added as if in afterthought: "Raphtontis will remain with you till the accomplishment of the geas and the end of your journey below Voormithadreth. He knows the secrets of the underworld and the lairing-places of the Old Ones. If our Lord Tsathoggua should disdain the blood-offering, or, in his generosity, should send you on to his brethren, Raphtontis will be fully competent to lead the way whithersoever is ordained by the god."

Ralibar Vooz found himself unable to answer this more than outrageous peroration in the style which it manifestly deserved. In fact, he could say nothing at all: for it seemed that a sort of lockjaw had afflicted him. Moreover, to his exceeding terror and bewilderment, this vocal paralysis was accompanied by certain involuntary movements of a most alarming type. With a sense of nightmare compulsion, together with the horror of one who feels that he is going mad, he began to divest himself of the various weapons which he carried. His bladed buckler, his mace, broadsword, hunting-knife, ax, and needle-tipped anlace jingled on the ground before the obsidian block.

"I shall permit you to retain your helmet and body-armor," said Ezdagor at this juncture. "Otherwise, I fear that you will not reach Tsathoggua in the state of corporeal intactness proper for a sacrifice. The teeth and nails of the Voormis are sharp, even as their appetites."

Muttering certain half-inaudible and doubtful-sounding words, the wizard turned from Ralibar Vooz and began to quench the tri-colored fire with a mixture of dust and blood from a shallow brass basin. Deigning to vouchsafe no farewell or sign of dismissal, he kept his back toward the hunter, but waved his left hand obliquely to the bird Raphtontis. This creature, stretching his murky wings and clacking his saw-like beak, abandoned his perch and hung poised in air with one amber-colored eye malignly fixed on Ralibar Vooz. Then, floating slowly, his long snakish neck reverted and his eye maintaining its vigilance, the bird flew among the lava-ridges toward the pyramidal cone of Voormithadreth; and Ralibar Vooz followed, driven by a compulsion that he could neither understand nor resist.

Evidently the demon fowl knew all the turnings of that maze of delusion with which Ezdagor had environed his abode; for the hunter was led with comparatively little indirection across the enchanted buttress. He heard the far-off shouting of his men as he went; but his own voice was faint and thin as that of a flittermouse when he sought to reply. Soon he found himself at the bottom of a great scarp of the upper mountain, pitted with cavern mouths. It was a part of Voormithadreth that he had never visited before.

Raphtontis rose toward the lowest cave, and hovered at its entrance while Ralibar Vooz climbed precariously behind him amid a heavy barrage of bones and glass-edged flints and other oddments of less mentionable nature hurled by the Voormis. These low, brutal savages, fringing the dark mouths of the dens with their repulsive faces and members, greeted the hunter's progress with ferocious howlings and an inexhaustible supply of garbage. However, they did not molest Raphtontis, and it seemed that they were anxious to avoid hitting him with their missiles; though the presence of this hovering, wide-winged fowl interfered noticeably with their aim as Ralibar Vooz began to near the nethermost den.

Owing to this partial protection, the hunter was able to reach the cavern without serious injury. The entrance was rather strait; and Raphtontis flew upon the Voormis with open beak and flapping wings, compelling them to withdraw into the interior while Ralibar Vooz made firm his position on the threshold-ledge. Some, however, threw themselves on their faces to allow the passage of Raphtontis; and, rising when the bird had gone by, they assailed the Commorian as he followed his guide into the fetid gloom. They stood only half erect, and their shaggy heads were about his thighs and hips, snarling and snapping like dogs; and they clawed him with hook-shaped nails that caught and held in the links of his armor.

Weaponless he fought them in obedience to his geas, striking down their hideous faces with his mailed fist in a veritable madness that was not akin to the ardor of a huntsman. He felt their nails and teeth break on the close-woven links as he hurled them loose; but others took their place when he won onward a little into the murky cavern; and their females struck at his legs like darting serpents; and their young beslavered his ankles with mouths wherein the fangs were as yet ungrown.

Before him, for his guidance, he heard the clanking of the wings of Raphtontis, and the harsh cries, half hiss and half caw, that were emitted by this bird at intervals. The darkness stifled him with a thousand stenches; and his feet slipped in blood and filth at every step. But anon he knew that the Voormis had ceased to assail him. The cave sloped downward; and he breathed an air that was edged with sharp, acrid mineral odors.

Groping for a while through sightless night, and descending a steep incline, he came to a sort of underground hall in which neither day nor darkness prevailed. Here the archings of rock were visible by an obscure glow such as hidden moons might yield. Thence, through declivitous grottoes and along perilously skirted gulfs, he was conducted ever downward by Raphtontis into the world beneath the mountain Voormithadreth. Everywhere was that dim, unnatural light whose source he could not ascertain. Wings that were too broad for those of the bat flew vaguely overhead; and at whiles, in the shadowy caverns, he beheld great, fearsome bulks having a likeness to those behemoths and giant reptiles which burdened the Earth in earlier times; but because of the dimness he could not tell if these were living shapes or forms that the stone had taken.

Strong was the compulsion of his geas on Ralibar Vooz; and a numbness had seized his mind; and he felt only a dulled fear and a dazed wonder. It seemed that his will and his thoughts were no longer his own, but were become those of some alien person. He was going down to some obscure but predestined end, by a route that was dark-some but foreknown.

⁂

At last the bird Raphtontis paused and hovered significantly in a cave distinguished from the others by a most evil potpourri of smells. Ralibar Vooz deemed at first that the cave was empty. Going forward to join Raphtontis, he stumbled over certain attenuated remnants on the floor, which appeared to be the skin-clad skeletons of men and various animals. Then, following the coalbright gaze of the demon bird, he discerned in a dark recess the formless bulking of a couchant mass. And the mass stirred a little at his approach, and put forth with infinite slothfulness a huge and toad-shaped head. And the head opened its eyes very slightly, as if half awakened from slumber, so that they were visible as two slits of oozing phosphor in the black, browless face.

Ralibar Vooz perceived an odor of fresh blood amid the many fœtors that rose to besiege his nostrils. A horror came upon him therewith; for, looking down, he beheld lying before the shadowy monster the lean husk of a thing that was neither man, beast, nor Voormi. He stood hesitant, fearing to go closer yet powerless to retreat. But, admonished by angry hissing from the archæopteryx, together with a slashing stroke of its beak between his shoulder-blades, he went forward till he could see the fine dark fur on the dormant body and sleepily porrected head.

With new horror, and a sense of hideous doom, he heard his own voice speaking without volition: "O Lord Tsathoggua, I am the blood-offering sent by the sorcerer Ezdagor."

There was a sluggish inclination of the toad-like head; and the eyes opened a little wider, and light flowed from them in viscous tricklings on the creased underlids. Then Ralibar Vooz seemed to hear a deep, rumbling sound; but he knew not whether it reverberated in the dusky air or in his own mind. And the sound shaped itself, albeit uncouthly, into syllables and words:

"Thanks are due to Ezdagor for this offering. But, since I have fed lately on a well-blooded sacrifice, my hunger is appeased for the present, and I require not the offering. However, it may be that others of the Old Ones are athirst or famished. And, since you came here with a geas upon you, it is not fitting that you should go hence without another. So I place you under this geas, to betake yourself downward through the caverns till you reach, after long descent, that bottomless gulf over which the spider-god Atlach-Nacha weaves his eternal webs. And there, calling to Atlach-Nacha, you must say: 'I am the gift sent by Tsathoggua.' "

So, with Raphtontis leading him, Ralibar Vooz departed from the presence of Tsathoggua by another route than that which had brought him there. The way steepened more and more; and it ran through chambers that were too vast for the searching of sight; and along precipices that fell sheer for an unknown distance to the black, sluggish foam and somnolent murmur of underworld seas.

At last, on the verge of a chasm whose farther shore was lost in darkness, the night-flying bird hung motionless with level wings and down-dropping tail. Ralibar Vooz went close to the verge and saw that great webs were attached to it at intervals, seeming to span the gulf with their multiple crossings and reticulations of gray, rope-thick strands. Apart from these, the chasm was bridgeless. Far out on one of the webs he discerned a darksome form, big as a crouching man but with long spider-like members. Then, like a dreamer who hears some nightmare sound, he heard his own voice crying loudly: "O Atlach-Nacha, I am the gift sent by Tsathoggua."

The dark form ran toward him with incredible swiftness. When it came near he saw that there was a kind of face on the squat ebon body, low down amid the several-jointed legs. The face peered up with a weird expression of doubt and inquiry; and terror crawled through the veins of the bold huntsman as he met the small, crafty eyes that were circled about with hair.

Thin, shrill, piercing as a sting, there spoke to him the voice of the spider-god Atlach-Nacha: "I am duly grateful for the gift. But, since there is no one else to bridge this chasm, and since eternity is required for the task, I can not spend my time in extracting you from those curious shards of metal. However, it may be that the antehuman sorcerer Haon-Dor, who abides beyond the gulf in his palace of primal enchantments, can somehow find a use for you. The bridge I have just now completed runs to the threshold of his abode; and your weight will serve to test the strength of my weaving. Go then, with this geas upon you, to cross the bridge and present yourself before Haon-Dor, saying: 'Atlach-Nacha has sent me.' "

With these words, the spider-god withdrew his bulk from the web and ran quickly from sight along the chasm-edge, doubtless to begin the construction of a new bridge at some remoter point.

Though the third geas was heavy and compulsive upon him, Ralibar Vooz followed Raphtontis none too willingly over the night-bound depths. The weaving of Atlach-Nacha was strong beneath his feet, giving and swaying only a little; but between the strands, in unfathomable space below, he seemed to descry the dim flitting of dragons with claw-tipped wings; and, like a seething of the darkness, fearful hulks without name appeared to heave and sink from moment to moment.

However, he and his guide came presently to the gulf's opposite shore, where the web of Atlach-Nacha was joined to the lowest step of a mighty stairway. The stairs were guarded by a coiled snake whose mottlings were broad as bucklers and whose middle volumes exceeded in girth the body of a stout warrior. The horny tail of this serpent rattled like a sistrum, and he thrust forth an evil head with fangs that were long as bill-hooks. But, seeing Raphtontis, he drew his coils aside and permitted Ralibar Vooz to ascend the steps.

Thus, in fulfilment of the third geas, the hunter entered the thousand-columned palace of Haon-Dor. Strange and silent were those halls hewn from the gray, fundamental rock of Earth. In them were faceless forms of smoke and mist that went uneasily to and fro, and statues representing monsters with myriad heads. In the vaults above, as if hung aloof in night, lamps burned with inverse flames that were like the combustion of ice and stone. A chill spirit of evil, ancient beyond all conception of man, was abroad in those halls; and horror and fear crept throughout them like invisible serpents, unknotted from sleep.

Threading the mazy chambers with the surety of one accustomed to all their windings, Raphtontis conducted Ralibar Vooz to a high room whose walls described a circle broken only by the one portal, through which he entered. The room was empty of furnishment, save for a five-pillared seat rising so far aloft without stairs or other means of approach, that it seemed only a winged being could ever attain thereto. But on the seat was a figure shrouded with thick, sable darkness, and having over its head and features a caul of grisly shadow.

The bird Raphtontis hovered ominously before the columned chair. And Ralibar Vooz, in astonishment, heard a voice saying: "O Haon-Dor, Atlach-Nacha has sent me." And not till the voice had ceased speaking did he know it for his own.

For a long time the silence seemed infrangible. There was no stirring of the high-seated figure. But Ralibar Vooz, peering trepidantly at the walls about him, beheld their former smoothness embossed with a thousand faces, twisted and awry like those of mad devils. The faces were thrust forward on necks that lengthened; and behind the necks malshapen shoulders and bodies emerged inch by inch from the stone, craning toward the huntsman. And beneath his feet the very floor was now cobbled with other faces, turning and tossing restlessly, and opening ever wider their demoniac mouths and eyes.

At last the shrouded figure spoke; and though the words were of no mortal tongue, it seemed to the listener that he comprehended them darkly:

"My thanks are due to Atlach-Nacha for this sending. If I appear to hesitate, it is only because I am doubtful regarding what disposition I can make of you. My familiars, who crowd the walls and floors of this chamber, would devour you all too readily: but you would serve only as a morsel amid so many. On the whole, I believe that the best thing I can do is to send you on to my allies, the serpent people. They are scientists of no ordinary attainment; and perhaps you might provide some special ingredient required in their chemistries. Consider, then, that a geas has been put upon you, and take yourself off to the caverns in which the serpent-people reside."

Obeying this injunction, Ralibar Vooz went down through the darkest strata of that primeval underworld, beneath the palace of Haon-Dor. The guidance of Raphtontis never failed him; and he came anon to the spacious caverns in which the serpent-men were busying themselves with a multitude of tasks. They walked lithely and sinuously erect on pre-mammalian members, their pied and hairless bodies bending with great suppleness. There was a loud and constant hissing of formulae as they went to and fro. Some were smelting the black nether ores; some were blowing molten obsidian into forms of flask and urn; some were measuring chemicals; others were decanting strange liquids and curious colloids. In their intense preoccupation, none of them seemed to notice the arrival of Ralibar Vooz and his guide.

After the hunter had repeated many times the message given him by Haon-Dor, one of the walking reptiles at last perceived his presence. This being eyed him with cold but highly disconcerting curiosity, and then emitted a sonorous hiss that was audible above all the noises of labor and converse. The other serpent-men ceased their toil immediately and began to crowd around Ralibar Vooz. From the tone of their sibilations, it seemed that there was much argument among them. Certain of their number sidled close to the Commorian, touching his face and hands with their chill, scaly digits, and prying beneath his armor. He felt that they were anatomizing him with methodical minuteness. At the same time, he perceived that they paid no attention to Raphtontis, who had perched himself on a large alembic.

After a while, some of the chemists went away and returned quickly, bearing among them two great jars of glass filled with a clear liquid. In one of the jars there floated upright a well-developed and mature male Voormi; in the other, a large and equally perfect specimen of Hyperborean manhood, not without a sort of general likeness to Ralibar Vooz himself. The bearers of these specimens deposited their burdens beside the hunter and then each of them delivered what was doubtless a learned dissertation on comparative biology.

This series of lectures, unlike many such, was quite brief. At the end the reptilian chemists returned to their various labors, and the jars were removed. One of the scientists then addressed himself to Ralibar Vooz with a fair though somewhat sibilant approximation of human speech:

"It was thoughtful of Haon-Dor to send you here. However, as you have seen, we are already supplied with an exemplar of your species; and, in the past, we have thoroughly dissected others and have learned all that there is to learn regarding this very uncouth and aberrant life-form.

"Also, since our chemistry is devoted almost wholly to the production of powerful toxic agents, we can find no use in our tests and manufactures for the extremely ordinary matters of which your body is composed. They are without pharmaceutic value. Moreover, we have long abandoned the eating of impure natural foods, and now confine ourselves to synthetic types of aliment. There is, as you must realize, no place for you in our economy.

"However, it may be that the Archetypes can somehow dispose of you. At least you will be a novelty to them, since no example of contemporary human evolution has so far descended to their stratum. Therefore we shall put you under that highly urgent and imperative kind of hypnosis which, in the parlance of warlockry, is known as a geas. And, obeying the hypnosis, you will go down to the Cavern of the Archetypes . . ."

The region to which the magistrate of Commoriom was now

conducted lay at some distance below the ophidian laboratories. The air of the gulfs and grottoes along his way began to increase markedly in warmth, and was moist and steamy as that of some equatorial fen. A primordial luminosity, such as might have dawned before the creation of any sun, seemed to surround and pervade everything.

All about him, in this thick and semi-aqueous light, the hunter discerned the rocks and fauna and vegetable forms of a crassly primitive world. These shapes were dim, uncertain, wavering, and were all composed of loosely organized elements. Even in this bizarre and more than doubtful terrain of the under-Earth, Raphtontis seemed wholly at home, and he flew on amid the sketchy plants and cloudy-looking boulders as if at no loss whatever in orienting himself. But Ralibar Vooz, in spite of the spell that stimulated and compelled him onward, had begun to feel a fatigue by no means unnatural in view of his prolonged and heroic itinerary. Also, he was much troubled by the elasticity of the ground, which sank beneath him at every step like an oversodded marsh, and seemed insubstantial to a quite alarming degree.

To his further disconcertion, he soon found that he had attracted the attention of a huge foggy monster with the rough outlines of a tyrannosaurus. This creature chased him amid the archetypal ferns and club-mosses; and overtaking him after five or six bounds, it proceeded to ingest him with the celerity of any latter-day saurian of the same species. Luckily, the ingestion was not permanent: for the tyrannosaurus' body-plasm, though fairly opaque, was more astral than material; and Ralibar Vooz, protesting stoutly against his confinement in its maw, felt the dark walls give way before him and tumbled out on the ground.

After its third attempt to devour him, the monster must have decided that he was inedible. It turned and went away with immense leapings in search of comestibles on its own plane of matter. Ralibar Vooz continued his progress through the Cavern of the Archetypes:

a progress often delayed by the alimentary designs of crude, misty-stomached allosaurs, pterodactyls, pteranodons, stegosaurs, and other carnivora of the prime.

At last, following his experience with a most persistent megalosaur, he beheld before him two entities of vaguely human outline. They were gigantic, with bodies almost globular in form, and they seemed to float rather than walk. Their features, though shadowy to the point of inchoateness, appeared to express aversion and hostility. They drew near to the Commorian, and he became aware that one of them was addressing him. The language used was wholly a matter of primitive vowel-sounds; but a meaning was forcibly, though indistinctly, conveyed:

"We, the originals of mankind, are dismayed by the sight of a copy so coarse and egregiously perverted from the true model. We disown you with sorrow and indignation. Your presence here is an unwarrantable intrusion; and it is obvious that you are not to be assimilated even by our most esurient dinosaurs. Therefore we put you under a geas: depart without delay from the Cavern of the Archetypes, and seek out the slimy gulf in which Abhoth, father and mother of all cosmic uncleanness, eternally carries on Its repugnant fission. We consider that you are fit only for Abhoth, which will perhaps mistake you for one of Its own progeny and devour you in accordance with that custom which It follows."

The weary hunter was led by the untirable Raphtontis to a deep cavern on the same level as that of the Archetypes. Possibly it was a kind of annex to the latter. At any rate, the ground was much firmer there, even though the air was murkier; and Ralibar Vooz might have recovered a little of his customary aplomb, if it had not been for the ungodly and disgusting creatures which he soon began to meet. There were things which he could liken only to monstrous one-legged toads, and immense myriad-tailed worms, and miscreated lizards. They came flopping or crawling through the gloom in a ceaseless procession;

and there was no end to the loathsome morphologic variations which they displayed. Unlike the Archetypes, they were formed of all too solid matter; and Ralibar Vooz was both fatigued and nauseated by the constant necessity of kicking them away from his shins. He was somewhat relieved to find, however, that these wretched abortions became steadily smaller as he continued his advance.

The dusk about him thickened with hot, evil steam that left an oozy deposit on his armor and bare face and hand. With every breath he inhaled an odor noisome beyond imagining. He stumbled and slipped on the crawling foulnesses underfoot. Then, in that reeky twilight, he saw the pausing of Raphtontis; and below the demoniac bird he descried a sort of pool with a margin of mud that was marled with obscene offal; and in the pool a grayish, horrid mass that nearly choked it from rim to rim.

Here, it seemed, was the ultimate source of all miscreation and abomination. For the gray mass quobbed and quivered, and swelled perpetually; and from it, in manifold fission, were spawned the anatomies that crept away on every side through the grotto. There were things like bodiless legs or arms that flailed in the slime, or heads that rolled, or floundering bellies with fishes' fins; and all manner of things malformed and monstrous, that grew in size as they departed from the neighborhood of Abhoth. And those that swam not swiftly ashore when they fell into the pool from Abhoth, were devoured by mouths that gaped in the parent bulk.

Ralibar Vooz was beyond thought, beyond horror, in his weariness: else he would have known intolerable shame, seeing that he had come to the bourn ordained for him by the Archetypes as most fit and proper. A deadness near to death was upon his faculties; and he heard as if remote and high above him a voice that proclaimed to Abhoth the reason of his coming; and he did not know that the voice was his own.

There was no sound in answer; but out of the lumpy mass there grew a member that stretched and lengthened toward Ralibar Vooz where he stood waiting on the pool's margin. The member divided to a flat, webby hand, soft and slimy, which touched the hunter and went over his person slowly from foot to head. Having done this, it seemed that the thing had served its use: for it dropped quickly away from Abhoth and wriggled into the gloom like a serpent together with the other progeny.

Still waiting, Ralibar Vooz felt in his brain a sensation as of speech heard without words or sound. And the import, rendered in human language, was somewhat as follows:

"I, who am Abhoth, the coeval of the oldest gods, consider that the Archetypes have shown a questionable taste in recommending you to me. After careful inspection, I fail to recognize you as one of my relatives or progeny; though I must admit that I was nearly deceived at first by certain biologic similarities. You are quite alien to my experience; and I do not care to endanger my digestion with untried articles of diet.

"Who you are, or whence you have come, I can not surmise; nor can I thank the Archetypes for troubling the profound and placid fertility of my existence with a problem so vexatious as the one that you offer. Get hence, I adjure you. There is a bleak and drear and dreadful limbo, known as the Outer World, of which I have heard dimly; and I think that it might prove a suitable objective for your journeying. I settle an urgent geas upon you: go seek this Outer World with all possible expedition."

Apparently Raphtontis realized that it was beyond the physical powers of his charge to fulfill the seventh geas without an interim of repose. He led the hunter to one of the numerous exits of the grotto inhabited by Abhoth: an exit giving on regions altogether unknown, opposite to the Cavern of the Archetypes. There, with significant gestures of his wings and beak, the bird indicated a sort of narrow alcove in the rock. The recess was dry and by no means uncomfortable as a sleeping-place. Ralibar Vooz was glad to lay himself down; and a black tide of slumber rolled upon him with the closing of his eyelids.

Raphtontis remained on guard before the alcove, discouraging with strokes of his bill the wandering progeny of Abhoth that tried to assail the sleeper.

Since there was neither night nor day in that subterrene world, the term of oblivion enjoyed by Ralibar Vooz was hardly to be measured by the usual method of time-telling. He was aroused by the noise of vigorously flapping wings, and saw beside him the fowl Raphtontis, holding in his beak an unsavory object, whose anatomy was that of a fish rather than anything else. Where or how he had caught this creature during his constant vigil was a more than dubious matter; but Ralibar Vooz had fasted too long to be squeamish. He accepted and devoured the proffered breakfast without ceremony.

After that, in conformity with the geas laid upon him by Abhoth, he resumed his journey back to the outer Earth. The route chosen by Raphtontis was presumably a short-cut. Anyhow, it was remote from the cloudy cave of the Archetypes, and the laboratories in which the serpent-men pursued their arduous toils and toxicological researches. Also, the enchanted palace of Haon-Dor was omitted from the itinerary. But, after long, tedious climbing through a region of desolate crags and over a sort of underground plateau, the traveler came once more to the verge of that far-stretching, bottomless chasm which was bridged only by the webs of the spider-god Atlach-Nacha.

For some time past he had hurried his pace because of certain of the progeny of Abhoth, who had followed him from the start and had grown steadily bigger after the fashion of their kind, till they were now large as young tigers or bears. However, when he approached the nearest bridge, he saw that a ponderous and sloth-like entity, preceding him, had already begun to cross it. The posteriors of this being were studded with unamiable eyes, and Ralibar Vooz was unsure for a little regarding its exact orientation. Not wishing to tread too closely upon the reverted talons of its heels, he waited till the monster had disappeared in the darkness; and by that time the spawn of Abhoth were hard upon him.

Raphtontis, with sharp admonitory cawings, floated before him above the giant web; and he was impelled to a rash haste by the imminently slavering snouts of the dark abnormalities behind. Owing to such precipitancy, he failed to notice that the web had been weakened and some of its strands torn or stretched by the weight of the sloth-like monster. Coming in view of the chasm's opposite verge, he thought only of reaching it, and redoubled his pace. But at this point the web gave way beneath him. He caught wildly at the broken, dangling strands, but could not arrest his fall. With several pieces of Atlach-Nacha's weaving clutched in his fingers, he was precipitated into that gulf which no one had ever voluntarily tried to plumb.

This, unfortunately, was a contingency that had not been provided against by the terms of the seventh geas.

THE HOLINESS
OF AZÉDARAC

I

"By the ram with a Thousand Ewes! By the Tail of Dagon and the Horns of Derceto!" said Azédarac, as he fingered the tiny, pot-bellied vial of vermilion liquid on the table before him. "Something will have to be done with this pestilential Brother Ambrose. I have now learned that he was sent to Ximes by the Archbishop of Averoigne for no other purpose than to gather proof of my subterraneous connection with Azazel and the Old Ones. He has spied upon my evocations in the vaults, he has heard the hidden formula, and beheld the veritable manifestation of Lilit, and even of Iog-Sotôt and Sodagui, those demons who are more ancient than the world; and this very morning, an hour agone, he has mounted his white ass for the return journey to Vyones. There are two ways—or, in a sense, there is one way—in which I can avoid the pother and inconvenience of a trial for sorcery: the contents of this vial must be administered to Ambrose before he has reached his journey's end—or, failing this, I myself shall be compelled to make use of a similar medicament."

Jehan Mauvaissoir looked at the vial and then at Azédarac. He was not at all horrified, nor even surprised, by the non-episcopal oaths and the somewhat uncanonical statements which he had just heard from the Bishop of Ximes. He had known the Bishop too long and too intimately, and had rendered him too many services of an unconventional nature, to be surprised at anything. In fact, he had known

Azédarac long before the sorcerer had ever dreamt of becoming a prelate, in a phase of his existence that was wholly unsuspected by the people of Ximes; and Azédarac had not troubled to keep many secrets from Jehan at any time.

"I understand," said Jehan. "You can depend upon it that the contents of the vial will be administered. Brother Ambrose will hardly travel post-haste on that ambling white ass; and he will not reach Vyones before tomorrow noon. There is abundant time to overtake him. Of course, he knows me—at least, he knows Jehan Mauvaissoir . . . But that can easily be remedied."

Azédarac smiled confidentially. "I leave the affair—and the vial— in your hands, Jehan. Of course, no matter what the eventuation, with all the Satanic and pre-Satanic facilities at my disposal, I should be in no great danger from these addlepated bigots. However, I am very comfortably situated here in Ximes; and the lot of a Christian Bishop who lives in the odor of incense and piety, and maintains in the meanwhile a private understanding with the Adversary, is certainly preferable to the mischancy life of a hedge-sorcerer. I do not care to be annoyed or disturbed, or ousted from my sinecure, if such can be avoided.

"May Moloch devour that sanctimonious little milksop of an Ambrose," he went on. "I must be growing old and dull, not to have suspected him before this. It was the horror-stricken and averted look he has been wearing lately that made me think he had peered through the keyhole on the subterranean rites. Then, when I heard he was leaving, I wisely thought to review my library; and I have found that the Book of Eibon, which contains the oldest incantations, and the secret, man-forgotten lore of Iog-Sotôt and Sodagui, is now missing. As you know, I had replaced the former binding of aboriginal, sub-human skin with the sheep-leather of a Christian missal, and had surrounded the volume with rows of legitimate prayer-books. Ambrose is carrying it away under his robe as proof conclusive that I am addicted to the Black Arts. No one in Averoigne will be able to read the immemorial Hyperborean script; but the dragon's-blood illuminations and drawings will be enough to damn me."

Master and servant regarded each other for an interval of significant silence. Jehan eyed with profound respect the haughty stature, the grimly lined lineaments, the grizzled tonsure, the odd, ruddy, crescent scar on the pallid brow of Azédarac, and the sultry points of orange-yellow fire that seemed to burn deep down in the chill and liquid ebon of his eyes. Azédarac, in his turn, considered with confidence the vulpine features and discreet, inexpressive air of Jehan, who might have been—and could be, if necessary—anything from a mercer to a cleric.

"It is regrettable," resumed Azédarac, "that any question of my holiness and devotional probity should have been raised among the clergy of Averoigne. But I suppose it was inevitable sooner or later— even though the chief difference between myself and many other ecclesiastics is, that I serve the Devil wittingly and of my own free will, while they do the same in sanctimonious blindness. However, we must do what we can to delay the evil hour of public scandal, and eviction from our neatly feathered nest. Ambrose alone could prove anything to my detriment at present; and you, Jehan, will remove Ambrose to a realm wherein his monkish tattlings will be of small consequence. After that, I shall be doubly vigilant. The next emissary from Vyones, I assure you, will find nothing to report but saintliness and bead-telling."

II

The thoughts of Brother Ambrose were sorely troubled, and at variance with the tranquil beauty of the sylvan scene, as he rode onward through the forest of Averoigne between Ximes and Vyones. Horror was nesting in his heart like a knot of malignant vipers; and the evil Book of Eibon, that primordial manual of sorcery, seemed to burn beneath his robe like a huge, hot, Satanic sigil pressed against his bosom. Not for the first time, there occurred to him the wish that

Clément, the Archbishop, had delegated someone else to investigate the Erebean turpitude of Azédarac. Sojourning for a month in the Bishop's household, Ambrose had learned too much for the peace of mind of any pious cleric, and had seen things that were like a secret blot of shame and terror on the white page of his memory. To find that a Christian prelate could serve the powers of nethermost perdition, could entertain in privity the foulnesses that are older than Asmodai, was abysmally disturbing to his devout soul; and ever since then he had seemed to smell corruption everywhere, and had felt on every side the serpentine encroachment of the dark Adversary.

As he rode on among the somber pines and verdant beeches, he wished also that he were mounted on something swifter than the gentle, milk-white ass appointed for his use by the Archbishop. He was dogged by the shadowy intimation of leering gargoyle faces, of invisible cloven feet, that followed him behind the thronging trees and along the umbrageous meanderings of the road. In the oblique rays, the elongated webs of shadow wrought by the dying afternoon, the forest seemed to attend with bated breath the noisome and furtive passing of innominable things. Nevertheless, Ambrose had met no one for miles; and he had seen neither bird nor beast nor viper in the summer woods.

His thoughts returned with fearful insistence to Azédarac, who appeared to him as a tall, prodigious Antichrist, uprearing his sable vans and giant figure from out the flaming mire of Abaddon. Again he saw the vaults beneath the Bishop's mansion, wherein he had peered one night on a scene of infernal terror and loathliness, had beheld the Bishop swathed in the gorgeous, coiling fumes of unholy censers, that mingled in midair with the sulfurous and bituminous vapors of the Pit; and through the vapors had seen the lasciviously swaying limbs, the bellying and dissolving features of foul, enormous entities . . . Recalling them, again he trembled at the pre-Adamite lubriciousness of Lilit, again he shuddered at the transgalactic horror of the demon Sodagui, and the ultra-dimensional hideousness of that being known as Iog-Sotôt to the sorcerers of Averoigne.

How balefully potent and subversive, he thought, were these immemorial devils, who had placed their servant Azédarac in the very bosom of the Church, in a position of high and holy trust. For nine years the evil prelate had held an unchallenged and unsuspected tenure, had befouled the bishopric of Ximes with infidelities that were worse than those of the Paynims. Then, somehow, through anonymous channels, a rumor had reached Clément—a warning whisper that not even the Archbishop had dared to voice aloud; and Ambrose, a young Benedictine monk, the nephew of Clément, had been dispatched to examine privily the festering foulness that threatened the integrity of the Church. Only at that time did any one recall how little was actually known regarding the antecedents of Azédarac; how tenuous were his claims to ecclesiastical preferment, or even to mere priestship; how veiled and doubtful were the steps by which he had attained his office. It was then realized that a formidable wizardry had been at work.

Uneasily, Ambrose wondered if Azédarac had already discovered the removal of the Book of Eibon from among the missals contaminated by its blasphemous presence. Even more uneasily, he wondered what Azédarac would do in that event, and how long it would take him to connect the absence of the volume with his visitor's departure.

At this point, the meditations of Ambrose were interrupted by the hard clatter of galloping hoofs that approached from behind. The emergence of a centaur from the oldest wood of paganism could scarcely have startled him to a keener panic; and he peered apprehensively over his shoulder at the nearing horseman. This person, mounted on a fine black steed with opulent trappings, was a bushy-bearded man of obvious consequence; for his gay garments were those of a noble or a courtier. He overtook Ambrose and passed on with a polite nod, seeming to be wholly intent on his own affairs.

The monk was immensely reassured, though vaguely troubled for some moments by a feeling that he had seen elsewhere, under circumstances which he was now unable to recall, the narrow eyes and sharp profile that contrasted so oddly with the bluff beard of the horseman. However, he was comfortably sure that he had never seen the man in Ximes. The rider soon vanished beyond a leafy turn of the arboreal highway. Ambrose returned to the pious horror and apprehensiveness of his former soliloquy.

As he went on, it seemed to him that the sun had gone down with untimely and appalling swiftness. Though the heavens above were innocent of cloud, and the low-lying air was free from vapors, the woods were embrowned by an inexplicable gloom that gathered visibly on all sides. In this gloom, the trunks of the trees were strangely distorted, and the low masses of foliage assumed unnatural and disquieting forms. It appeared to Ambrose that the silence around him was a fragile film through which the raucous rumble and mutter of diabolic voices might break at any moment, even as the foul and sunken driftage that rises anon above the surface of a smoothly-flowing river.

With much relief, he remembered that he was not far from a wayside tavern, known as the Inn of Bonne Jouissance. Here, since his journey to Vyones was little more than half completed, he resolved to tarry for the night.

A minute more, and he saw the lights of the inn. Before their benign and golden radiance, the equivocal forest shadows that attended him seemed to halt and retire, and he gained the haven of the tavern courtyard with the feeling of one who has barely escaped from an army of goblin perils.

Committing his mount to the care of a stable-servant, Ambrose entered the main room of the inn. Here he was greeted with the deference due to his cloth by the stout and unctuous taverner; and, being assured that the best accommodations of the place were at his disposal, he seated himself at one of several tables where other guests had already gathered to await the evening meal.

Among them, Ambrose recognized the bluff-bearded horseman who had overtaken him in the woods an hour agone. This person was sitting alone, and a little apart. The other guests, a couple of travelling mercers, a notary, and two soldiers, acknowledged the presence of the monk with all due civility; but the horseman arose from his table, and coming over to Ambrose, began immediately to make overtures that were more than those of common courtesy.

"Will you not dine with me, sir monk?" he invited, in a gruff but ingratiating voice that was perplexingly familiar to Ambrose, and yet, like the wolfish profile, was irrecognizable at the time.

"I am the Sieur des Émaux, from Touraine, at your service," the man went on. "It would seem that we are travelling the same road—possibly to the same destination. Mine is the cathedral city of Vyones. And yours?"

Though he was vaguely perturbed, and even a little suspicious, Ambrose found himself unable to decline the invitation. In reply to the last question, he admitted that he also was on his way to Vyones. He did not altogether like the Sieur des Émaux, whose slitted eyes gave back the candle-light of the inn with a covert glitter, and whose manner was somewhat effusive, not to say fulsome. But there seemed to be no ostensible reason for refusing a courtesy that was doubtless well-meant and genuine. He accompanied his host to their separate table.

"You belong to the Benedictine order, I observe," said the Sieur des Émaux, eyeing the monk with an odd smile that was tinged with furtive irony. "It is an order that I have always admired greatly—a most noble and worthy brotherhood. May I not inquire your name?"

Ambrose gave the requested information with a curious reluctance.

"Well, then, Brother Ambrose," said the Sieur des Émaux, "I suggest that we drink to your health and the prosperity of your order in the red wine of Averoigne while we are waiting for supper to be served. Wine is always welcome, following a long journey, and is no less beneficial before a good meal than after."

Ambrose mumbled an unwilling assent. He could not have told why, but the personality of the man was more and more distasteful to him. He seemed to detect a sinister undertone in the purring voice, to surprise an evil meaning in the low-lidded glance. And all the while his brain was tantalized by intimations of a forgotten memory. Had he seen his interlocutor in Ximes? Was the self-styled Sieur des Émaux a henchman of Azédarac in disguise?

Wine was now ordered by his host, who left the table to confer with the innkeeper for this purpose, and even insisted on paying a visit to the cellar, that he might select a suitable vintage in person. Noting the obeisance paid to the man by the people of the tavern, who addressed him by name, Ambrose felt a certain measure of reassurance. When the taverner, followed by the Sieur des Émaux, returned with two earthen pitchers of wine, he had well-nigh succeeded in dismissing his vague doubts and vaguer fears.

Two large goblets were now placed on the table, and the Sieur des Émaux filled them immediately from one of the pitchers. It seemed to Ambrose that the first of the goblets already contained a small amount of some sanguine fluid, before the wine was poured into it; but he could not have sworn to this in the dim light, and thought that he must have been mistaken.

"Here are two matchless vintages," said the Sieur des Émaux, indicating the pitchers. "Both are so excellent that I was unable to choose between them; but you, Brother Ambrose, are perhaps capable of deciding their merits with a finer palate than mine."

He pushed one of the filled goblets toward Ambrose. "This is the wine of La Frenaie," he said. "Drink, it will verily transport you from the world by virtue of the mighty fire that slumbers in its heart."

Ambrose took the proffered goblet, and raised it to his lips. The Sieur des Émaux was bending forward above his own wine to inhale its bouquet; and something in his posture was terrifyingly familiar to Ambrose. In a chill flash of horror, his memory told him that the thin, pointed features behind the square beard were dubiously similar to those of Jehan Mauvaissoir, whom he had often seen in the household of Azédarac, and who, as he had reason to believe, was implicated in the Bishop's sorceries. He wondered why he had not placed the resemblance before, and what wizardry had drugged his powers of recollection. Even now he was not sure; but the mere suspicion terrified him as if some deadly serpent had reared its head across the table.

"Drink, Brother Ambrose," urged the Sieur des Émaux, draining his own goblet. "To your welfare and that of all good Benedictines."

Ambrose hesitated. The cold, hypnotic eyes of his interlocutor were upon him, and he was powerless to refuse, in spite of all his apprehensions. Shuddering slightly, with the sense of some irresistible compulsion, and feeling that he might drop dead from the virulent working of a sudden poison, he emptied his goblet.

An instant more, and he felt that his worst fears had been justified. The wine burned like the liquid flames of Phlegeton in his throat and on his lips; it seemed to fill his veins with a hot, infernal quicksilver. Then, all at once, an unbearable cold had inundated his being; an icy whirlwind wrapped him round with coils of roaring air, the chair melted beneath him, and he was falling through endless glacial gulfs. The walls of the inn had flown like receding vapors; the lights went out like stars in the black mist of a marsh; and the face of the Sieur des Émaux faded with them on the swirling shadows, even as a bubble that breaks on the milling of midnight waters.

III

It was with some difficulty that Ambrose assured himself that he was not dead. He had seemed to fall eternally, through a gray night that was peopled with ever-changing forms, with blurred unstable masses that dissolved to other masses before they could assume definitude.

For a moment, he thought there were walls about him once more; and then he was plunging from terrace to terrace of a world of phantom trees. At whiles, he thought also that there were human faces; but all was doubtful and evanescent, all was drifting smoke and surging shadow.

Abruptly, with no sense of transition or impact, he found that he was no longer falling. The vague fantasmagoria around him had returned to an actual scene—but a scene in which there was no trace of the Inn of Bonne Jouissance, or the Sieur des Émaux.

Ambrose peered about with incredulous eyes on a situation that was truly unbelievable. He was sitting in broad daylight on a large square block of roughly hewn granite. Around him, at a little distance, beyond the open space of a grassy glade, were the lofty pines and spreading beeches of an elder forest, whose boughs were already touched by the gold of the declining sun. Immediately before him, several men were standing.

These men appeared to regard Ambrose with a profound and almost religious amazement. They were bearded and savage of aspect, with white robes of a fashion he had never before seen. Their hair was long and matted, like tangles of black snakes; and their eyes burned with a frenetic fire. Each of them bore in his right hand a rude knife of sharply chiseled stone.

Ambrose wondered if he had died after all, and if these beings were the strange devils of some unlisted Hell. In the face of what had happened, and the light of Ambrose's own beliefs, it was a far from unreasonable conjecture. He peered with fearful trepidation at the supposed demons, and began to mumble a prayer to the God who had abandoned him so inexplicably to his spiritual foes. Then he remembered the necromantic powers of Azédarac, and conceived another surmise—that he had been spirited bodily away from the Inn of Bonne Jouissance, and delivered into the hands of those pre-Satanic entities that served the sorcerous Bishop. Becoming convinced of his own physical solidity and integrity, and reflecting that such was scarcely the appropriate condition of a disincarnate soul, and also that the sylvan scene about him was hardly characteristic of the infernal regions, he accepted this as the true explanation. He was still alive, and still on earth, though the circumstances of his situation were more than mysterious, and were fraught with dire, unknowable danger.

The strange beings had maintained an utter silence, as if they were too dumbfounded for speech. Hearing the prayerful murmurs of Ambrose, they seemed to recover from their surprise, and became not only articulate but vociferous. Ambrose could make nothing of their harsh vocables, in which sibilants and aspirates and gutturals were often combined in a manner difficult for the normal human tongue to imitate. However, he caught the word *taranit,* several times repeated, and wondered if it were the name of an especially malevolent demon.

The speech of the weird beings began to assume a sort of rude rhythm, like the intonations of some primordial chant. Two of them stepped forward and seized Ambrose, while the voices of their companions rose in a shrill, triumphant litany.

Scarcely knowing what had happened, and still less what was to follow, Ambrose was flung supine on the granite block, and was held down by one of his captors, while the other raised aloft the keen blade of chiseled flint which he carried. The blade was poised in air above Ambrose's heart, and the monk realized in sudden terror that it would fall with dire velocity and pierce him through before the lapse of another moment.

Then, above the demoniac chanting, which had risen to a mad, malignant frenzy, he heard the sweet and imperious cry of a woman's voice. In the wild confusion of his terror, the words were strange and meaningless to him; but plainly they were understood by his captors, and were taken as an undeniable command. The stone knife was lowered sullenly, and Ambrose was permitted to resume a sitting posture on the flat slab.

His rescuer was standing on the edge of the open glade, in the wide-flung umbrage of an ancient pine. She came forward now; and the white-garmented beings fell back with evident respect before her. She was very tall, with a fearless and regal demeanor, and was gowned in a dark, shimmering blue, like the star-laden blue of nocturnal summer skies. Her hair was knotted in a long golden-brown braid, heavy as the glistening coils of some Eastern serpent. Her eyes were a strange amber, her lips a vermilion touched with the coolness of woodland shadow, and her skin was of alabastrine fairness. Ambrose saw that she was beautiful; but she inspired him with the same awe that he would have felt before a queen, together with something of the fear and consternation which a virtuous young monk would conceive in the perilous presence of an alluring succubus.

"Come with me," she said to Ambrose, in a tongue that his monastic studies enabled him to recognize as an obsolete variant of the French of Averoigne—a tongue that no man had supposedly spoken for many hundred years. Obediently and in great wonder, he arose and followed her, with no hindrance from his glowering and reluctant captors.

❖

The woman led him to a narrow path that wound sinuously away through the deep forest. In a few moments, the glade, the granite block, and the cluster of white-robed men were lost to sight behind the heavy foliage.

"Who are you?" asked the lady, turning to Ambrose. "You look like one of those crazy missionaries who are beginning to enter Averoigne nowadays. I believe that people call them Christians. The Druids have sacrificed so many of them to Taranit, that I marvel at your temerity in coming here."

Ambrose found it difficult to comprehend the archaic phrasing; and the import of her words was so utterly strange and baffling that he felt sure he must have misunderstood her.

"I am Brother Ambrose," he replied, expressing himself slowly and awkwardly in the long-disused dialect. "Of course, I am a Christian; but I confess that I fail to understand you. I have heard of the pagan Druids; but surely they were all driven from Averoigne many centuries ago."

The woman stared at Ambrose, with open amazement and pity. Her brownish-yellow eyes were bright and clear as a mellowed wine.

"Poor little one," she said. "I fear that your dreadful experiences have served to unsettle you. It was fortunate that I came along when I did, and decided to intervene. I seldom interfere with the Druids and their sacrifices; but I saw you sitting on their altar a little while agone, and was struck by your youth and comeliness."

Ambrose felt more and more that he had been made the victim of a most peculiar sorcery; but, even yet, he was far from suspecting the true magnitude of this sorcery. Amid his bemusement and consternation, however, he realized that he owed his life to the singular and lovely woman beside him, and began to stammer out his gratitude.

"You need not thank me," said the lady, with a dulcet smile. "I am Moriamis, the enchantress, and the Druids fear my magic, which is more sovereign and more excellent than theirs, though I use it only for the welfare of men and not for their bale or bane."

The monk was dismayed to learn that his fair rescuer was a sorceress, even though her powers were professedly benignant. The knowledge added to his alarm; but he felt that it would be politic to conceal his emotions in this regard.

"Indeed, I am grateful to you," he protested. "And now, if you can tell me the way to the Inn of Bonne Jouissance, which I left not long ago, I shall owe you a further debt."

Moriamis knitted her light brows. "I have never heard of the Inn of Bonne Jouissance. There is no such place in this region."

"But this is the forest of Averoigne, is it not?" inquired the puzzled Ambrose. "And surely we are not far from the road that runs between the town of Ximes and the city of Vyones?"

"I have never heard of Ximes, or Vyones, either," said Moriamis. "Truly, the land is known as Averoigne, and this forest is the great wood of Averoigne, which men have called by that name from primeval years. But there are no towns such as the ones whereof you speak, Brother Ambrose. I fear that you still wander a little in your mind."

Ambrose was aware of a maddening perplexity. "I have been most damnably beguiled," he said, half to himself. "It is all the doing of that abominable sorcerer, Azédarac, I am sure."

The woman started as if she had been stung by a wild bee. There was something both eager and severe in the searching gaze that she turned upon Ambrose.

"Azédarac?" she queried. "What do you know of Azédarac? I was once acquainted with some one by that name; and I wonder if it could be the same person. Is he tall and a little gray, with hot, dark eyes, and a proud, half-angry air, and a crescent scar on the brow?"

Greatly mystified, and more troubled than ever, Ambrose admitted the veracity of her description. Realizing that in some unknown way he had stumbled upon the hidden antecedents of the sorcerer, he confided the story of his adventures to Moriamis, hoping that she would reciprocate with further information concerning Azédarac.

The woman listened with the air of one who is much interested but not at all surprised.

"I understand now," she observed, when he had finished. "Anon I shall explain everything that mystifies and troubles you. I think I know this Jehan Mauvaissoir, also; he has long been the man-servant of Azédarac, though his name was Melchire in other days. These two have always been the underlings of evil, and have served the Old Ones in ways forgotten or never known by the Druids."

"Indeed, I hope you can explain what has happened," said Ambrose. "It is a fearsome and strange and ungodly thing, to drink a draft of wine in a tavern at eventide, and then find one's self in the heart of the forest by afternoon daylight, among demons such as those from whom you succored me."

"Yea," countered Moriamis, "it is even stranger than you dream. Tell me, Brother Ambrose, what was the year in which you entered the Inn of Bonne Jouissance?"

"Why, it is the year of our Lord, 1175, of course. What other year could it be?"

"The Druids use a different chronology," replied Moriamis, "and their notation would mean nothing to you. But, according to that which the Christian missionaries would now introduce in Averoigne, the present year is 475 A. D. You have been sent back no less than seven hundred years into what the people of your era would regard as the past. The Druid altar on which I found you lying is probably located on the future site of the Inn of Bonne Jouissance."

Ambrose was more than dumbfounded. His mind was unable to grasp the entire import of Moriamis's words.

"But how can such things be?" he cried. "How can a man go backward in time, among years and people that have long turned to dust?"

"That, mayhap, is a mystery for Azédarac to unriddle. However, the past and the future co-exist with what we call the present, and are merely the two segments of the circle of time. We see them and name them according to our own position in the circle."

Ambrose felt that he had fallen among necromancies of a most unhallowed and unexampled sort, and had been made the victim of diableries unknown to the Christian catalogues.

Tongue-tied by a consciousness that all comment, all protest or even prayer would prove inadequate to the situation, he saw that a stone tower with small lozenge-shaped windows was now visible above the turrets of pine along the path which he and Moriamis were following.

"This is my home," said Moriamis, as they came forth from beneath the thinning trees at the foot of a little knoll on which the tower was situated. "Brother Ambrose, you must be my guest."

Ambrose was unable to decline the proffered hospitality, in spite of his feeling that Moriamis was hardly the most suitable of chatelaines for a chaste and God-fearing monk. However, the pious misgivings with which she inspired him were not unmingled with fascination. Also, like a lost child, he clung to the only available protection in a land of fearful perils and astounding mysteries.

The interior of the tower was neat and clean and home-like, though with furniture of a ruder sort than that to which Ambrose was accustomed, and rich but roughly woven arrases. A serving-woman, tall as Moriamis herself, but darker, brought to him a huge bowl of milk and wheaten bread, and the monk was now able to assuage the hunger that had gone unsatisfied in the Inn of Bonne Jouissance.

As he seated himself before the simple fare, he realized that the Book of Eibon was still heavy in the bosom of his gown. He removed the volume, and gave it gingerly to Moriamis. Her eyes widened, but she made no comment until he had finished his meal. Then she said:

"This volume is indeed the property of Azédarac, who was formerly a neighbor of mine. I knew the scoundrel quite well—in fact, I knew him all too well." Her bosom heaved with an obscure emotion as she paused for a moment. "He was the wisest and the mightiest of sorcerers, and the most secret withal; for no one knew the time and the manner of his coming into Averoigne, or the fashion in which he had procured the immemorial Book of Eibon, whose runic writings were beyond the lore of all other wizards. He was master of all enchantments and all demons, and likewise a compounder of mighty potions. Among these were certain philtres, blended with potent spells and possessed of unique virtue, that would send the drinker backward or forward in time. One of them, I believe, was administered to you by Melchire, or Jehan Mauvaissoir; and Azédarac himself, together with this manservant, made use of another—perhaps not for the first time—when they went onward from the present age of the Druids into that age of Christian authority to which you belong. There was a blood-red vial for the past, and a green for the future. Behold! I possess one of each—though Azédarac was unaware that I knew of their existence."

She opened a little cupboard, in which were the various charms and medicaments, the sun-dried herbs and moon-compounded essences that a sorceress would employ. From among them she brought out the two vials, one of which contained a sanguine-colored liquid, and the other a fluid of emerald brightness.

"I stole them one day, out of womanly curiosity, from his hidden store of philtres and elixirs and magistrals," continued Moriamis. "I could have followed the rascal when he disappeared into the future, if I had chosen to do so. But I am well enough content with my own age; and moreover, I am not the sort of woman who pursues a wearied and reluctant lover."

"Then," said Ambrose, more bewildered than ever, but hopeful, "if I were to drink the contents of the green vial, I should return to my own epoch."

"Precisely. And I am sure, from what you have told me, that your return would be a source of much annoyance to Azédarac. It is like the fellow, to have established himself in a fat prelacy. He was ever the master of circumstance, with an eye to his own accommodation and comfort. It would hardly please him, I am sure, if you were to reach the Archbishop . . . I am not revengeful by nature . . . but on the other hand—"

"It is hard to understand how any one could have wearied of you," said Ambrose, gallantly, as he began to comprehend the situation.

Moriamis smiled. "That is prettily said. And you are really a charming youth, in spite of that dismal-looking robe. I am glad that I rescued you from the Druids, who would have torn your heart out and offered it to their demon, Taranit."

"And now you will send me back?"

Moriamis frowned a little, and then assumed her most seductive air.

"Are you in such a hurry to leave your hostess? Now that you are living in another century than your own, a day, a week or a month will make no difference in the date of your return. I have also retained the formulas of Azédarac; and I know how to graduate the potion, if necessary. The usual period of transportation in time is exactly seven hundred years; but the philtre can be strengthened or weakened a little."

The sun had fallen beyond the pines, and a soft twilight was beginning to invade the tower. The maid-servant had left the room. Moriamis came over and seated herself beside Ambrose on the rough bench he was occupying. Still smiling, she fixed her amber eyes upon him, with a languid flame in their depths—a flame that seemed to brighten as the dusk grew stronger. Without speaking, she began slowly to unbraid her heavy hair, from which there emanated a perfume that was subtle and delicious as the perfume of grape-flowers.

Ambrose was embarrassed by this delightful proximity. "I am not sure that it would be right for me to remain, after all. What would the Archbishop think?"

"My dear child, the Archbishop will not even be born for at least six hundred and fifty years. And it will be still longer before you are born. And when you return, anything that you have done during your stay with me will have happened no less than seven centuries ago . . . which should be long enough to procure the remission of any sin, no matter how often repeated."

Like a man who has been taken in the coils of some fantastic dream, and finds that the dream is not altogether disagreeable, Ambrose yielded to this feminine and irrefutable reasoning. He hardly knew what was to happen; but, under the exceptional circumstances indicated by Moriamis, the rigors of monastic discipline might well be relaxed to almost any conceivable degree, without entailing spiritual perdition or even a serious breach of vows.

IV

A month later, Moriamis and Ambrose were standing beside the Druid altar. It was late in the evening; and a slightly gibbous moon had risen upon the deserted glade and was fringing the treetops with wefted silver. The warm breath of the summer night was gentle as the sighing of a woman in slumber.

"Must you go, after all?" said Moriamis in a pleading and regretful voice.

"It is my duty. I must return to Clément with the Book of Eibon and the other evidence I have collected against Azédarac." The words sounded a little unreal to Ambrose as he uttered them; and he tried very hard, but vainly, to convince himself of the cogency and validity of his arguments. The idyll of his stay with Moriamis, to which he was oddly unable to attach any true conviction of sin, had given to all that preceded it a certain dismal insubstantiality. Free from all responsibility or restraint, in the sheer obliviousness of dreams, he had lived like a happy pagan; and now he must go back to the drear existence of a mediæval monk, beneath the prompting of an obscure sense of duty.

"I shall not try to hold you," Moriamis sighed. "But I shall miss you, and remember you as a worthy lover and a pleasant playmate. Here is the philtre."

The green essence was cold and almost hueless in the moonlight, as Moriamis poured it into a little cup and gave it to Ambrose.

"Are you sure of its precise efficacy?" the monk inquired. "Are you sure that I shall return to the Inn of Bonne Jouissance, at a time not far subsequent to that of my departure therefrom?"

"Yea," said Moriamis, "for the potion is infallible. But stay, I have also brought along the other vial—the vial of the past. Take it with you—for who knows, you may sometime wish to return and visit me again."

❧

Ambrose accepted the red vial and placed it in his robe beside the ancient manual of Hyperborean sorcery. Then, after an appropriate farewell to Moriamis, he drained with sudden resolution the contents of the cup.

The moonlit glade, the gray altar, and Moriamis, all vanished in a swirl of flame and shadow. It seemed to Ambrose that he was soaring endlessly through fantasmagoric gulfs, amid the ceaseless shifting and melting of unstable things, the transient forming and fading of irresoluble worlds. At the end, he found himself sitting once more in the Inn of Bonne Jouissance, at what he assumed to be the very same table before which he had sat with the Sieur des Émaux. It was daylight, and the room was full of people, among whom he looked in vain for the rubicund face of the innkeeper, or the servants and fellow-guests he had previously seen. All were unfamiliar to him; and the furniture was strangely worn, and was grimier than he remembered it.

Perceiving the presence of Ambrose, the people began to eye him with open curiosity and wonderment. A tall man with dolorous eyes and lantern jaws came hastily forward and bowed before him with an air that was half servile but full of a prying impertinence.

"What do you wish?" he asked.

"Is this the Inn of Bonne Jouissance?"

The innkeeper stared at Ambrose. "Nay, it is the Inn of Haute Espérance, of which I have been the taverner these thirty years. Could you not read the sign? It was called the Inn of Bonne Jouissance in my father's time, but the name was changed after his death."

Ambrose was filled with consternation. "But the inn was differently named, and was kept by another man when I visited it not long ago," he cried in his bewilderment. "The owner was a stout, jovial man, not in the least like you."

"That would answer the description of my father," said the taverner, eyeing Ambrose more dubiously than ever. "He has been dead for the full thirty years of which I speak; and surely you were not even born at the time of his decease."

Ambrose began to realize what had happened. The emerald potion, by some error or excess of potency, had taken him many years beyond his own time into the future!

"I must resume my journey to Vyones," he said in a bewildered voice, without fully comprehending the implications of his situation. "I have a message for Archbishop Clément—and must not delay longer in delivering it."

"But Clément has been dead even longer than my father," exclaimed the innkeeper. "From whence do you come that you are ignorant of this?" It was plain from his manner that he had begun to doubt the sanity of Ambrose. Others, overhearing the strange discussion, had begun to crowd about, and were plying the monk with jocular and sometimes ribald questions.

"And what of Azédarac, the Bishop of Ximes? Is he dead, too?" inquired Ambrose, desperately.

"You mean St. Azédarac, no doubt. He outlived Clément, but nevertheless he has been dead and duly canonized for thirty-two years. Some say that he did not die, but was transported to Heaven alive, and that his body was never buried in the great mausoleum reared for him at Ximes. But that is probably a mere legend."

Ambrose was overwhelmed with unspeakable desolation and confusion. In the meanwhile, the crowd about him had increased, and in spite of his robe, he was being made the subject of rude remarks and jeers.

"The good Brother has lost his wits," cried some. "The wines of Averoigne are too strong for him," said others.

"What year is this?" demanded Ambrose, in his desperation.

"The year of our Lord, 1230," replied the taverner, breaking into a derisive laugh. "And what year did you think it was?"

"It was the year 1175 when I last visited the Inn of Bonne Jouissance," admitted Ambrose.

His declaration was greeted with fresh jeers and laughter. "Hola, young sir, you were not even conceived at that time," the taverner said. Then, seeming to remember something, he went on in a more thoughtful tone: "When I was a child, my father told me of a young monk, about your age, who came to the Inn of Bonne Jouissance one evening in the summer of 1175, and vanished inexplicably after drinking a draft of red wine. I believe his name was Ambrose. Perhaps you are Ambrose, and have only just returned from a visit to nowhere." He gave a derisory wink, and the new jest was taken up and bandied from mouth to mouth among the frequenters of the tavern.

Ambrose was trying to realize the full import of his predicament. His mission was now useless, through the death or disappearance of Azédarac; and no one would remain in all Averoigne to recognize him or believe his story. He felt the hopelessness of his alienation among unknown years and people.

Suddenly he remembered the red vial given him at parting by Moriamis. The potion, like the green philtre, might prove uncertain in its effect; but he was seized by an all-consuming desire to escape from the weird embarrassment and wilderment of his present position. Also, he longed for Moriamis like a lost child for its mother; and the charm of his sojourn in the past was upon him with an irresistible spell. Ignoring the ribald faces and voices about him, he drew the vial from his bosom, uncorked it, and swallowed the contents.

He was back in the forest glade, by the gigantic altar. Moriamis was beside him again, lovely and warm and breathing; and the moon was still rising above the pine-tops. It seemed that no more than a few moments could have elapsed since he had said farewell to the beloved enchantress.

"I thought you might return," said Moriamis. "And I waited a little while."

Ambrose told her of the singular mishap that had attended his journey in time.

Moriamis nodded gravely. "The green philtre was more potent than I had supposed," she remarked. "It is fortunate, though, that the red philtre was equivalently strong, and could bring you back to me through all those added years. You will have to remain with me now, for I possessed only the two vials. I hope you are not sorry."

Ambrose proceeded to prove, in a somewhat unmonastic manner, that her hope was fully justified.

Neither then nor at any other time did Moriamis tell him that she herself had strengthened slightly and equally the two philtres by means of the private formula which she had also stolen from Azédarac.

THE BEAST
OF AVEROIGNE

Old age, like a moth in some fading arras, will gnaw my memories oversoon, as it gnaws the memories of all men. Therefore I, Luc le Chaudronnier, sometime known as astrologer and sorcerer, write this account of the true origin and slaying of the Beast of Averoigne. And when I have ended, the writing shall be sealed in a brazen box, and the box be set in a secret chamber of my house at Ximes, so that no man shall learn the verity of this matter till many years and decades have gone by. Indeed, it were not well for such evil prodigies to be divulged while any who took part in them are still on the earthward side of Purgatory. And at present the truth is known only to me and to certain others who are sworn to maintain secrecy.

As all men know, the advent of the Beast was coeval with the coming of that red comet which rose behind the Dragon in the early summer of 1369. Like Satan's rutilant hair, trailing on the wind of Gehenna as he hastens worldward, the comet streamed nightly above Averoigne, bringing the fear of bale and pestilence in its train. And soon the rumor of a strange evil, a foulness unheard of in any legend, passed among the people.

To Brother Gerome of the Benedictine Abbey of Perigon it was given to behold this evil ere the horror thereof became manifest to others. Returning late to the monastery from an errand in Ste. Zenobie, Gerome was overtaken by darkness. No moon arose to lantern his way through the forest; but, between the gnarled boughs of antic oaks, he saw the vengefully streaming fire of the comet, which seemed to pursue him as he went. And Gerome felt an eerie fear of the pit-deep shadows, and he made haste toward the abbey postern.

Passing among the ancient trees that towered thickly behind Perigon, he thought that he discerned a light from the windows, and was much cheered thereby. But, going on, he saw that the light was near at hand, beneath a lowering bough. It moved as with the flitting of a fen-fire, and was of changeable color, being pale as a corposant, or ruddy as new-spilled blood, or green as the poisonous distillation that surrounds the moon.

Then, with terror ineffable, Gerome beheld the thing to which the light clung like a hellish nimbus, moving as it moved, and revealing dimly the black abomination of head and limbs that were not those of any creature wrought by God. The horror stood erect, rising to more than the height of a tall man; and it swayed like a great serpent, and its members undulated, bending like heated wax. The flat black head was thrust forward on a snakish neck. The eyes, small and lidless, glowing like coals from a wizard's brazier, were set low and near together in a noseless face above the serrate gleaming of such teeth as might belong to a giant bat.

This much, and no more, Gerome saw, ere the thing went past him with its nimbus flaring from venomous green to a wrathful red. Of its actual shape, and the number of its limbs, he could form no just notion. Running and slithering rapidly, it disappeared among the antique oaks, and he saw the hellish light no more.

Nigh dead with fear, Gerome reached the abbey postern and sought admittance. And the porter, hearing the tale of that which he had met in the moonless wood, forbore to chide him for his tardiness.

Before nones, on the morrow, a dead stag was found in the forest behind Perigon. It had been slain in some ungodly fashion, not by wolf or poacher or hunter. It was unmarked by any wound, other than a wide gash that had laid open the spine from neck to tail. The spine itself had been shattered and the white marrow sucked therefrom; but no other portion had been devoured. None could surmise the nature of the beast that slew and ravened in such fashion. But the good Brothers, heedful of the story told by Gerome, believed that some creature from the Pit was abroad in Averoigne. And Gerome marveled at the mercy of God, which had permitted him to escape the doom of the stag.

Now, night by night, the comet greatened, burning like an evil mist of blood and fire, while the stars blenched before it. And day by day, from peasants, priests, woodcutters, and others who came to the abbey, the Benedictines heard tales of fearsome and mysterious depredations. Dead wolves were found with their chines laid open and the white marrow gone; and an ox and a horse were treated in like fashion. Then, it seemed, the unknown beast grew bolder—or else it wearied of such humble prey as the creatures of farm and forest.

At first, it did not strike at living men, but assailed the dead like some foul eater of carrion. Two freshly buried corpses were found lying in the cemetery at Ste. Zenobie, where the thing had dug them from their graves and had bared their vertebrae. In each case, only a little of the marrow had been eaten; but, as if in rage or disappointment, the cadavers had been torn asunder, and the tatters of their flesh were mixed with the rags of their cerements. From this, it would seem that only the spinal marrow of creatures newly killed was pleasing to the monster.

Thereafterward, the dead were not again molested. But on the night following the desecration of the graves, two charcoal-burners, who plied their trade in the forest not far from Perigon, were slain in their hut. Other charcoal-burners, dwelling near by, heard the shrill screams that fell to sudden silence; and peering fearfully through the chinks of their bolted doors, they saw anon in the starlight the departure of a black, obscenely glowing shape that issued from the hut. Not till dawn did they dare to verify the fate of their fellows, who had been served in the same manner as the stag, the wolves, and the corpses.

Theophile, the abbot of Perigon, was much exercised over this evil that had chosen to manifest itself in the neighborhood and whose depredations were all committed within a few hours' journey of the abbey. Pale from over-strict austerities and vigils, he called the monks before him in assembly; and a martial ardor against the minions of Asmodai blazed in his hollowed eyes as he spoke.

"Truly," he said, "there is a great devil among us, that has risen with the comet from Malebolge. We, the Brothers of Perigon, must go forth with cross and holy water to hunt the devil in its hidden lair, which lies haply at our very portals."

So, on the forenoon of that same day, Theophile, together with Gerome and six others chosen for their hardihood, sallied forth and made search of the forest for miles around. They entered with lit torches and lifted crosses the deep caves to which they came, but found no fiercer thing than wolf or badger. Also, they searched the crumbling vaults of the deserted castle of Faussesflammes, which was said to be haunted by vampires. But nowhere could they trace the monster or find any sign of its lairing.

With nightly deeds of terror, beneath the comet's blasting, the middle summer went by. Men, women, children, to the number of more than forty, were done to death by the Beast, which, though seeming to haunt mainly the environs of the abbey, ranged afield at times even to the shores of the river Isoile and the gates of La Frenâie and Ximes. There were those who beheld it by night, a black and slithering foulness clad in changeable luminescence; but no man saw it by day. And always the thing was silent, uttering no sound; and was swifter in its motion than the weaving viper.

Once, it was seen by moonlight in the abbey garden, as it glided toward the forest between rows of peas and turnips. Then, coming in darkness, it struck within the walls. Without waking the others, on whom it must have cast a Lethean spell, it took Brother Gerome, slumbering on his pallet at the end of the row, in the dormitory. And the fell deed was not discovered till daybreak, when the monk who slept nearest to Gerome awakened and saw his body, which lay face downward with the back of the robe and the flesh beneath in bloody tatters.

A week later, it came and dealt likewise with Brother Augustin. And in spite of exorcisms and the sprinkling of holy water at all doors and windows, it was seen afterward, gliding along the monastery halls; and it left an unspeakably blasphemous sign of its presence in the chapel. Many believed that it menaced the abbot himself; for Brother Constantin the cellarer, returning late from a visit to Vyones, saw it by starlight as it climbed the outer wall toward that window of Theophile's cell which faced the great forest. And seeing Constantin, the thing dropped to the ground like a huge ape and vanished among the trees.

Great was the scandal of these happenings, and the consternation of the monks. Sorely, it was said, the matter preyed on the abbot, who kept his cell in unremitting prayer and vigil. Pale and meager as a dying saint he grew, mortifying the flesh till he tottered with weakness; and a feverish illness devoured him visibly.

More and more, apart from this haunting of the monastery, the horror fared afield, even invading walled towns. Toward the middle of August, when the comet was beginning to decline a little, there occurred the grievous death of Sister Therese, the young and beloved niece of Theophile, killed by the hellish Beast in her cell at the Benedictine convent of Ximes. On this occasion the monster was met by late passers in the streets, and others watched it climb the city ramparts, running like some enormous beetle or spider on the sheer stone as it fled from Ximes to regain its hidden lair.

In her dead hands, it was told, the pious Therese held tightly clasped a letter from Theophile in which he had spoken at some length of the dire happenings at the monastery, and had confessed his grief and despair at being unable to cope with the Satanic horror.

All this, in the course of the summer, came to me in my house at Ximes. From the beginning, because of my commerce with occult things and the powers of darkness, the unknown Beast was the subject of my concern. I knew that it was no creature of earth or of the terrene hells; but regarding its actual character and genesis I could learn no more at first than any other. Vainly I consulted the stars and made use of geomancy and necromancy; and the familiars whom I interrogated professed themselves ignorant, saying that the Beast was altogether alien and beyond the ken of sublunar spirits.

Then I bethought me of that strange, oracular ring which I had inherited from my fathers, who were also wizards. The ring had come down from ancient Hyperborea, and had once been the property of the sorcerer Eibon. It was made of a redder gold than any that the Earth had yielded in latter cycles, and was set with a large purple gem, somber and smoldering, whose like is no longer to be found. In the gem an antique demon was held captive, a spirit from pre-human worlds, which would answer the interrogation of sorcerers.

So, from a rarely opened casket, I brought out the ring and made such preparations as were needful for the questioning. And when the purple stone was held inverted above a small brazier filled with hotly burning amber, the demon made answer, speaking in a shrill voice that was like the singing of fire. It told me the origin of the Beast, which had come from the red comet, and belonged to a race of stellar devils that had not visited the Earth since the foundering of Atlantis; and it told me the attributes of the Beast, which, in its own proper form, was invisible and intangible to men, and could manifest itself only in a fashion supremely abominable. Moreover, it informed me of the one method by which the Beast could be vanquished, if overtaken in a tangible shape. Even to me, the student of darkness, these revelations were a source of horror and surprise. And for many reasons, I deemed the mode of exorcism a doubtful and perilous thing. But the demon had sworn that there was no other way.

Musing on that which I had learned, I waited among my books and alembics; for the stars had warned me that my intervention would be required in good time.

To me, following the death of Sister Therese, there came privily the marshal of Ximes, together with the abbot Theophile, in whose worn features and bowed form I descried the ravages of mortal sorrow and horror and humiliation. And the two, albeit with palpable hesitancy, asked my advice and assistance in the laying of the Beast.

"You, Messire le Chaudronnier," said the marshal, "are reputed to know the arcanic arts of sorcery, and the spells which summon and dismiss demons. Therefore, in dealing with this devil, it may be that you shall succeed where all others have failed. Not willingly do we employ you in the matter, since it is not seemly for the church and the law to ally themselves with wizardry. But the need is desperate, lest the demon should take other victims. In return for your aid we can promise you a goodly reward of gold and a guarantee of lifelong immunity from all inquisition which your doings might otherwise invite. The Bishop of Ximes, and the Archbishop of Vyones, are privy to this offer, which must be kept secret."

"I ask no reward," I replied, "if it be in my power to rid Averoigne of this scourge. But you have set me a difficult task, and one that is haply attended by strange perils."

"All assistance that can be given you shall be yours to command," said the marshal. "Men-at-arms shall attend you, if need be."

Then Theophile, speaking in a low, broken voice, assured me that all doors, including those of the abbey of Perigon, would be opened at my request, and that everything possible would be done to further the laying of the fiend.

I reflected briefly, and said:

"Go now, but send to me, an hour before sunset, two men-at-arms, mounted, and with a third steed. And let the men be chosen for their valor and discretion: for this very night I shall visit Perigon, where the horror seems to center."

Remembering the advice of the gem-imprisoned demon, I made no preparation for the journey, except to place upon my index finger the ring of Eibon, and to arm myself with a small hammer, which I placed at my girdle in lieu of a sword. Then I awaited the set hour, when the men and the horses came to my house, as had been stipulated.

The men were stout and tested warriors, clad in chain-mail, and carrying swords and halberds. I mounted the third horse, a black and spirited mare, and we rode forth from Ximes toward Perigon, taking a direct and little-used way which ran through the werewolf-haunted forest.

My companions were taciturn, speaking only in answer to some question, and then briefly. This pleased me; for I knew they would maintain a discreet silence regarding that which might occur before dawn. Swiftly we rode, while the sun sank in a redness as of welling blood among the tall trees; and soon the darkness wove its thickening webs from bough to bough, closing upon us like some inexorable net of evil. Deeper we went, into the brooding woods; and even I, the master of sorceries, trembled a little at the knowledge of all that was abroad in the darkness.

Undelayed and unmolested, however, we came to the abbey at late moonrise, when all the monks, except the aged porter, had retired to their dormitory. The abbot, returning at sunset from Ximes, had given word to the porter of our coming, and he would have admitted us; but this, as it happened, was no part of my plan. Saying I had reason to believe the Beast would re-enter the abbey that very night, I told the porter my intention of waiting outside the walls to intercept it, and merely asked him to accompany us in a tour of the building's exterior, so that he could point out the various rooms. This he did, and during the tour, he indicated a certain window in the second story as being that of Theophile's cell. The window faced the forest, and I remarked the abbot's rashness in leaving it open. This, the porter told me, was his invariable custom, in spite of the oft-repeated demoniac invasions of the monastery. Behind the window we saw the glimmering of a taper, as if the abbot were keeping late vigil.

We had committed our horses to the porter's care. After he had conducted us around the building and had left us, we returned to the space before Theophile's window and began our long watch.

Pale and hollow as the face of a corpse, the moon rose higher, swimming above the somber oaks, and pouring a spectral silver on the gray stone of the abbey walls. In the west the comet flamed among the lusterless signs, veiling the lifted sting of the Scorpion as it sank.

We waited hour by hour in the shortening shadow of a tall oak, where none could see us from the windows. When the moon had passed over, sloping westward, the shadow began to lengthen toward the wall. All was mortally still, and we saw no movement, apart from the slow shifting of the light and shade. Half-way between midnight and dawn the taper went out in Theophile's cell, as if it had burned to the socket; and thereafter the room remained dark.

Unquestioning, with ready weapons, the men-at-arms companioned me in that vigil. Well they knew the demonian terror which they might face before dawn; but there was no trepidation in their bearing. And knowing much that they could not know, I drew the ring of Eibon from my finger, and made ready for that which the demon had directed me to do.

The men stood nearer than I to the forest, facing it perpetually according to a strict order that I had given. But nothing stirred in the fretted gloom; and the slow night ebbed; and the skies grew paler, as if with morning twilight. Then, an hour before sunrise, when the shadow of the great oak had reached the wall and was climbing toward Theophile's window, there came the thing I had anticipated. Very suddenly it came, and without forewarning of its nearness, a horror of hellish red light, swift as a kindling, wind-blown flame, that leapt from the forest gloom and sprang upon us where we stood stiff and weary from our night-long vigil.

One of the men-at-arms was borne to the ground; and I saw above him, in a floating redness as of ghostly blood, the black and semi-serpentine form of the Beast. A flat and snakish head, without ears or nose, was tearing at the man's armor with sharp, serrate teeth, and I heard the teeth clash and grate on the linked iron. Swiftly I laid the ring of Eibon on a stone I had placed in readiness, and broke the dark jewel with a blow of the hammer that I carried.

From the pieces of the lightly shattered gem, the disemprisoned demon rose in the form of a smoky fire, small as a candle-flame at first, and greatening like the conflagration of piled faggots. And, hissing softly with the voice of fire, and brightening to a wrathful, terrible gold, the demon leapt forward to do battle with the Beast, even as it had promised me, in return for its freedom after cycles of captivity.

It closed upon the Beast with a vengeful flaring, tall as the flame of an auto-da-fé, and, the Beast relinquished the man-at-arms on the ground beneath it, and writhed back like a burnt serpent. The body and members of the Beast were loathfully convulsed, and they seemed to melt in the manner of wax and to change dimly and horribly beneath the flame, undergoing an incredible metamorphosis. Moment by moment, like a werewolf that returns from its beasthood, the thing took on the wavering similitude of man. The unclean blackness flowed and swirled, assuming the weft of cloth amid its changes, and becoming the folds of a dark robe and cowl such as are worn by the Benedictines. Then, from the cowl, a face began to peer; and the face, though shadowy and distorted, was that of the abbot Theophile.

This prodigy I beheld for an instant; and the men also beheld it. But still the fire-shaped demon assailed the abhorrently transfigured thing, and the face melted again into waxy blackness, and a great column of sooty smoke arose, followed by an odor as of burning flesh commingled with some mighty foulness. And out of the volumed smoke, above the hissing of the demon, there came a single cry in the voice of Theophile. But the smoke thickened, hiding both the assailant and that which it assailed; and there was no sound, other than the singing of fed fire.

At last, the sable fumes began to lift, ascending and disappearing amid the boughs, and a dancing golden light, in the shape of a will-o'-the-wisp, went soaring over the dark trees toward the stars. And I knew that the demon of the ring had fulfilled its promise, and had now gone back to those remote and ultra-mundane deeps from which the sorcerer Eibon had drawn it down in Hyperborea to become the captive of the purple gem.

The stench of burning passed from the air, together with the mighty foulness; and of that which had been the Beast there was no longer any trace. So I knew that the horror born of the red comet had been driven away by the fiery demon. The fallen man-at-arms had risen, unharmed beneath his mail, and he and his fellow stood beside me, saying naught. But I knew that they had seen the changes of the Beast, and had divined something of the truth. So, while the moon grew gray with the nearness of dawn, I made them swear an awful oath of secrecy, and enjoined them to bear witness to the statement I must make before the monks of Perigon.

Then, having settled this matter, so that the good renown of the holy Theophile should suffer no calumny, we aroused the porter. We averred that the Beast had come upon us unaware, and had gained the abbot's cell before we could prevent it, and had come forth again, carrying Theophile with its snakish members as if to bear him away to the sunken comet. I had exorcised the unclean devil, which had vanished in a cloud of sulfurous fire and vapor; and, most unluckily, the abbot had been consumed by the fire. His death, I said, was a true martyrdom, and would not be in vain: the Beast would no longer plague the country or bedevil Perigon, since the exorcism I had used was infallible.

This tale was accepted without question by the Brothers, who grieved mightily for their good abbot. Indeed, the tale was true enough, for Theophile had been innocent, and was wholly ignorant of the foul change that came upon him nightly in his cell, and the deeds that were done by the Beast through his loathfully transfigured body. Each night the thing had come down from the passing comet to assuage its hellish hunger; and being otherwise impalpable and powerless, it had used the abbot for its energumen, molding his flesh in the image of some obscene monster from beyond the stars.

It had slain a peasant girl in Ste. Zenobie on that night while we waited behind the abbey. But thereafter the Beast was seen no more in Averoigne; and its murderous deeds were not repeated.

⚜

In time the comet passed to other heavens, fading slowly; and the black terror it had wrought became a varying legend, even as all other bygone things. The abbot Theophile was canonized for his strange martyrdom; and they who read this record in future ages will believe it not, saying that no demon or malign spirit could have prevailed thus upon true holiness. Indeed, it were well that none should believe the story: for thin is the veil betwixt man and the godless deep. The skies are haunted by that which it were madness to know; and strange abominations pass evermore between earth and moon and athwart the galaxies. Unnamable things have come to us in alien horror and will come again. And the evil of the stars is not as the evil of Earth.

THE EMPIRE OF
THE NECROMANCERS

The legend of Mmatmuor and Sodosma shall arise only in the latter cycles of Earth, when the glad legends of the prime have been forgotten. Before the time of its telling, many epochs shall have passed away, and the seas shall have fallen in their beds, and new continents shall have come to birth. Perhaps, in that day, it will serve to beguile for a little the black weariness of a dying race, grown hopeless of all but oblivion. I tell the tale as men shall tell it in Zothique, the last continent, beneath a dim sun and sad heavens where the stars come out in terrible brightness before eventide.

I

Mmatmuor and Sodosma were necromancers who came from the dark isle of Naat, to practice their baleful arts in Tinarath, beyond the shrunken seas. But they did not prosper in Tinarath: for death was deemed a holy thing by the people of that gray country; and the nothingness of the tomb was not lightly to be desecrated; and the raising up of the dead by necromancy was held in abomination.

So, after a short interval, Mmatmuor and Sodosma were driven forth by the anger of the inhabitants, and were compelled to flee toward Cincor, a desert of the south, which was peopled only by the bones and mummies of a race that the pestilence had slain in former time.

The land into which they went lay drear and leprous and ashen below the huge ember-colored sun. Its crumbling rocks and deathly solitudes of sand would have struck terror to the hearts of common men; and, since they had been thrust in that barren place without food or sustenance, the plight of the sorcerers might well have seemed a desperate one. But, smiling secretly, with the air of conquerors who tread the approaches of a long-coveted realm, Sodosma and Mmatmuor walked steadily on into Cincor.

Unbroken before them, through fields devoid of trees and grass, and across the channels of dried-up rivers, there ran the great highway by which travelers had gone formerly between Cincor and Tinarath. Here they met no living thing; but soon they came to the skeletons of a horse and its rider, lying full in the road, and wearing still the sumptuous harness and raiment which they had worn in the flesh. And Mmatmuor and Sodosma paused before the piteous bones, on which no shred of corruption remained; and they smiled evilly at each other.

"The steed shall be yours," said Mmatmuor, "since you are a little the elder of us two, and are thus entitled to precedence; and the rider shall serve us both and be the first to acknowledge fealty to us in Cincor."

Then, in the ashy sand by the wayside, they drew a threefold circle; and standing together at its center, they performed the abominable rites that compel the dead to arise from tranquil nothingness and obey henceforward, in all things, the dark will of the necromancer. Afterward they sprinkled a pinch of magic powder on the nostril-holes of the man and the horse; and the white bones, creaking mournfully, rose up from where they had lain and stood in readiness to serve their masters.

So, as had been agreed between them, Sodosma mounted the skeleton steed and took up the jeweled reins, and rode in an evil mockery of Death on his pale horse; while Mmatmuor trudged on beside him, leaning lightly on an ebon staff; and the skeleton of the man, with its rich raiment flapping loosely, followed behind the two like a servitor.

After a while, in the gray waste, they found the remnant of another horse and rider, which the jackals had spared and the sun had dried to the leanness of old mummies. These also they raised up from death; and Mmatmuor bestrode the withered charger; and the two magicians rode on in state, like errant emperors, with a lich and a skeleton to attend them. Other bones and charnel remnants of men and beasts, to which they came anon, were duly resurrected in like fashion; so that they gathered to themselves an ever-swelling train in their progress through Cincor.

Along the way, as they neared Yethlyreom, which had been the capital, they found numerous tombs and necropoli, inviolate still after many ages, and containing swathed mummies that had scarcely withered in death. All these they raised up and called from sepulchral night to do their bidding. Some they commanded to sow and till the desert fields and hoist water from the sunken wells; others they left at diverse tasks, such as the mummies had performed in life. The century-long silence was broken by the noise and tumult of myriad activities; and the lank liches of weavers toiled at their shuttles; and the corpses of plowmen followed their furrows behind carrion oxen.

Weary with their strange journey and their oft-repeated incantations, Mmatmuor and Sodosma saw before them at last, from a desert hill, the lofty spires and fair, unbroken domes of Yethlyreom, steeped in the darkening stagnant blood of ominous sunset.

"It is a goodly land," said Mmatmuor, "and you and I will share it between us, and hold dominion over all its dead, and be crowned as emperors on the morrow in Yethlyreom."

"Aye," replied Sodosma, "for there is none living to dispute us here; and those that we have summoned from the tomb shall move and breathe only at our dictation, and may not rebel against us."

So, in the blood-red twilight that thickened with purple, they entered Yethlyreom and rode on among the lofty, lampless mansions, and installed themselves with their grisly retinue in that stately and abandoned palace, where the dynasty of Nimboth emperors had reigned for two thousand years with dominion over Cincor.

In the dusty golden halls, they lit the empty lamps of onyx by means of their cunning sorcery, and supped on royal viands, provided from past years, which they evoked in like manner. Ancient and imperial wines were poured for them in moonstone cups by the fleshless hands of their servitors; and they drank and feasted and reveled in fantasmagoric pomp, deferring till the morrow the resurrection of those who lay dead in Yethlyreom.

They rose betimes, in the dark of dawn, from the opulent palace-beds in which they had slept; for much remained to be done. Everywhere in that forgotten city, they went busily to and fro, working their spells on the people that died in the last year of the pest and had lain unburied. And having accomplished this, they passed beyond Yethlyreom into that other city of high tombs and mighty mausoleums, in which lay the Nimboth emperors and the more consequential citizens and nobles of Cincor.

Here they bade their skeleton slaves to break in the sealed doors with hammers and then, with their sinful, tyrannous incantations, they called forth the imperial mummies, even to the eldest of the dynasty, all of whom came walking stiffly, with lightless eyes, in rich swathings sewn with flame-bright jewels. And also, later, they brought forth to a semblance of life many generations of courtiers and dignitaries.

Moving in solemn pageant, with dark and haughty and hollow faces, the dead emperors and empresses of Cincor made obeisance to Mmatmuor and Sodosma, and attended them like a train of captives through all the streets of Yethlyreom. Afterward, in the immense throne-room of the palace, the necromancers mounted their high double throne, where the rightful rulers had sat with their consorts. Amid the assembled emperors, in gorgeous and funereal state, they were invested with sovereignty by the sere hands of the mummy of Hestaiyon, earliest of the Nimboth line, who had ruled in half-mythic years. Then all the descendants of Hestaiyon, crowding the room in a great throng, acclaimed with toneless, echo-like voices the dominion of Mmatmuor and Sodosma.

Thus did the outcast necromancers find for themselves an empire and a subject people in the desolate, barren land where the men of Tinarath had driven them forth to perish. Reigning supreme over all the dead of Cincor, by virtue of their malign magic, they exercised a baleful despotism. Tribute was borne to them by fleshless porters from outlying realms; and plague-eaten corpses, and tall mummies scented with mortuary balsams, went to and fro upon their errands in Yethlyreom, or heaped before their greedy eyes, from inexhaustible vaults, the cobweb-blackened gold and dusty gems of antique time.

Dead laborers made their palace-gardens to bloom with long-perished flowers; liches and skeletons toiled for them in the mines, or reared superb, fantastic towers to the dying sun. Chamberlains and princes of old time were their cupbearers, and stringed instruments were plucked for their delight by the slim hands of empresses with golden hair that had come forth untarnished from the night of the tomb. Those that were fairest, whom the plague and the worm had not ravaged overmuch, they took for their lemans and made to serve their necrophilic lust.

II

In all things, the people of Cincor performed the actions of life at the will of Mmatmuor and Sodosma. They spoke, they moved, they ate and drank as in life. They heard and saw and felt with a similitude of the senses that had been theirs before death; but their brains were enthralled by a dreadful necromancy. They recalled but dimly their former existence; and the state to which they had been summoned was empty and troublous and shadow-like. Their blood ran chill and sluggish, mingled with water of Lethe; ant the vapors of Lethe clouded their eyes.

Dumbly they obeyed the dictates of their tyrannous lords, without rebellion or protest, but filled with a vague, illimitable weariness such as the dead must know, when having drunk of eternal sleep, they are called back once more to the bitterness of mortal being. They knew no passion or desire or delight, only the black languor of their awakening from Lethe, and a gray, ceaseless longing to return to that interrupted slumber.

Youngest and last of the Nimboth emperors was Illeiro, who had died in the first month of the plague, and had lain in his high-built mausoleum for two hundred years before the coming of the necromancers.

Raised up with his people and his fathers to attend the tyrants, Illeiro had resumed the emptiness of existence without question and had felt no surprise. He had accepted his own resurrection and that of his ancestors as one accepts the indignities and marvels of a dream. He knew that he had come back to a faded sun, to a hollow and spectral world, to an order of things in which his place was merely that of an obedient shadow. But at first he was troubled only, like the others, by a dim weariness and a pale hunger for the lost oblivion.

Drugged by the magic of his overlords, weak from the age-long nullity of death, he beheld like a somnambulist the enormities to which his fathers were subjected. Yet, somehow, after many days, a feeble spark awoke in the sodden twilight of his mind.

Like something lost and irretrievable, beyond prodigious gulfs, he recalled the pomp of his reign in Yethlyreom, and the golden pride and exultation that had been his in youth. And recalling it, he felt a vague stirring of revolt, a ghostly resentment against the magicians who had haled him forth to this calamitous mockery of life. Darkly he began to grieve for his fallen state, and the mournful plight of his ancestors and his people.

Day by day, as a cup-bearer in the halls where he had ruled aforetime, Illeiro saw the doings of Mmatmuor and Sodosma. He saw their caprices of cruelty and lust, their growing drunkenness and gluttony. He watched them wallow in their necromantic luxury, and become lax with indolence, gross with indulgence. They neglected the study of their art, they forgot many of their spells. But still they ruled, mighty and formidable; and, lolling on couches of purple and rose, they planned to lead an army of the dead against Tinarath.

Dreaming of conquest, and of vaster necromancies, they grew fat and slothful as worms that have installed themselves in a charnel rich with corruption. And pace by pace with their laxness and tyranny, the fire of rebellion mounted in the shadowy heart of Illeiro, like a flame that struggles with Lethean damps. And slowly, with the waxing of his wrath, there returned to him something of the strength and firmness that had been his in life. Seeing the turpitude of the oppressors, and knowing the wrong that had been done to the helpless dead, he heard in his brain the clamor of stifled voices demanding vengeance.

Among his fathers, through the palace-halls of Yethlyreom, Illeiro moved silently at the bidding of the masters, or stood awaiting their command. He poured in their cups of onyx the amber vintages, brought by wizardry from hills beneath a younger sun; he submitted to their contumelies and insults. And night by night he watched them nod in their drunkenness, till they fell asleep, flushed and gross, amid their arrogated splendor.

There was little speech among the living dead; and son and father, daughter and mother, lover and beloved, went to and fro without sign of recognition, making no comment on their evil lot. But at last, one midnight, when the tyrants lay in slumber, and the flames wavered in the necromantic lamps, Illeiro took counsel with Hestaiyon, his eldest ancestor, who had been famed as a great wizard in fable and was reputed to have known the secret lore of antiquity.

— ❧ —

Hestaiyon stood apart from the others, in a corner of the shadowy hall. He was brown and withered in his crumbling mummy-cloths; and his lightless obsidian eyes appeared to gaze still upon nothingness. He seemed not to have heard the questions of Illeiro; but at length, in a dry, rustling whisper, he responded:

"I am old, and the night of the sepulcher was long, and I have forgotten much. Yet, groping backward across the void of death, it may be that I shall retrieve something of my former wisdom; and between us we shall devise a mode of deliverance." And Hestaiyon searched among the shreds of memory, as one who reaches into a place where the worm has been and the hidden archives of old time have rotted in their covers; till at last he remembered, and said:

"I recall that I was once a mighty wizard; and among other things, I knew the spells of necromancy, but employed them not, deeming their use and the raising up of the dead an abhorrent act. Also, I possessed other knowledge; and perhaps, among the remnants of that ancient lore, there is something which may serve to guide us now. For I recall a dim, dubitable prophecy, made in the primal years, at the founding of Yethlyreom and the empire of Cincor. The prophecy was, that an evil greater than death would befall the emperors and the people of Cincor in future time; and that the first and the last of the Nimboth dynasty, conferring together, would effect a mode of release and the lifting of the doom. The evil was not named in the prophecy; but it was said that the two emperors would learn the solution of their problem by the breaking of an ancient clay image that guards the nethermost vault below the imperial palace in Yethlyreom."

Then, having heard this prophecy from the faded lips of his forefather, Illeiro mused a while, and said:

"I remember now an afternoon in early youth, when searching idly through the unused vaults of our palace, as a boy might do, I came to the last vault and found therein a dusty, uncouth image of clay, whose form and countenance were strange to me. And, knowing not the prophecy, I turned away in disappointment, and went back as idly as I had come, to seek the moted sunlight."

Then, stealing away from their heedless kinfolk, and carrying jeweled lamps they had taken from the hall, Hestaiyon and Illeiro went downward by subterranean stairs beneath the palace; and, threading like implacable furtive shadows the maze of nighted corridors, they came at last to the lowest crypt.

Here, in the black dust and clotted cobwebs of an immemorial past, they found, as had been decreed, the clay image, whose rude features were those of a forgotten earthly god. And Illeiro shattered the image with a fragment of stone; and he and Hestaiyon took from its hollow center a great sword of unrusted steel, and a heavy key of untarnished bronze, and tablets of bright brass on which were inscribed the various things to be done, so that Cincor should be rid of the dark reign of the necromancers and the people should win back to oblivious death.

So, with the key of untarnished bronze, Illeiro unlocked, as the tablets had instructed him to do, a low and narrow door at the end of the nethermost vault, beyond the broken image; and he and Hestaiyon saw, as had been prophesied, the coiling steps of somber stone that led downward to an undiscovered abyss, where the sunken fires of earth still burned. And leaving Illeiro to ward the open door, Hestaiyon took up the sword of unrusted steel in his thin hand, and went back to the hall where the necromancers slept, lying a-sprawl on their couches of rose and purple, with the wan, bloodless dead about them in patient ranks.

Upheld by the ancient prophecy and the lore of the bright tablets, Hestaiyon lifted the great sword and struck off the head of Mmatmuor and the head of Sodosma, each with a single blow. Then, as had been directed, he quartered the remains with mighty strokes. And the necromancers gave up their unclean lives, and lay supine, without movement, adding a deeper red to the rose and a brighter hue to the sad purple of their couches.

Then, to his kin, who stood silent and listless, hardly knowing their liberation, the venerable mummy of Hestaiyon spoke in sere murmurs, but authoritatively, as a king who issues commands to his children. The dead emperors and empresses stirred, like autumn leaves in a sudden wind, and a whisper passed among them and went forth from the palace, to be communicated at length, by devious ways, to all the dead of Cincor.

All that night, and during the blood-dark day that followed, by wavering torches or the light of the failing sun, an endless army of plague-eaten liches, of tattered skeletons, poured in a ghastly torrent through the streets of Yethlyreom and along the palace-hall where Hestaiyon stood guard above the slain necromancers. Unpausing, with vague, fixed eyes, they went on like driven shadows, to seek the subterranean vaults below the palace, to pass through the open door where Illeiro waited in the last vault, and then to wend downward by a thousand thousand steps to the verge of that gulf in which boiled the ebbing fires of earth. There, from the verge, they flung themselves to a second death and the clean annihilation of the bottomless flames.

But, after all had gone to their release, Hestaiyon still remained, alone in the fading sunset, beside the cloven corpses of Mmatmuor and Sodosma. There, as the tablets had directed him to do, he made trial of those spells of elder necromancy which he had known in his former wisdom, and cursed the dismembered bodies with that perpetual life-in-death which Mmatmuor and Sodosma had sought to inflict upon the people of Cincor. And maledictions came from the pale lips, and the heads rolled horribly with glaring eyes, and the limbs and torsos writhed on their imperial couches amid clotted blood. Then, with no backward look, knowing that all was done as had been ordained and predicted from the first, the mummy of Hestaiyon left the necromancers to their doom, and went wearily through the nighted labyrinth of vaults to rejoin Illeiro.

So, in tranquil silence, with no further need of words, Illeiro and Hestaiyon passed through the open door of the nether vault, and Illeiro locked the door behind them with its key of untarnished bronze. And thence, by the coiling stairs, they wended their way to the verge of the sunken flames and were one with their kinsfolk and their people in the last, ultimate nothingness.

But of Mmatmuor and Sodosma, men say that their quartered bodies crawl to and fro to this day in Yethlyreom, finding no peace or respite from their doom of life-in-death, and seeking vainly through the black maze of nether vaults the door that was locked by Illeiro.

THE DISINTERMENT
OF VENUS

I

Prior to certain highly deplorable and scandalous events in the year 1550, the vegetable garden of Perigon was situated on the southeast side of the abbey. After these events, it was removed to the northwest side, where it has remained ever since; and the former garden-site was given to weeds and briars which, by strict order of the successive abbots, no one has ever tried to eradicate or curb.

The happenings which compelled this removal of the Benedictines' turnip and carrot patches became a popular tale in Averoigne. It is hard to say how much or how little of the legend is apocryphal.

One April morning, three monks were spading lustily in the garden. Their names were Paul, Pierre, and Hughes. The first was a man of ripe years, hale and robust; the second was in his early prime; the third was little more than a boy, and had but recently taken his final vows.

Being moved with an especial ardor, in which the vernal stirring of youthful sap may have played its part, Hughes proceeded to dig the loamy soil even more diligently than his comrades. The ground was almost free of stones, owing to the careful tillage of many generations of monks; but anon, through the muscular zeal with which it was wielded, the spade of Hughes encountered a hard and well-buried object of indeterminate size.

Hughes felt that this obstruction, which in all likelihood was a small boulder, should be removed for the honor of the monastery and the glory of God. Bending busily, he shoveled away the moist, blackish loam in an effort to uncover it. The task was more arduous than he had expected; and the supposed boulder began to reveal an amazing length and a quite singular formation as he bared it by degrees. Leaving their own toil, Pierre and Paul came to his assistance. Soon, through the zealous endeavors of the three, the nature of the buried object became all too manifest.

In the large pit they had now dug, the monks beheld the grimy head and torso of what was plainly a marble woman goddess from antique years. The pale stone of shoulders and arms, tinged faintly as if with a living rose, had been scraped clean in places by their shovel but the face and breasts were still black with heavily caked loam.

The figure stood erect, as if on a hidden pedestal. One arm was raised caressing with a shapely hand the ripe contour of shoulder and bosom; the other, hanging idly, was still plunged in the earth. Digging deeplier, the monk uncovered the full hips and rounded thighs; and finally, taking turns in the pit, whose rim was now higher than their heads, they came to the sunken pedestal which stood on a pavement of granite.

During the course of their excavation the Brothers had felt a strange, powerful excitement whose cause they could hardly have explained, but which seemed to arise, like some obscure contagion, from the long-buried arms and bosom of the image. Mingled with a pious horror due to the infamous paganry and nudity of the statue, there was an unacknowledged pleasure which the three would have rebuked in themselves as vile and shameful if they had recognized it.

Fearful of chipping or scratching the marble, they wielded their spades with much chariness; and when the digging was completed and the comely feet were uncovered on their pedestal, Paul, the oldest, standing beside the image in the pit, began to wipe away with a handful of weeds and grass the maculations of dark loam that still clung to its lovely body. This task he performed with great thoroughness; and he ended by polishing the marble with the hem and sleeves of his black robe.

He and his fellows, who were not without classic learning, now saw that the figure was evidently a statue of Venus, dating no doubt from the Roman occupation of Averoigne, when certain altars to this divinity had been established by the invaders.

The vicissitudes of half-legendary time, the long dark years of inhumation, had harmed the Venus little if at all. The slight mutilation of an ear-tip half hidden by rippling curls, and the partial fracture of a shapely middle toe, merely served to add, if possible, a keener seduction to her languorous beauty.

She was exquisite as the succubi of youthful dreams, but her perfection was touched with inenarrable evil. The lines of the mature figure were fraught with a maddening luxuriousness; the lips of the full, Circean face were half pouting, half smiling with ambiguous allure. It was the masterpiece of an unknown, decadent sculptor; not the noble maternal Venus of heroic times, but the sly and cruelly voluptuous Cytherean of dark orgies, ready for her descent into the Hollow Hill.

A forbidden enchantment, an unhallowed thralldom, seemed to flow from the flesh-pale marble and to weave itself like invisible hair about the hearts of the Brothers. With a sudden, mutual feeling of shame, they recalled their monkhood, and began to debate what should be done with the Venus, which, in a monastery garden, was somewhat misplaced. After brief discussion, Hughes went to report their find to the abbot and await his decision regarding its disposal. In the meanwhile, Paul and Pierre resumed their garden labors, stealing, perhaps, occasional covert glances at the pagan goddess.

II

Augustin the abbot came presently into the garden, accompanied by those monks who were not, at that hour, engaged in some special task. With a severe mien, in silence, he proceeded to inspect the statue; and those with him waited reverently, not venturing to speak before their abbot had spoken.

Even the saintly Augustin, however, in spite of his age and rigorous temper, was somewhat discomfited by the peculiar witchery which seemed to emanate from the marble. Of this he gave no sign, and the natural austerity of his demeanor deepened. Curtly he ordered the bringing of ropes, and directed the raising of the Venus from her loamy bed to a standing position on the garden ground beside the hole. In this task, Paul, Pierre, and Hughes were assisted by two others.

Many of the monks now pressed forward to examine the figure closely; and several were even prompted to touch it, till rebuked for this unseemly action by their superior. Certain of the elder and more austere Benedictines urged its immediate destruction, arguing that the image was a heathen abomination that defiled the abbey garden by its presence. Others, the most practical, pointed out that the Venus, being a rare and beautiful example of Roman sculpture, might well be sold at a goodly price to some rich and impious art-lover.

Augustin, though he felt that the Venus should be destroyed as an impure pagan idol, was filled with a queer and peculiar hesitation which led him to defer the necessary orders for her demolishment. It was as if the subtly wanton loveliness of the marble were pleading for clemency like a living form, with a voice half human, half divine. Averting his eyes from the white bosom, he spoke harshly, bidding the Brothers to return to their labors and devotions, and saying that the Venus could remain in the garden till arrangements were made for her ultimate disposition and removal. Pending this, he instructed one of the Brothers to bring sackcloth and drape therewith the unseemly nudity of the goddess.

The disinterment of this antique image became a source of much discussion and some perturbation and dissension amid the quiet Brotherhood at Perigon. Because of the curiosity shown by many monks, the abbot issued an injunction that no one should approach the statue, other than those whose labors might compel an involuntary proximity. He himself, at that time, was criticized by some of the deans for his laxness in not destroying the Venus immediately. During the few years that remained to him, he was to regret bitterly the remissness he had shown in this matter.

No one, however, dreamt of the grave scandals that were to ensue shortly. But, on the day following the discovery of the statue, it became manifest that some evil and disturbing influence was abroad. Heretofore, breaches of discipline had been rare among the Brothers; and cardinal offenses were quite unknown; but now it seemed that a spirit of unruliness, impiety, ribaldry, and wrong-doing had entered Perigon.

Paul, Pierre, and Hughes were the first to undergo penance for their peccancies. A shocked dean had overheard them discussing with impure levity, certain matters that were more suitable for the conversation of worldly gallants than of monks. By way of extenuation, the three Brothers pleaded that they had been obsessed with carnal thoughts and images ever since their exhumation of the Venus; and for this they blamed the statue, saying that a pagan witchcraft had come upon them from its flesh-white marble.

On that same day, others of the monks were charged with similar offenses; and still others made confession of lubric desires and visions such as had tormented Anthony during his desert vigil. Those, too, were prone to blame the Venus. Before evensong, many infractions of monastic rule were reported; and some of them were of such nature as to call for the severest rebuke and penance. Brothers whose conduct had heretofore been exemplary in all ways were found guilty of transgressions such as could be accounted for only by the direct influence of Satan or some powerful demon.

Worst of all, on that very night, it was found that Hughes and Paul were absent from their beds in the dormitory; and no one could say whither they had gone. They did not return on the day following. Inquiries were made by the abbot's order in the neighboring village of Sainte Zenobie, and it was learned that Paul and Hughes had spent the night at a tavern of unsavory repute, drinking and wenching; and they had taken the road to Vyones, chief city of the province, at early dawn. Later, they were apprehended and brought back to the monastery, protesting that their downfall was wholly due to some evil contagion which they had incurred by touching the statue.

In view of the unexampled demoralization which prevailed at Perigon, no one doubted that a diabolic pagan charm was at work. The source of the charm was all too obvious. Moreover, queer tales were told by monks who had labored in the garden or had passed within sight of the image. They swore that the Venus was no mere sculptured idol but a living woman or she-devil who had changed her position repeatedly and had rearranged the folds of the sackcloth in such manner as to lay bare one shapely shoulder and a part of her bosom. Others avowed that the Venus walked in the garden by night; and some even affirmed that she had entered the monastery and appeared before them like a succubus.

Much fright and horror was created by these tales, and no one dared to approach the image closely. Though the situation was supremely scandalous, the abbot still forbore to issue orders for the statue's demolition, fearing that any monk who touched it, even with a motive so pious, would court the baleful sorcery that had brought Hughes and Paul to disaster and disgrace, and had led others into impurity of speech or actual impiety.

It was suggested, however, that some laymen should be hired to shatter the idol and remove and bury its fragments. This, no doubt, would have been accomplished in good time, if it had not been for the hasty and fanatic zeal of Brother Louis.

III

This Brother, a youth of good family, was conspicuous among the Benedictines both for his comely face and his austere piety. Handsome as Adonis, he was given to ascetic vigils and prolonged devotions, outdoing in this regard the abbot and the deans.

At the hour of the statue's disinterment, he was busily engaged in copying a Latin testament; and neither then nor at any later time had he cared to inspect a find which he considered more than dubious. He had expressed disapprobation on hearing from his fellows the details of the discovery; and feeling that the abbey garden was polluted by the presence of an obscene image, he had purposely avoided all windows through which the marble might have been visible to his chaste eyes.

When the influence of heathen evil and corruption became manifest amid the Brothers, he had shown great indignation, deeming it a most insufferable thing that virtuous, God-fearing monks should be brought to shame through the operation of some hellish pagan spell. He had reprobated openly the hesitation of Augustin and his delay in destroying the maleficent idol. More mischief, he said, would ensue if it were left intact.

In view of all this, extreme surprise and alarm were felt at Perigon when, on the fourth day after the exhumation of the statue, Brother Louis was discovered missing. His bed had not been occupied on the previous night; but it seemed impossible that he could have fled the monastery, yielding to such desires and impulsions as had caused the ruin of Paul and Hughes.

The monks were strictly interrogated by their abbot, and it was revealed that Brother Louis, when last seen, had been loitering about the abbey workshop. Since, formerly, he had shown small interest in tools or manual labor, this was deemed a peculiar thing. Forthwith a visit was made to the workshop; and the monk in charge of the smithy soon found that one of his heaviest hammers had been removed.

The conclusion was obvious to all: Louis, impelled by virtuous ardor and holy wrath, had gone forth during the night to demolish the baleful image of Venus.

Augustin and the Brothers who were with him repaired immediately to the garden. There they were met by the gardeners, who, noticing from afar that the image no longer occupied its position beside the pit, were hurrying to report this matter to the abbot. They had not dared to investigate the mystery of its disappearance, believing firmly that the statue had come to life and was lurking somewhere about the garden.

Made bold by their number and by the leadership of Augustin, the assembled monks approached the pit. Beside its rim they beheld the missing hammer, lying on the clodded loam as if Louis had cast it aside. Near by was the sacking that had clothed the image; but there were no fragments of broken marble such as they had thought to see. The footprints of Louis were clearly imprinted upon the pit's margin, and were discernible in strangely close proximity to the mark left by the pedestal of the statue.

All this was very peculiar, and the monks felt that the mystery had begun to assume a more than sinister tinge. Then, peering into the hole itself, they beheld a thing that was explicable only through the machinations of Satan—or one of Satan's most pernicious and seductive she-demons.

Somehow, the Venus had been overturned and had fallen back into the broad deep pit. The body of Brother Louis, with a shattered skull and lips bruised to a sanguine pulp, was lying crushed beneath her marble breasts. His arms were clasped about her in a desperate, lover-like embrace, to which death had now added its own rigidity. Even more horrible and inexplicable, however, was the fact that the stone arms of the Venus had changed their posture and were now folded closely about the dead monk as if she had been sculptured in the attitude of an amorous enlacement!

The horror and consternation felt by the Benedictines were inexpressible. Some would have fled from the spot in panic, after viewing this frightful and most abominable prodigy; but Augustin restrained them, his features stern with the religious ire of one who beholds the fresh handiwork of the Adversary. He commanded the bringing of a cross, an aspergillus, and holy water, together with a ladder for use in descending into the pit; saying that the body of Louis must be redeemed from the baleful and dolorous plight into which it had fallen. The iron hammer, lying beside the hole, was proof of the righteous intention with which Louis had gone forth; but it was all too plain that he had succumbed to the hellish charms of the statue. Nevertheless, the Church could not abandon an erring servant to the powers of Evil.

When the ladder was brought, Augustin himself led the descent, followed by three of the stoutest and most courageous Brothers, who were willing to risk their own spiritual safety for the redemption of Louis. Regarding that which ensued, the legends vary slightly. Some say that the aspersions of holy water made by Augustin on the statue and victim were without palpable effect, while others relate that the drops turned to infernal steam when they struck the recumbent Venus, and blackened the flesh of Louis like that of a month-old cadaver, thus proving him wholly claimed by perdition. But the tales agree in this, that the strength of the three Brothers, laboring in unison at their abbot's direction, was impotent to loosen the marble clasp of the goddess from about her prey.

So, by the order of Augustin, the pit was filled hastily to its rim with earth and stones; and the very spot where it had been, being left without mound or other mark, was quickly overgrown by grass and weeds along with the rest of the abandoned garden.

THE DEVOTEE
OF EVIL

The old Larcom house was a mansion of considerable size and dignity, set among oaks and cypresses on the hill behind Auburn's Chinatown, in what had once been the aristocratic section of the village. At the time of which I write, it had been unoccupied for several years and had begun to present the signs of desolation and dilapidation which untenanted houses so soon display. The place had a tragic history and was believed to be haunted. I had never been able to procure any first-hand or precise accounts of the spectral manifestations that were accredited to it. But certainly it possessed all the necessary antecedents of a haunted house. The first owner, Judge Peter Larcom, had been murdered beneath its roof back in the seventies by a maniacal Chinese cook; one of his daughters had gone insane; and two other members of the family had died accidental deaths. None of them had prospered: their legend was one of sorrow and disaster.

Some later occupants, who had purchased the place from the one surviving son of Peter Larcom, had left under circumstances of inexplicable haste after a few months, moving permanently to San Francisco. They did not return even for the briefest visit; and beyond paying their taxes, they gave no attention whatever to the place. Everyone had grown to think of it as a sort of historic ruin, when the announcement came that it had been sold to Jean Averaud, of New Orleans.

My first meeting with Averaud was strangely significant, for it revealed to me, as years of acquaintance would not necessarily have done, the peculiar bias of his mind. Of course, I had already heard some odd rumors about him; his personality was too signal, his advent too mysterious, to escape the usual fabrication and mongering of village tales. I had been told that he was extravagantly rich, that he was a recluse of the most eccentric type, that he had made certain very singular changes in the inner structure of the old house; and last, but not least, that he lived with a beautiful mulatress who never spoke to anyone and who was believed to be his mistress as well as his housekeeper. The man himself had been described to me by some as an unusual but harmless lunatic, and by others as an all-round Mephistopheles.

I had seen him several times before our initial meeting. He was a sallow, saturnine Creole, with the marks of race in his hollow cheeks and feverish eyes. I was struck by his air of intellect, and by the fiery fixity of his gaze—the gaze of a man who is dominated by one idea to the exclusion of all else. Some medieval alchemist, who believed himself to be on the point of attaining his objective after years of unrelenting research, might have looked as he did.

I was in the Auburn library one day when Averaud entered. I had taken a newspaper from one of the tables and was reading the details of an atrocious crime—the murder of a woman and her two infant children by the husband and father, who had locked his victims in a clothes-closet, after saturating their garments with oil. He had left the woman's apron-string caught in the shut door, with the end protruding, and had set fire to it like a fuse.

Averaud passed the table where I was reading. I looked up, and saw his glance at the headlines of the paper I held. A moment later he returned and sat down beside me, saying in a low voice:

"What interests me in a crime of that sort is the implication of unhuman forces behind it. Could any man, on his own initiative, have conceived and executed anything so gratuitously fiendish?"

"I don't know," I replied, somewhat surprised by the question and by my interrogator. "There are terrifying depths in human nature—more abhorrent than those of the jungle."

"I agree. But how could such impulses, unknown to the most brutal progenitors of man, have been implanted in his nature, unless through some ulterior agency?"

"You believe, then, in the existence of an evil force or entity—a Satan or an Ahriman?"

"I believe in evil—how can I do otherwise when I see its manifestations everywhere? I regard it as an all-controlling power; but I do not think that the power is personal in the sense of what we know as personality. A Satan? No. What I conceive is a sort of dark vibration, the radiation of a black sun, of a center of malignant eons—a radiation that can penetrate like any other ray—and perhaps more deeply. But probably I don't make my meaning clear at all."

I protested that I understood him; but, after his burst of communicativeness, he seemed oddly disinclined to pursue the conversation. Evidently he had been prompted to address me; and no less evidently, he regretted having spoken with so much freedom. He arose; but before leaving, he said:

"I am Jean Averaud—perhaps you have heard of me. You are Philip Hastane, the novelist. I have read your books and I admire them. Come and see me sometime—we may have certain tastes in common."

Averaud's personality, the conception he had avowed, and the intense interest and value which he so obviously attached to these conceptions, made a singular impression on my mind, and I could not forget him. When, a few days later, I met him on the street and he repeated his invitation with a cordialness that was unfeignedly sincere, I could do no less than accept. I was interested, though not altogether attracted, by his bizarre, well-nigh morbid individuality, and was impelled by a desire to learn more concerning him. I sensed a mystery of no common order—a mystery with elements of the abnormal and the uncanny.

The grounds of the old Larcom place were precisely as I remembered them, though I had not found occasion to pass them for some time. They were a veritable tangle of Cherokee rose-vines, arbutus, lilac, ivy, and crepe-myrtle, half overshadowed by the great cypresses and somber evergreen oaks. There was a wild, half-sinister charm about them—the charm of rampancy and ruin. Nothing had been done to put the place in order, and there were no outward repairs in the house itself, where the white paint of bygone years was being slowly replaced by mosses and lichens that flourished beneath the eternal umbrage of the trees. There were signs of decay in the roof and pillars of the front porch; and I wondered why the new owner, who was reputed to be so rich, had not already made the necessary restorations.

I raised the gargoyle-shaped knocker and let it fall with a dull, lugubrious clang. The house remained silent; and I was about to knock again, when the door opened slowly and I saw for the first time the mulatress of whom so many village rumors had reached me.

The woman was more exotic than beautiful, with fine, mournful eyes and bronze-colored features of a semi-negroid irregularity. Her figure, though, was truly perfect, with the curving lines of a lyre and the supple grace of some feline animal. When I asked for Jean Averaud, she merely smiled and made signs for me to enter. I surmised at once that she was dumb.

Waiting in the gloomy library to which she conducted me, I could not refrain from glancing at the volumes with which the shelves were congested. They were an ungodly jumble of tomes that dealt with anthropology, ancient religions, demonology, modern science, history, psychoanalysis, and ethics. Interspersed with these were a few romances and volumes of poetry. Beausobre's monograph on Manichaeism was flanked with Byron and Poe; and *Les Fleurs du mal* jostled a late treatise on chemistry.

Averaud entered, after several minutes, apologizing profusely for his delay. He said that he had been in the midst of certain labors when I came; but he did not specify the nature of these labors. He looked even more hectic and fiery-eyed than when I had seen him last. He was patently glad to see me, and eager to talk.

"You have been looking at my books," he observed immediately. "Though you might not think so at first glance, on account of their seeming diversity, I have selected them all with a single object: the study of evil in all its aspects, ancient, medieval, and modern. I have traced it in the religions and demonologies of all peoples; and, more than this, in human history itself. I have found it in the inspiration of poets and romancers who have dealt with the darker impulses, emotion, and acts of man. Your novels have interested me for this reason: you are aware of the baneful influences which surround us, which so often sway or actuate us. I have followed the working of these agencies even in chemical reactions, in the growth and decay of trees, flowers, minerals. I feel that the processes of physical decomposition, as well as the similar mental and moral processes, are due entirely to them.

"In brief, I have postulated a monistic evil, which is the source of all death, deterioration, imperfection, pain, sorrow, madness, and disease. This evil, so feebly counteracted by the powers of good, allures and fascinates me above all things. For a long time past, my life-work has been to ascertain its true nature, and trace it to its fountain-head. I am sure that somewhere in space there is the center from which all evil emanates."

He spoke with a wild air of excitement, of morbid and semimaniacal intensity. His obsession convinced me that he was more or less unbalanced; but there was an unholy logic in the development of his ideas; and I could not but recognize a certain disordered brilliancy and range of intellect.

Scarcely waiting for me to reply, he continued his monologue:

"I have learned that certain localities and buildings, certain arrangements of natural or artificial objects, are more favorable to the reception of evil influences than others. The laws that determine the degree of receptivity are still obscure to me; but at least I have verified the fact itself. As you know, there are houses or neighborhoods notorious for a succession of crimes or misfortunes; and there are also articles, such as certain jewels, whose possession is accompanied by disaster. Such places and things are receivers of evil . . . I have a theory, however, that there is always more or less interference with the direct flow of the malignant force; and that pure, absolute evil has never yet been manifested.

"By the use of some device which would create a proper field or form a receiving station, it should be possible to evoke this absolute evil. Under such conditions, I am sure that the dark vibration would become a visible and tangible thing, comparable to light or electricity." He eyed me with a gaze that was disconcertingly exigent. Then:

"I will confess that I have purchased this old mansion and its grounds mainly on account of their baleful history. The place is unusually liable to the influences of which I have spoken. I am now at work on an apparatus by means of which, when it is perfected, I hope to manifest in their essential purity the radiations of malign force."

At this moment, the mulatress entered and passed through the room on some household errand. I thought that she gave Averaud a look of maternal tenderness, watchfulness, and anxiety. He, on his part seemed hardly to be aware of her presence, so engrossed was he in the strange ideas and the stranger project he had been expounding. However, when she had gone, he remarked:

"That is Fifine, the one human being who is really attached to me. She is mute, but highly intelligent and affectionate. All my people, an old Louisiana family, are long departed . . . and my wife is doubly dead to me." A spasm of obscure pain contracted his features, and vanished. He resumed his monologue; and at no future time did he again refer to the presumably tragic tale at which he had hinted: a tale in which, I sometimes suspect, were hidden the seeds of the strange moral and mental perversion which he was to manifest more and more.

I took my leave, after promising to return for another talk.

Of course, I considered now that Averaud was a madman; but his madness was of a most uncommon and picturesque variety. It seemed significant that he should have chosen me for a confidant. All others who met him found him uncommunicative and taciturn to an extreme degree. I suppose he had felt the ordinary human need of unburdening himself to someone; and had selected me as the only person in the neighborhood who was potentially sympathetic.

I saw him several times during the month that followed. He was indeed a strange psychological study; and I encouraged him to talk without reserve—though such encouragement was hardly necessary. There was much that he told me—a strange medley of the scientific and the mystic. I assented tactfully to all that he said, but ventured to point out the possible dangers of his evocative experiments, if they should prove successful. To this, with the fervor of an alchemist or a religious devotee, he replied that it did not matter—that he was prepared to accept any and all consequences.

More than once he gave me to understand that his invention was progressing favorably. And one day he said, with abruptness:

"I will show you my mechanism, if you care to see it." I protested my eagerness to view the invention, and he led me forthwith into a room to which I had not been admitted before. The chamber was large, triangular in form, and tapestried with curtains of some sullen black fabric. It had no windows. Clearly, the internal structure of the house had been changed in making it; and all the queer village tales, emanating from carpenters who had been hired to do the work, were now explained. Exactly in the center of the room, there stood on a low tripod of brass—the apparatus of which Averaud had so often spoken.

The contrivance was quite fantastic, and presented the appearance of some new, highly complicated musical instrument. I remember that there were many wires of varying thickness, stretched on a series of concave sounding-boards of some dark, unlustrous metal; and above these, there depended from three horizontal bars a number of square, circular, and triangular gongs. Each of these appeared to be made of a different material; some were bright as gold, or translucent as jade; others were black and opaque as jet. A small, hammerlike instrument hung opposite each gong, at the end of a silver wire.

Averaud proceeded to expound the scientific basis of his mechanism. The vibrational properties of the gongs, he said, were designed to neutralize with their sound-pitch all other cosmic vibrations than those of evil. He dwelt at much length on this extravagant theorem, developing it in a fashion oddly lucid. He ended his peroration:

"I need one more gong to complete the instrument; and this I hope to invent very soon. The triangular room, draped in black, and without windows, forms the ideal setting for my experiment. Apart from this room, I have not ventured to make any change in the house or its grounds, for fear of deranging some propitious element or collocation of elements."

More than ever, I thought that he was mad. And, though he had professed on many occasions to abhor the evil which he planned to evoke, I felt an inverted fanaticism in his attitude. In a less scientific age he would have been a devil-worshiper, a partaker in the abominations of the Black Mass; or would have given himself to the study and practice of sorcery. His was a religious soul that had failed to find good in the scheme of things; and lacking it, was impelled to make of evil itself an object of secret reverence.

"I fear that you think me insane," he observed in a sudden flash of clairvoyance. "Would you like to watch an experiment? Even though my invention is not completed, I may be able to convince you that my design is not altogether the fantasy of a disordered brain."

I consented. He turned on the lights in the dim room. Then he went to an angle of the wall and pressed a hidden spring or switch. The wires on which the tiny hammers were strung began to oscillate, till each of the hammers touched lightly its companion gong. The sound they made was dissonant and disquieting to the last degree—a diabolic percussion unlike anything I have ever heard, and exquisitely painful to the nerves. I felt as if a flood of finely broken glass was pouring into my ears.

The swinging of the hammers grew swifter and heavier; but, to my surprise, there was no corresponding increase of loudness in the sound. On the contrary, the clangor became slowly muted, till it was no more than an undertone which seemed to be coming from an immense depth or distance—an undertone still full of disquietude and torment, like the sobbing of far-off winds in Hell, or the murmur of demonian fires on coasts of eternal ice.

Said Averaud at my elbow:

"To a certain extent, the combined notes of the gongs are beyond human hearing in their pitch. With the addition of the final gong, even less sound will be audible."

While I was trying to digest this difficult idea, I noticed a partial dimming of the light above the tripod and its weird apparatus. A vertical shaft of faint shadow, surrounded by a still fainter penumbra, was forming in the air. The tripod itself, and the wires, gongs, and hammers, were now a trifle indistinct, as if seen through some obscuring veil. The central shaft and its penumbra seemed to widen; and looking down at the floor, where the outer adumbration, conforming to the room's outline, crept toward the walls, I saw that Averaud and myself were now within its ghostly triangle.

At the same time there surged upon me an intolerable depression, together with a multitude of sensations which I despair of conveying in language. My very sense of space was distorted and deformed as if some unknown dimension had somehow been mingled with those familiar to us. There was a feeling of dreadful and measureless descent, as if the floor were sinking beneath me into some nether pit; and I seemed to pass beyond the room in a torrent of swirling, hallucinative images, visible but invisible, felt but intangible, and more awful, more accurst than that hurricane of lost souls beheld by Dante.

Down, down, I appeared to go, in the bottomless and phantom

hell that was impinging upon reality. Death, decay, malignity, madness, gathered in the air and pressed me down like Satanic incubi in that ecstatic horror of descent. I felt that there were a thousand forms, a thousand faces about me, summoned from the gulfs of perdition. And yet I saw nothing but the white face of Averaud, stamped with a frozen and abominable rapture as he fell beside me.

Like a dreamer who forces himself to awaken, he began to move away from me. I seemed to lose sight of him for a moment in the cloud of nameless, immaterial horrors that threatened to take on the further horror of substance. Then I realized that Averaud had turned off the switch, and that the oscillating hammers had ceased to beat on those infernal gongs. The double shaft of shadow faded in mid-air, the burden of terror and despair lifted from my nerves, and I no longer felt the damnable hallucination of nether space and descent.

"My God!" I cried. "What was it?"

Averaud's look was full of a ghastly, gloating exultation as he turned to me.

"You saw and felt it, then?" he queried—"that vague, imperfect manifestation of the perfect evil which exists somewhere in the cosmos? I shall yet call it forth in its entirety, and know the black, infinite, reverse raptures which attend its epiphany."

I recoiled from him with an involuntary shudder. All the hideous things that had swarmed upon me beneath the cacophonous beating of those accursed gongs drew near again for an instant; and I looked with fearful vertigo into hells of perversity and corruption. I saw an inverted soul, despairing of good, which longed for the baleful ecstasies of perdition. No longer did I think him merely mad: for I knew the thing which he sought and could attain; and I remembered, with a new significance, that line of Baudelaire's poem—"The Hell wherein my heart delights."

Averaud was unaware of my revulsion, in his dark rhapsody. When I turned to leave, unable to bear any longer the blasphemous atmosphere of that room, and the sense of strange depravity which emanated from its owner, he pressed me to return as soon as possible.

"I think," he exulted, "that all will be in readiness before long. I want you to be present in the hour of my triumph."

I do not know what I said, nor what excuses I made to get away from him. I longed to assure myself that a world of unblasted sunlight and undefiled air could still exist. I went out; but a shadow followed me; and execrable faces leered or mowed from the foliage as I left the cypress-shaded grounds.

For days afterward I was in a condition verging upon neurotic disorder. No one could come as close as I had been to the primal effluence of evil and go thence unaffected. Shadowy noisome cobwebs draped themselves on all my thoughts, and presences of unlineamented fear, of shapeless horror, crouched in the half-lit corners of my mind but would never fully declare themselves. An invisible gulf, bottomless as Malebolge, seemed to yawn before me wherever I went.

Presently, though, my reason reasserted itself, and I wondered if my sensations in the black triangular room had not been wholly a matter of suggestion or auto-hypnosis. I asked myself if it were credible that a cosmic force of the sort postulated by Averaud could really exist; or, granting it existed, could be evoked by any man through the absurd intermediation of a musical device. The nervous terrors of my experience faded a little in memory; and, though a disturbing doubt still lingered, I assured myself that all I had felt was of purely subjective origin. Even then, it was with supreme reluctance, with an inward shrinking only to be overcome by violent resolve, that I returned to visit Averaud once more.

For an even longer period than usual, no one answered my knock. Then there were hurrying footsteps, and the door was opened abruptly by Fifine. I knew immediately that something was amiss, for her face wore a look of unnatural dread and anxiety, and her eyes were wide, with the whites showing blankly, as if she gazed upon horrific things.

She tried to speak, and made that ghastly inarticulate sound which the mute is able to make on occasion as she plucked my sleeve and drew me after her along the somber hall to the triangular room.

The door was open; and as I approached it, I heard a low, dissonant, snarling murmur, which I recognized as the sound of the gongs. It was like the voice of all the souls in a frozen hell, uttered by lips congealing slowly toward the ultimate torture of silence. It sank and sank till it seemed to be issuing from pits below the nadir.

Fifine shrank back on the threshold, imploring me with a pitiful glance to precede her. The lights were all turned on; and Averaud, clad in a strange medieval costume, in a black gown and cap such as Faustus might have worn, stood near the percussive mechanism. The hammers were all beating with a frenzied rapidity; and the sound became still lower and tenser as I approached. Averaud did not seem to see me: his eyes, abnormally dilated, and flaming with infernal luster like those of one possessed, were fixed upon something in mid-air.

Again the soul-congealing hideousness, the sense of eternal falling, of myriad harpy-like incumbent horrors, rushed upon me as I looked and saw. Vaster and stronger than before, a double column of triangular shadow had materialized and was becoming more and more distinct. It swelled, it darkened, it enveloped the gong-apparatus and towered to the ceiling. The double column grew solid and opaque as ebony; and the face of Averaud, who was standing well within the broad penumbral shadow, became dim as if seen through a film of Stygian water.

I must have gone utterly mad for a while. I remember only a teeming delirium of things too frightful to be endured by a sane mind, that peopled the infinite gulf of hell-born illusion into which I sank with the hopeless precipitancy of the damned. There was a sickness inexpressible, a vertigo of redeemless descent, a pandemonium of ghoulish phantoms that reeled and swayed about the column of malign omnipotent force which presided over all. Averaud was only one more phantom in this delirium, when with arms outstretched in his perverse adoration, he stepped toward the inner column and passed into it till he was lost to view. And Fifine was another phantom when she ran by me to the wall and turned off the switch that operated those demoniacal hammers.

As one who re-emerges from a swoon, I saw the fading of the dual pillar, till the light was no longer sullied by any tinge of that satanic radiation. And where it had been, Averaud still stood beside the baleful instrument he had designed. Erect and rigid he stood, in a strange immobility; and I felt an incredulous horror, a chill awe, as I went forward and touched him with a faltering hand. For that which I saw and touched was no longer a human being but an ebon statue, whose face and brow and fingers were black as the Faust-like raiment or the sullen curtains. Charred as by sable fire, or frozen by black cold, the features bore the eternal ecstasy and pain of Lucifer in his ultimate hell of ice. For an instant, the supreme evil which Averaud had worshipped so madly, which he had summoned from the vaults of incalculable space, had made him one with itself; and passing, it had left him petrified into an image of its own essence. The form that I touched was harder than marble; and I knew that it would endure to all time as a testimony of the infinite Medusean power that is death and corruption and darkness.

Fifine had now thrown herself at the feet of the image and was clasping its insensible knees. With her frightful muted moaning in my ears, I went forth for the last time from that chamber and from that mansion. Vainly, through delirious months and madness-ridden years, I have tried to shake off the infrangible obsession of my memories. But there is a fatal numbness in my brain as if it too had been charred and blackened a little in that moment of overpowering nearness to the dark ray of the black statue that was Jean Averaud, the impress of awful and forbidden things has been set like an everlasting seal.

THE ENCHANTRESS
OF SYLAIRE

"Why, you big ninny! I could never marry you," declared the demoiselle Dorothée, only daughter of the Sieur des Flèches. Her lips pouted at Anselme like two ripe berries. Her voice was honey—but honey filled with bee-stings.

"You are not so ill-looking. And your manners are fair. But I wish I had a mirror that could show you to yourself for the fool that you really are."

"Why?" queried Anselme, hurt and puzzled.

"Because you are just an addle-headed dreamer, poring over books like a monk. You care for nothing but silly old romances and legends. People say that you even write verses. It is lucky that you are at least the second son of the Comte du Framboisier—for you will never be anything more than that."

"But you loved me a little yesterday," said Anselme, bitterly. A woman finds nothing good in the man she has ceased to love.

"Dolt! Donkey!" cried Dorothée, tossing her blonde ringlets in pettish arrogance. "If you were not all that I have said, you would never remind me of yesterday. Go, idiot—and do not return."

Anselme, the hermit, had slept little, tossing distractedly on his hard, narrow pallet. His blood, it seemed, had been fevered by the sultriness of the summer night.

Then, too, the natural heat of youth had contributed to his unease. He had not wanted to think of women—a certain woman in particular. But, after thirteen months of solitude, in the heart of the wild woodland of Averoigne, he was still far from forgetting. Crueler even than her taunts was the remembered beauty of Dorothée des Flèches: the full-ripened mouth, the round arms and slender waist, the breast and hips that had not yet acquired their amplest curves.

Dreams had thronged the few short intervals of slumber, bringing other visitants, fair but nameless, about his couch.

He rose at sundawn, weary but restless. Perhaps he would find refreshment by bathing, as he had often done, in a pool fed from the river Isoile and hidden among alder and willow thickets. The water, deliciously cool at that hour, would assuage his feverishness.

His eyes burned and smarted in the morning's gold glare when he emerged from the hut of wattled osier withes. His thoughts wandered, still full of the night's disorder. Had he been wise, after all, to quit the world, to leave his friends and family, and seclude himself because of a girl's unkindness? He could not deceive himself into thinking that he had become a hermit through any aspiration toward sainthood, such as had sustained the old anchorites. By dwelling so much alone, was he not merely aggravating the malady he had sought to cure?

Perhaps, it occurred to him belatedly, he was proving himself the ineffectual dreamer, the idle fool that Dorothée had accused him of being. It was weakness to let himself be soured by a disappointment.

Walking with downcast eyes, he came unaware to the thickets that fringed the pool. He parted the young willows without lifting his gaze, and was about to cast off his garments. But at that instant the nearby sound of splashing water startled him from his abstraction.

With some dismay, Anselme realized that the pool was already occupied. To his further consternation, the occupant was a woman. Standing near to the center, where the pool deepened, she stirred the water with her hands till it rose and rippled against the base of her bosom. Her pale wet skin glistened like white rose-petals dipped in dew.

Anselme's dismay turned to curiosity and then to unwilling delight. He told himself that he wanted to withdraw but feared to frighten the bather by a sudden movement. Stooping with her clear profile and her shapely left shoulder toward him, she had not perceived his presence.

⸙

A woman, young and beautiful, was the last sight he had wished to see. Nevertheless, he could not turn his eyes away. The woman was a stranger to him, and he felt sure that she was no girl of the village or countryside. She was lovely as any chatelaine of the great castles of Averoigne. And yet surely no lady or demoiselle would bathe unattended in a forest pool.

Thick-curling chestnut hair, bound by a light silver fillet, billowed over her shoulders and burned to red, living gold where the sun-rays searched it out through the foliage. Hung about her neck, a light golden chain seemed to reflect the lusters of her hair, dancing between her breasts as she played with the ripples.

The hermit stood watching her like a man caught in webs of sudden sorcery. His youth mounted within him, in response to her beauty's evocation.

Seeming to tire of her play, she turned her back and began to move toward the opposite shore, where, as Anselme now noticed, a pile of feminine garments lay in charming disorder on the grass. Step by step she rose up from the shoaling water, revealing hips and thighs like those of an antique Venus.

Then, beyond her, he saw that a huge wolf, appearing furtively as a shadow from the thicket, had stationed itself beside the heap of clothing. Anselme had never seen such a wolf before. He remembered the tales of werewolves, that were believed to infest that ancient wood, and his alarm was touched instantly with the fear which only preternatural things can arouse. The beast was strangely colored, its fur being a glossy bluish-black. It was far larger than the common gray wolves of the forest. Crouching inscrutably, half hidden in the sedges, it seemed to await the woman as she waded shoreward.

Another moment, thought Anselme, and she would perceive her danger, would scream and turn in terror. But still she went on, her head bent forward as if in serene meditation.

"Beware the wolf!" he shouted, his voice strangely loud and seeming to break a magic stillness. Even as the words left his lips, the wolf trotted away and disappeared behind the thickets toward the great elder forest of oaks and beeches. The woman smiled over her shoulder at Anselme, turning a short oval face with slightly slanted eyes and lips red as pomegranate flowers. Apparently she was neither frightened by the wolf nor embarrassed by Anselme's presence.

"There is nothing to fear," she said, in a voice like the pouring of warm honey. "One wolf, or two, will hardly attack me."

"But perhaps there are others lurking about," persisted Anselme. "And there are worse dangers than wolves for one who wanders alone and unattended through the forest of Averoigne. When you have dressed, with your permission I shall attend you safely to your home, whether it be near or far."

"My home lies near enough in one sense, and far enough in another," returned the lady, cryptically. "But you may accompany me there if you wish."

She turned to the pile of garments, and Anselme went a few paces away among the alders and busied himself by cutting a stout cudgel for weapon against wild beasts or other adversaries. A strange but delightful agitation possessed him, and he nearly nicked his fingers several times with the knife. The misogyny that had driven him to a woodland hermitage began to appear slightly immature, even juvenile. He had let himself be wounded too deeply and too long by the injustice of a pert child.

By the time Anselme finished cutting his cudgel, the lady had completed her toilet. She came to meet him, swaying like a lamia. A bodice of vernal green velvet, baring the upper slopes of her breasts, clung tightly about her as a lover's embrace. A purple velvet gown, flowered with pale azure and crimson, moulded itself to the sinuous outlines of her hips and legs. Her slender feet were enclosed in fine soft leather buskins, scarlet-dyed, with tips curling pertly upward. The fashion of her garments, though oddly antique, confirmed Anselme in his belief that she was a person of no common rank.

Her raiment revealed, rather than concealed, the attributes of her femininity. Her manner yielded—but it also withheld.

Anselme bowed before her with a courtly grace that belied his rough country garb.

"Ah! I can see that you have not always been a hermit," she said, with soft mockery in her voice.

"You know me, then," said Anselme.

"I know many things. I am Sephora, the enchantress. It is unlikely that you have heard of me, for I dwelt apart, in a place that none can find—unless I permit them to find it."

"I know little of enchantment," admitted Anselme. "But I can believe that you are an enchantress."

For some minutes they had followed a little used path that serpentined through the antique wood. It was a path the hermit had never come upon before in all his wanderings. Lithe saplings and low-grown boughs of huge beeches pressed closely upon it. Anselme, holding them aside for his companion, came often in thrilling contact with her shoulder and arm. Often she swayed against him, as if losing her balance on the rough ground. Her weight was a delightful burden, too soon relinquished. His pulses coursed tumultuously and would not quiet themselves again.

Anselme had quite forgotten his eremitic resolves. His blood and his curiosity were excited more and more. He ventured various gallantries, to which Sephora gave provocative replies. His questions, however, she answered with elusive vagueness. He could learn nothing, could decide nothing, about her. Even her age puzzled him: at one moment he thought her a young girl, the next, a mature woman.

Several times, as they went on, he caught glimpses of black fur beneath the low, shadowy foliage. He felt sure that the strange black wolf he had seen by the pool was accompanying them with a furtive surveillance. But somehow his sense of alarm was dulled by the enchantment that had fallen upon him.

Now the path steepened, climbing a densely wooded hill. The trees thinned to straggly, stunted pines, encircling a brown, open moorland as the tonsure encircles a monk's crown. The moor was studded with Druidic monoliths, dating from ages prior to the Roman occupation of Averoigne. Almost at its center, there towered a massive cromlech, consisting of two upright slabs that supported a third like the lintel of a door. The path ran straight to the cromlech.

"This is the portal of my domain," said Sephora, as they neared it. "I grow faint with fatigue. You must take me in your arms and carry me through the ancient doorway."

Anselme obeyed very willingly. Her cheeks paled, her eyelids fluttered and fell as he lifted her. For a moment he thought that she had fainted; but her arms crept warm and clinging around his neck. Dizzy with the sudden vehemence of his emotion, he carried her through the cromlech. As he went, his lips wandered across her eyelids and passed deliriously to the soft red flame of her lips and the rose pallor of her throat. Once more she seemed to faint, beneath his fervor.

His limbs melted, and a fiery blindness filled his eyes. The earth seemed to yield beneath them like an elastic couch as he and Sephora sank down.

Lifting his head, Anselme looked about him with swiftly growing bewilderment. He had carried Sephora only a few paces—and yet the grass on which they lay was not the sparse and sun-dried grass of the moor, but was deep, verdant, and filled with tiny vernal blossoms! Oaks and beeches, huger even than those of the familiar forest, loomed umbrageously on every hand with masses of new, golden-green leafage, where he had thought to see the open upland. Looking back, he saw that the gray, lichened slabs of the cromlech itself alone remained of that former landscape.

Even the sun had changed its position. It had hung at Anselme's left, still fairly low in the east, when he and Sephora had reached the moorland. But now, shining with amber rays through a rift in the forest, it had almost touched the horizon on his right.

He recalled that Sephora had told him she was an enchantress. Here, indeed, was proof of sorcery! He eyed her with curious doubts and misgivings.

"Be not alarmed," said Sephora, with a honeyed smile of reassurance. "I told you that the cromlech was the doorway to my domain. We are now in a land lying outside of time and space as you have hitherto known them. The very seasons are different here. But there is no sorcery involved, except that of the great ancient Druids, who knew the secret of this hidden realm and reared those mighty slabs for a portal between the worlds. If you should weary of me, you can pass back at any time through the doorway—But I hope that you have not tired of me so soon —"

Anselme, though still bewildered, was relieved by this information. He proceeded to prove that the hope expressed by Sephora was well-founded. Indeed, he proved it so lengthily and in such detail that the sun had fallen below the horizon before Sephora could draw a full breath and speak again.

"The air grows chill," she said, pressing against him and shivering lightly. "But my home is close at hand."

They came in the twilight to a high round tower among trees and grass-grown mounds.

"Ages ago," announced Sephora, "there was a great castle here. Now the tower alone remains, and I am its chatelaine, the last of my family. The tower and the lands about it are named Sylaire."

Tall dim tapers lit the interior, which was hung with rich arrasses, vaguely and strangely pictured. Aged, corpse-pale servants in antique garb went to and fro with the furtiveness of specters, setting wines and foods before the enchantress and her guest in a broad hall. The wines were of rare flavor and immense age, the foods were curiously spiced. Anselme ate and drank copiously. It was all like some fantastic dream, and he accepted his surroundings as a dreamer does, untroubled by their strangeness.

The wines were potent, drugging his senses into warm oblivion. Even stronger was the inebriation of Sephora's nearness.

However, Anselme was a little startled when the huge black wolf he had seen that morning entered the hall and fawned like a dog at the feet of his hostess.

"You see, he is quite tame," she said, tossing the wolf bits of meat from her plate. "Often I let him come and go in the tower; and some-times he attends me when I go forth from Sylaire."

"He is a fierce-looking beast," Anselme observed doubtfully.

It seemed that the wolf understood the words, for he bared his teeth at Anselme, with a hoarse, preternaturally deep growl. Spots of red fire glowed in his somber eyes, like coals fanned by devils in dark pits.

"Go away, Malachie," commanded the enchantress, sharply. The wolf obeyed her, slinking from the hall with a malign backward glance at Anselme.

"He does not like you," said Sephora. "That, however, is perhaps not surprising."

Anselme, bemused with wine and love, forgot to inquire the meaning of her last words.

⁂

Morning came too soon, with upward-slanting beams that fired the tree-tops around the tower.

"You must leave me for awhile," said Sephora, after they had break-fasted. "I have neglected my magic of late—and there are matters into which I should inquire."

Bending prettily, she kissed the palms of his hands. Then, with backward glances and smiles, she retired to a room at the tower's top beside her bedchamber. Here, she had told Anselme, her grimoires and potions and other appurtenances of magic were kept.

During her absence, Anselme decided to go out and explore the woodland about the tower. Mindful of the black wolf, whose tameness he did not trust despite Sephora's reassurances, he took with him the cudgel he had cut that previous day in the thickets near the Isoile.

There were paths everywhere, all leading to fresh loveliness. Truly, Sylaire was a region of enchantment. Drawn by the dreamy golden light, and the breeze laden with the freshness of spring flowers, Anselme wandered on from glade to glade.

He came to a grassy hollow, where a tiny spring bubbled from beneath mossed boulders. He seated himself on one of the boulders, musing on the strange happiness that had entered his life so unexpectedly. It was like one of the old romances, the tales of glamor and fantasy, that he had loved to read. Smiling, he remembered the gibes with which Dorothée des Flèches had expressed her disapproval of his taste for such reading-matter. What, he wondered, would Dorothée think now? At any rate, she would hardly care—

His reflections were interrupted. There was a rustling of leaves, and the black wolf emerged from the boscage in front of him, whining as if to attract his attention. The beast had somehow lost his appearance of fierceness.

Curious, and a little alarmed, Anselme watched in wonder while the wolf began to uproot with his paws certain plants that somewhat resembled wild garlic. These he devoured with palpable eagerness.

Anselme's mouth gaped at the thing which ensued. One moment the wolf was before him. Then, where the wolf had been, there rose up the figure of a man, lean, powerful, with blue-black hair and beard, and darkly flaming eyes. The hair grew almost to his brows, the beard nearly to his lower eye-lashes. His arms, legs, shoulders, and chest were matted with bristles.

"Be assured that I mean you no harm," said the man. "I am Malachie du Marais, a sorcerer, and the one-time lover of Sephora. Tiring of me, and fearing my wizardry, she turned me into a were-wolf by giving me secretly the waters of a certain pool that lies amid this enchanted domain of Sylaire. The pool is cursed from old time with the infection of lycanthropy—and Sephora has added her spells to its power. I can throw off the wolf shape for a little while during the dark of the moon. At other times I can regain my human form, though only for a few minutes, by eating the root that you saw me dig and devour. The root is very scarce."

Anselme felt that the sorceries of Sylaire were more complicated than he had hitherto imagined. But amid his bewilderment he was unable to trust the weird being before him. He had heard many tales of werewolves, who were reputedly common in medieval France. Their ferocity, people said, was that of demons rather than of mere brutes.

"Allow me to warn you of the grave danger in which you stand," continued Malachie due Marais. "You were rash to let yourself be enticed by Sephora. If you are wise, you will leave the purlieus of Sylaire with all possible dispatch. The land is old in evil and sorcery, and all who dwell within it are ancient as the land, and are equally accursed. The servants of Sephora, who waited upon you yestereve, are vampires that sleep by day in the tower vaults and come forth only by night. They go out through the Druid portal, to prey on the people of Averoigne."

He paused as if to emphasize the words that followed. His eyes glittered balefully, and his deep voice assumed a hissing undertone. "Sephora herself is an ancient lamia, well-nigh immortal, who feeds on the vital forces of young men. She has had many lovers through-out the ages—and I must deplore, even though I cannot specify, their ultimate fate. The youth and beauty that she retains are illusions. If you could see Sephora as she really is, you would recoil in revulsion, cured of your perilous love. You would see her—unthinkably old, and hideous with infamies."

"But how can such things be?" queried Anselme. "Truly, I cannot believe you."

Malachie shrugged his hairy shoulders. "At least I have warned you. But the wolf-change approaches, and I must go. If you will come to me later, in my abode which lies a mile to the westward of Sephora's tower, perhaps I can convince you that my statements are the truth. In the meanwhile, ask yourself if you have seen any mirrors, such as a beautiful young woman would use, in Sephora's chamber. Vampires and lamias are afraid of mirrors—for a good reason."

Anselme went back to the tower with a troubled mind. What Malachie had told him was incredible. Yet there was the matter of Sephora's servants. He had hardly noticed their absence that morning—and yet he had not seen them since the previous eve—And he could not remember any mirrors among Sephora's various feminine belongings.

He found Sephora waiting him in the tower's lower hall. One glance at the utter sweetness of her womanhood, and he felt ashamed of the doubts with which Malachie had inspired him.

Sephora's blue-gray eyes questioned him, deep and tender as those of some pagan goddess of love. Reserving no detail, he told her of his meeting with the werewolf.

"Ah! I did well to trust my intuitions," she said. "Last night, when the black wolf growled and glowered at you, it occurred to me that he was perhaps becoming more dangerous than I had realized. This morning, in my chamber of magic, I made use of my clairvoyant powers—and I learned much. Indeed, I have been careless. Malachie has become a menace to my security. Also, he hates you, and would destroy our happiness."

"Is it true, then," questioned Anselme, "that he was your lover, and that you turned him into a werewolf?"

"He was my lover—long, long ago. But the werewolf form was his own choice, assumed out of evil curiosity by drinking from the pool of which he told you. He has regretted it since, for the wolf shape, while giving him certain powers of harm, in reality limits his actions and his sorceries. He wishes to return to human shape, and if he succeeds, will become doubly dangerous to us both.

"I should have watched him well—for I now find that he has stolen from me the recipe of antidote to the werewolf waters. My clairvoyance tells me that he has already brewed the antidote, in the brief intervals of humanity regained by chewing a certain root. When he drinks the potion, as I think that he means to do before long, he will regain human form—permanently. He waits only for the dark of the moon, when the werewolf spell is at its weakest."

"But why should Malachie hate me?" asked Anselme. "And how can I help you against him?"

"That first question is slightly stupid, my dear. Of course, he is jealous of you. As for helping me—well, I have thought of a good trick to play on Malachie."

She produced a small purple glass vial, triangular in shape, from the folds of her bodice.

"This vial," she told him, "is filled with the water of the werewolf pool. Through my clairvoyant vision, I learned that Malachie keeps his newly brewed potion in a vial of similar size, shape, and color. If you can go to his den and substitute one vial for the other without detection, I believe that the results will be quite amusing."

"Indeed, I will go," Anselme assured her.

"The present should be a favorable time," said Sephora. "It is now within an hour of noon; and Malachie often hunts at this time. If you should find him in his den, or he should return while you are there, you can say that you came in response to his invitation."

She gave Anselme careful instructions that would enable him to find the werewolf's den without delay. Also, she gave him a sword, saying that the blade had been tempered to the chanting of magic spells that made it effective against such beings as Malachie. "The wolf's temper has grown uncertain," she warned. "If he should attack you, your alder stick would prove a poor weapon."

It was easy to locate the den, for well used paths ran toward it with little deviation. The place was the mounded remnant of a tower that had crumbled down into grassy earth and mossy blocks. The entrance had once been a lofty doorway: now it was only a hole, such as a large animal would make in leaving and returning to its burrow.

Anselme hesitated before the hole. "Are you there, Malachie du Marais?" he shouted. There was no answer, no sound of movement from within. Anselme shouted once more. At last, stooping on hands and knees, he entered the den.

Light poured through several apertures, latticed with wandering tree-roots, where the mound had fallen in from above. The place was a cavern rather than a room. It stank with carrion remnants into whose nature Anselme did not inquire too closely. The ground was littered with bones, broken stems, and leaves of plants, and shattered or rusted vessels of alchemic use. A verdigris-eaten kettle hung from a tripod above ashes and ends of charred faggots. Rain-sodden grimoires lay mouldering in rusty metal covers. The three-legged ruin of a table was propped against the wall. It was covered with a medley of oddments, among which Anselme discerned a purple vial resembling the one given him by Sephora.

In one corner was a litter of dead grass. The strong, rank odor of a wild beast mingled with the carrion stench.

Anselme looked about and listened cautiously. Then, without delay, he substituted Sephora's vial for the one on Malachie's table. The stolen vial he placed under his jerkin.

There was a padding of feet at the cavern's entrance. Anselme turned—to confront the black wolf. The beast came toward him, crouching tensely as if about to spring, with eyes glaring like crimson coals of Avernus. Anselme's fingers dropped to the hilt of the enchanted sword that Sephora had given him.

The wolf's eyes followed his fingers. It seemed that he recognized the sword. He turned from Anselme, and began to chew some roots of the garlic-like plant, which he had doubtless collected to make possible those operations which he could hardly have carried on in wolfish form.

This time, the transformation was not complete. The head, arms, and body of Malachie du Marais rose up again before Anselme; but the legs were the hind legs of a monstrous wolf. He was like some bestial hybrid of antique legend.

"Your visit honors me," he said, half snarling, with suspicion in his eyes and voice. "Few have cared to enter my poor abode, and I am grateful to you. In recognition of your kindness, I shall make you a present."

With the padding movements of a wolf, he went over to the ruinous table and groped amid the confused oddments with which it was covered. He drew out an oblong silver mirror, brightly burnished, with jeweled handle, such as a great lady or damsel might own. This he offered to Anselme.

"I give you the mirror of Reality," he announced. "In it, all things are reflected according to their true nature. The illusions of enchantment cannot deceive it. You disbelieved me when I warned you against Sephora. But if you hold this mirror to her face and observe the reflection, you will see that her beauty, like everything else in Sylaire, is a hollow lie—the mask of ancient horror and corruption. If you doubt me, hold the mirror to my face—now: for I, too, am part of the land's immemorial evil."

Anselme took the silver oblong and obeyed Malachie's injunction. A moment, and his nerveless fingers almost dropped the mirror. He had seen reflected within it a face that the sepulcher should have hidden long ago—

The horror of that sight had shaken him so deeply that he could not afterwards recall the circumstances of his departure from the werewolf's lair. He had kept the werewolf's gift; but more than once he had been prompted to throw it away. He tried to tell himself that what he had seen was merely the result of some wizard trick. He refused to believe that any mirror would reveal Sephora as anything but the young and lovely sweetheart whose kisses were still warm on his lips.

All such matters, however, were driven from Anselme's mind by the situation that he found when he re-entered the tower hall. Three visitors had arrived during his absence. They stood fronting Sephora, who, with a tranquil smile on her lips, was apparently trying to explain something to them. Anselme recognized the visitors with much amazement, not untouched with consternation.

One of them was Dorothée des Flèches, clad in a trim traveling habit. The others were two serving men of her father, armed with longbows, quivers of arrows, broadswords, and daggers. In spite of this array of weapons, they did not look any too comfortable or at home. But Dorothée seemed to have retained her usual matter-of-fact assurance.

"What are you doing in this queer place, Anselme?" she cried. "And who is this woman, this chatelaine of Sylaire, as she calls herself?"

Anselme felt that she would hardly understand any answer that he could give to either query. He looked at Sephora, then back at Dorothée. Sephora was the essence of all the beauty and romance that he had ever craved. How could he have fancied himself in love with Dorothée, how could he have spent thirteen months in a hermitage because of her coldness and changeability? She was pretty enough, with the common bodily charms of youth. But she was stupid, wanting in imagination—prosy already in the flush of her girlhood as a middle-aged housewife. Small wonder that she had failed to understand him.

"What brings you here?" he countered. "I had not thought to see you again."

"I missed you, Anselme," she sighed. "People said that you had left the world because of your love for me, and had become a hermit. At last I came to seek you. But you had disappeared. Some hunters had seen you pass yesterday with a strange woman, across the moor of Druid stones. They said you had both vanished beyond the cromlech, fading as if in air. Today I followed you with my father's serving men. We found ourselves in this strange region, of which no one has ever heard. And now this woman—"

The sentence was interrupted by a mad howling that filled the room with eldritch echoes. The black wolf, with jaws foaming and slavering, broke in through the door that had been opened to admit Sephora's visitors. Dorothée des Flèches began to scream as he dashed straight toward her, seeming to single her out for the first victim of his rabid fury.

Something, it was plain, had maddened him. Perhaps the water of the werewolf pool, substituted for the antidote, had served to redouble the original curse of lycanthropy.

The two serving men, bristling with their arsenal of weapons, stood like effigies. Anselme drew the sword given him by the enchantress, and leaped forward between Dorothée and the wolf. He raised his weapon, which was straight-bladed, and suitable for stabbing. The mad werewolf sprang as if hurled from a catapult, and his red, open gorge was spitted on the outthrust point. Anselme's hand was jarred on the sword-hilt, and the shock drove him backward. The wolf fell threshing at Anselme's feet. His jaws had clenched on the blade. The point protruded beyond the stiff bristles of his neck.

Anselme tugged vainly at the sword. Then the black-furred body ceased to thresh—and the blade came easily. It had been withdrawn from the sagging mouth of the dead ancient sorcerer, Malachie du Marais, which lay before Anselme on the flagstones. The sorcerer's face was now the face that Anselme had seen in the mirror, when he held it up at Malachie's injunction.

"You have saved me! How wonderful!" cried Dorothée. Anselme saw that she had started toward him with outthrust arms. A moment more, and the situation would become embarrassing.

He recalled the mirror, which he had kept under his jerkin, together with the vial stolen from Malachie du Marais. What, he wondered, would Dorothée see in its burnished depths?

He drew the mirror forth swiftly and held it to her face as she advanced upon him. What she beheld in the mirror he never knew but the effect was startling. Dorothée gasped, and her eyes dilated in manifest horror. Then, covering her eyes with her hands, as if to shut out some ghastly vision, she ran shrieking from the hall. The serving men followed her. The celerity of their movements made it plain that they were not sorry to leave this dubious lair of wizards and witches.

Sephora began to laugh softly. Anselme found himself chuckling. For awhile they abandoned themselves to uproarious mirth. Then Sephora sobered.

"I know why Malachie gave you the mirror," she said. "Do you not wish to see my reflection in it?"

Anselme realized that he still held the mirror in his hand. Without answering Sephora, he went over to the nearest window, which looked down on a deep pit lined with bushes, that had been part of an ancient, half-filled moat. He hurled the silver oblong into the pit.

"I am content with what my eyes tell me, without the aid of any mirror," he declared. "Now let us pass to other matters, which have been interrupted too long."

Again the clinging deliciousness of Sephora was in his arms, and her fruit-soft mouth was crushed beneath his hungry lips.

The strongest of all enchantments held them in its golden circle.

PUBLICATION HISTORY

"The Return of the Sorcerer" first appeared in *Strange Tales of Mystery and Terror*, (September 1931)

"The City of Singing Flame" first appeared in *Wonder Stories*, (July 1931)

"Beyond the Singing Flame" first appeared in *Wonder Stories*, (November 1931)

"The Vaults of Yoh-Vombis" first appeared in *Weird Tales*, (May 1932)

"The Double Shadow" first appeared in *The Double Shadow and Other Fantasies*, Auburn Journal (1933)

"The Monster of the Prophecy" first appeared in *Weird Tales*, (January 1932)

"The Hunters from Beyond" first appeared in *Strange Tales of Mystery and Terror*, (October 1932)

"The Isle of the Torturers" first appeared in *Keep on the Light*, Selwyn & Blount (1933)

"A Night in Malnéant" first appeared in *The Double Shadow and Other Fantasies*, Auburn Journal (1933)

"The Chain of Aforgomon" first appeared in *Weird Tales*, (December 1935)

"The Dark Eidolon" first appeared in *Weird Tales*, (January 1935)

"The Seven Geases" first appeared in *Weird Tales*, (October 1934)

"The Holiness of Azédarac" first appeared in *Weird Tales*, (November 1933)

"The Beast of Averoigne" first appeared in *Weird Tales*, (May 1933)

"The Empire of the Necromancers" first appeared in *Weird Tales*, (September 1932)

"The Disinterment of Venus" first appeared in *Weird Tales* (July 1934)

"The Devotee of Evil" first appeared in *The Double Shadow and Other Fantasies*, Auburn Journal (1933)

"The Enchantress of Sylaire" first appeared in *Weird Tales*, (July 1941)

ABOUT THE AUTHOR

Clark Ashton Smith (13 January 1893 – 14 August 1961) was a poet, sculptor, painter and author of fantasy, horror and science fiction short stories. It is for these stories, and his literary friendship with H. P. Lovecraft from 1922 until Lovecraft's death in 1937, that he is mostly remembered today. With Lovecraft and Robert E. Howard, also a friend and correspondent, Smith remains one of the most famous contributors to the pulp magazine *Weird Tales*.